Perry

MW01674222

Overland Explorations in Siberia, Northern Asia, and The Great Amoor River Country

SALZWASSER
VERLAG

Perry McDonough Collins

Overland Explorations in Siberia, Northern Asia, and The Great Amoor River Country

Reprint of the original, first published in 1864.

1st Edition 2022 | ISBN: 978-3-75259-126-2

Verlag (Publisher): Salzwasser Verlag GmbH, Zeilweg 44, 60439 Frankfurt, Deutschland
Vertretungsberechtigt (Authorized to represent): E. Roepke, Zeilweg 44, 60439 Frankfurt, Deutschland
Druck (Print): Books on Demand GmbH, In de Tarpen 42, 22848 Norderstedt, Deutschland

OVERLAND EXPLORATIONS

IN

SIBERIA, NORTHERN ASIA,

AND THE GREAT

AMOOR RIVER COUNTRY;

INCIDENTAL NOTICES OF

MANCHOORIA, MONGOLIA, KAMSCHATKA, AND JAPAN,

WITH

MAP AND PLAN OF AN OVERLAND TELEGRAPH AROUND
THE WORLD, VIA BEHRING'S STRAIT AND
ASIATIC RUSSIA TO EUROPE.

BY

MAJOR PERRY McD. COLLINS.

RIVER,

NEW YORK

1864.

TO

LIEUTENANT-GENERAL MOURAVIEFF,

GOVERNOR-GENERAL OF EASTERN SIBERIA, COUNT OF THE AMOOR,
ETC., ETC.,

THIS VOLUME IS RESPECTFULLY INSCRIBED,

IN TOKEN OF ADMIRATION AND GRATITUDE,

BY ONE WHO HAS SHARED HIS GENEROUS HOSPITALITY,

AND WITNESSED THE NOBLE RESULTS OF HIS PROFOUND AND BENEFICENT POLICY
ON THE AMOOR RIVER.

PREFACE.

My attention was first turned towards Siberia by the perusal of Lieutenant Von Wrangel's narrative of an expedition to the Polar Sea. Reflecting on the vast extent of the country, its mighty rivers, its stately and boundless forests, its immense mineral wealth, I was struck with the magnitude of its natural resources, and with its possible value to the commerce of the world, if it could only obtain an easy outlet to the ocean.

For several years previous to 1855, while residing in California, I had given much study to the commercial resources of the Pacific side of the United States, especially in connection with the opposite coast of Asia. I had already fixed in my own mind upon the river Amoor as the destined channel by which American commercial enterprise was to penetrate the obscure depths of Northern Asia, and open a new world to trade and civilization, when news arrived in 1855 that the Russians had taken possession of the Amoor country, and formed a settlement at the mouth of the river. Greatly interested by this event, the important consequences of which my previous speculations enabled me fully to comprehend, I proceeded to Washington in search of accurate information on the subject. Little was known in California about the Amoor, with which no direct communication had then been effected. To have gone to the mouth of the river myself, as I was strongly inclined to do, would have required me to charter a vessel for the express purpose, and this I was scarcely able to afford. And besides, on arriving there, a private adventurer, without credentials, I could have no assurance of being permitted to ascend the river or explore the country. What I chiefly desired was to examine the whole length of the Amoor, and ascertain its fitness for steamboat navigation. That point settled in the affirmative, everything else was sure to follow as a matter of course.

At Washington, I had conferences with President Pierce, Secretary Marcy, and the Russian Ambassador, which resulted in my appointment, March 24, 1856, as Commercial Agent of the United States for the Amoor River.

Armed with this commission, and with letters to influential personages at St. Petersburg, I started without delay for the Russian Capital, resolved to traverse the empire from West to East, cross Siberia, enter Tartary, and, if possible, descend the Amoor river from its source to its mouth. I sailed from New York April 12, 1856, and the result of my travels and voyages is here submitted to the public.

CONTENTS.

A VOYAGE DOWN THE AMOOR.

CHAPTER I.

DEPARTURE FOR SIBERIA.

On the 17th of May, 1856, I reached Cronstadt in the first steamer that had entered the port that year, and was the only passenger on board. For three days we had been detained by ice in the Gulf of Finland. For two more days I was kept at Cronstadt in consequence of my passport having no visé of a Russian Consul in the United States, as is required by the police regulations of the empire. At the end of that time, however, the matter was satisfactorily explained, and I was permitted to enter St. Petersburg.

My main object at the Russian capital was to get the permission of the imperial government to traverse Siberia and explore the Amoor River, which I was resolved to descend, if possible, from its head waters to its mouth. Little, however, could be done in this direction during the absence of General Mouravieff, the distinguished Governor-General of Eastern Siberia, to whom my application had been referred by the imperial government, and who was then on a visit to Germany. I waited patiently for his return through the months of June and July, occupying myself with observing the manners and customs and studying the language of the Russians, and in enjoying the hospitalities with which I was honored through the kindness of the United States Minister, Governor Seymour of Connecticut.

Early in August General Mouravieff reached St. Petersburg. I waited upon him at his lodgings in company with Governor Seymour. He received me with great kindness, and warmly expressed his approbation of my designs, saying that he was most happy to have the opportunity to introduce an American to the Amoor. He promised that I should see the whole country and have every facility that his power and influence could procure. He intended himself to leave Moscow early in November for Irkutsk, the capital of his province. The winter was the proper season for travelling in Siberia, as the roads were then in the best condition and could easily be traversed by sleighs. I could accompany him on the journey, he said, or, if I preferred, could go somewhat earlier in company with an officer despatched to Siberia on public service.

In the latter part of August I went, with all the rest of the world of Russia, to Moscow to attend the coronation of His Imperial Majesty Alexander II. After witnessing that superb ceremonial, September 7, I remained in Moscow nearly three months, waiting till the usual fall of snow should make the roads to the eastward practicable for winter travel. I continually practised myself in the Russian language, wandering daily about the streets, markets, bazaars, and shops of the city, taking my meals at the native eating-houses, many of them sufficiently curious places, drinking great quantities of tea in the tea-houses, and visiting theatres, gardens, and all kind of places where I could acquire the tongue and study the habits of the people. Moscow, above all other cities, is the best index to Russia. There the character, the manners, and the disposition of the true Russian are seen in the highest perfection. There are found the written and the architectural records of the past history of the empire, and there are preserved, in all their freshness, the traditions which have such potent influence over the Russian mind. There lie buried the great princes and czars of the empire, from Rurik down to the little murdered Demetrius, and there the emperors come to be crowned from their glittering metropolis on the marshy Neva. Every Russian looks upon Moscow with patriotic enthusiasm as the holy city, the true, national, and religious capital of his country. The emperor is not invested with full Imperial authority until he has been formally crowned in its ancient cathedral. And, besides, the political importance which this fact, and its old associations with the national history, give to it, Moscow is rapidly acquiring additional importance as a commercial capital. It is the centre of the interior trade of the country, and affords peculiar facilities, of which I endeavored fully to avail myself, in order to become acquainted with the nature and extent of the overland trade and commerce with Siberia, and the Chinese Empire.

I had good advice respecting the nature of the preparations to be made for Siberian travel, and, in company with Mr. Peyton, a countryman and friend, who had agreed to make the journey with me as far as Irkutsk, and with Captain Anakoff, an officer of the staff of General Mouravieff, I quitted Moscow December 3, 1856.

We had received from General Mouravieff the following passport, which we soon found was of almost magical efficiency in smoothing down difficulties and removing obstacles on the road :

"The bearers of this, citizens of the United States of America, Messrs. Collins and Peyton, are proceeding from Moscow to Irkutsk with the authorization of the imperial government.

"I have the honor to request all the chief authorities to give a free passage to Messrs. Collins and Peyton, and, in case of need, to offer to them legal protection, and to contribute to the celerity of their journey. In faith of which I have given them this open passport, with my signature, and to which I have attached my seal.

"MOURAVIEFF,
"Governor-General of Eastern Siberia."

This passport or *poderojina* authorized us to demand post horses at the stations on the road. Captain Anakoff, however, carried his own *poderojina*, and, so far as our way lay together, relieved us of all care or responsibility.

We purchased in Moscow a stock of the warmest clothing we could find and laid in provisions and supplies of both a solid and liquid nature. We carried our own tea, sugar, salt, spices, together with hams, biscuits, and other substantial provender.

It is the invariable custom in Russia to start on a journey in the evening instead of the morning. We therefore spent the last day of our residence in Moscow in making farewell calls upon our friends and acquaintances, and at the approach of darkness we were sufficiently fatigued to be glad to take refuge in our sleigh, and sufficiently warmed by the farewell glasses we had emptied to face with indifference the chill air of a Russian winter night.

CHAPTER II.

FROM MOSCOW TO NIJNE-NOVGOROD.

The bells attached to the yoke of our shaft-horse jingled merrily; our sleigh slid upon the slippery road from one side to the other; the driver selected the smoothest places, and the clatter of the horses' feet grew faster and faster, as, answering to the command of the captain —*poshol! poshol-skoro!*—go! go quick! he applied the lash to his frosty horses.

The road on which we were travelling is the artery of an extensive commerce, dotted with villages, towns and cities. At every change of horses at the post-stations, we found a warm room, where we could prepare our own tea, from the quickly-steaming *samovar*, and procure such fare as the house afforded, in addition to what we had in our own provision-box. Night or day, these rooms are always heated, and if not quite as comfortable or as luxuriously furnished as the hotels we left behind us in New York, Paris, or St. Petersburg, they were nevertheless very acceptable.

Post after post, and station after station succeeded; night hung heavy and chill upon me; morning came, but I had not closed an eye. In fact, I did not require sleep, my mind was so busy with the future; for more than a year I had been straining every nerve to reach the goal of my ambition—the Amoor. I was now on the high road to it; with the Czar's permission in my pocket, and an officer of General Mouravieff's staff seated in my sleigh —what could I wish more? my highest hopes were accomplished, and if I could survive the rigors of a Siberian winter, and the fatigue of five thousand miles of travel, after the lapse of a few months I should be afloat upon the waters of the Amoor, on my way to the Eastern Ocean, opposite to the shores of my own country.

My mind was busy with the future, and I saw that night, as if by inspiration, the deep snows open before me; the forests waved and toppled; long and beautiful vistas stretched out in the dim distance; great rivers, with broad and gentle currents, invited me on, and a great ocean seemed to bound the extended horizon. I dreamed, but my eyes were open; I saw, though the night was dark.

We discovered, before the close of the day, that the interior arrangement of our sleigh was far from being comfortable; we had left the seats in the body of the carriage-top; these should have been removed, our baggage placed as evenly as possible on the bottom, over which our extra furs and skins should have been spread upon a good coating of straw, or covered with a mattrass, on which we could, as convenience prompted, have sat or stretched ourselves at length.

The best Russian travellers (the couriers) seldom lie down in the vehicle, wagon, or sleigh, but with a pillow or two, or a leathern cushion placed behind them, sit upright all the time, sleeping or waking; this, I understand, is considered the safest and best mode, and less fatiguing in long journeys, as many persons have their spines injured by the motion of the vehicle or the roughness of the roads, in those long and terrible Siberian expeditions.

Eight or ten stations were passed before we reached Vlademir, one hundred and twelve miles from Moscow. It is a pleasant-looking city, with many fine churches and public buildings, and is situated on the Kliazma branch of the Oka, a tributary of the Volga. It was founded in the eleventh century, and the present population is ten thousand. It was the capital of the Principality of Vlademir from A.D. 1157 to 1328, when it was annexed to the grand duchy of Moscow. The cathedral of St. Dmetre once formed a part of its ancient palace;. the cathedral of the Assumption was built in 1169, and contains the ancient regalia of its princes; many of its buildings are of great antiquity. The ancient city is supposed to have extended as far as the convent of Bogholubeskoy, a distance of seven miles. The trade is in linen, feathers, cherries, etc. The bricklayers and carpenters of this city are in great request. Vlademir is said to have been the burial-place of Saint Alexander Nevsky, whose remains were removed to St. Petersburg by order of Peter the Great, to give *eclat* to his new capital.

It is said that the Saint, not liking the new and miserable quarters assigned to him on the banks of the Neva, picked up his *wet* bones one bright moonlight night, and made his way back to his old resting-place—the monks declaring that he never would rest quietly on the Neva. Peter, hearing of this "monkish theoric," whispered into their ears a very different story, and told them that if the Saint did not find his way back to the Neva, and that in right good time, he would teach them a lesson in ghost-walking that they would not soon forget.

Peter was not to be baulked in his plans on the Neva, and St. Alexander, being the hero of the great triumph of Russia over her enemies upon the shores of that river, or perhaps upon the very spot where he proposed to found his city, it was highly proper, and certainly much to the Saint's worldly honor, that he should take up his abode in the new capital. Peter was right; the monks reported the Saint all snug and dry enough again on the Neva; and now his remains repose at the Convent of the Nevsky, at the foot of the Nevsky-prospective in St. Petersburg, under a silver tomb, richly ornamented, and in one of the most pleasant places in the city of palaces.

Our horses were yoked to the sleigh, and the postmaster poked his head in at the door and said *gotovey!* We passed through Sood-ogh-da-Moor-om, founded by the Sarmatians before the eleventh century. There are rich mines of iron and copper here. There is much trade in corn, leather, and skins, and the annual fair is held in June, for ten days. The population is from five to seven thousand. The town stands on the Oka, the sands of which were formerly rich in gold, and is one of the most ancient places in Muscovy.

Night arrived again, but we hurried on, regardless of the darkness; the frost was severe, with a piercing wind, and the road far from good. The driver beat the jaded horses into an unwilling gallop, upon the promise of an extra *grevna,* as we were anxious to reach Nijne-

Novgorod very early in the morning. The beasts were so poor, and so jaded from previous hard driving, that it had, even at the start, taken a thousand "*chorts*" and "*duraks*" to get them out of a snail's pace. It was, therefore, well along towards noon before the gilded domes and silver spires of Nijne arose from the snowy horizon. We galloped rapidly through the broad and well-built streets, up to the door of the *Gostennitsah*, the best hotel in the city.

CHAPTER III.

NIJNE-NOVGOROD—THE GREAT FAIR.

We bore a letter from Governor-General Mouravieff, of Siberia, to General Mouravieff, his kinsman, governor of Nijne-Novgorod. Immediately upon our arrival, we sent the letter to him, and it was not long before a messenger was at our lodgings, with an invitation to dine with the governor.

He entertained us with great kindness and hospitality. His palace stands within the citadel, and every thing about it had a military air.

The governor has seen much service in Asia and on the Kuban and among the Georgians ; is a gallant soldier, and a man of great talent, and one in whom the present Czar has much confidence. He has taken an active and influential part in the great measure for the emancipation of the serfs, which is now being carried out by the imperial government.

The governor's wife and niece were present at the dinner, and we found their society very agreeable. The niece spoke English ; in fact, English, French, and German were spoken by different members of the governor's family. The niece mentioned the few Americans who had visited Nijne and those she had seen at Moscow during the coronation. She had kept the cards of those with whom she had become acquainted, and at her request we added ours to the collection. We spent a very pleasant evening in conversation with this accomplished family, among other things speaking of the commerce of the city, a subject with which the ladies seemed well acquainted. We parted reluctantly from these agreeable people, and were sorry that we could not remain a few days longer in the city.

We took a drive around the town in company with the chief of police, seeing what we could of it in so short a time. The weather was far from agreeable. The wind blew fiercely, and considerable snow fell during the day. The object of greatest interest connected with this city is the yearly fair held here. Not having been so fortunate as to have witnessed it, I subjoin the following animated description, from Murray's excellent Handbook for Russia :—

"Twenty-four hours' travelling from Murom will bring the stranger within sight of the white walls and blue domes of Novgorod. The fair is held in the autumn, and the weather is at that season generally fine, so that dust, not mud, will be the misery; but if there has been any rain, the road for the last nine miles will exceed, in depth of the latter, all that the tourist has ever been dragged through; and one traveller states that he was five hours performing the last five miles. This is caused by the carriages, kibitkas, and telegas of the different streams of traders and merchandise converging to the central point. Long lines of these vehicles will assure the stranger that he is approaching the town; bands of Cossacks, stationed by way of police in rude tents along the road, with their long lances glittering among the trees, are seen in larger numbers; and crowds of Russians and wild eastern-looking men, in singular and varied costumes, become every moment more dense, until, on reaching Nijni itself, the crowd and turmoil surpasses all description.

"The town of Nijni is situated on a high triangular promontory, standing between the Volga and the confluence of the Oka with that river. The Oka at this point seems as large as the former, and is, in fact, a magnificent stream, and navigable for a great portion of its length. The position of Novgorod is so admirably adapted for commerce, and so central in regard to Asiatic as well as European Russia, that Peter the Great intended, at one time, to make it the seat of the capital of the empire, instead of the mouths of the Neva. The country round it is also highly picturesque; nevertheless those who founded the city do not seem to have courted the opportunities of enriching themselves by means of the two great rivers which flow by it, for the old town lies back behind the ridge. This mistake struck the present emperor very forcibly when he paid Nijni his first visit; and he is said to have remarked, that 'nature had done everything, man nothing.' To remedy this, a suburb has been built along the face, and at the foot, of the high ground which forms the southern bank of the Oka. The principal part of the city lies on the summit of the triangular height, and is chiefly composed of three handsome streets, converging towards an irregular open space in front of the Kremlin, which covers the lofty point of the triangle immediately overhanging the Volga. There is a beautiful terrace above this river, from whence is seen one of the most singular and extensive views in Europe; as far as the eye can reach extends a vast plain of corn and forest land. The city contains no fewer than 26 churches, some of which are of great size and beauty, two monasteries, and a nunnery. The Kremlin, with its low arched gates and jagged walls, is one of the most remarkable of these ancient structures now remaining in Russia. Curious, however, as the Kremlin and the various churches are, they possess, to one who has seen all the wonders in this way at Moscow and St. Petersburgh, little interest compared with the views from the spot on which they stand, and the two mighty rivers on which the traveller looks down, flowing so near that it seems as if a pebble could be thrown into either from this lofty eminence. Turning, however, from the far east, the stranger must look in a contrary direction, and across the Oka, to the triangular piece of land between that river and the Volga, a low, and sometimes inundated flat, exposed to the waters of both these rivers, where, during the fair, is exhibited a picture of human life unparalleled in any other portion of the globe. Here is then seen a vast town of shops, laid out in regular streets, with churches, hospitals, barracks, and theatres, the whole tenanted by no less than from 250,000 to 300,000 souls, destined, however, in six weeks to be as silent and lifeless as the forest steppes of which we have just made mention; for, when the fair is over, not an inhabitant of Nijni ever traverses the spot which annually swarms with foreigners. It must not be supposed that these shops are constructed like the English booth, of canvas, ropes, and poles; they are, on the contrary, regular houses, built of the most substantial materials, generally of one story, with large shops to the front, and sleeping rooms for the merchant and his servants in the rear. The interior portion of the fair is regularly laid out in twelve or thirteen streets of shops, terminating in a Russian church and twelve Chinese pavilions, from the summits of which there is a good view. It is said that a person would have to walk twenty-five miles if he promenaded every street; and this does not include what may be termed the suburbs of the fair. The business of this fair is of such importance that the governor of the province takes up his residence in it during the two months it lasts, that is to say, July and August. His house, which is in the centre, is a handsome building, and accommodates a large train of secretaries and other officials. A dozen Chinese pagodas rise above the shops, and the whole stands upon vaulted cloacæ, into which dirt of every description is conveyed. These sewers, which are constructed of hewn stone, are cleaned out several times a day by pumps, which draw the water from the adjoining rivers, and are entered at several points by handsome staircases. They were constructed by the Emperor Alexander, and are worthy of the Morpeths of ancient Rome. Any one who shows a disposition to defile the streets is quickly enjoined by a Cossack to retire to the lower regions. A portion of the sums expended on these sewers, which, from the nature of the swampy soil, must have been enormous, would have been economized had a better site been selected; but there seems to be a fatality attending the choice of position for public edifices all over the world, our own barracks in the West Indies included. The first view of this fair from the Kremlin is very striking; but we must descend from that elevated spot and take the traveller into the busy scene itself; this is about a mile from the centre of the city, though less from the outskirts, to which it is in fact united by a long and wide bridge of boats across the Oka, and a line of good houses along the steep and difficult slope leading to the bank of that river. Here will be met a countless throng of every kind of vehicle, for this is the only bridge that connects the town of Nijni with the fair; and the space between the street in question and the entrance to it is one of the very few spots in Russia where large masses of the population can be seen congregated together, always excepting the military portion of it. On each side of the bridge, and for more than a mile and a half above it, the river is wider than the Thames at Westminster, and so completely covered with boats, that the element on which they float is scarcely visible. These barges, of every variety of shape and tonnage, are either discharging or taking in their cargoes. The shops in the fair near the bank thus receive their goods at once from the two rivers, and at the more remote parts of it there are canals which serve the same purpose. An aquatic community, amounting to 40,000 persons, from every corner of this side of the earth, inhabit this floating camp; and their countenances and costumes are as varied and strange as the vessels they navigate. On the Volga, near the mouth of the Oka, and up and down the former river, extends a similar scene. Immediately on leaving the bridge, the fair ground begins; this part is crowded with mujiks looking out for employment, with a good sprinkling of Cossacks to keep order; then come lines of temporary booths, displaying beads, trinkets, and articles of dress for the lower orders, particularly caps from Tartary, Kirghis bonnets, made of black wool, and flat gold-figured cowls from Kazan. These booths stand in front of the tea houses laid out with little tables; and traktirs, or *restaurants*, large enough for two or three hundred persons to dine in with comfort, at any price from ten silver kopeks to twelve silver rubles. This being the great entrance to the fair, it is always the most crowded part of it, consequently the most interesting to the traveller; and if he can squeeze himself into some corner, or under the projecting roof of some booth, no easy matter in such a whirlpool of promenaders, he will pass in review as strange a scene as he ever witnessed, or is likely to do again. It is scarcely accurate to apply the word tame to such a stream of human beings, but the stranger must not expect to witness the *diablerie* of an English, German, or French fair; no clown, grinning from ear to ear, is to be seen, nor is the peculiar squeak that announces the peripatetic Punch to be heard, no quack dentist to pull teeth and dispense his nostrums. The fair of Nijni is not an idle holiday meeting, but a place of business, a gathering of merchants, traders, and bankers, who have their whole fortunes at stake, and who meet here once a year to deal and barter in commodities which may be valued at not less than fifteen millions sterling. It should also be mentioned that a great blank exists in the crowd, caused by the scarcity of female faces. From the space in front of the bridge the stranger enters into the regular quarters of the fair, and unless he has studied costumes, various will be his inquiries as to those he meets at every turn. Amongst the traders which may probably fall under his observation is the white-faced, flat-nosed merchant of Archangel, come to sell his furs; the bronze and long-eared Chinese his tea; Tartars, Crim and Nogai, with their muslins; Cossacks with their hides from the Ukraine; and others from the Aktuba with caviare; Persians with their scents and amulets; Bukarians with their turquoises and precious stones; Bashkirs, Calmucks, Turkomans, Kirghisses, Circassians, Turks, and other eastern etcetera. There is, indeed, no spot in the world where so many individuals meet belonging to such different divisions of the globe. The number of Mahometans is so great that a handsome mosque has been built for them at the end of the fair, in which worship is performed as regularly as in those of their native cities. The Bukharians, who inhabit the country near Thibet, consume nearly a year in their journey out and home. The Kalmucks and Kirghisses are many of them horse-dealers, and bring here droves of their little wild steeds; these animals are very active and strong, and singularly attached to each other, so much so that when sold it is necessary to separate them by force. Amongst the European merchants and dealers may be cited those of Manchester; German jewellers; Swiss watchmakers; Frankfort wine merchants; Hamburgh leech buyers; dealers in amber from the Baltic; pipe-makers from Dresden; furriers from Warsaw; French fancy dealers; Jews from Poland and the south of the empire, in their long black caftans; and, though we did not meet with one, there is no doubt, when so many dollars are changing hands, a delegate or two from Boston and New York. Many of the bulky articles occupy a large space of ground, and to that called the tea quarter we will now conduct the traveller through streets as long and as wide as some of the best in London, many of which have elegant light arcades on each side, supported in front by thousands of cast iron columns, where purchasers can walk about well sheltered in all kinds of weather, and make purchases, or gossip, as they feel disposed. The shops, generally very handsome, extend, in some instances, like Swan and Edgar's, from street to street, so as to have two fronts; they present nothing of the confusion of a fair, and the goods of every kind are as neatly arranged as in the shops of a large capital. This tea quarter is one of the most interesting in the fair, not only from the number of Chinese seen in it, but also from the large demand there is for this article. The Russians are, after the English, the most inveterate tea drinkers in Europe; and we believe that the tea sold at Nijni is the finest imported from China—it is, certainly, the most fragrant and perfumed, and, therefore, to the English palate generally perhaps not so agreeable; to our own, however, the Russian tea is delicious. It is introduced into this country by Kiatka, on the frontiers of China, a very insignificant place, and separated from it and the Chinese town of Mamaia by a small brook. At this first depot it is exchanged for goods; and from thence transported by land in packages of about two feet square, and covered with skin, to Koursk, in Siberia; here the tea is put into barges, which navigate the Irtish and the Tobol, until it arrives at the town of Tourmine, where it is disembarked and transported again by land to Perm, in Siberia; there it is once more embarked in boats that descend the Kama to the Volga, by which river it arrives at Nijni. From 90,000 to 100,000 chests are annually imported; half of these remain in Siberia, and reach Moscow by sledges during the winter, while the remainder are sold at this fair. The importation from China to England is upwards of 350,000 chests annually; but it should be observed that a pound of the tea sold at Nijni would go farther, that is make more tea, than two pounds of that sold in England; the very finest fetches sometimes as much as thirty or forty shillings a pound. Next in interest to the tea quarter is that of the Persians, situated in a suburb on the opposite side of an arm of the Oka, in which are sold costly shawls, small carpets, and silk pieces. Then there is the quarter for the dealers in skins and furs; here the outside garment of pretty nearly every beast that claims the arctic circle for a home may be seen, from a sable to a bear; and a pelisse of the choicest skins of the latter animal will fetch as much as five hundred pounds. Near this is the quarter for the sale of Siberian iron—a perfect metal town; one may walk for nearly half a league surrounded by every species of bar-iron, palisades, pots, agricultural, and other instruments. The outskirts, in which most of the foregoing articles are sold, is by far the most animated portion of the fair; there is more movement there, carriages and carts are passing to and fro, the tones of the dealers are louder, venders of kvass and refreshments ply their trade with unceasing energy, and the crowd rolls backwards and forwards in one uninterrupted stream; every tongue going; and earnestness or drollery in every face. In the interior of the fair there is an air of regularity and order which savors more of real business; even the features of the Cossacks, who do the duties of policemen, are scarcely ever seen to relax into a smile. There is also a theatre, and sometimes a good company."

CHAPTER IV.

FROM NIJNE TO EKATERINBURG.

CAPT. ANAKOFF, whom we had found a very pleasant companion, partèd from us here on his way to visit his friends further to the south. So eager was he to go on, that he would not even take time to call on the governor. From his extreme haste, I was induced to surmise that there was a fair lady waiting for him at his point of destination.

Before leaving Moscow, it was arranged that a party of officers, who were going to Siberia, and who were to leave the next morning after our departure, should overtake us at Nijne, and that we should go on under their guidance and protection as far as Irkutsk. Our new friends arrived during the evening—Messrs. Leutke, Paul Malavertsky, and Belchekoff, officers belonging to the civil service; their *podorojnaya* was to be our passport to the "further east," and we willingly resigned ourself to their care. A pleasant, kind, and clever set of fellows they proved to be. Only those who have experienced the difficulties and perplexities of travelling in strange and unfrequented countries, can estimate or appreciate the thousand-and-one troubles that we were saved from by this arrangement, which we owed to the kindness of General Mouravieff.

After a hearty warm supper and plentiful cups of tea, our *podorojnaya* having been despatched to the post station for horses, we were prepared for our second stage on the journey. We were kept waiting but a short time, the bells were jingling in the yard, and soon the pleasant word "*gotovey*" was spoken. It was about midnight when we set out from Nijne-Novgorod. The night was very dark, with a thick atmosphere, though the snow had ceased to fall.

We passed immediately from the town down on the Volga, upon the frozen surface of which our drivers proposed to travel during the night. They said we should be able to keep upon the river all the way to Kazan, which would facilitate our journey a full day. We passed along very well for some miles, occasionally getting a good shaking up in deep holes under the bank of the river where the water had receded, leaving the ice broken into considerable inequalities.

It was not long before the sledge of our companions stopped, stuck hard and fast in a hole and half buried in the loose snow, the horses floundering, tugging, and snorting under the heavy lash and severe blows of the driver. A half hour elapsed before they were extricated, and then not till the horses from our sleigh were hitched to the hind part of theirs, which was thus pulled backwards out of the hole.

Our drivers now went along the banks, crossing and recrossing to find the best road. If any track there was, it had been covered by the recent fall of snow, and the only guide they had was to avoid the black-looking places where the water was upon the ice. At length, one runner of our sleigh broke through, and the horses fell floundering in broken ice and water. This looked rather serious, and we got out of the sleigh as soon as possible, and found hard and dry footing near by. Fortunately it was near the shore and the water shallow. The horses were turned towards the land, and finally succeeded in gaining a solid footing. At a point lower down we recrossed the river, and after meeting a gang of freight sleds, with the drivers of which ours held a short conference, we found a slope leading up the bank, and making the best of our way through fields where there was no sign of a track, we gained at length the high road, which we were very glad to pursue for the rest of the night, and not try further navigation upon the river.

The fact was, our drivers were experimenting upon the sufficiency of the ice to bear us, and in the darkness of the night it was a miracle that we were not plunged into dangers from which it might have been difficult to escape. The trouble was, there had first been a severe frost, by which the river was sufficiently frozen for travel, after which there had been a thaw, a rise in the river, and a breaking up of the ice, succeeded by the present cold spell, leaving many holes and much water on the ice beneath the snow.

We kept the post-road and made tolerable time after we left the river, but it was a tough night, cold and raw, and from having to get out of our well stowed places several times, we suffered considerably. We were until near daylight in getting to the first station, twenty-one miles distant, where we fortified ourselves with several cups of hot tea, which revived us very much.

We dashed along through many towns and villages, over a comparatively level country, sometimes gently undulating, with but little forest. This is a fine grain and stock country. The post-horses were generally in good condition, and we made some rapid drives.

From Nijne-Novgorod to Kazan we were two days and a half, stopping only to change horses, drink tea, or take a hasty meal. We changed horses more than twenty times.

Kazan is 208 miles east by south of Nijne, and stands on high ground, near the Kama, about four miles above the Volga. It is chiefly built of brick, and has broad and winding streets. The population is about 60,000, of whom about ten or twelve thousand are Tartars. There is a very large bazaar and a handsome college, built of white stone. It is a place of considerable trade, being the central point of commerce between Moscow and St. Petersburgh on the west, Archangel on the north, Astrakhan on the south, and Siberia on the east.

Before we reached Kazan we had shivered one of the runners of our sleigh, where it turned up in front, this needed repair, and we also wanted a new shaft and more rope. The jolts and thumps we had received since leaving Moscow had satisfied us that we were far from being properly prepared for a Siberian journey, upon which we had, as it were, only just entered.

We here purchased a mattress to put in the bottom of our sleigh, and two pillows to support our backs and protect our heads and necks when sitting up from coming in contact with the wood-work in the jolts and thumps we received in rough parts of the road.

We added also to our wardrobe Kazan sheep-skin coats, which are warm, with the wool turned in, and are generally worn beneath an outer garment. I wore mine as an outer coat, having chosen it long and large for the purpose, so that it completely enveloped me from head to foot. The skin is dressed better here than elsewhere, and is soft, pliable, and silky. We found these coats, upon trial, exceedingly warm and comfortable; and with them and the bedding, we felt as if we certainly could keep out the cold, and sleep without having our necks dislocated or our backs broken. Mr. Peyton had a splendid buffalo robe, which he had brought from the United States, and by spreading this partly upon the mattress, and using the rest of it to cover our feet and legs, we protected our feet from the draft of air that came in at the fore part of the sleigh.

We set out from Kazan at midnight for Ekaterinburg, the next great stage of our journey. It was six days since we had left Moscow, and we had not slept anywhere but in our sleigh during the time. We proceeded now at a more rapid pace, the horses improving in speed and flesh the further we penetrated to the eastward; and even the roads appeared to grow better the further we passed from the capital, though perhaps the change was owing to the fact that we were now somewhat hardened to the roughness of the travelling, and besides, we were now fairly domiciliated in our vehicle, and felt quite at home in it. There was also more snow, and it lay evenly on the roads, with the absence of those dreadful *Oukhabas* lying in our track like a miniature frozen sea, with the waves frozen just as they were under the lash of the winds.

The most of the way between Kazan and Ekaterinburg the road was broad, smooth, and well beaten. For several hundred miles it is planted with double rows of trees on each side, and a foot-way between, painted verst-posts, water-ways, and bridges, as on a turnpike road. We were astonished by the beauty and regularity of the road, the perfect manner in which it is kept in repair, its regular grades, and the precision of engineering observed in its structure. It very seldom forms curves, but makes angles of various degrees, according to the face of the country, so that you have long stretches before you, the curves only occurring in ascending or descending abrupt hills or mountainous districts, where it is graded to suit the nature of the ground.

Town after town, village after village, and station after station, were passed as we hurried forward towards the ridge that divides Europe from Asia. Nothing occurred of any great interest on the way, except, as in Kazan, we frequently saw a large mixture of Tartar faces and costumes in several of the villages, and occasionally a mosque, denoting the prevalence of Mahommedanism yet among these people. We observed some really good faces among the girls, who, with their silver necklaces, girdles, and high, ornamented head-gear, were not by any means destitute of attraction. I saw several with fine teeth, lively countenances, and well-turned busts. Before reaching Kongour our sleigh was further damaged, our side-windows and lamps were smashed, our boxes thrown from the top to lighten it, and our baggage and traps settled down, jammed, and confined to the least possible space. A trunk lashed on the front part was filled with useless trash purchased in Moscow, taken from the inside, and all made firm and secure with ropes. Shaft ropes were renewed, wider and heavier fenders were lashed to the sides, like out-riggers to a canoe, to keep us from upsetting, and on we sped as fast as Tartar horse-flesh and Tartar drivers could hurry us.

CHAPTER V.

FROM EKATERINBURG TO OMSK.

We reached Ekaterinburg on the 16th December, 1856, on the thirteenth day out from Moscow, not having as yet slept in a house on the road. We found a very comfortable hotel here, in which we obtained rooms without beds, but provided with sofas and lounges, chairs, tables, mirrors, and warmed to a pleasant summer heat. It seems to be the practice in Russia for persons on the road to furnish their own bedding. A traveller through Eastern Russia and Siberia soon learns to get along without warm beds and downy couches, which would only tend to unfit him for the hardships of the road. We, however, found it no hardship to sleep on our own furs and skins, and to make our own bed upon the floor of a warm room, after having passed twelve nights in our sleigh.

Ekaterinburg is 1122 miles from Moscow; contains 25,000 inhabitants, and is situated on the river Iset, near some lakes. It is well built, with several fine churches, magazines, stores, and markets; and is the seat of much industry in copper, iron, glass, marble, and precious stones. There appears to be much wealth here, and the markets are plentifully supplied with meats, game, fish, and vegetables. We laid in a supply of fresh fish, quails, and white bread, for the road, at reasonable prices, and our friends did not forget a little *vodka*, or brandy. The weather was pleasant, because there was no wind, yet the atmosphere was hazy, so that the surrounding country was shut from view. The thermometer indicated 2° below zero. Our time was spent agreeably in visiting various workshops, and in looking about the town, to say nothing of the real, substantial, downright hard-sleeping that we luxuriated in during the two nights we remained in the city.

Ekaterinburg, perched upon the very summit of the Ural chain, half European, half Asiatic, takes one by surprise as he is entering into dreary and frozen Siberia. Its appearance would do credit to any country in Europe or America. The works in marbles and precious stones are very extensive and remarkable, and a stranger might occupy himself profitably for a month in their inspection. But my pathway lay so far to the east, and time being a great object with me just then, I was constrained to hurry away from this as I had from other places of interest on the road.

We departed from Ekaterinburg by daylight, the first time we had done so at any stopping-place since we left Moscow ; the country was covered with snow, but not in the least so as to impede travel ; the roads were well beaten, and our Asiatic horses fairly flew over the streets and out at the eastern gate. Our driver was a merry fellow, and sung, coaxed, and talked his horses to the very acme of speed. We did not forget him at the next change of drivers.

The descent of the Ural is so easy and regular, that with but little grading a railroad track would take the place of the present post-road: as an impediment to a railroad from Europe into Asia, the Ural Mountains amount to nothing. Much of the descent was well wooded, and had the appearance of having been subjected to the axe at regular periods, the trees were so uniform in their growth.

Twelve stations brought us to Tumen, a handsomely situated city, on the western branch of the Oby, and about 160 miles in a south-westerly direction from Tobolsk, and now its rival as one of the storehouses of the carrying-trade of the great Asiatic-European commerce. It is here that the two streams of trade meet from the east and from the west, one to rest before setting out on its great journey thousands of miles to the east; the other, to gather strength to cross the Ural into Europe, after its fatigue and hardships on the steppes and rivers of Asia.

Viewed by snow and moonlight, it appeared a well-built place, on navigable water, with wide streets, and large public squares. I walked from the station down to the bank of the river, and found the sidewalks paved, and bordered with trees. The watchmen, guardians of the night, were rendering it hideous by the deafening clatter of their *tam-tams*, arousing the dogs of the town, a numerous pack, whose barking kept time and tune to the tam-tams' din.

The town is 198 miles from Ekaterinburg, 1758 from St. Petersburg, and has a population of twenty thousand; of late years it has superseded Tobolsk in the eastern transit trade, and hence its growth in importance and population. Tobolsk formerly monopolized the entire transit of the eastern trade.

The weather had not, as yet, been very cold, only on the western side of the mountains, coming up from Kazan, on the steppes, with piercing wind blowing from the north and north-east—then the mercury was at 10° below zero. The cold was steady at Ekaterinburg, but was not in the least unpleasant, because the atmosphere was calm.

We rode out through the eastern portal of Tumen at full speed, our driver no doubt benefited by the stirrup-cup we had volunteered to give him, and enlivened by the tam-tams and the barking of the dogs ;—the clatter that the watchmen keep up must be admirably calculated to give thieves warning of their whereabouts, like the lighted lanterns of our Knickerbocker watchmen ; the custom is probably Tartar or Chinese. A faint relic of this is still observed in St. Petersburg, where you hear the *dvorniks* at night before their gateways, when not *asleep*, knocking on the pavement with their heavy pole-clubs, five or six feet long, and of formidable thickness.

We left the old beaten track by way of Tobolsk, and turned southerly, directly towards Omsk. The country here is populous, with evidences of Tartar origin among the people, though they are pretty thoroughly Sclavonized. Much of this country would be interesting, if traversed in summer, but the interminable horizon of snow is very monotonous. The country evidently contains much well-cultivated land, as we judged from the amount of stock and the good condition of the horses.

We crossed the steppe of Ischem, which lies between

the main western branch of the Oby and a southeast branch of the Irtish; this is a prolongation of the great Kirgeese Steppe; the road was well beaten, and we made very good time over a portion of it.

After a long, cold drive, with the mercury at 15° below zero, we reached Ischem, a town of five or six thousand inhabitants. It was market day, and the streets presented a lively and grotesque appearance as we passed along through the crowd of sledges, horses, men, and women, with an indescribable medley of provisions and merchandise exposed for sale in the open streets, either arranged on frames or rude tables, or spread upon the ground. It was evident, from the looks of the people, that we were quite as great curiosities to them, as they and their wares were to us.

Ischem is not far to the north of the Kirgeese country, consequently we found the real pure Tartar face somewhat prominently mixed up with the Sclavonic; in fact, this was formerly the seat of a formidable Tartar nation, where the successors of Gengis Khan held sway over a numerous and warlike people.

We rested at a *trakter* for several hours; had our sleigh repaired and new ropes put to the shafts; walked about the streets; saw several pretty Tartar-Sclavic girls, made them laugh and shew fine white teeth in our attempts to talk Russ; bought more rope and wrought-nails; packed into our sleigh, and separated from Ischem on the third day since we entered Asia.

We were whirled along at full speed during most of the day and night, along frozen water-courses or over lakes, seeming to have abandoned the regular road, but we came regularly to villages, where we obtained horses, and again sped merrily on. The road was often narrow, and the snow outside of the tracks was deep. At night we thumped and jolted against innumerable freight-sleds either going from or towards Ischem, and were frequently detained in the road waiting for them to yield us the track. All other vehicles must give way to the "post;" this does not necessarily mean that you are in a vehicle carrying the mail, but you are driving "post" horses, for which privilege you have paid the government half a kopyek per verst.

In the day time you are not often detained, because you can see the approaching train, or at the sound of your bells they clear the track, but at night, where the road is narrow or the banks steep with deep snow, the drivers find it difficult to force their horses off the road, or they themselves are half asleep sitting on their sleds, wrapped up in their great skin coats, and the horses having it all their own way, it is only by loud and long shouts and curses that your driver succeeds in getting a half clear track. The horses, from their own instinct, trying to avoid the unbeaten road-side, where hidden holes and pitfalls, covered deep with treacherous snow, await them, resist to the last the lashes and outcries with which they are assailed. The half-sleeping and frozen drivers of the sleds, equally unwilling to leave their seats or rouse from their snooze, stick to their places, and let your driver and their horses fight it out as best they can. They are generally sharp enough though, in the last resort, to keep out of the reach of the whip of your post-man, who is fully authorized, in case you back him up, to slash them right and left.

Many an animated chase we have witnessed between our *yamschek*, when willing to exercise his power, and some calf-skin-coated sled-driver, who had refused or neglected to give the road after the often-repeated shouts of the post-man. Sometimes the horse and sled would roll down the bank in one direction, the combatants in another, while we were left standing in the road witnessing this frequently amusing performance. On more than one occasion horses went down, sleds were overturned, broken, or stuck fast into holes; and in one case a poor horse's leg was broken. This accident, however, seemed to involve no very serious loss. Several of the drivers were Tartars, and the horse was knocked in the head, the hide stripped off, and the smoking carcase quartered and deposited on the same sled that, but a few minutes previously, he had drawn himself. At the next stopping-place the flesh afforded good steaks or soup, while the hide would be exchanged for a bottle or two of *vodka*.

These sleds generally run in gangs of ten to fifty, most commonly drawn by a single horse each, with one driver to every third or fourth sled; the cargo weighs from seven to ten hundred pounds. The second horse is tied to the tail of the first sled, and so on to the end. A thousand of these sleds have been passed by us in one day's travel, and at this season of the year the majority of those going west were loaded with tea from Kyachta.

We reached Omsk in the night, unfortunately, for I wished to see it by daylight. It is apparently a well built place, covering a large extent of ground, and seems to be regularly laid out. It is the seat of government for the district of Tobolsk and has about 20,000 inhabitants.

We found a very comfortable *trakter*, and while our horses were changing, had tea and beefsteaks for dinner. One of our companions, Capt. Malavetsky, was taken suddenly ill, which detained us several hours. We were, however, off again long before daylight.

CHAPTER VI

FROM OMSK TO IRKUTSK.

After leaving Omsk we hastened along over the terrible Barabinsky Steppe, which is much dreaded by Siberian travellers. We were caught here at night in a furious snow-storm, and our companion's sleigh was swamped in a drift, the driver having missed the road. Our yamschek, after driving on some time, stopped and listened for the tinkling bells. He presently got down, and thrusting his head into the window of our sleigh, said: "Baren nyat kolokel, nyat drogay vashok; snyag ochen mnogo." "Schto tam takoy?" we asked, What is the matter? He again repeated "that he heard no bells; that the other vashok was not coming, and that the snow was very great." "Well," said we, "what is to be done? We must not go on without our companions; it is necessary that we go in company; go back and see what has happened." He reached to us the rope reins through the window, and hastened back on the road. Before leaving us, however, he called loudly by name his brother yamschek, but received no answer. We remained in this position two long hours before we heard the bells and the shouts of the drivers

As our companions came up we started off, the snow falling in fitful, blinding showers. I feared that we should certainly lose the road, and have a horrible night in the snow-drifts, but either the driver or the horses possessed a kind of instinct for finding roads where none was visible, and after a most tedious and uncomfortable journey of several hours, we reached the next station, nearly used up. Hot tea was quickly provided, and we regained our spirits and our warmth.

Fresh horses rapidly carried us to the next station, which we reached about daybreak. In the morning our friends, or the yamschecks, took it into their heads to explore a new and shorter route than the regular post-road—one more to the south. We floundered along over unbeaten roads, or rather no roads at all, through a terrible waste of country, flushing a great many white partridges, upon which we experimented with our six-shooters. The result was, that after a very long and cold stage, on empty stomachs, half starved, and with worn-out horses, we stuck fast in a snow-drift at a village cross fence, but luckily the village, a very small, poor looking one, was in view. A bareheaded, skin-clad peasant, seeing our dilemma, came out from the village on horseback to see what we wanted, which he soon ascertained, for we had already broken two or three fence-rails in trying to prize the sleigh out. One horse was down, and it was thought best to let him use his own pleasure about getting up again, as when up he was of no service. The new and fresh horse of our village friend, with the assistance of additional stout and willing arms from the village, soon put us on a gallop towards it, where we found the whole population assembled to witness our entrance. Our driver told them his story, which must have been satisfactory, for they very readily offered us horses to assist us on our journey; besides which, we were kindly invited into the best house in the place. We found it warm, but its odor was very offensive after coming in from the open air.

Our companions having disappeared, a runner was despatched to seek them with fresh horses while we were waiting to have the tea got ready. It was soon steaming, and our companions having been dug out of a drift some miles in the rear, we gave them a warm reception, and such other creature comforts as our kind hostess could command were added to make out our last night's supper and the day's breakfast and dinner. The repast comprised tea, black-bread, fish-bread, boiled milk, and honey, to which was added, from our own stores, a little *vodka*, and we fared sumptuously.

It was difficult to decide among the crowd whose horses and drivers we should choose, so we managed to leave it with the villagers to arrange among themselves. Every thing was satisfactorily arranged, and after paying our hostess we took our departure.

We passed over a considerable extent of country before coming to the postroad again. Our companions supposed that we had gained something in distance by leaving the highway, but my private opinion was that, like the country girl in the dance, we had made it all up in turning round.

We, however, at length regained the postroad, and at several of the stations found horses ready harnessed awaiting the arrival of General Mouravieff, who, from the report of a courier, was hourly expected. In many villages and towns at night we found watch-fires burning, and in places where there were military stations there were officers awaiting his arrival. We made most excellent time over this portion of the road, being considered the avant-couriers of the general, as our party held special podorojnaya from him. We experienced on this part of the road the severest cold yet met with—50° below zero.

We reached Tomsk after the worst, the coldest, and the most tiresome, but the fastest night's ride since we left Moscow. The snow had been at least three feet deep on the road, and was rolled in waves like a miniature frozen sea, over which we rapidly dashed from station to station, each new yamschek seeming to be determined to exceed his predecessor in the punishment of horse flesh.

I thought it impossible that our sleigh could withstand the thousand-and-one shocks, and feared a breakdown or a smash-up every moment, and that our spinal-columns or neck-joints would certainly be dislocated ; but on we sped, our drivers being determined to spend as little time as possible on the road, a resolution which we heartily commended, for it was really a bitter and biting frost. We gave them extra kopyeks at every change of horses, which sent the next driver off in high spirits, talking to and praising his hardy little horses.

We were compelled to alight at every station and warm ourselves, examine the condition of our sleigh as well as the state of our half-frozen faces and feet, dislocated bones, and sprained and battered muscles. In fact, we had determined to make the journey a frolic, intending to have a good time of it, or at least the best possible under the circumstances; we therefore took every thing as we found it, mended it if we could, grumbled at nothing, kept as warm as possible, and paid the yamschecks liberally for fast driving. On the last day before coming to Tomsk we drove over two hundred miles and would have even increased upon that if the road had not become wretchedly bad.

On the morning of the 25th December, 1856, we galloped through the streets of Tomsk and drove into the court-yard of the "Gostennitzah Inostranetz." We found warm rooms and with the ever-welcome *samovar*, and real genuine Chinese tea soon made ourselves as comfortable as possible.

Our meals were served in our rooms, and as usual we made our sleeping-places ourselves with our own furs, cloaks, and skins. We found a wine list and billiard room in an adjoining building, and succeeded, with their help, in reviving and strengthening our worn-out frames. On the whole we contrived to spend a tolerably pleasant Christmas night in the city of Tomsk.

After getting thoroughly thawed out we rode and walked about the city, and it being the commencement of the annual fair, we had a good opportunity to witness something of the traffic and see many of the people from the southern borders. Tomsk has about twenty thousand inhabitants, and is the centre of a very extensive, and for Siberia, well-peopled country. The land is fertile, abounding in stock and grain. There are a large number of mines to the south and east and considerable trade, extending into Tartary, which, with its annual fair, makes the city the seat of an extensive commerce. At all events we found here many stores and warehouses, markets and bazars, with fish, flesh, and fowl, all effectually preserved by freezing. The fish when being handled rattled like so many bricks. Loads of iron, tea, wool, tallow, honey, hides, skins, furs, hay, grain, chickens, turkeys, and fish, filled the streets and lined the approaches to the city, and thousands of chests of tea lay piled in the streets, being transshipped on its way from Kyachta to Nijne-Novgorod. Bukarians, Songarians, Kalmuks, and other Tartar tribes added variety to the costumes of the people and excitement to the scene.

We purchased some Persian powder for exterminating vermin, which we were told would be very useful at times in such lodgings as a traveller might chance upon on the road. We also added to our store of provisions, and after spending a part of three days and two whole nights within doors, the first since leaving Ekaterinburg, we renewed our journey in as good if not better condition and health than when we left Moscow twenty-five days previous.

We left Tomsk rather reluctantly, that is, speaking for myself, I did. It was a bitter cold day, but the air was still, and we wrapped ourselves up as warmly as possible, deposited a teaspoonful of red pepper inside of our socks next to our feet, and rode on determined to make the rest of the journey to Irkutsk in quick time. We were now fairly in Siberia, with whole bones, not frost-bitten, and the coldest point reached, so that we felt as if the worst of the journey was over, having but the matter of ten or twelve hundred miles between us and Irkutsk, with a fund of experience and hard knocks sufficient to justify us in the belief that we could at least hold out till we reached our place of destination.

However, one pitch-dark night, with a thick hazy atmosphere, and bitter cold, we were descending a long hill before reaching Krasnoyarsk when our yamschek, either being asleep or the horses becoming unmanageable, we were thrown off the side of the road into a deep chasm; there we stuck hard and fast, our horses tugging and pulling and twisting to get out, but in spite of shifting of horses, with blows, coaxing, and swearing, we still stuck harder and deeper, with our sleigh, by this time, half buried in the snow. After an hour spent in all sorts of experiments and expedients our companions came up, having themselves met with some mishap which had detained them. With their assistance and the drivers of some freight-sleds which had very luckily come up, we were finally hauled out of the hole; but while all the men with our driver were about the sides and behind the sleigh, prizing and shouting, encouraging the horses, they gained a hard footing, and glad to get out of the scrape, went down the hill at full gallop. Seeing that the horses were off and the driver left behind, all we dared do, at the fearful speed at which we were rushing, was to sit still and see what would turn up; in fact, we could do nothing else. We thought of divesting ourself of our furs and trying to get from the door to the box to see if we could not recover the reins, but the speed was so great, and the motion of the sleigh bounding from one side of the road to the other, was so violent, that we concluded not to make the attempt. But we hoped that with the downhill inclination there would be a corresponding up hill, and so consoled ourselves with the reflection that if we did not turn over we would be able to stop on the next rise of ground if there should happen to be one before reaching the station.

We chiefly feared meeting with other sleighs and being thrown off the road and dashed to pieces ; however, on we went ; but how far, or what dangers were on either hand, the darkness prevented us from observing. In an instant there was a crash and a stop, as if the whole sleigh had been torn to atoms, yet we found ourselves occupying our accustomed places, and no bones broken, though pretty thoroughly shaken up. We got out of the sleigh as soon as possible, for one is not absolutely master of his own motions in a moment, with a Siberian winter-dress about him. The tinkling of bells and a harsh growl, like the snarl of a grizzly bear, was heard in the dim distance, which evidently came from the inmate of the sled going in the opposite direction, with which we had come in collision.

One horse was down, apparently lifeless, while two others had turned around and were standing at the back part of the sleigh entangled in the ropes and broken harness, while the fourth was *non est.* The shafts were shattered and the fore part of our craft knocked into a cocked-hat.

Seeing that all the damage was done that could be for the present (there being no danger of the two live horses getting off again with the sleigh), we awaited calmly and *very coolly* the advent of our driver. In due course of time, distance considered, he came up with his companion on the other sleigh, whereupon a council of war was held and a *post mortem* examination of vehicle and horse had, upon which it was decided to send to the nearest village for help and the necessary timber to bind up the wounds and splinter the breaks in our vehicle. Upon examination, our running gear was found in good condition, which was the most important of all.

All this was effected in the course of time, though not so soon as I tell it, nor did the night grow any warmer during the operation, and we became thoroughly chilled from standing in the road while the repairs were going on, but we survived to drink tea at the next station.

Our next halt was at Krasnoyarsk, a town of 6,000 inhabitants, and the centre of the mining operations of a very extensive region of country north and south. We rode about the town in a hack-sleigh, had a good dinner, with a bottle of sherry, at a *gostennitzah*, kept by a German, drank tea before leaving, and with the mercury at zero set out for Irkutsk.

We hastened on, making some very good days' works; passed through Kansk, Nijne Udinsk, and many other considerable towns, without any thing worthy of note, and arrived on the banks of the Angara, opposite Irkutsk, the capital of Eastern Siberia, on the 7th day of January, 1857, at four o'clock, P. M., making, within a few hours of thirty-five days since leaving Moscow, a distance of 3,545 miles; having slept out of our sleigh only three whole nights in that time, with an atmosphere ranging from 50° below zero to 10° above. We changed horses 210 times, and drove over 700 on the journey, with some 210 drivers, and twenty-five postilions. The actual time employed in the journey, including ordinary delay, was about twenty-eight days and nights, averaging, therefore, a speed of 126 miles every twenty-four hours, or five miles and a fraction per hour.

The river opposite Irkutsk was yet unfrozen, but large fields of ice were sweeping past with a rapid current. We were placed in a ferry-boat, propelled by oars and poles, and watching a favorable opportunity, when the river was partially free of ice, crossed to the opposite shore.

We came near camping out in the street the first night in Irkutsk. There is only one house that bears the name of hotel, Shultz's, kept by a German, and there was not a room to be had in it. Our kind companions, the Russian officers, succeeded, after some delay, in renting the upper story of a large house recently vacated, in which we were quickly domiciliated. Our whole cargo, for the first time since we left Moscow, was removed from our sleigh, and deposited in the room, where it made a queer enough medley. The old trunk that I had tied on to the fore part of the sleigh, and which had stood the voyage from San Francisco, was filled with the odds and ends of a cook shop, plates, knives, forks, spoons, cups, glasses, &c., and as we were about to enter upon housekeeping, were now all displayed, and a portion brought into requisition; our cloaks, *shoobas*, boots, mattress, skins, ropes, trunks, bags, and carpet-bags, were stowed in various corners, or hung up on convenient pegs or nails, and we were at home. The ever-grateful *samovar* was soon steaming on a table, tea was prepared, and we were soon warmed up and fortified until a servant was despatched to Shultz's to see if he could furnish us some dinner; but it was too late; dinner was over, and the arrival of five hungry men at one time created quite a panic in the kitchen; Shultz, however, sent us all he had to spare, which, with a portion of ham, some broken sausages, and some other odds and ends left of our old Moscow stock of provisions, kept us from absolute starvation.

It was really a joyous time with us, after such a long journey at the coldest season of a Siberian winter, to reach a house where we had the prospect of a few days and *nights* rest in a warm, comfortable room, where we could strip off the cumbrous furs and skins, and have again the free use of our limbs. Irkutsk, too, looked so pleasant and comfortable, with its fine wide streets, its substantial and spacious buildings, and numerous churches, that it appeared to us more like a pleasant dream than an actual, enjoyable reality. This beautiful city, seated on one of the finest rivers in the world, with its turrets, steeples, towers, domes, and crosses, gilded and burnished, and painted in different colors, took us so completely by surprise, that it really seemed like enchantment. We visited the theatre in the evening, and witnessed a very creditable performance.

CHAPTER VII.

IRKUTSK.

A FEW days after our arrival, we moved our quarters to really a fine and pleasant suite of rooms, fronting on the Angara, where we lived quite as comfortably as we would in places much nearer home. The hospitality of the principal citizens was unbounded, the people kind and civil, society agreeable, ladies handsome, wine good, and dinners excellent—what could a traveller ask more? We had hot baths, sleigh rides, pic-nics, ice-hills, suppers, routs, balls, and sleigh-promenades, to refresh and divert us.

General Mouravieff arrived on the 24th January, which was the signal for general gayety; dinners, balls, and parties, followed in quick succession. The day after his arrival he gave a reception dinner, to which we were invited. Captain Hudson had departed several days previously. At this dinner there were about sixty persons present—all, except Peyton and myself, Russians. There were no ladies.

The palace of the governor-general, in which the banquet was held, is a large, finely-proportioned building, situated on, and fronting the Angara River. At each flank of the building sentinels were standing in their gray overcoats, looking rather cold, shouldering their muskets, with large mittens on their hands, to protect them from the frosty steel.

We drove up in our sleigh, and entering the outer door, our cloaks, caps, and overshoes were taken by servants in military garb, and we were then ushered up a broad and spacious flight of stairs, into a large hall, in which the tables were already spread, and at the upper end of which were congregated a number of guests. Our friend Colonel Martenoff, aid to the governor-general, met us, and conducted us to the door leading from the hall, and through it to the reception room. We made our way through a crowd of elegantly-dressed officers, in full uniform, until, from within a third room, General Mouravieff made his appearance. He received us with great cordiality, in the midst of a brilliant staff and the high officers of his government, and welcomed us as Americans to Siberia, and as the pioneers to the Amoor, embracing us in the true Russian style, giving us a friendly hug, and kissing us at the same time.

Dinner was soon announced, and the General led the way to the dining-hall, an apartment about seventy-five feet long and thirty wide, with a very lofty ceiling. A military band of music occupied an overhanging gallery. The dinner was extremely well served, and I doubt whether a better could be got in Paris or London. The wines were choice and abundant, and the champagne and white wines in particular were of rare excellence and quality.

The dinner went on with great good humor, amid a tempest of conversation, while in the overhanging gallery the band at intervals discoursed most capital music.

General Mouravieff sat at the centre of the table, General Venzel, Governor of Irkutsk, sat on his right, and on his left was General Korsackoff, Governor of the Province of Trans Baikal. I sat opposite to General Mouravieff, and Mr. Peyton a little to the right of me. It was intended that we should have sat together, but some accident in seating the guests prevented this.

During the dinner, after the regular and national toasts were given, to which there was no reply but *vivas*, music, and cheers—speaking at dinner not being the custom in Russia—General Mouravieff proposed the toast, "America and Russia;" the whole company rose to their feet, and it was drank standing, with cheers. All eyes were turned in the direction of the two solitary Americans. I looked pleadingly at Peyton, who shook his head. I thought it too good an opportunity to be lost, though I did not feel like speaking; however, as I did not know how it would be regarded on such an occasion, I stood hesitating a moment, until I caught the approving smile of my friend Captain Martenoff, who had been placed near me, and who spoke English well; I then said:

"General Mouravieff, in responding to the sentiment just proposed by you, and which has met with such a generous and hearty response, you must pardon me if I o'erleap the bounds of custom, or trespass upon the usages of society here, a stranger among you, and not cognizant of the particular customs on occasions like the present. I shall act precisely as I would on a similar occasion in my own country.

"The sentiment proposed by you, 'America and Russia,' is particularly agreeable to the American heart, because

America recognizes in Russia, from the earliest records of her national existence, a true and steadfast friend. In the different angry and complicated questions, involving the rights of a new power, just emerging from the depths of a new world, Young America found in Old Russia a friend and co-laborer in the cause of 'Free trade and sailors' rights.' From the reign of the great Catharine, down to the present sovereign of Russia, America has received from Russia only the most friendly offices. In Alexander I., of glorious memory, and in Nicholas I., we recognized true friends, as is evidenced by our willingness to refer or submit to them complicated questions and grave disputes between the United States and a powerful European nation.

"The sentiment you have given is also most agreeable, because it brings up other and more recent remembrances of peace and good will between Russia and America; but on this occasion I shall not revert at length to the past, however agreeable and instructive it might be—it is with us to deal with the present.

"In a country so remote as Siberia from the centre of European civilization—a country so little known in my own, where to speak of Siberia causes a freezing sensation to steal over you—it is doubly agreeable to find one's native land so cordially and warmly regarded.

"We have now, in our time, and in our generation, a new epoch in the history of the world presented to us; Siberia, heretofore regarded as a *terra incognita*, and only *used* by geographers to fill up uncertain and waste space on the map of the globe, has emerged from that Egyptian darkness that enveloped her. Tartar rule and Tartar supremacy have passed away under the civilizing and enlightened rule of the Sclavonic race, spreading Christianity, the arts and sciences, trade and commerce, where all before was darkness, disorder, and superstition. A new era has dawned upon Siberia, under the enlightened guidance, and far-seeing and statesman-like policy of General Mouravieff. I stand here to-day, a living monument of that sagacious policy, to testify to the world that to General Mouravieff must be accorded the honor of making Siberia approachable from the Pacific Ocean by way of the Amoor River, and hereafter it will be recorded on the imperishable page of history as but a just tribute to his honor.

"What strikes a stranger particularly with amazement, is the vast extent and wonderful resources of this country, and one is equally amazed that they should have lain so long comparatively dormant and scarcely recognized by the world at large. But we are at the same time reminded that it was reserved for a Mouravieff to develop the resources and the knowledge of Siberia and the country of the Amoor. The Russian nation will owe, the world will owe, to the man whose genius has achieved this, true and lasting honor, because it must mark an epoch in history. Russia descending from the heights of the Altai to the great Eastern Ocean by way of this mighty river, and the United States descending to its opposite shores from the heights of the Sierra Nevada, will shake the friendly hand in commercial intercourse upon that mighty sea, and these two great nations will only vie with each other in developing the resources of their respective countries."

I closed by giving the health of "Nicolai Nicolaivitch, Lieutenant-General Mouravieff III., Governor-General of

Eastern Siberia, by whose enlightened, sagacious, and far-seeing policy in the opening of the Amoor River to commerce, this great hitherto unknown country is destined to become one of the most important on the map of the world." This was cheered by the guests, and the band struck up a lively Russian march.

Some further time was occupied in the dessert, when the champagne again flowed, and General Mouravieff, rising, proposed as a toast the health of the two Americans—Messrs. Peyton and Collins. This was drank with all the honors, and Peyton refusing to respond, I spoke again briefly. The banquet soon after closed, and we returned to our lodgings.

CHAPTER VIII.

IRKUTSK CONTINUED.

A RUSSIAN ice-hill is a very popular, cheap, innocent, healthful, and funny amusement.

I missed seeing the ice-hills at Moscow, as the season had not yet properly arrived before I left there. The ice hill at Irkutsk was elevated by a scaffolding of timber about twenty-five feet high, on the surface of the river in front of the city. An inclined plane, made of planks, upon which water is poured until a sufficient coating of ice is produced, runs off from the raised platform in an angle of 20°. Steps made along on both sides of the plane, reach a platform or landing sufficiently capacious to accommodate twenty or thirty persons with rude seats of plank, and a strong railing to prevent accidents. Up these steps swarm a living stream of persons of both sexes, who, arriving at the platform, take their regular turn to commence the descent, regulated by police officers to prevent accident or confusion. Arriving at the platform, and seated or lying upon small hand-sleighs, down this inclined plane they rush like lightning till they reach the surface of the river, where there is a clear wide track fenced off and scraped smooth, and cleared of all irregularities, along which, with the impetus received in coming down the hill, they glide for several hundred yards.

Along on each side of this icy track stand the spectators to witness the sport and laugh and shout at the mishaps, the upsetting and spillings that frequently occur. Around and on all sides are sleighs, with their fair loads of furred and rosy-cheeked dames and damsels, with their lovers, suitors, and gallants, all making themselves as agreeable and as happy as possible. The sport of riding down the hill here was mostly indulged in by the common people. I did not see either military men or fashionable ladies engaged in it ; though I think it is a favorite amusement among the upper classes in Western Russia.

Near this ice hill was cleared a wide double track for a race course, of near a mile in circuit, upon which all the fast nags, fast men, and handsome women, ride and race in their sleighs, which was really a very gay and pretty sight, and well worth spending an hour after dinner in witnessing.

The Angara closed opposite Irkutsk on the night of the 18th January, 1857, with the temperature 12° below zero. Why this river remains open so much longer than other water courses in Siberia over which we had been riding for a month past, and even when the whole surface of the lake from which it flows is frozen over, is worthy of investigation. It cannot be because of the rapidity of the current, for other rivers are frozen which are quite as rapid, and even the Angara itself at points lower down is frozen where the current is even more rapid than it is at Irkutsk. We must therefore account for this phenomenon in some other way. The Angara is the sole outlet to a large body of water, Lake Baikal, which is fed by many rivers; it is also fed by innumerable springs, and, besides, many warm springs are said to be submerged, which are connected with volcanic action beneath the surface of the lake, which is fully attested by the fact of large quantities of asphaltum being thrown up from the bottom; or it may be a natural result where large and deep bodies of water have but a narrow and confined outlet, that when the surface becomes frozen, the deep water being much warmer than the surface, and protected from the cold atmosphere by its shield of ice, that the escape water would not be below the freezing point. Consequently, it would have to be some time exposed to the atmosphere before it would become cold enough to congeal.

There is a large space just at the outlet of the lake where the river forms, which I was informed never froze. This open space is sending up volumes of vapor, and innumerable ducks and divers are sporting there the whole winter, while there is not a drop of uncongealed water to be found elsewhere in Siberia. This water extends for several miles down the river. I passed the lake and its outlet three times during the winter, and found it clear of ice and full of water fowl.

CHAPTER IX.

IRKUTSK CONTINUED.

Irkutsk, the capital of Eastern Siberia, has a population of about twenty thousand, and is situated on the northern or right bank of the Angara River, about forty miles by the course of the river from the lake, and opposite the mouth of the Irkut, which flows into the Angara from the south. It has many churches and public institutions, is well built, lighted, and paved.

The Angara is the only outlet to the pent-up waters of Lake Baikal, which is five hundred miles long by forty to sixty wide, and in portions of it of an unfathomable depth. The rivers emptying into Baikal drain an extensive country, and draw their sources from that chain of mountains which divide the waters of the Frozen Ocean from those of the Pacific. The Selenga River penetrating far into the regions of Mongolia, is only separated from the waters of the Ho-ang-ho, the great river of Northern China, by the mountain ridges of Cobi. Many rivers, from more than three hundred sources, unite to make up this beautiful sheet of water.

To appreciate the peculiar and singularly fortunate position of this city, one must study a good map of

Northern Asia. The Angara falls into the Upper Tonguska several hundred miles to the north-west of Irkutsk; the Tonguska again falls into the Enesei not far above the town of Eneseysk, from whence by a comparatively short portage you reach an eastern branch of the Oby, which, leading still in the main a westerly course, conducts you into the Irtish, which you ascend to the very foot of the Ural; thus having passed by water, with one very short portage, across the whole western extent of Siberia. To the east and north, within a few hundred miles, are the navigable waters of the Lena, which conducts by Yakutsk towards the sea of Okhotsk, and soon by the Aldan to the Okhotsk, and thence across it to Kamschatka. All these great northern rivers flow with a navigable breadth and depth into the waters of the Frozen Ocean, and are, even up to this day, quite unused in much of their course, though for some months in the year free of ice, because their length and rapidity of current render them unavailable to any agent but steam, and that as yet has not been introduced. It may be said that commerce can never enter into this cold and inhospitable region, or that there is nothing upon which commerce may subsist. On the contrary, bread and meat are quite as cheap in Siberia as they were upon the banks of the Wabash before Fitch built the first steamer on the Ohio. The rivers are flanked with fine forests, the banks yield iron and coal, gold, silver, and copper, while the waters and forests are abundantly stocked with fish, fowl, and game, only awaiting the advance of population and the introduction of steamboats and railroads.

To the south you have the noble Angara, connecting

with the Baikal, and leading off to the plains of Mongolia by the Selenga, connecting the great Russian Chinese marts of Kyachta and Mia-mat-tschin with a population of twenty millions, whose trade must all pass through the gates of Irkutsk, pulsating and circulating regularly between the imperial cities of Moscow and Pekin.

To the east of Kyachta, not many hundreds of miles, and if a railroad were constructed only twenty-four hours distant, you come upon the great outlet of Northern Asia —the river Amoor.

Irkutsk thus situated, with a salubrious climate, a productive soil, noble rivers, and oriental commerce, rich in gold and silver, iron and coal, copper and lead, salt and asphalt, and ivory, presents to us a queenly little city, seated upon the beautiful shores of the Angara, to whose future grandeur and prosperity it is not easy at present to assign limits.

The necessities incident to Asiatic Russia are quite reversed by the laws of nature; having within her borders the noblest system of rivers in the world; they are yet, in a great degree, unavailable to her necessities, from the fact that their entrance into the ocean is so far north as to render them, in consequence of the severity of the climate, wholly unavailable during nine months in every twelve; owing to this, and to the fact that the ocean into which they flow, to its high northern latitude, is nearly useless in a commercial point of view, being, as its name implies, "the Frozen Ocean," they can only be reached at great expense, delay, hardship, and privation. The trade, then, of Siberia, in seeking an outlet for its commerce, as well as an inlet to its wants, must seek it against all precedent, and all example, towards the sources of her great rivers; and these again, mostly in their general course, being from south to north, have their origin in that great back-bone of Asia, which divides the waters of that continent between Northern and Southern Asia. The commerce, then, of this vast country, seeking a channel of communication with other countries and nations, must, of necessity, seek the sources of new rivers for an outlet; and in case of failure to meet the required facilities of water communication, must content itself with the more difficult and costly route by land, the only resort left to it. Hitherto, the close and jealous policy of the people inhabiting the more southern portions of Asia, has forced the trade of that country westward, in order to seek an outlet. This route, which would be absolutely impracticable under any other than the government of Russia, has, under the fostering and thoughtful wisdom of that government, become one of the greatest commercial arteries in the world.

Concentrating, as it does, at Kyachta, where it gathers the trade of Manchooria, Mongolia, and China, settling the balances, and arranging the exchanges, it then flows westward in a steady stream by land and by water, often slow, tedious, and expensive, until it becomes lost in the great ocean of European-Russian commerce at Nijne-Novgorod; there it commingles, increasing and perfecting that immense system of Russian inland commerce flowing towards the imperial marts of Moscow and St. Petersburg.

This trade, although great, is absolutely one of complete necessity, and flows only in a necessitous and restricted current, not at present susceptible of world-wide expansion, or of much interest out of its immediate local influence. What, then, does this country want? The question is easily answered—It wants a cheaper, an easier, a more rapid, and a more constant communication to the sea. What sea? Not the Polar Sea—nature has laid a prohibition in that direction; not the Baltic, or the Caspian, or the Black Seas, which would lead to the Atlantic Ocean—that she has now by the present overland route. What then remains? The overland route to Pekin. Yes; but the land carriage is too great to reach the sea that way, even if permitted by China.

What, then, is left? There is no communication eastward, in Siberia, into the Pacific Ocean by water; if there was, the intense severity of the climate renders it impracticable. It seems, then, that there is no escape. East, west, north, south, all seem to be barred by nature, or by man. But do not be too hasty; look upon that map once again. There is a chain of mountains, not very high, that skirts the south-eastern horizon; look once again, you will see that two great systems of waters are forming upon their gentle sides, and interlocking their rivulets within their ravines and gorges; gathering the dew-drops, embracing the bubbling springs, absorbing the murmuring brooks, and presently, on either hand, course great rivers, on their way to far distant, far different, and far divided oceans. Lake Baikal receives the drainage of these waters on the north, while the Amoor receives the waters from the eastern and southern sheds, gathering, in its mighty course, the accumulated streams of a hitherto unknown little world, and onward rolling its unbroken and majestic course for 2,500 miles, towards the rising sun, and the mild waters of the Pacific Ocean. Throw yourself with confidence upon its flowing tide, for upon this generous river shall float navies, richer and more powerful than those of Tarshish; mines shall be found upon its shore richer than those of Ophir, and the timbers of its forests more precious than the *Almugim* of Scripture; a mighty nation shall rise upon its banks and within its valleys, and at its mouth shall arise a vast city, wherein shall congregate the merchant princes of the earth, seeking the trade of millions of people.

CHAPTER X.

FROM IRKUTSK TO KYACHTA.

On the 3d of February we partook, by invitation of the *Golovah*, or Mayor of Irkutsk, of a dinner given by him to General Mouravieff. It was a very elegant and costly affair, and numerously attended. After dinner we made some evening calls, and, retiring to our lodgings, prepared for our journey to Kyachta and Mia-mat-tschin.

For some reason or other a Russian has a very great distaste to set out on a journey in the day-time. I got into the habit, or rather yielded to the necessity, while in Siberia, of commencing most journeys in the night-time; the fact being that the day previous to setting out was generally occupied in making calls, receiving company, or in entertainments, and besides the day is so short that the hours allotted to business matters are few. The night, therefore, was really the most pröper time for starting, as you did not have to get out of a warm bed, and dress and wash, but merely to tumble out at the station and await the change of horses.

We left Irkutsk at 1½ A. M., on the 4th February, for Kyachta and Mia-mat-tschin, travelling upon and beside the Angara until we reached Lake Baikal, and then partly on that and partly on its western shore for some 40 miles to the point of crossing. Our driver arranged so that we had daylight to cross in. It had been reported at Irkutsk that there were still openings and fissures in the lake which would make crossing at night dangerous, and at all events it would have been unpleasant to take a bath in such icy waters twenty miles from land.

We drank tea at the last station on the north-west shore of the lake under a high steep mountain, and caught a fine view of the opposite shore, beyond which the crest of the Altai range peeped out from a cloudy horizon long enough to give us a fleeting view of great beauty and grandeur.

There were now three of us in the same sleigh in which we had travelled from Moscow, but we were not encumbered with any baggage except a few clean shirts. It was severely cold, and, wrapping ourselves up in our furs, we packed closely into the sleigh while our horses were being held by the head to keep them from starting, our driver being already on the box. The word was given, *poshol horoshinkey*, and off we dashed from the front of the station down the bank and on to the lake at full speed, with four tough, frosty, shagged little white horses, whose sharp-shod feet clattered merrily upon the firm smooth ice, on which the track was marked by green pine boughs.

Certain loud reports, like the booming of cannon, which we had heard in the early morning as we came up the shore of the lake, together with the clouds which we had seen arising from its surface, had prepared us to encounter an ice-wall, or rather a ditch and moat in the very midst of the lake. Accordingly, when about ten miles from shore, we encountered one of these "ice-walls," thrown up during the previous night by the collapsing of the ice. This brought us to a stand, for the ridge was too abrupt to be passed. Our driver, however, jumped from the sleigh, and while his horses were gathering a little breath, beat down the rampart with an iron instrument he carried for the purpose. In a very few minutes we were again gliding over the ice at full speed. Mr. Beetsov, the diplomatic secretary of General Mouravieff, carried a courier's pass, with dispatches for Pekin via Kyachta, and therefore had the right to kill as many horses as he chose, if they did not keep up to time.

The clattering of the horses' sharply-shod feet, accompanied by the sonorous and hollow sound as the sleigh passed along, had a strangely soothing effect, so that I could scarcely keep my eyes open ; or it might have been that I had not slept the previous night ; however, determined not to miss the novel scenery around me, I kept my eyes alert by the occasional application of a handful of snow.

We only stopped once more to brush the ice and frost from the nostrils of our puffing horses, and went on again at a round gallop, the ice thundering and cracking under our horses' feet more than once in a way that greatly accelerated their pace. The shore where the river Selenga comes in is low and uninteresting, but to the north and south the scenery is very grand. The lake was passed, and our station in Trans-Baikal reached, in somewhat more than three hours. This may be considered very good driving with one set of four horses, without even a sup of water or a moment's rest, except the two short halts of not over five minutes on the way, a distance of 45 miles, or nearly 15 miles an hour.

We now traversed a thickly-settled country, keeping along the banks of the main Selenga, but frequently taking to the ice on small streams, lakes, or ponds. We saw much grain in stacks, and barns well filled, plenty of cattle, sheep and horses, hemp and flax.

At Verchne-Udinsk, which is about two hundred miles from Irkutsk, and the most important town on the Trans-Baikal side of the lake, except Kyachta, we took the frozen surface of the Selenga, nor did we leave it till within a few miles of Kyachta. This river is rich in wild and beautiful scenery, has almost continuous settlements along its banks, and large flocks of sheep were grazing upon the mountain sides. We only stopped to change horses at the regular stations, which were generally convenient to the river, and frequently our sleigh was left standing upon the river until a change of horses was provided. We saw in the distance Old Selenginsk, once the capital of this country before Irkutsk was founded, but now shorn of much of its former greatness by the march of empire eastward. It stands, nevertheless, in a fine agricultural and stock country, and still has some of its former trade.

The scenery on this river is fine, even in the winter; it must be really enchanting in spring and summer. The mountains are lofty, with beautiful valleys interspersed, and there is much forest. Yet some of the mountains form steep precipices, whose bare and almost perpendicular sides quite overhang the river. As the river winds through this beautiful country, you see many vistas where the landscape would well reward the pencil of an artist.

Old Selenginsk, the scene of very early Russian power and settlement in these regions, looks deserted, and has lost rank since the settlement of New Selenginsk on the opposite side of the river, a mile or more distant. This is the point to which the early ambassadors came on their way to Pekin, and where troops and munitions were gathered to be used in Tartar warfare.

The river abounds in fish, and great quantities are taken by the people in the spring and summer; particularly a fish called *omully*, which comes up out of Baikal to spawn, like the herring in our rivers on the Atlantic coast. Whether these fish come from the sea I could not learn, but I believe it is said that the lake is to them the sea. Seals also are found in the lake the year round, and are caught by the people in the winter for their skins. There are many varieties of fish in Baikal—one especially interesting, which at certain periods is cast dead upon the shores of the lake. A live one has never been seen. This fish is a mere mass of fat, from which the inhabitants make quantities of oil, which is largely used for domestic purposes, and is burned for light. Bitumen or asphalt is also thrown up from the depths of the lake and cast upon the shores, and from this also the people easily obtain oil. The shock of an earthquake was felt here on the 10th of August last. Baikal was called the Holy Sea by the native Tartars; and the fact of these migrating fish and seal living in it the year round, would justly entitle it to be classed as a sea.

We reached the mouth of Kyachta creek, where it falls into the Selenga, about 10 P. M., on the second day after leaving Irkutsk. Here we had to leave our sleigh, as the road was practicable only for wheel-vehicles. The police master of Kyachta had passed us on the road, and at this point, without our knowledge, had already provided the necessary means of conveyance for us to Kyachta, and was also prepared to render us all the aid and comfort in his power within his bailiwick. A merchant of the place sent for us to his house, where supper was provided, and we were treated with every civility; but I was too unwell to enjoy the supper, and wanted a doctor more than a cook.

The tarantass, a large partially-covered, four-wheeled vehicle, swung on elastic poles between the wheels, which were at least twelve feet apart, was ready with four black horses, and we set forth about midnight. The night was raw and cold, 15° below zero, with a piercing freezing wind. The police master and Captain Beetsov rode on before us in another vehicle, so as to have our quarters prepared before we should reach Kyachta, as we learned afterwards.

The road proved long, tiresome, and heavy, the horses having at times as much as they could do to pull us at a walk. We reached Troitzkosavsk about 5 A. M., on the second morning from Irkutsk, nearly frozen, sick, and miserable. I had not felt so uncomfortable since leaving Moscow; in fact, it was the worst five hours that I had passed in Siberia.

CHAPTER XI.

KYACHTA AND MIA-MAT-TSCHIN.

We found our friends at the house prepared for our lodgings just on the outskirts of the town. It turned out that this house belonged to Mr. Egouminoff, the oldest and one of the chief merchants of Kyachta, and had been appropriated to our use while we should remain in the place—how, why, or by what means, I never could fully learn—but I attributed the whole affair to the magic wand of our friend, General Mouravieff; which, in Siberia, is almost equal in potency to the lamp of Aladdin.

Fires were soon lighted in our lodgings, and we made our beds upon sofas, with our furs and pillows, and rested for several hours. The rattle of crockery and the stir of attendance soon indicated that we were not to starve, and presently we had before us a charming breakfast: delicious tea, light crisp bread, steaks, and cold fowl.

We had slept a little since our arrival, but yet my head continued to ache, and I felt really sick; but the tea seemed to revive me, to which I added a teaspoonful of magnesia with a little vinegar, which in the course of an hour relieved me very much.

So soon as we were rested we called upon our host, Mr. Egouminoff, who had sent his own vehicle for our use; this was a very genteel *drojke* on four wheels, with a seat running fore and aft, on which half a dozen persons could be seated back to back—a well-dressed driver and a really fine and spirited horse made up a capital turn-out.

We found Mr. Egouminoff at his own residence in the city of Kyachta, two miles distant from Troitzkosavsk, where he received us with great cordiality and hospitality. After remaining a short time with him, we drove over the Russo-Chinese line to take a hurried look at the Celestials in the city of Mia-mat-tschin. We had many cups of tea and some cups of hot wine with the merchants of "The Flowery Kingdom," looked at their shops and storehouses, their temples and idols, walked through their streets, very closely eyed by the curious people, and, by appointment, returned to dine with Mr. Egouminoff.

The dinner was excellent, with several kinds of wine, closing with champagne. We had also the pleasure of the company of Mrs. E. and daughter, and several other guests, besides a handsome widow. We saw what we could of the little city, and retired to our quarters to get a night's rest, which, after the three previous nights, mostly spent on the road, we found very desirable indeed. That night was one of the nights to be recollected, and we did not wake up till late the following day, when we accompanied a party of Russians who were invited to dine with a Chinese merchant in Mia-mat-tschin.

We had a bountiful number of dishes, and I have no doubt it was a good dinner, if we could have known how to have eaten it. Wine and spirits were also served, and tea afterwards, to which I did full justice—pure and simple tea out of nice little China cups. After dinner the ladies went shopping, as ladies will do in all countries, the fair dames and damsels of Siberia being every whit as fond of the amusement as our own wives and sisters on this side of the water.

Porcelain jars and vases, fancy laquered boxes, fans, and other little Celestial notions, just from Pekin and Nankin, Moukden and Canton, with musk from Thibet, and shawls from Cashmere, rubies and garnets, pearls and opals from Bukaria, Cabul, and Balk—all these little notions, with a thousand others, were priced and examined, some purchases were made, and after a visit to a tea warehouse and the capacious kitchen of our host, where our dinner had been prepared, we retired to Kyachta.

I do not know who proposed to make a visit of inspection to the kitchen, but the ladies eagerly seconded the motion, anxious to get a glimpse at the interior of Chinese cookery. A glance was sufficient. The ladies silently retreated the instant they reached the threshold, and we followed them with little delay. The walls of the kitchen were covered with paintings, as large as life, of the most grossly obscene character.

Mr. Egouminoff, judging rightly that our Mia-mattschin repast was one more satisfying to curiosity than to the stomach, had a sumptuous dinner prepared for the party upon our return, to which we sat down soon after reaching his house.

CHAPTER XII.

THE FEAST OF LANTERNS.

MR. DESPOT ZENOVITCH, the commissioner of the *frontier*, an office nearly equivalent to that of consul-general and collector of the customs combined, showed us much attention and civility, and, among other clever acts, invited us to accompany him to the "Feast of Lanterns," the new year or white moon of the Chinese, to which he was invited by the governor of Mia-mat-tschin, Pah-Loyah, the "Zar-gots-tschay." We were introduced as Russian merchants from St. Petersburg; the party consisted of some twenty merchants and other guests.

We were introduced as Russians, because had it been as Americans, it would have led to explanations on the part of the commissioner, which he wished to avoid. Captain Beetsov explained this to us, and said that further west than St. Petersburg the Zar-gots-tschay would not be able to comprehend. I was perfectly willing to forego my nationality for the time, in order to attend the "Feast of Lanterns."

In company with the commissioner, in a vehicle, escorted by a troop of Cossacks, we passed out of the southern gate of Kyachta, over the neutral ground, to the northern gate of Mai-mat-tschin. Here we were received

4

by a Mongol guard of honor, and, preceded by a band of music, we entered the principal street on our way to the hall of entertainment. The houses are well built, generally around a court, are mostly of one story, and entered through a gateway, or port, before you reach the residence of the owner. The streets are narrow, say fifteen feet in width, but very clean, and covered with a kind of cement for pavement. As we passed, the streets were crowded with Chinese and Mongol faces to get a sight of the "outside barbarians."

Arriving at the entrance of the court leading to the residence of the Zar-gots-tschay, we alighted from our carriage, and, amid the squeaking of fiddles, the rattle of drums, and the clang of gongs, entered through courts and corridors into the dining-hall, or "room of feasts." Here we found the chief, an aged, tall man, of the Manchoo race, who received us with great cordiality. We were soon seated, and tea being served with confectionery, the "feast" commenced. I sat next but one to the chief on his right hand; wine being served, he motioned us to drink. A very burning kind of spirit was also served in small cups, and the number, kind, and quality of the dishes, or rather bowls, which were constantly being served, was absolutely beyond computation. Each guest was furnished with a saucer half filled with a kind of soy, or diluted vinegar, into which the delicious morsels taken from the aforesaid bowls by the little soup-ladle or chopsticks at the side of your saucer were to be dipped; the chief frequently selecting with his own *chops* dainty morsels, which he conveyed to my now overflowing saucer in the most patronizing and gracious manner.

After these innumerable courses, the table was cleared, when, from the upper end of the room, came attendants, bearing tables, on which were several whole pigs, roasted in the most approved style, and approaching quite to the front of the chief, exhibited to the guests this crowning glory of the "feast," all smoking hot. The chief bowed approvingly to the cook, and the pigs disappeared by a side door. Then came clean saucers and more soy, and soon followed well filled bowls of the aforesaid pigs, all finely cut into thin strips, with pieces of the crisped skin broken into small squares. Finally, small bowls of plain boiled rice, perfectly dry, were served, and the feast closed in honor of the Russian guests with sparkling champagne.

A few minutes before we sat down to dinner, we were invited into the court in front of the hall to witness the performance of a band of players, among whom were several men dressed as women, in a native Mongol dance. During the dinner the band of musicians were piping their music, and performing their antics for the gratification of the crowd on the outside. After champagne was freely drank, the chief invited the company to visit the theatre. This we did on foot; and here was presented a scene worthy of the pencil. The chief, preceded by a few Mongol guards to clear the way of the crowding multitude, conducted us to an open pavilion in front of the theatre, where we were seated on wooden benches around a table. The theatre is simply a stage open in front and on the sides, with screens for the performers to retire behind. The audience stand in the open air. The players were already in the midst of some grand scene when we arrived.

The Mongol guards cleared, and kept free a space in

front of the chief's box. Tea, confectionery, and dried fruit were served to us during the performance of the play. The crowd of spectators swayed to and fro like the surges of the ocean. The united breath of the multitude ascended like steam from a boiling caldron, the temperature being at 12° of Fahrenheit below zero.

After some time spent here we visited the great pagoda. By this time night had set in, and the illumination by lanterns had commenced in good earnest. Passing through a court immediately in front of the theatre, we were conducted by the Zar-gots-tschay into the temple. On tables in front of the different idols a great variety of dishes were spread, with whole carcasses of sheep, as a repast for the gods. At night these dishes are taken by the priests and eaten in the recesses of the temple. The sheep, I suppose, go the way of all flesh, and serve for the priestly dinner next day.

From the temple we returned to the dining-room, where a party of Russian ladies from Kyachta and Irkutsk had been invited to meet us to take tea, and then to partake with us of the "Feast of Lanterns." They soon arrived. Tea, confectionery, and fruits were served. Some children that were along were loaded with sweet things by the good-hearted old chief. We were now very soon on our way to see and partake of the "Feast of Lanterns." But how shall I describe the indescribable! Led on by the Zar-gots-tschay, preceded by the whole band of musicians, actors, and mountebanks, with two special lantern-bearers carrying great round lanterns immediately in front of the chief, and followed and pressed on all sides by a motley crowd of Tartars, we commenced the promenade of the evening.

The streets were beautifully ornamented with colored paper suspended from the roofs of the buildings on cords, and lanterns of every imaginable size, shape, and color, lighted the streets and illuminated the buildings and temples.

Thus led on, pressed by the crowd, to the tune of the unmusical Mongol music, we proceeded through one of the principal streets to the residence of the first merchant with whom we were to "feast," and this was to be repeated eight times in different parts of the city at as many different establishments. But it will not do to describe the eight suppers or feasts; they were but little removed in style or fashion from the dinner. Of course, eating was out of the question and impossible; but tasting and drinking innumerable cups of tea and hot Chinese wine was absolutely necessary, in order to satisfy the pressing invitations of the various hosts, who frequently added Madeira and champagne.

At the entrance of each establishment the musicians ranged themselves in open order, piping us into each house, and during the repast continued their antics and music for the amusement of the crowd without. At our exit they took up the line of march, the lantern-bearers resumed their station, and on we went amid fireworks, fire-crackers, plays, and lanterns, to the next feast, and so on to the end.

The concluding feast was near the gate. The Zargots-tschay and the host of the feast bid us good night. We reached our vehicle at the outer port, the Mongol guard and music conducting us. Here the commissioner's Cossack escort were mounted, waiting, and, amid the shouts of the crowd, we crossed the "neutral ground," and passed the gate of Kyachta, put the commissioner down at his residence, and reached my lodgings, three miles distant, all the better for the ride, in a clear frosty night, with the thermometer at 12° below zero, which helped much to counteract the effects of the various Chinese potations.

CHAPTER XIII.

A RUSSIAN DINNER.

On the day previous to our departure, we were invited by the merchants of Kyachta to a public dinner, to be given at their club-rooms, to the two Americans, the first that had ever been in their city.

The club-house is handsome and spacious, and the dining-hall capable of seating a hundred guests. When we arrived, at four P. M., a numerous party were already assembled. The military were well represented, and the principal civil functionaries of the city were present.

A band of music struck up as we entered, and, passing into the room, we were received by the Golovah, who welcomed us in the name of the merchants of Kyachta to their city, as the pioneers of American commerce, and the heralds of steamboats on the Amoor.

We passed along through the dining-room, to an adjoining apartment, where most of the company were assembled. Here we were introduced to various gentlemen, among whom we also found several old acquaintances from Irkutsk. About sixty persons sat down to dinner, after having observed a custom which is nearly universal throughout the empire. Either in the hall, in an adjoining room, or upon a side-table in the dining-room, is prepared what we would call a luncheon, composed of bread, salted fish, caviar, ham, butter, brandy, wines, and cordials. Each guest partakes of this, as an appetitive, just before going to dinner, in fact, on his way to the table—a true Russian dinner is not complete without it.

The dining-room swarmed with servants, and the band of musicians and a choir of singers gave us instrumental and vocal music at intervals. The dinner proved to be a regular drinking-bout, and I soon saw that in all probability we were fairly in for a debauch, at least if we drank but one toast out of ten. To avoid drinking was out of the question, among such a lot of good fellows, and our only salvation was to touch as lightly as possible before the champagne came, which is generally towards the close of the entertainment, at which time you are expected to drink bumpers. But unfortunately the champagne began to flow before the dinner was half over, and as bumpers must be drank out of respect and politeness, as well for the host as the subject toasted, I began to fear that I should really run over before the dinner closed.

The emperor always receives the first toast, after which there appears to be no regularity in the form and manner of toasting. The name of General Mouravieff was next given, and without a moment's consideration whether it was proper or not, though knowing that the custom of responding to toasts does not prevail in Russia, I rose to reply, and said as follows:

"Gentlemen-merchants of Kyachta, you have done well in drinking to the health of Nicolai Nicolaivitch Lieutenant-General Mouravieff, and with your permission,

I cannot refrain from saying a few words when I hear his name mentioned.—(Clapping of hands, and horosho! horosho!! good! good!!)—Because I have had an opportunity to see what he has done for your country. In him Russia has a true, a faithful, a vigilant, and sagacious public servant. He knows the wants, the interests, and the rights of Russia, and how to provide for the one, to advance the other, to defend her when in peril.

"In opening up Siberia to the commerce of the world, through that magnificent river the Amoor, whose head waters drain yonder snow-clad mountains, he has done more for your country than any of his predecessors. Look upon the map, and regard the peculiar situation of Siberia, and you must at once perceive that it is only through this river that you can have communication with the great ocean, and thus an extended commerce with all the nations of the world.

"This great river, and its tributaries in the possession of Russia, with steam upon their waters, and a railroad connecting you and it with Lake Baikal, and steamers upon this magnificent sheet of water, and the more western rivers of Siberia, would open up a system of inland navigation, wonderful in extent, and absolutely past calculation in its commercial results.

"Siberia, then, would be able to contend with England for the commerce of China and of India. Peter the Great and Catharine II. thought the Chinese commerce worthy of their consideration, and the existence of your own beautiful, rich, and prosperous little city, attests the wisdom of their policy; and I shall be very much mistaken if your present sagacious emperor does not increase your

4*

wealth by increasing the borders and commerce of your country also, and that before a very long period.

"I am no prophet, nor the son of a prophet; but if General Mouravieff does what I think he will do, and what I believe Russia ought to allow him to do, I believe that his country will hereafter accord to him the honor of creating a new era in the history of Siberia, for the occupation of the Amoor River by Russia must become celebrated in history as the event of an age.

"It is with great pleasure, then, that I have drank his health, because through his policy in opening the Amoor, the Americans will become acquainted with Siberia and Siberians, and with the great trade of your own city, and from what I have already witnessed, that acquaintance will prove of mutual advantage, and a great commerce must spring up between the two countries, beneficial to both."

This speech created a lively sensation, and was well received; hands were shaken prodigiously, and champagne flowed fiercely. After some little time spent in animated conversation, the Golovah proposed the health of the President (elect) of the United States, Mr. Buchanan. This was of course drank standing, with cheers and bumpers, and as my companion would not respond, I rose to the call from all sides of the house, and let off a little of the champagne in the following speech:

"Gentlemen-merchants of Kyachta, it gives me unalloyed pleasure, as an American citizen, in a land so far remote from my native country, and one so distant as this is from the active scenes of our national politics, to reply to the toast just proposed, 'the President of the United

States of America.' In proposing this toast, you have, as Russians, done honor to a friend, because I know personally the sentiments of the President towards your country.

"If it were possible for Russia to want proof of our determination to act justly and fairly with her, we could point triumphantly to the fact that our President recently dismissed the minister of one of the most powerful nations of Europe, because he violated a principle of our national law, wherein Russia was concerned during the late allied war against her.

"But you want no extraordinary or recent proof of our friendship and good-fellowship towards your country, for the United States have been your true and tried friends since our national existence.

"It is truly gratifying to us, as Americans, to respond here in Kyachta, ground on which no American ever stood before, to so friendly a sentiment. It revives in us reciprocal feelings towards your sovereign, who has manifested the most friendly feelings towards our country.

"The President of the United States but reflects the will, and gives utterance to the voice, of the American people in his friendly relations with Russia. Receive, then, gentlemen, from us, the reciprocal assurances of friendship towards your own beloved country."

By this time every thing had disappeared from the table except bottles and glasses, and bumpers were exchanged between neighboring parties, just in order to keep their hands in for the next regular toast. Presently the Golovah rose, and glasses all being filled to the brim, and running over, silence was restored, and he gave, "Our guests, the Americans."

I was now ready and willing to resign to my companion the oratorical field, and retire upon my honors, but Peyton would not speak, so off I went for the honor of the nation. The toast was drank with hearty good-will, and all eyes were turned upon us. I said:

"Mr. Golovah, and your associates, merchants of Kyachta, it becomes me to reply to the toast just proposed for my friend Mr. Peyton and myself, who have been so kindly, so hospitably, and so nobly entertained by you.

"We cannot receive this magnificent banquet as *solely* for ourselves, because it is too much for us to assume, and we know that individually it is more than we could ask of your generous hospitality, but we receive it as Americans for America, for that country of which we are proud to be citizens, and as an earnest of the friendly feelings that you are willing to extend to our countrymen.

"We shall ever cherish in our hearts this spontaneous expression of your kindness towards us, and of the noble and generous hospitality of Kyachta. I wish it were possible for me to speak the feelings of my heart to you in your own native and expressive tongue, then I could do justice to myself and my feelings, and thank you in becoming language for your generous kindness; but, as it is, I must content myself with but few words.

'In conclusion, Mr. Mayor, receive for yourself and your brother-merchants of Kyachta, our warm and heartfelt thanks."

I now gave, "the Golovah and Merchants of Kyachta," all glasses were refilled, and it was drank with bumpers. The Golovah then said:

"It gives me much pleasure to meet Americans in

Siberia, and we hope that now you have shown your countrymen the way, that they will hereafter come to our country. We thank you, also, for the sentiments you have spoken in regard to Russia and Siberia; we have always believed that the Americans were friendly towards us, and we are pleased that that sentiment still prevails in the United States.

"You have paid a just tribute to the genius and sagacity of General-Governor Mouravieff. We all feel that he has done great things for Siberia. The opening of the Amoor alone ought to prove to everybody his great desire for the prosperity of Siberia and the grandeur of Russia. Through this great river we hope that, upon your return to your country, you will be able to tell your merchants that they will be able to reach Siberia, and exchange trade with us. We believe it can be made mutually beneficial to both countries."

Though the wine continued to flow, I really hoped that the dinner was over. I could not now see much room for its continuance, and I was sure there could not be much more room within the company. Finally, the Golovah rose, and the dinner ended, and with it, as I supposed, the drinking also; but I was mistaken. We adjourned to the coffee-room, where tea and coffee were both served; the tea really delicious, the purest herb of China. I drank very freely of it, for I hoped that it would counteract the effects of the wine. As soon as politeness would seem to justify, we rose to depart. In the mean time, the dining-room had been cleared of every vestige of the dinner, tables and all, and was now occupied by groups in animated conversation. As soon as we entered the apartment, servants, bearing trays loaded with glasses, foaming with champagne, approached us, and the Golovah pressed us to take the parting glass. This it was idle to refuse, so we drank, as we supposed, for really the last time. Presently I noticed a pretty dense circle encompassing Peyton, and in an instant he was seized by half-a-dozen stout, jolly merchants, and tossed up in the direction of the ceiling. Fortunately it was not a very low one, or else he must have gone through to the roof. Down he came, however, into the hands of his tormentors, who sent him up again, if any thing, higher than ever, the most uproarious mirth and laughter prevailing. My companion was not a small man, or a light one, but he was no more than a feather in the hands of these portly Siberians.

This sport is called in Russian *podkeedovate*, or tossing-up, and is considered a mark of great respect. General Mouravieff told me, after our return, that he had had *podkeedovate* performed upon him in the same room.

During the performance, I stood half-aghast, looking at the figure Peyton was cutting, a man six feet high and well proportioned, going up and down like a trap-ball, his coat-tail flying sky-high, and his face as red as a brick. I was all the time consoling myself that they had administered this extra touch of hospitality to Peyton because they considered him the most worthy, and the best able to stand it, and I said to Beetsov, "I hope one tossing for the American nation will be considered honor enough." He replied, "Your turn will very likely come too."

After a while Peyton came down, and staid down. Servants again came around, and again we had to drink champagne. I had just emptied my glass, and placed it on the waiter, when, without a moment's warning, I was seized, and up I went. Being much lighter than Peyton, and handled after him by these stout, and now very jovial and mellow fellows, I have a distinct recollection of touching the ceiling. My coat-tail certainly did, and what I thought at first a piece of good fortune, now proved to be otherwise, for, having taken Peyton's guage with regard to weight, they did not take into consideration my lightness, and I came near going through the top of the house. Up I went and down I came, only to go up again, until my friends were satisfied that if I was not drunk before, my head would certainly swim now. However, I was able to stand when I came to my feet, which was more than I calculated upon when tossing between the floor and ceiling.

Of course we all had to take another drink. By this time Peyton and I were working our way towards the door, in order to evacuate this citadel of hospitality, and finally succeeded in reaching our sleigh, which was standing near the entrance of the house; we had, however, to partake of the stirrup cup after we were seated; and thus ended one of the most extraordinary, and, barring the overflow of wine, one of the most agreeable dinners I ever partook of.

As we had made arrangements to leave for Irkutsk that night, it was our duty to call on Mr. Egoumenoff, and thank him for his hospitality while in Kyachta. However, we first rode to our lodgings, about two miles distant, in order to breathe the cold air, and relieve us a little from the effects of the banquet.

Late in the evening we repaired to Mr. Egoumenoff's,

but before he would listen to our adieus we were compelled to take a last and parting glass of champagne. We parted with our kind host, and at half-past one A. M. were seated in our *tarantass*, and galloping out of the northern street of Troitzkosavsk, on our return to Irkutsk. But we were fated to be disappointed in having drank the final glass of champagne for the night, and I had hoped for a month, for our constant and most obliging friend, Golovachevsky, was at the northern gate of the town, with what I verily hoped was the last bottle of champagne in Siberia, which of course had to be drank, but as we were now in the open, frosty air, and a long, cold ride before us, it perhaps did us no harm; at all events, it went the way of all champagne, and shaking the offered hand of our kind friend, we bade farewell to Kyachta.

CHAPTER XIV.

RETURN TO IRKUTSK.

We passed back in the direction of Irkutsk over the same road we came, killing one horse on the way, though how many more died from hard driving afterwards, we had no account of. The death of that horse was a singular circumstance. We were galloping rapidly, and were approaching the station, when the animal dropped as if struck by lightning. We were in such rapid motion upon the smooth ice of the river, that though several yards from the stopping point, the other horses kept on, dragging the dead horse, nor did the driver attempt to stop them, but seemed determined to reach the station at full speed. As soon as we had stopped I got out and examined the body. It was as stiff as a poker, and stirred not a muscle, the eyes being cold and glassy. The fact is, the horse must have been dead before he fell, and his muscular action was kept up some time after life had departed. We inquired of Captain Beetsov as to our responsibility for the loss, but he said as he was riding as a courier, if any damage had been done, the accounts could be presented at Irkutsk —we had nothing to do with it.

The driver put on a very sorry face, and in order tc cheer his drooping spirits, we gave him a few roubles, which seemed to have all the vivifying qualities requisite, and produced in the new driver very great alacrity in yoking in the fresh horses, and a speedy departure from the station.

We performed the return journey in about forty-eight hours, crossing Lake Baikal at night in three hours and a half, and reached Irkutsk about 2 A. M., on the morning of February 14th, 1857.

After our return there were balls, suppers, parties, sleigh-rides, dinners, and theatricals in profusion. The weather was generally pleasant, dry, cold, and clear, without wind, the air bracing and healthy, and time passed off pleasantly, though slowly to me, as I was impatient to turn my face once more to the east. But to depart before March was worse than useless, as I should have to remain on the head waters of the Amoor until May before being able to proceed as I wished by water.

On the 7th March, we took our farewell dinner with General Mouravieff, and Peyton departed for the United States, via Moscow, on the 8th. I was now "solitary and alone," the only American between Irkutsk and San Francisco. On the 9th I had a very agreeable conversation with General Mouravieff, and in the course of the morning made as many adieus as possible, conforming to the Russian custom.

It was a beautiful day, and the sun was shining in a clear sky. After many adieus to very pleasant acquaintances, we partook of breakfast at the residence of Colonel Kleminoff, the general director or governor of the mines of Yenisaisk. Colonel Kleminoff has a large family, and one of the most agreeable and accomplished in Irkutsk.

The impatient post-horses were soon at the door, Gourieff received his papers, and as it was 3 P. M., and we were to dine next day at Verchne-Udinsk, some two hundred miles distant, we hurried through the streets and out of the north-eastern gate of the capital of Eastern Siberia.

CHAPTER XV.

FROM IRKUTSK TO PETROVSKEY.

We galloped along for some time upon the margin of the frozen Angara, and again upon its banks, changing horses once before we reached Lake Baikal, along the left shore of which, changing horses again, we reached the jumping-off station where the lake must be crossed, about forty miles over, with one set of horses. It was now night, and the sky had seemingly closed down upon us, with a dull, heavy, impenetrable sort of canopy, the atmosphere of which was so intensely cold and thick, that the breathing of it seemed to make up for the vacuum within, consequent upon nothing to eat since breakfast. We, however, fortified ourselves by drinking of a dozen or so of cups of hot tea before we launched our sleigh upon this frozen sea. Our four sprightly, snorting, shaggy little horses were already at the door, our driver was seated, *golovey* was the word, and, wrapping ourselves snugly in our furs and skins, with the merry little bells ringing at the yoke of our shaft-horse, we were soon speeding at full gallop over Baikal.

It was not so cold as I had before experienced, yet I felt it more than on the first occasion when I crossed the lake, owing to the peculiarly raw state of the atmosphere. The darkness was frightful; there was danger of gaps or fissures in the ice, but my companion, Captain Gourieff, berated the driver until the smoking breath and sweat of the horses fairly rained upon us in frozen particles and enveloped us in a sort of frozen mist; but the nimble clattering feet of our horses, assisted and hastened by blows, and the curses of the driver, in something more than three hours brought us to the next station on the eastern shore of the lake. Fresh horses being quickly procured (for a courier's pass opens every door and removes all difficulties), we hastened along frozen water-courses, through open fields and sleeping villages, and, after daylight, procuring hot tea and a slice of bread, we hurried on.

We arrived at Verchne-Udinsk in time to dine, by invitation of the merchants, at a public dinner given to General Korsackoff, the governor of this province, who had preceded us by a day on his way from Irkutsk to Chetah. The dinner, as well as the company, were all one could desire, and after the twenty-four hours' drive it was a very comforting affair to my inner man. Champagne and other wines were plenty, and both General Korsackoff and myself had to answer to the drinking of our healths. Captain Gourieff, a good English scholar, rendered my speech into Russian, which was received with apparent satisfaction as well as applause.

After a very pleasant time, we set out at 11 P. M., for Petrovskey iron works, taking the same road, or rather river, we had traversed on our way to Kyachta. After a couple of stations on the river, we left it on the right, and commenced ascending the mountains. We had gone along fairly while on the river, but, once upon the land, we found the road frequently bare of snow. After toiling on very slowly for some time, and the night bitterly cold and in an open *vashok*, we came to a dead halt, the horses refusing or being unable to pull us over the bare ground any longer. Our driver, with whip and oaths, did all he could to make them go on, but to no purpose. There we stuck on the side of the mountain. Gourieff scolded the driver soundly for daring to set out with runners when he knew that there was no snow upon the ground; but he contended that there had been snow, or ought to have been, and that the devil had blown it away, or done something else with it. It was bitterly cold, the wind blowing fiercely, and it was yet several hours to morning and ten miles to the next village or station. The driver finally gave up and declared that his horses could not pull the vehicle. Nothing was left for us to do but to wait until the driver could go to the next station and procure fresh horses. Off he went, leaving us desolate enough. I had vague and discouraging reminiscenses in my memory of travellers in the wilds of Siberia being attacked and devoured by wolves, and not anticipating any danger or detention on the road, we had not so much as a pocket-knife for defence. We, however, had some consolation in the fact that the three remaining horses would serve for a lunch for a tolerably hungry pack before trying Gourieff and myself.

The hours wore away cold, dreary, tedious, but finally the rattling of wheels and the shout of the driver were heard coming down the mountain. We were soon transferred into the wagon and once more under way. We rode along over the mountains which flank immediately on the river, and afterwards came into a rolling country, with fine valleys, along which we rode, sometimes changing our *telyaga* for a *vashok*, or *vice versa*, as the snow, or ground, or ice would justify. We drank tea at a peasant's cabin, and the good housewife furnished us with cream, bread, and fresh eggs, of which we made a pleasant and hearty breakfast.

We galloped along through valleys and over hills, and towards night reached the Zavod of Petrovskey, one hundred miles to the southeast of Verchne-Odinsk. We were received with hospitality by the superintendent, our baggage was deposited in a room provided for our special accommodation, and, after making a comfortable toilet in a warm room, we were regaled with a good dinner and excellent wine.

CHAPTER XVI.

FROM PETROVSKEY TO VERCHNE-ODINSUSK.

PETROVSKEY is the seat of a government iron works and the nucleus of a large village, which has grown up from liberated convicts and the industrial interest of the iron mines. We spent a very pleasant evening with the superintendent, and a German engineer, who was superintending the construction of machinery for a steamer on the Amoor, and with one or two other gentlemen connected with the works, after which we retired and enjoyed a good night's rest in a warm room. No person can estimate reasonably the amount of satisfaction derived from comfortable sleep after a cold and dreary night upon the road.

We found ourselves much revived in the morning. Our host had a breakfast of cutlets and other creature comforts prepared, after which we walked out to look at the iron works. We found a considerable degree of skill exhibited in the various departments, though the establishment is in rather a dilapidated condition. The works produce about one thousand *poods* of bar-iron yearly, which goes into the consumption of this section of the country. There are also castings of hollow ware, ploughs, and some machinery made of limited amount.

These works were established in the reign of Peter the Great, and belong to the crown, and are worked mostly by convicts. Mineral coal is found in abundance in this vicinity, but timber being also plentiful, charcoal is used in smelting the ore. The ore is certainly of good quality, and specimens of the bar-iron I saw looked well; yet it is said the quality is not good, and the price is so high that large quantities of iron are brought from the Ural, two thousand miles distant.

We saw here the iron framework of a building in progress of construction, manufactured on the spot, which, when completed, will augment the capacities of the present establishment, and also afford a machine shop in which steam engines can be built. It is anticipated that under the new impetus given to everything here by the Amoor movement that these works will receive such aid from the government as will enable it to become a first-rate establishment.

My object was accomplished in seeing with my own eyes a large iron foundery, smelting furnaces, trip hammers, rolling-mill, and brass, copper, and iron fittings being turned, polished, cast, and fitted here at the foot of the mountains, from whose summits the Amoor could be descried, and could be reached by a wagon-road within a few days. Coal and iron are there in inexhaustible quantities; and with coal and iron man can do wonders. The machinery was worked with water, though there is a steam engine attached to the works, and in the improved and enlarged works steam will be used as auxiliary.

We were treated with great politeness, and were courteously shown everything, and spent an agreeable day with the intelligent superintendent. In the afternoon, after dinner, we set out on our return and rode briskly through the valleys and over the mountains, and, having now the descent in our favor, reached Verchne-Udinsk the following day.

Having tried the post station at this place once before, and finding no accommodation for man or beast, Captain Gourieff concluded that the best plan was to drive to the house of our friend Mr. Korbatoff, the banker and merchant prince of this section. We were very kindly received by him, and, in due time, dinner was prepared for us, which was washed down with champagne, sherry, claret, and ale. This generous repast set us up again after the previous night's ride, and we were now prepared to go on our way rejoicing.

CHAPTER XVII.

FROM VERCHNE-UDINSK TO CHETAH.

I HAD met Mr. Korbatoff before at Irkutsk and also as I passed up to Petrovskey at the dinner given to General Korsackoff, and found him a very agreeable gentleman. He had invited me to call upon him, and I intended to do so, but I did not expect to drive into his yard, and, with bag and baggage, occupy his house as a hotel. That, however, is the style in Siberia. In travelling, you quarter upon your friends without ceremony, stay as long as you choose, and leave when it suits you.

Mr. Korbatoff was evidently very much pleased to see us. General Mouravieff had spoken in the highest terms of the probity and character of this gentleman, and had procured an interview between us on a previous occasion at Irkutsk to talk over the commercial affairs of Siberia. We, therefore, felt ourselves at home under his roof.

Mr. Korbatoff is very wealthy—a millionnaire, in fact. He is engaged in extensive commercial, manufacturing, and mining enterprises, and has also contracts for supplying the army. He lives in princely style in a house that may be called a palace. We had our supper before setting out, and the horses being at the door, we emptied a parting bottle of champagne, bade him farewell, and drove on towards Chetah at 11 P. M.

Just above the town, as we were making our way upon the surface of the river, we suddenly found the horses splashing along through water knee deep. The driver had slacked their pace, and it was not long before we called a halt, as the water appeared to be deepening and the horses were themselves unwilling to proceed.

We held a council to see what was to be done. The driver declared that this was the only safe road to reach the opposite side of the river, and that the water was caused by a recent thaw of the snow further up. But this explanation did not help the matter much. At length a horse was unhitched, and the driver mounted, and was despatched ahead to try the depth and practicability of the proposed ford. He was soon lost to view in the distance and the darkness, and even the splash of his horse's feet died away, and there we sat, heaven knew how far from shore, with the water nearly touching our feet. However, after some fifteen or twenty minutes, we heard the returning splash of the driver, who reported that the water would not be deeper than the bed of our wagon. To return would be unpleasant, besides involving considerable delay and a probability of an increased depth of water. We concluded, therefore, to go ahead, and on we splashed through the water in the dark, standing up in the wagon to keep from being submerged. We, however, succeeded in reaching the opposite shore without any serious consequences, and drove up the bank and set foot upon dry land as soon as possible, well pleased to get out of the scrape so cheaply. The driver said that at that season of the year it sometimes happened that a delay of a week occurred in crossing the river.

We dashed along at a rattling pace, and under the good influence of the last bottle of champagne, I slept soundly, and was only awoke at the next station. We had been, since leaving Irkutsk, riding in the vehicles belonging to the post, which are changed at every station along with the horses, so that my nap was broken here, much against my inclination.

These little wagons are very hard riding vehicles, especially if the road be rough. There is a box placed between the wheels on two poles, and in the better ones a cover on the hind part to protect the head, and some of them have an apron to button up from the foot, so as to cover you partly in case of stormy weather; but you are jolted and stirred up so effectually that you must go through a seasoning before you can rest much in one of them.

We hurried along during the day and found the road tolerably good ; in truth, we could scarcely realise the fact that we were approaching the great Altai chain, or, indeed, crossing it, then ; but the range is very much depressed and broken in this region, where the Selenga breaks through and waters the "land of grass," as the Tartars call Mongolia. The scenery at some points was beautiful, though the atmosphere was too thick and hazy to let us see the distant elevated ridges. Handsome openings, with scattered timber and rounded hills, with fine valleys, were seen to the right, while much of the land to the north ran off into an undulating prairie country.

We passed through many Burat villages, and changed

horses and vehicles at their stations, while we obtained very active and most excellent drivers. These Tartars inhabit a large section of this portion of Siberia. They formerly constituted a kingdom or khanate, lying north of Mongolia proper, but have been entirely absorbed by Russia.

We were making very good time, and drove rapidly over the mountains or among the hills. The road was generally good, and we met with no delay at the stations. General Mouravieff's courier was quickly despatched. Gourieff gave the drivers no rest, and our little Tartar horses fairly flew over the road. After becoming a little more familiar with Russian and Siberian travelling, I found it expedient to have as little baggage as possible, and to be satisfied with what I could find to eat at the stations or towns on the road. In Siberia I found it better to provide nothing but tea and sugar.

When riding in the post-vehicles you should be as little encumbered as possible, because at every station out goes everything from the old to the new vehicle, and this is troublesome and annoying if you have much baggage. Gourieff generally succeeded well with the good woman at the stations, and if any thing was to be had in the kitchen or larder we did not starve. Eggs, cream, cheese, black-bread, fish, and sometimes cutlets or steaks, made up the bill of fare.

On the following day we were dashing along in the midst of a severe blinding snow-storm on the very summit of the mountains, and had sleighs instead of wagons for several stations. Towards noon the storm came thicker and faster, and Gourieff swore lustily at the driver, fearing that we might have to spend the day in a snow-drift. We lost our way at one time, the driver becoming completely bewildered, as all signs of the track were buried under the snow, while the atmosphere was so thick that no object ten paces off could be seen. We finally came among some trees and bushes, which enabled the driver to regain the road, upon which he hurried us on with increased speed.

Nothing could be seen of the mountains, and we were now upon the descent, going down into the valley of the Ingodah. We saw fine timber and well wooded districts as we passed down, for we had got below the snow-cloud, and could form some idea of the country. There was no difficulty in the descent of the mountains, the road being well graded, and we succeeded in reaching the station at the post before night. Here we drank tea, and found ourselves at last on the eastern slope of the Altaï chain. The water at our feet was running towards the Pacific Ocean. The clouds broke away from the eastern horizon, and we had a view of the first valley on the head waters of the Amoor. A well-defined range of mountains bounded the horizon to the east, while to the north and south the valley stretched out to a great extent. The scene, for a moment, was very fine, as a struggling ray from the setting sun gilded the opposite mountains.

We were only delayed at the station a few minutes, while we fortified ourselves with a few cups of tea for the evening's ride. Our driver said *gotovey*, and, leaping into the wagon, we were off at full speed. We bounded along over a rolling prairie, where we saw herds of cattle and flocks of sheep grazing on the natural grasses of the country, as I have seen them in California during the winter.

We were very anxious to reach Chetah, and Captain Gourieff gave the drivers no rest, till they whipped their horses to their highest speed. The road was really fine, and we dashed along, watching for the first light that should disclose Chetah to our view.

At 8 P. M. we were at the police master's door. Our lodgings had already been provided, by order of the governor, General Korsackoff, to which we drove, and in a few minutes we were seated in a warm room, drinking hot tea to the health of the governor of the province of Trans-Baikal. A supper of cutlets and potatoes was soon forthcoming, in paying our respects to which we forgot the discomforts of the passage of the Altaï.

To cross the great chain in forty-five hours, a distance of nearly three hundred miles, was not bad driving, with about twenty changes of horses, vehicles, and drivers. I was the first American—in fact, the first white man, except of Russian race, who ever crossed the frontiers of the Amoor, and descended to its valley.

The first thing in order, on the following morning, March 16th, 1857, was to pay my respects to General Korsackoff. He met me with great cordiality, and welcomed me warmly to the valley of the Ingodah, congratulating me upon being the first of my countrymen who had visited this distant out-post of the Russian Empire.

The time, however, passed off heavily at Chetah, notwithstanding General Korsackoff's kind invitation to dine with him daily, and the presence besides of several old Irkutsk acquaintances, and some very pleasant new ones. I was anxious to be off to the Amoor. There were many Russian officers arriving and passing through Chetah, to points further on, some to stations in the country, and others to join the Amoor expedition under Colonel Oushakoff. I longed to be on the great river, and so the time passed heavily.

Meanwhile, we hunted the goat, *kozel*, upon the mountains, and had wild goose hunts upon the plains. Governor Korsackoff in person, with his Cossacks, gave us two gazelle hunts, in which the horsemen beat the bush and mountain side, while the guests took stands upon the mountains or in the gorges and passes, to shoot the fleet and beautiful antelopes, as they passed, fleeing from the whoop and horn of the Cossacks. An impromptu lunch of sandwiches and brandy came very opportune, at the foot of the mountain, after a tedious walk and stand of an hour or two. But the gazelles escaped us, and the polite general proposed that we should try them on the other side of the mountain. I saw no antelope fall, but we had venison for dinner the next day. The hunt, in spite of our scanty success, was very satisfactory to me, and very amusing.

CHAPTER XVIII.

A VISIT TO THE MINES OF NERCHINSK.

THE frozen chains of winter still held in bondage the waters of the Altaï; and, after becoming conversant with the country, and being satisfied that the Ingodah might be navigable hence to the Amoor, I determined to make Chetah my starting point by water to the Pacific Ocean. First, however, I paid a visit to the great mines of Nerchinsk.

Captain Gourieff made all the necessary arrangements, and, provided with a courier's *podorojenaya*, we set forth from Chetah on the 3d April, 1857. Sometimes we were on the river on runners, again we were on land, bounding over hill and dale in the telyaga, making our way over hill, valley, and mountain, without any consideration for horse flesh. We left Chetah in the daytime, consequently we had an opportunity to look at the country, and admire the beautiful scenery of the Ingodah.

The mountains to the right were generally wooded, while those on the left, except the most lofty, were bare of timber, but covered with grass. We rolled along through the Cossack villages and stations, until the following morning, when old Nerchinsk rose to our view.

The surrounding country is of much picturesque beauty, and has a rich soil. Hill, valley, river, mountain, all combine to make it an interesting spot, aside from its legendary and historic associations.

It is about 5000 miles east of St. Petersburg, and contains six thousand inhabitants. It is on the river Nercha, near where it falls into the Schilkah. The upper town is built at the end of a long sweeping prairie, and exposed to all the winds that blow up through the valley or down from the snow-clad summits of the Yoblonovey mountains.

There are churches, and magazines, and several large straggling government houses in the upper town ; but the principal part of the city lies on the banks of the Nercha, and is mostly built of logs, but nevertheless has some very comfortable houses.

We drove up to the post station for a change of horses and a little rest, intending also to look at the town. The *smotretal* informed Gourieff that he had no accommodation for travellers, not even a room where we could wash or change our dress, or even sit while the horses were being changed.

Gourieff immediately ordered the driver to drive to the police-master. On arriving at his quarters our wants were made known, and a Cossack was ordered to procure us lodgings. Gourieff raised quite a breeze in the place, and orders were given on the spot, that hereafter a room should be provided at the post station for travellers to rest in during the change of horses.

In many of the interior towns in Siberia, as well as in Russia, there are no hotels. There are seldom any travellers but officers or merchants. Officers apply to the police master of the town, or village, who appoints them quarters in any house in the town that he may choose, while merchants either stop with their friends or hire lodgings the best way they can.

After some delay the Cossack returned, and conducted us to a large house, through a narrow hall, into a small room, where we sat down cheerless and disconsolate. Gourieff was so angry that he would not talk. We sat for a considerable time here, no one coming or paying the least attention to us. Gourieff was too enraged to ask for any thing, though we were half famished, having eaten nothing since the previous night, so that we were really not only in bad humor, but in bad plight. There were a number of people passing back and forth through the hall, and up a flight of steps, among whom we caught a glimpse of a pretty face, and a neat, gaitered foot, and heard the soft voice and merry laugh of a woman, which somewhat tended to break in upon the wofulness of our situation.

From appearances, I judged that we were in the house of a merchant, and having been thrust upon him against his will, we were likely to fare but poorly, as Gourieff, in this instance, would not exercise his prerogative, or condescend to ask for any thing, where our presence seemed to be so unwelcome.

After a long hour the horses were ready, and just as we were ready to start, an old lady came into the room and wanted to know if we would not have some tea, and made an apology for not offering us any thing before. I was quite willing to accept the offer, tardy as it was, but Gourieff would make no concession, and off we drove.

The weather was very unpleasant, a savagely cold wind, with a bluish-grey atmosphere, and the next station was nearly twenty miles distant. Before leaving the town we drove up to a store, and Gourieff purchased some small jars of preserved cherries and currants. The grass did not grow under our horses' feet this post, for Gourieff was at the top of his humor, and he swore at the driver until we fairly flew along the road, and along the frozen surface of the river, until we reached Bankin.

The country north-east of Nerchinsk rises and runs off to the mountains in an extensive steppe, and, where the soil had been turned up by the plow, it looked black and rich.

We were cold, hungry, and out of temper, when we reached Bankin; but we found at the post-station two officers, whom we had met both in Irkutsk and Chetah, now on their way to Schilkah. They had been dining, and we found their *samovar* steaming upon the table, and, with the assistance of a little *vodka*, we succeeded in thawing out, and our long faces, in company of our old friends, with plentiful glasses of tea, were reduced to their proper proportions. We lunched on biscuits and preserves, while the people were getting dinner for us, and found the cheese of our friends very acceptable.

We remained here at least two hours, thawing out. Gourieff emptied a jar or two of preserves, while I paid my respects to several pounds of very tough beef; but we had left a long hungry day behind us, and had high mountains and a long, bleak night before us, which promised to be one of the worst of the season; and it became necessary to fortify the inner man against the dreary passage of the mountain—the highest in this region. Our friends had departed, and it was near night when we set out. We found the telyaga the merest apology for a vehicle we had yet met with on the road. It was very small, without back, top, or seat—a mere box on wheels. Our baggage filled the box, and on the top of that we seated ourselves, and drove off, liable to be jolted or shaken from our seats at any moment. We soon reached the mountain, where the road was both steep and narrow, which rendered it not only tedious but dangerous, as we made our way along the narrow track cut out of the sides of the mountain. At times there were only a few inches between our wheels and a yawning gulf of hundreds of feet in depth.

The night was cold, the road frightful, and our conveyance detestable. I finally was compelled to abandon the attempt to sit up without support, and turned my back against that of the driver, who sat half in and half out, upon the front part of the box. I got some support in this way, and partial shelter from the keen wind, which increased in intensity as we ascended the mountain.

We toiled on, winding along the sides and crossing the heads of ravines on bridges, for over two hours before we reached the summit. We called a short halt here, and arranged our places as well as we could, wrapped ourselves well in our furs, and started downwards. The driver, determined to make up for lost time, now dashed along, quite heedless of the probability of broken bones from the yawning gulfs, into which the least mishap would have plunged us. However, we did not check him, and on we rattled, at a fearful pace. Sitting upright was out of the question, and I coiled myself down on the bottom and tried to forget cold, fatigue, and danger. It was a long, long time before we reached the next station, and I felt as if I would give a kingdom for one hour's sleep in a warm bed.

We found a clean warm room at the station, and drowned our troubles, and fortified ourselves against the next stage of twenty miles, with abundant cups of hot tea. *Gotovey!* was pronounced from the half open door, by the *smotretal*, and we left the comfortable room reluctantly. The road lay along valleys and down a considerable stream, with some fine-looking land, but generally bare of timber, except upon the higher mountains. I was much struck with the resemblance of this country to the regions round about Knight's Ferry on the Stanislaus, in California. In fact, this whole country may find its counterpart in different sections of California, north and south.

We came regularly to stations, and to thrifty-looking villages, and, passing one gold washing establishment, reached Great Nerchinsk Zavod on the third day from Chetah.

Gourieff directed our driver to take us to the chief of police, in order to procure lodgings. We dashed through a long narrow street and up to the station, which was surmounted with the double-headed eagle. A Cossack received Gourieff's orders and disappeared within the building. After half an hour's delay, we turned upon our track, a quarter of a mile, and were deposited in the private house of a merchant, where we found a good room, with two sofas, a few chairs, and a table. As usual, there were no beds. Our host received us very civilly, and ordered tea immediately, of which we stood much in need.

After supper we called upon the governor of the mines, whom I had met before at Irkutsk. He received us cordially, but was sorry that at that season of the year there were no mines immediately in the vicinity that he could show me. But he prepared a sketch of a route further to the south, where I could find accessible mines.

We slept soundly that night, on our host's sofas. After our terrible ride of four hundred miles, to say nothing of the passage of the mountains, it was a real luxury to be able to throw off skins, cloaks, and clothing, and stretch out in a warm, comfortable room, and know that we need not get up or wake up till morning.

The next day we dined sumptuously at the governor's, with his family and two officers, whom we had known at Irkutsk. The governor's wife was an intelligent and agreeable lady, and had a most interesting family of children. It was really like a dream—here, in the very depths of northern Asia, five thousand miles from St. Petersburg, to find such comfort, such luxury, and such charming people, and such refined hospitality.

The governor offered us his own private *tarantass*, in which to make the tour of the southern mines on the Argoon. We had determined to set out that evening, so we very reluctantly bade adieu to our friend and his family, and rode to our lodgings to pack up again and be off. I am very sorry that I have forgotten the name of the governor of Nerchinsk, which deserves to be recorded, were it only for his extreme kindness to a stranger.

CHAPTER XIX.

THE SILVER MINES OF ZARENTUNSKIE.

GREAT Nerchinsk Zavod is situated on a small stream that empties into the Argoon, a tributary of the Amoor. It is about five thousand two hundred and fifty miles east of St. Petersburg, and about seven hundred miles nearly due north of Pekin, and about four hundred and eighty north of the Chinese Wall. The population is about six thousand. It is the principal mining town in the district of Nerchinsk, and the seat of the general direction for the mines.

The town is built under some high, rounded hills. The ore principally worked is silver, though gold, lead, and copper are also worked here. The shops and warehouses are well supplied with merchandise from Europe and China, and the merchants appear to be in a prosperous condition. The attention of the traders is now beginning to be directed to the commerce of the Amoor, and I was shown samples of various kinds of provisions which were being prepared for shipment on the opening of navigation.

We passed out through the southern portion of the town, and rode along the sides of great rounded hills, bare of timber, but covered with bushes or grass. We saw at every few hundred yards mining shafts and excavations on the sides of the mountains or hills. The country has much the appearance of the mountain region east of Los Angeles, in California. The soil is rich, and produces vegetables, grain, and grass in abundance. The country is well stocked with cattle, sheep, and horses.

We reached the silver *rudnik* of Zarentunskie in a drive of two or three hours, and were politely received by Mr. Eichwald, the superintendent and engineer, who had spent some time in the mines of Germany, studying his profession, and was recently sent here by the Russian government, to carry out practically such alterations and improvements in working the silver mines as his knowledge and experience might suggest. The mines are of great richness, but, from careless working and improper engineering, many of them have been abandoned to water and foul air. From the plans and drawings of this engineer, and his practical turn of mind, I am inclined to believe that he will create a revolution in their working and productiveness. He was very eager in his inquiries in regard to the mines of California, concerning which I readily gave him full details.

We visited a mine on the side of the mountain, half a mile from the little village. There was a building over the entrance to the shaft, where the guard was on duty, and a room for tools and implements and for the raised ore. Two men lighted candles, of which we each took one, and commenced the descent. We found adits at different depths, and flights of steps, until we reached the bottom, where we passed along a horizontal shaft, tortuous, and somewhat uneven on the floor, until we came to a long chamber perfectly sheathed with ice and icy stalactites, which gave us rather a cool reception. Not far beyond we came to several side shafts, and two men working. We were shown here, in the sides of the adit, rich veins of ore, blue and sparkling, and one of the attendants dug some pieces out on the spot. We now passed out of the mine by a drift in a different direction, and, after a walk altogether of certainly five or six hundred yards, came out on the side of the mountain several hundred feet below where we entered. Mr. Eichwald had an excellent dinner prepared for us, of beef, veal, fish, and dessert, with *na-lifka* of excellent flavor and pleasant to drink. There were maps, drawings, plans, models, and a fine cabinet of minerals, curiosities, and specimens, attached to his quarters.

Bidding adieu to our mining friend, we pursued our course still to the south and west, nearer the Argoon, the great south-western tributary of the Amoor. We were not far from Zuruchaitu, the old "fortress of commerce" before Kyachta sprung into existence, where merchants from Pekin and Bukaria were wont to congregate and trade with the Russians—a place something like Santa Fé, in New Mexico, in old times, when adventurous traders crossed the plains from Missouri to exchange their merchandise for Mexican silver.

The next point of interest was Zarentoonsky *roodnik*. We met with a very warm reception from the *smotretal*, who seemed to be post-master, chief of police, *nachalnik*—in fact, every thing. The first thing he did was to offer us some excellent brandy; then we must drink tea, to which the good woman contributed nice bread. It was growing late, and we wished to visit the mines, but our hospitable friend pressed us to pass the night with him and take the next day to look at the mines. He said we had better take a comfortable night's rest. But we had become accustomed to living and sleeping in a tarantass, or even a telyaga, and preferred to see what we could in the day and travel at night, which would greatly expedite us in our journey. Against his earnest protestations, therefore, we declined to stop, and after another drink, to fortify us in our visit underground, we set out in a telyaga which he furnished us. We did not have to ride far before we came to the entrance of the mine. Several men from a neighboring building took candles themselves, and, providing us also with lights, proceeded at once to enter the drift. We were soon passing along a vaulted way, which continued for several hundred yards, when we came to a shaft, down which we descended by simple ladders, covered with ice, and dripping with water. On the walls were pendant icicles, and the rounds of the ladders were clammy and slippery, the air chill, damp, and foul. Gourieff looked rather horrified, and asked how much deeper we had to go. "*Ne dalako,*" said our host, and down we went.

"*Chort!*" exclaimed Gourieff, "get me out of this, and I shall be done with silver mines for the rest of my life. The devil! another flight of those slippery steps."

"*Ne dalako, ne dalako, ochen blezk*—not far, very near!" shouted our guide, and down we went again.

We now came to a passage, at the turn of which were four men—convicts—two pumping and two resting. "This, for the present," said the overseer, "is all the work we are doing. This pumping goes on night and day; the men are relieved regularly every four hours. We are only keeping the water down to a certain point."

We now passed along another drift, and found nothing unpleasant in this underground passage, and finally, after a descent of two hundred and eighty feet, our way led into a dark, deep, and hollow-sounding cavern, in which our voices and our footsteps were reverberated in thunder tones. The men now lighted pine torches, which, in addition to our candles, revealed a scene which well repaid us for the descent down cold, slippery ladders, and along wet and narrow passages. Gourieff acknowledged it, but said, nevertheless, he would hereafter be satisfied with the bare recital of what was hidden within the depths of the mountains, without descending to look at them himself.

The torches revealed to us a palace whose roof and sides were fretted silver, and whose floor was inlaid with silver and ivory (hornblende). Silver was above our heads, under our feet, and all around us. The wealth and splendor here disclosed, rivalled the most gorgeous tales of Oriental romance. It was a true Aladdin's cave of riches.

No ore has been allowed to be taken from this mine for several years, on account of some defect in the drainage, and the fear that further mining in a certain direction would lead to an accumulation of water above their power to carry it off; it, therefore, awaits the talent of some new engineer to propose and carry out a new system of drainage. The superintendent said the whole mountain was rich in silver as far as it had been explored. Nor is it a very small mountain, for it stretched off to the south and east as far as we could see.

We returned along those gloomy and slippery passages, which made a horrid contrast to the bright scene we had just left. They afforded a truthful and lively picture of the dark, tortuous, and slippery paths which often lead to wealth. We found our telyaga awaiting our reappearance on upper earth, and, seating ourselves, we drove back to the house of our host. That worthy gentleman talked so fast, and would have us drink so often, and was so lively, and had so rich and soft a brogue, that I was half inclined to think he was an Irishman, who had somehow strayed off to Siberia. He really looked like an Irishman, and was so free and open-hearted in his hospitality, that it was with great difficulty that we could prevail on him to send for horses that we might pursue our journey. He fairly forced us to eat and drink again and again, until we tore ourselves away.

CHAPTER XX.

THE COSSACKS OF THE ARGOON.

It was now night, and snow was falling fast. Our driver became somewhat bewildered, for we awoke after a very long nap, and found we were standing motionless on the road. Gourieff swore at the driver, who said the snow was falling so fast that he could not find the road, and that he had been on ahead to look for it. We proceeded slowly, and arrived at a village about midnight, where we stopped to get a change of horses and inquire concerning the Zavod of Alexandrovsky.

We were yet some distance from it, but learned that it would be useless to visit it, as there were no workmen there, and, of course, the mills were idle. Gourieff became satisfied that we could see nothing further in this direction, unless, as he said, I would like to take a ride down to the Great Wall, or to Pekin.

After some delay, we procured fresh horses and drove on. The night was dark, though not very cold, and we found the road rough, but comparatively level. We now rode through the border Cossack villages on the Argoon, near the frontier of Mongolia, and had a pretty tedious night of it, making but little progress. We, however, had a good opportunity to witness the economy of Cossack border life, to inspect their dwellings, and to witness the simplicity of their sleeping arrangements, during this and several other nights which we spent in this region.

The houses are built of logs, and are of one story, with two or four rooms, and a passage between. The doors are low and wide, and if I ever said d—n in my life, with emphasis, it was when I thumped my head against the top log of one of these detestable Siberian doorways. I said then, and, with a vivid recollection of the thump, I still adhere to it, that if I were emperor of Russia, or governor of Siberia, I would compel the people, in building their houses, to have every door at least six feet and a half in the clear.

In one end of the house the family live permanently, and eat, drink, and sleep. If there is a small back room partitioned from this, you may find a bed in it, and the wealth of the household, consisting of clothing and other valuables, secured in a trunk or box. But it is not always that you find so effeminate an article as a bed in a Cossack's house. The sleeping is done on or along the sides of the oven or stove, by which the room is warmed, or around the sides of the room on narrow benches, or upon the floor or under the benches ; sometimes the floor is covered several inches deep with hay or straw, and on this the whole family sleep. Coming into one of these houses out of the cold fresh air, the stove steaming hot, the accumulated breath and perspiration of a dozen or two of skin-clad people, is almost pestilential, and generally makes one sicken immediately. I have, on many occasions, had to escape into the open air to catch my breath. You will see in this manner whole families for two or three generations, packed in pairs and fours, and in sixes, around the room. You walk in, and the mistress of the house gets up and strikes a light, frequently of splinters of wood, and there you see the family lying heads and tails, arms and legs, odds and evens, dressed, half dressed, and not dressed at all, snoring, sleeping, groaning, coughing, stewing, squirming, and sweating. That they don't all die of fevers, is a strong proof of the salubrity of the climate and the robust constitution of the people.

One end of the better houses in the larger villages has a room generally kept as a spare room, with a few chairs, a small table or two, and a rough sofa. In such a house you can get tea, and, if the good woman is applied to, you may get eggs, cream, milk, fish, and sometimes meat and vegetables, or cabbage-soup, and perhaps *quass*. In some of the larger villages you will also find a peasant who is the rich man of his tribe, and in his house you will find a good and clean spare room. These rooms are kept for the accommodation of officers, or such other transient travellers as may happen to pass. The officers of government are always furnished with accommodation by applying to the *starosta*, the head peasant of the village, or to the police master. They are quartered on any person who has a house or a suitable room, as we were in Nerchinsk and other places.

CHAPTER XXI.

THE GOLD MINES OF THE ONON.

We had now made a considerable circuit up the Argoon, and were turning more to the north in the direction of Onon. We had seen some good country, where grain and vegetables thrive well, and where there is fine grazing for cattle and sheep. We had mountains in the distance on the north, but the country generally was undulating and favorable to agriculture and stock.

We stopped to change horses in a small village, and, in the mean time, to drink tea and get what we could to eat. We had a dozen hard-boiled eggs, black-bread and milk, which, with our tea, made us breakfast and dinner both. Gourieff's preserves, which held out, served for a dessert. It was some time before the horses were ready, and we had considerable conversation with the women about the house in relation to the Amoor country. Some of the men had been in the expedition of the previous year, and the people feared that the whole village might be called upon to emigrate in the summer to the Amoor.

These border Cossacks are, under their own peculiar constitution, liable to be moved by their Hetman from time to time, as the necessities of their service demand,

and frequently migrate in tribes, or battalions, as they are now organized.

After much delay the horses came, and we drove off, with only a very dim wagon track for a road, through a country of undulating prairie, with rounded hills on the right and left, and a high mountain in the distance in front. After an hour's drive, we came to a long, wooded slope, and then across meadow land, and along a creek, with ploughed land, and then over a fine sweep of rolling prairie. Gourieff questioned the driver, to know why he was taking us through such by-roads and, apparently, in such a roundabout direction, but he answered constantly, "*nechevo nechevo, sechass sechass, bolshey dorogah*—never mind, never mind, have no fear, we shall have the great road directly," and, cracking his whip, sent his horses off at a gallop.

Four hours brought us to a small village at the foot of the mountain we had had in view all day. Driving up to the principal house, we went in, while our driver unyoked his horses and started on his return to his village. After waiting some time for the man of the house to arrive, in order to procure fresh horses, we were told that there was neither road or track over, through, or around, or under, the great mountain before us, and that to reach our road the nearest, and indeed the only way, was to go exactly back on the same track over which we had come.

We drank tea on the strength of this information, while the Cossack yoked a team of four sturdy little horses to take us back. Gourieff instead of swearing, as I expected, was as demure and contented as a Methodist preacher going to camp-meeting. I accounted for this by the recollection of a very pretty Cossack girl at the village we were returning to. For myself, it was a matter of indifference, for I had become interested in these border Cossacks, and a few days and nights more or less would make no difference in my journey towards the Amoor, for which it was yet some weeks too early to set off.

We made the return trip rapidly, and reached the residence of the pretty Cossack in good time and fine spirits. Our former driver and the people of the house were not in the least surprised at our return, as they all told the Captain, or Prince, as the girl called Gourieff, that there was no road over the mountains, and they were expecting us back during the night. While a new set of horses was being procured, we drank tea and swallowed milk and eggs to fortify us for the night's ride. I left the Captain, the girl, and her mother talking about the roads and the villages further on, and went into another part of the house, where I found a woman spinning, with whom I talked as much Russian as I was master of, and tried to talk much more, at which she laughed heartily, though she tried hard to add a few words to my vocabulary.

When the horses were ready, we set off in the direction of Chetah. The night was frosty, but the stars were twinkling brightly, our new driver was in good spirits, and drove us over a smooth good road at a full gallop. Three hours brought us to a village, whose watch-dogs barked fiercely while we alighted in front of a house, the driver calling out loudly for the people to get up. We discovered the door and went in. A light was soon struck, and we found ourselves in an encampment of men, women, children, pigs, calves, and chickens. The air was so terribly close and stifling that both of us were compelled to back out in a few minutes to take breath.

After an hour's delay fresh horses were ready, and off we went at full speed, the driver talking to his horses as they flew over the hard frosty road. We made a couple of stations before morning, dashing along through several villages on our route. At an early hour we reached the post-road that we had passed over on our way to Nerchinsk Zavod, and came to the station where we were to leave the tarantass of our friend, the governor of Nerchinsk. Fortifying ourselves with many glasses of tea, we again set forth in the post telyaga to visit the gold mines of the Onon. We left the main road, and taking a mere track over the roughest country I had seen in Asia, made all haste towards the "diggings." Much of the way was in creek-beds and along mountain torrents and ravines, over loose and broken rock, and along the sides of mountains like the worst mule trail in California. We arrived at the diggings, and were shown into a room, where we washed and made our toilet, and were soon invited to the superintendent's quarters. He ordered his tarantass, in which we were soon seated and on our way through a straggling village, beyond which we came to the mines where the convicts were at labor. They were working on the machines, which are used for separating the gold from the earth, and preparing the earth ready to be washed. On the previous night cord-wood had been spread upon the ground in a trench and set fire to, for the purpose of thawing the earth. A number of men were now removing the dirt that had been thus softened.

The machines used here, I have no doubt, are very efficient. They simply consist of a wheel, turned by water, which sets in motion a vertical shaft, having four large arms, to which are attached pieces of iron, chains, or drags, which revolve in a bason, having an iron bottom, pierced with small holes. The earth is cast into this bason, water being, at the same time, led into it from above. Here the earth is crushed and separated from the stones, which are precipitated through an opening in the side, while the washed earth, sand, and gravel, pass down through the holes in the bottom of the bason, and are carried by the water over a wooden apron, inclined at an angle of about 35°, having grooves or pockets in it, which catch the heavier portions of the sand, and the gold, while the water and refuse matter pass off, and the tailings are borne away by men stationed at the tail-race. These machines are placed along, at intervals, according to the number of men employed.

The bed of the stream in which the gold is found, is first drained of its water, by means of a canal tapping it at the proper point above, and brought along the bank of the stream, and used to propel these machines.

This was a convict establishment, like all the mines east of Lake Baikal. The men were well clad, and, in visiting the hospital, prison, and quarters, I found the arrangements for their health and sleeping, clean and comfortable. Cooks were preparing dinner for the prisoners. I tasted of the soup, bread, and *kassia*, or grits, made from buckwheat, and found them good and well prepared. There were a number on the sick list, mostly those who had recently arrived, but they were in a warm, clean room, with clean beds and clothing, and with a separate kitchen, where proper diet was prepared for them.

These mines are considered rich. There were only three hundred men at work at this time, and the requisition for the year was only one hundred thousand rubles. They are on a branch of the Onon, which falls into the Ingodah, and have been worked but a few years. They are quite extensive, and lie in creek and gulch bottoms, as in California, and would be worked with us precisely as our creeks are there, with long-toms and sluices. The gold is mostly fine, though coarse gold is found mixed with it. I could not ascertain the yield per man. They calculate by the *pood* of dirt (36 pounds); perhaps five cents to the pan. The mountains are rugged, but I saw no quartz. There were heavy boulders of trap and granite in the creek, and much more sand than is generally found in California.

CHAPTER XXII.

PASSAGE OF MOUNT BORNORSKOY.

On returning from our tour of inspection, we found a good dinner prepared for us, with native wine, and, after spending a social hour or two with the superintendent, we ordered our horses, and succeeded in reaching the post-road before night. We now took the post telyagas again, and were on the road to Bankin. We wished to have returned by another route, higher up the river, but the recent thaw in the mountains had rendered the rivers difficult to pass, and we were, therefore, compelled to cross Bornorskoy Krebet, the same terrible mountain that we had encountered upon our entrance into the country; but we hoped that we should not have so unpleasant a night as we had before. We determined, however, to go on and cross it again in the night. We paid dearly for our temerity. We advanced, making changes of horses at several stations, and, at about 3 A. M., came to the last one before reaching the dreaded mountain. The night was cold and cloudy, with considerable wind. The ascent was slow and tedious, and, by the time we got half way up, the freezing north wind was blowing through the gorges and sweeping along the sides of the mountain most fearfully, and right in our faces. It was pitch dark, and the nearer we approached to the summit, the fiercer the storm raged. I feared that as we came to narrow and exposed parts of the road, our wagon, horses, and all might be blown off into the gulf beneath. The air was so icy and chill that our clothing gave us no warmth, and, above all, I was fearful that our horses might give out on the road, or refuse to go in the face of the storm ; for it was only by the constant application of the lash that they could be got to move, and that at a snail's pace. A portion of the harness also gave way, and it was some time before the driver, benumbed and half frozen as he was, could repair it. The very worst weather I experienced in Siberia was these cold, freezing winds. Forty degrees below zeio, in a still atmosphere, is nothing to it, as I had the opportunity more than once to experience. Our harness being again in a state of repair, we wrapped ourselves up as closely as possible, and finally reached the summit. In descending the opposite side, upon some portions of the road, we made tolerable speed. I turned my back to the wind, but the jolting of the telyaga over the rocks was so violent, that I could scarcely retain my seat, and our baggage was all in a jumble. However, we reached the foot of the mountain, and the driver did all in his power to hurry on the horses. It was daylight before we reached the station. We were pretty nearly used up, and Gourieff, though accustomed to a Siberian climate, was fully as well satisfied as myself at finding a warm room, where, with a steaming *samovar* and plenty of tea, we forgot the horrors of a night passage of Mount Bornorskoy.

Bankin is on the Schilkah, twenty-five miles below Old Nerchinsk. It was a place formerly of considerable note, on account of its being the only point from whence the mines could be reached, and, consequently, had all the overland trade. It was the point also for the reshipment and storage of merchandise and provisions to other points further down the river.

After resting sufficiently long to become perfectly thawed out, we ordered horses, and started for Nerchinsk. The river being unsafe to travel upon, we kept the high road over the country. At Nerchinsk, while changing horses, we sat in the police office until the horses were ready. Gourieff was determined to teach these people that it was necessary to have a place to accommodate travellers, and took this mode of giving them a practical lesson. Papers were written and instructions given, while we were there, to the postmaster, that, hereafter, a room must be provided for travellers to rest in at the station. I think the authorities were somewhat struck with our audacity, for sharp words passed between Gourieff and the police master. We were seated in a room, where several clerks were writing and officers passing in and out. When the horses were forthcoming, shaking the dust off our feet, as a testimony against the town and its officers, we galloped towards Chetah.

CHAPTER XXIII.

FROM NERCHINSK TO CHETAH.

NERCHINSK, as you approach from the east, presents a pretty appearance, the country to the west being a long stretch of rolling prairie, with the high wooded mountains of the Ingodah and Onon in the distance, on the left, while the high mountains to the north lay like a wall against the horizon. The large public buildings, a *gosteney-dvor*, or row of shops, and a large church, with painted dome, looked rather imposing, while the town itself lay modestly below the plateau along the margin of the river Nercha. The place has a very bleak location, and is one of the coldest in Southern Siberia. The wind blows with great force through the gorges of the Yablonovoy mountains from the north, and sweeps in dusty clouds over the steppe from the west, making it altogether an uncomfortable place in the winter. We took some pride, however, in having created a revolution in the city in favor of future travellers.

We had an excellent vehicle to the next station, the road was good, and we dashed over the smooth steppe in fine style. Yet we had a hard drive before us, for we were forced to take the mountain road, as the river was impracticable. As hard luck, too much haste, or slow driving, would have it, we had another mountain to cross in the night, but, after having crossed the Bankin mountains, we were not to be stopped by those of the Ingodah, and, after steaming up with deep potations of tea, and breakfasting on a dozen of boiled eggs, we set out. We had several changes of good horses, over a fine country, and drove on, making good time.

At night we reached the mountain, which is one of the most rugged in this section of the country, abutting upon the Ingodah in precipitous crags. Nothing daunted by our previous night's experience, we drove on with good horses. The way proved a long one, but the time was not lost, for I slept like a top, as warm and as snug as possible. The night air was nipping and frosty, but we had a large leather apron over us, and, shutting ourselves up, let the driver take his own time, which I am under the impression he did to the fullest extent, for the chickens were crowing when we alighted at the next station.

We found a clean, warm room, containing a rough plank bed, on which we rested until the horses were ready. We rode on all day, over a broken, well-timbered country, and arriving at Chetah after nightfall, we drove to the police master's in order to procure lodgings. After considerable delay, we were shown the upper story room in a house in the lower part of the town, where, upon a bare and very dirty floor, without fire, we were told that we might, as a great favor, rest that night, but that the next day we must vacate it for parties who had previously engaged it. I told Gourieff that we had better pay the driver for his telyaga and lodge in that; but this, it seemed, could not be done, as the driver was compelled to return quickly to his station, in accordance with the regulations of the service.

Captain Alarofsky's rooms would have been at our service, but, unfortunately, they were undergoing repair during his absence with General Korsackoff at Kyachta, and it was too late at night to seek for any better quarters than the police master had shown us. Our luggage was brought from the telyaga, and deposited in the room. We spread our *vailok* upon the floor, wrapped ourselves in our cloaks, and awaited the coming of daylight. General Korsackoff was absent at Kyachta, where he had gone to meet General Mouravieff and Admiral Puchachin, who was on his way as ambassador to Pekin, and had gone to Kyachta to try to induce the Chinese authorities of Mia-mat-tschin to permit him to proceed to Pekin overland. The number of officers and merchants on their way to the Amoor, or who had been brought here in consequence of the Amoor movement, was the cause of the scarcity of lodgings in the city.

The next day we changed our quarters to Captain Alarofsky's house, which had been newly scrubbed, washed, and whitewashed, and a very hot fire kept up in the *peck* all day, in order to dry it for our reception. The room smelt like a lime-kiln, and the evaporation made it quite like a real steam-bath; but we had no choice, and, being rather worn and tired after ten days, spent mostly on the road, night and day, we were soon asleep, and this time on a bedstead, with white sheets—a luxury I now saw for the first time in Siberia. I awoke in the night, nearly suffocated, and with a most maddening headache. The fire in the stove had not been properly attended to, and, probably, some pieces of wood had been left uncharred previous to closing the chimney. The gas from this, and the steam and heat of the room, came very near killing both Gourieff and myself. I was very sick the next day, in consequence, and did not recover from the effects for several days afterwards.

We moved our quarters the next day to a house in the new portion of the town, near the governor's residence.

It was now the 15th of April, and having made up my mind that I had seen enough of the country to fully understand its resources and wants, and having travelled in all, since I left St. Petersburg, between five and six thousand miles, and, being at last on the head waters of the Amoor, I was naturally anxious to proceed, but the icy band of winter was yet upon its sources, and I must await patiently the genial influences of spring for the movement of the waters.

Spring was really at hand. The wild goose, the harbinger of open water and springing grass, was with us, and his deep, guttural voice was heard at night, as he winged his way to his favorite northern haunts on the shores of the icy ocean.

CHAPTER XXIV.

RESIDENCE AT CHETAH.

GOVERNOR KORSACKOFF being absent, Gourieff and I amused ourselves as best we could. We practised pistol shooting in the skirt of woods opposite our lodgings, rode on horseback to the adjacent villages, and, with goat hunts on the mountains of the Ingodah, and pleasant meetings occasionally among our friends, contrived to pass the time agreeably enough.

I also made a pleasant visit with Mr. Linan, wife, and friends to his establishment on the Ingodah, where he was preparing beef, pork, and bread for shipment to the Amoor. We had an agreeable time, and paid a visit also to the river near Mr. Linan's place, where he had several barges building for the descent into the Amoor, which he would load with such produce and merchandise as he expected to sell down the river, or to barter with the natives for furs and skins.

After some time spent in looking about the premises, and an impromptu dinner, we returned at 11 P. M. Mr. Linan is an enterprising merchant and a spirited speculator, and, if he had the necessary capital, would proceed immediately to build steamers on his own account, and place them at once on the Amoor; but, like many other bold, shrewd, clear-headed men, he has not the means himself to engage in an undertaking where so much money is required. I dined frequently with him, and he was constantly dwelling on the great advance in commercial prosperity Siberia would make so soon as steam could be placed on the Amoor, and the great increase in the wealth and the industrial pursuits of the country consequent thereon.

We also rowed down upon the Ingodah, several miles below the town, where there are some obstructions to the navigation of the river, which we examined in order to suggest a remedy. The river makes a sudden bend at a rocky island, and on the opposite side forms a wide and shoal rapid. In the main channel, which is wide enough for a steamer, are some boulders, which have either tumbled down from the opposite mountain, or have been deposited there by some passing field of ice from a higher source. The whole difficulty appeared to me to be easy to remedy. In the winter the river freezes nearly solid at this place, as in most shoal places, and at times is perhaps perfectly solid. The remedy, then, would be to remove the ice, apply powder to the rocks, and blow them up. In the second place, in order to deepen the water in the right-main channel, a dam should be built from the head of the bar, or island, diagonally to the opposite shore, which would throw sufficient water into the main channel to increase the required depth, making it equal in depth to other bars and shoals on the river. This plan was afterward suggested to Governor Korsackoff, who thought favorably of it, and, as far as removing the rocks is concerned, he said it would be put in execution the coming winter; the other, and more costly improvement, of course must take time and await the action of government.

Mr. Linan, and his very pretty and accomplished wife, are both from European Russia. He himself had been engaged in the commerce of the Kuban and countries upon the Caspian and Volga. His wife, I believe, is a native of Nijne-Novgorod, and of noble blood. She speaks French fluently, draws well, and plays upon the piano and guitar—what more could a merchant ask in a wife upon the banks of the Ingodah, nearly six thousand miles east of Paris, and twelve thousand miles west of New York?

I met also at Chetah a very remarkable character, one of the political exiles of the *emeute* against Nicholas, in 1826, at his accession to the throne. This gentleman had lived in Siberia thirty years, and was yet a hale, hearty, sprightly, active man. He was, of course, young at the accession of Nicholas, but years had sat more lightly on the exile than on his Emperor—free from care and ambition he had passed a generation in Siberia, apparently contented and happy. He had his home, his books, and friends; lived very comfortably, "taught the young idea how to shoot," interested himself very much in the progress and prosperity of his country, and was quite conversant with American affairs. In early days, when a boy, attached to the public service under Alexander I., he had visited the Pacific and California, and was delighted to see one who had been there, and especially since the discovery of gold and the conquest by the United States.

He was now free to return to Russia, by the ukase of

Alexander II. at his coronation, but he loves Siberia, and thinks it a better country than Russia, and the probability is that he will remain on the head waters of the Amoor and participate in its development and coming prosperity.

CHAPTER XXV.

A BURAT LAMA.

A Burat Lama called upon me at Chetah. He was a fine-looking man, with a very agreeable face, and was dressed in the heavy fur-lined yellow silk robe of the priesthood, bound about the loins by a red silk sash. It had a few gilt or brass buttons on the upper front, and a black velvet collar and facings. Yellow leather boots, with wide loose breeches, tucked inside, completed his apparel. On his head he wore a small Chinese skull-cap, with a blue rosette, or button, at the top. He could speak Russian a little, nevertheless he was accompanied by an interpreter and body servant. Captain Gourieff spoke in Russian, and, when the Lama could not comprehend, he would call for explanation upon his interpreter, a Burat, who understood Russian well. He was very anxious to know something concerning my country, and if I was from the "Sea of the West," and how long it took me to reach Chetah. He was greatly surprised when I told him that my country was to the east, though I had come from the west, but, having passed about two-thirds of the distance round the world, I was nearer home now than I had been for some time, and that, by descending the Amoor and falling into the great sea to the east of China and Japan, my country would be just opposite, across the ocean.

"How much will it cost me," said he, "to go down the Sak-hah-lin on one of your *parohads*?" This is the only name they use for a steam-vessel, which they have learned from the Russians. "How much would it cost to go to Thibet, if these *parohads* you speak of were navigating the Sak-hah-lin?"

I had told him previously that it was my intention to induce an American company to place steamers on the Amoor. I told him it would take ten days perhaps to go to the sea. He then asked me how many days it would take to go from the sea to Thibet? I explained to him that Thibet could not be reached by the sea, but that he could pass by way of China and the English possessions in India, and reach Thibet in that way.

"Ah," said he, "this is most excellent; how valuable it is to be a great traveller, and to know all these things. How much will the whole of this journey cost?"

I told him "about a thousand rubles."

"Oh!" cried he, "this is not much, one can afford to pay that much to visit the country of his God and to see the Grand Lama."

"How long," asked he, "before these wonderful things will be done?"

I told him "in the course of three years perhaps steam would be introduced on the Amoor, and that, if he would go with me down the Amoor to the sea, he would find American ships that would convey him to China, from whence he could find an English steamer to carry him to Calcutta."

"Ah," said he, "this is truly wonderful, but I am not yet prepared for so great a journey; when you return, I will then go with you."

I told him that "when I again visited Chetah, it would, perhaps, be on a *parohad*, when he would be able to reach the sea in a few days, when our ships would certainly be there to carry him to any part of the world."

"How wonderful!" he exclaimed; "your countrymen must be powerful and happy, to be able thus to visit every part of the earth."

I had been writing, and, seeing the pen, ink, and paper, he asked me to write my name on a piece of paper that he might preserve it. I wrote my name on a card, and gave him a few steel pens, with which he was highly delighted. Wrapping them up carefully, he placed them beneath the folds of his robe in his bosom. I now requested him to write his name. This he joyfully assented to, and, taking the pen with which I had written, asked me "whether I would have him write in Thibetian or Mongol?" I answered, in the latter. He wrote with great ease, in the Mongol character, his name. He then took from his neck, beneath his dress, a rosary of beads of various sizes and shapes, and, untying it, selected one of the beads, and, placing it in my hand, said it would be a token by which I should keep him in remembrance.

This Lama lived about forty miles distant, at a Burat village. He invited me to visit him, but I could not make it convenient to do so during my stay at Chetah. He called again to see Captain Gourieff, to get his aid in some business affair he had with the government concerning his people. In a few days he left for his village, promising to visit us again after our return from Nerchinsk, but I saw no more of him.

The Burats were a tribe, or nation, of the Northern Mongols, subjugated and cut off by Russia from the more powerful hordes of the south. They inhabit the region round about the Baikal, and were once a large and powerful nation.

I believe there are no Lamisaries, or communities of Buddhist priests, among the tribes under Russian dominion, except at Selenginsk ; but to the south of Mai-mat-tschin, about one hundred and fifty miles, on the Orchan, which falls into the Selenga, there is an immense Lamisary, and a large city, situated in a beautiful valley, surrounded by a fertile country. This Buddhist society of priests number many thousands. A large city has sprung up in the vicinity, and it is a place of great trade. The Jesuit Huc, who was to the south further than I was to the north of it, describes it as a singularly interesting and important place, both as regards trade and political influences.

I had in my possession a Buddhist hand-bell and sceptre, that Governor Korsackoff had presented to me, under the following circumstances. Previous to my leaving Moscow, General Mouravieff had written to General Korsackoff that the Americans were coming, and told him to give them one of those bells—which are highly valued because they are considered to be very fine in metal and tone, and the workmanship excellent—to the first American who should cross the Altai and penetrate into his province. One day, when dining with him, he gave me this bell, the metal of which is said to be pretty well mellowed with silver, while the clapper is of fine polished steel, tied with red silk thread to the staple on which it swings.

These bells are used in religious ceremonies by the Lamas, and are considered very sacred, and much value is attached to them. This priest, at Chetah, showed me the use of the bell. He took it in his left hand, holding the handle between the thumb and fore finger, with the palm of the hand open, and the muzzle of the bell turned towards the body. In the right hand he took the mace, or sceptre, and, with much swaying of the body back and forth, he repeated, in a sing-song tone, *om mani*, or some other pious invocation, and rang the bell at intervals to accompany the prayer, while he was rolling the mace back and forth within the palm of his right hand. He then told us that it was a very holy instrument, and, in using it, much good could be done ; he also explained to us that, in the right hand, some grains of wheat, or other grain, are generally held, and sprinkled on the ground from time to time in front of the altar, or image, before which the ceremony is performed.

CHAPTER XXVI.

A WILD-GOOSE CHASE.

GOVERNOR KORSACKOFF was still in Kyachta, Alarofsky was absent, and "winter lingered in the lap of spring." I wished and hoped and prayed for rain, a real drenching, soaking rain, to raise the waters and set free the ice. The climatology of this section, however, was to me a puzzle. February and March and April had passed, and out of Irkutsk there had been snow only three times, and not a drop of rain. It must be recollected, however, that, on the east and south of the great Altai range, the physical causes of climate are very different from those on the north and west. On the north, the great Polar Sea, immense tracts of swamp, lakes, and rivers, all supply the atmosphere with moisture and swell abundantly the rain and snow clouds, while the prevailing winds in seasons of change are from the north. But upon the south there are few lakes or rivers, while the land in general is dry, rolling, or mountainous, and remote from the ocean. The water-charged clouds, coming down from the north, pass over a region of more than one thousand miles in breadth, where they precipitate much of their moisture, and, as they approach the purer and cooler air of the

Altai, and in the process of elevating themselves to pass the mountains, they part with almost their last drops, which fall in snows and rains along the northern sides of the range, or upon the crest and southern and eastern water-sheds.

Looking to the south and west, we find a high, dry, rolling country, with lofty mountains intervening between it, the Caspian Sea and the Indian Ocean. The winds and the rain clouds that gather there fall upon the mountains of Thibet and Bucharia, and, before they have reached the desert of Kobi, have but little moisture left, and, consequently, the country upon the head of the Amoor, in a south-westerly direction, receives very little water from them, and the south-westerly winds that sweep so regularly over the steppes of the Ingodah, Onon, and Argoon, are harsh and rainless, and it is only when the softening influence of spring has given to the north wind sufficient warmth, that rain descends in reviving showers from the summits and slopes of the Altai. This country, in many respects, is much like portions of California. From the causes enumerated heretofore, very little snow falls in the valleys, and even on the lower mountains, not enough to interfere with the grazing of sheep, cattle, or horses, where I have seen them feeding on native grasses during my sojourn on both sides of the Altai, in the Trans-Baikal country, during the winter and spring.

Wheat, buckwheat, rye, barley, and oats, hemp and flax, yield good crops on both sides of the mountains. Potatoes, cabbages, turnips, lettuce, radishes, onions, spinach, and horse-radish, are also cultivated.

The prices of the staple products have been heretofore

regulated merely upon domestic consumption, because export was out of the question, except to a very limited extent. A few thousand poods of rye, wheat, butter, cheese, tallow, and honey found their way to the Okhotsk, Kamschatka, and Russian America, by the tedious and expensive overland route north of Irkutsk via Yakoutsk, to the ports of Okhotsk or Ayan, while a still less quantity, of late years, found a market through the gates of Mia-mattschin, in exchange for Chinese produce.

Rye has been sold, of late years, at ten kopyeks the pood*, or about ten cents the bushel (American), and wheat twenty-five cents the pood, cattle at five to ten rubles a head, and sheep at seventy kopyeks.

Governor Korsackoff and suite returned from Kyachta on the 5th of May, which gave a more lively turn to affairs, and hastened the movements in the direction of the Amoor. We had agreeable reunions at his hospitable board, where I met several of my old friends and acquaintances, not only from Irkutsk, Verchne-Udinsk, and Kyachta, but also from Russia.

One day Captain Alarofsky invited me to witness a goose hunt. Early in the morning Gourieff and myself proceeded to his lodgings, where were guns, ammunition, provisions, telyaga, and horses, all in readiness for the expedition. Before setting out, each of us provided himself with arms and ammunition, and, in order to practise a little, one of our party, a midshipman on his way to join the Amoor fleet, let off his rifle, full charged, into the floor of the room in which we were all stand-

* 36 lbs. American.

ing, missing Aryefaky's toes by scarcely an inch, while Stewpan jumped as if he were shot, letting fall, in his fright, my gun, which he was bringing to me. However, we got off without further accident, and, crossing the main Chetah creek, yet frozen, with the water from the recent thaws running over the ice about three feet deep, we made across the intervening ground towards a village on the Ingodah. Here we had to cross a branch of the Chetah, at its entrance into the river, and, plunging in, the water was deep enough to float our provisions and extra baggage, but, seizing our guns, we stood up in the telyaga and escaped with moist feet.

Our road now lay along the base of a mountain. We soon came to some small lakes, where Aryefaky got down, and stole along, half bent, to get a shot at a number of geese feeding on the margin of one of the lakes, but an old gray gander was on the look-out, and, with *kronk! kronk!* the whole flock were up and off in an instant. We now went at full gallop over the broad plain to the west towards lofty, snow-capped mountains. The day was mild and pleasant, the sun shining brightly, larks were singing merrily, and occasional flights of geese and ducks gave us encouragement of good sport ahead. After a ride of several miles, we came in view of a ridge of low hills to the left, with the valley of the Chetah opening up broad and blue away to far distant, brilliant, snow-capped peaks to the north, where Pacific and Frozen Ocean waters were locked in icy embrace.

We soon saw some small lakes skirting along at the foot of low hills. Here Alarofaky called a halt, and, pointing in the direction of the water, said, "*Goo-se smat-vot ! vot !"*—look at the geese !—"*Dalako,*" said I; "*Nyat, nyat,*" said he, "*blezke*"—no, no, near by. Gourieff had seen them with his quick eye, and was out of the wagon and off before I saw a feather. Aryefsky followed, and then Alarofsky, while I took a direction between the two lakes, hoping that, if they flushed the birds, I could give them a shot on the wing as they passed over; but the best of calculations sometimes fail, and so it was in this case. Bang, bang, bang, went the guns of my friends on the right, and away went the geese in the wrong direction for me, seeking the higher, instead of the lower, waters of the Chetah, leaving us gooseless in the solitary plain. Gourieff now took a wide circuit to the front and left, Alarofsky and Aryefsky to the front and right, while I satisfied myself with skirting a lake to the rear and left. We were in a perfectly open prairie, not a shrub or bush to conceal our approach to the game. I had made up my mind, from the shyness of the first flock that we had seen in the morning, that our chances for success with the geese were rather slim, so I began to shoot larks, and bagged quite a number.

However, the party, after an hour, began to draw in towards the point where our driver had located a camp, by unhitching his horses, and, gathering a few scanty chips of *bois de vache*, raised a smoke, if not much fire. It was not long before a Burat came into camp with a pair of geese for sale; they were purchased, and, with the camp appliances that Alarofsky's soldier-like precaution had provided, our driver was soon in the midst of a grand stew, diversified by roasting of beef on ramrods.

Gourieff was now seen on the opposite side of the lake,

and the question was how he was to reach us, without a great circuit to the east, or retracing his steps to the north, but the difficulty was soon settled, by his mounting a bullock which the Burat huntsman had brought with him. The Burats train bullocks to assist them in hunting, using them with great success to stalk geese and wild ducks. The hunter, walking behind the bullock, drives the animal slowly along until he is near enough to the birds to make sure of his aim. Being accustomed to the presence of cattle the birds are easily approached in this way.

We returned by a different road, fording the creek at a point much higher up, where we got the assistance of some peasants in a cart to carry ourselves and traps over dry, while our low wagon was submerged in crossing.

CHAPTER XXVII.

DEPARTURE FROM CHETAH.

A REGIMENT of infantry of the line, from beyond the mountains, halted at Chetah on their way to Schilkah, the rendezvous for the Amoor expedition. They were regaled with a public dinner of meat, soup, bread, quass, and vodka. After a few days' rest they moved on towards the Amoor. In the movement of materiel and troops towards Schilkah, I was doomed to suffer a heavy loss. The services of my friend, Captain Gourieff, became absolutely necessary to Governor Korsackoff, and he was despatched as courier to the different military posts below. It was really a sad loss to me. We had been together since my arrival at Irkutsk, almost daily, except when I was at Kyachta. He spoke three languages fluently, and English tolerably well; was intelligent, inquiring, active, and well versed in every thing pertaining to his own country, and had proved to be in every way an agreeable and most valuable companion. I had hoped that, by some turn in the necessities of the public service, he would accompany me on to the mouth of the Amoor. We parted, with the hope of meeting either at Bankin or Schilkah, as I passed down the river. I hope that his government may appreciate his talents and worth; at all events, I think that his own force of character will bring him to the favorable notice of his superiors; in fact, I am sure of this, under so discriminating and active a chief as General Mouravieff.

Though I had lost Gourieff, good fortune favored me, as it had from the first since I entered Russia, with agreeable companions and kind and noble friends. Captain Fulyhelm, of the Imperial Russian Navy, Governor of Ayan, in the service of the Russian-American Company, to whom I had been introduced at Irkutsk by Gen-eneral Mouravieff, was now here on his way to the Amoor, under instructions from St. Petersburg to descend the river, for the purpose of observation connected with the general interests of the company. Heretofore, the whole commerce of this company had been carried either around the Cape of Good Hope, or by the shorter but more expensive transit of Yakutsk and the Okhotsk, but now the recent occupation of the Amoor had opened to them a new route to their possessions on the Pacific, and Captain Fulyhelm was, like myself, awaiting the moving of the waters to proceed on his mission.

This gentleman spoke four languages fluently, had travelled much, cruised on the Pacific Ocean, visited California and the Sandwich Islands, and, as governor of Ayan, had seen much of our whalemen there, and was also conversant generally with affairs in our country.

On the 11th May, General Korsackoff and staff departed for Schilkah, which again made delay more irksome to me, a feeling in which Captain Fulyhelm participated. A small boat, or skiff, by direction of General Korsackoff, had been ordered to be constructed for us at a place thirty miles distant up the river, and we were now anxiously awaiting its completion.

On the 7th, Colonel Oushakoff announced to us that the river was open, and that we might certainly expect our boat by the 13th. I walked down to the river bank, and saw the Ingodah flowing past. It was a pleasant and suggestive sight, and I anticipated with pleasure the hour when I should be afloat upon its dark and sweeping tide.

Two or three days after the first opening of the river, the flow of ice was checked both above and below Chetah, which dampened for the time our prospects of departure ; but before the 13th it was again all clear, and we anxiously awaited the arrival of our skiff. The 13th came and passed, as did the 14th, 15th, and 16th, and the boat did not come: Colonel Oushakoff was confident that it must arrive without further delay. We had been notified that it was coming, with others built for officers who were also waiting, but come it did not. It was now the 18th day of May, just one year since I had entered Russia at Kronstadt.

"What shall we do?" asked Captain Fulyhelm. "Gospodeen Zemin is here, whom you know, from Irkutsk, and offers us passage in his barge to Bankin, or perhaps Schilkah. Our skiff don't come, and Colonel Oushakoff is discouraged and vexed at the delay, but can do nothing to prevent it."

"By all means," I replied, "accept Mr. Zemin's kind offer, and take our chances, if he does not proceed to Schilkah to procure conveyance from Bankin, as best we can."

In five minutes we were packing up, and, after despatching several cart-loads of stores, provisions, and baggage, we bade farewell to friends and acquaintances, and set out in a telyaga, with post horses, for the point of embarkation.

We spent the night at Ataman, eight miles east of Chetah, in a peasant's cabin, on a tolerably soft pine plank against the wall; the husband and wife were in an adjoining room. She was crying the fore part of the night, and talking to her husband concerning his going to the Amoor, and how long he would be absent. She was much distressed, and had been speaking to Captain Fulyhelm in the afternoon, to intercede with the chief to procure the release of her husband, as he had been upon the Amoor once before, and, therefore, ought to be exempt this year. The captain made a memorandum of his name, and wife's statement, and promised to do what he could in the premises.

The barge we were to embark in was flat-bottomed, about forty feet long and twelve feet wide, with high sides, and partially roofed with plank, open between the roof and sides, and drawing two feet and a half of water. This was intended to be used below Schilkah as a lighter, to accompany a fleet of forty large freight barges, which were building at different villages on the Ingodah and Schilkah, belonging to Mr. Zemin, and to be freighted for the Russian-American Company and the Russian Government.

These barges are constructed from the pine and spruce timber of the country, growing in abundance upon the shores of the rivers, and are about sixty feet long, and sixteen feet wide, very heavily and strongly built, and capable of carrying fifty or sixty tons, and, when fully loaded, draw from six to seven feet of water. They carry a crew of ten men each, a large lug-sail, two side oars, a steering oar, and anchor, and will make the passage to the mouth of the Amoor in about sixty to ninety days.

The Ingodah, at this point, is about two hundred yards wide, the shores well timbered, and mountainous; the color of the water is dark, almost black, when looked at from the shore; when dipped up in a glass, it is clean, with a slight yellow tinge, and pleasant and agreeable to drink. We took our tea in the yard, to which the captain's servant, Evan, added some excellent chicken soup, which made up for the loss of our dinner; the good woman added milk, eggs, and black-bread, which furnished us an excellent meal. Our table was a pile of logs.

Tuesday, May 19. The long looked-for day broke bright and glorious over the rugged, pine-clad, eastern mountains, and, having slept rather badly on my plank during the night, I was glad when the morning came:—the day on which I should embark upon the waters of the Amoor, after a three-fourths circuit of the globe, and sixteen months eastward travel, was to me an eventful one.

During the morning I wandered along the banks of a beautiful creek, that came laughing down through a mountain gorge behind the village, and passing through the centre of it; as I ascended along it among the spurs, I found the shores yet covered in places with heavy masses of ice, the accumulation of the previous winter, and which the spring sun, amid the shades of the mountain, had as yet been too feeble to dissipate. Flowers were springing up along its margin in sunny spots, where a southern exposure admitted the full force of the sun; and wild ducks were trying its banks for the tender grass of spring.

CHAPTER XXVIII.

DOWN THE INGODAH.

AT 3 P. M. Mr. Zemin arrived, with the announcement that we would depart immediately. Bags, boxes, trunks, guns, pistols, knives, chicken-coops, bundles, cloaks, skins, pots, kettles, pans, bottles, with an indescribable variety of et ceteras, only known to Siberian travellers, were quickly in carts and on their way to the beach where the boat lay. We were all on board by 5 P. M., and, amid the shouts of some hundred peasants and boatmen, we pushed off into the Ingodah, the men sprung to their oars, and, with the assistance of the current, we were soon gliding rapidly along the beautiful shores of this river.

This was really a joyous moment to me, after the long and terrible land journeys I had made during a Siberian winter, and I felt as proud of our little pine barge, as she floated past the beautiful shores of the head waters of the Amoor, as if I were on one of the finest floating-palaces on the great "Father of Waters."

The river proved easy to navigate in this description of craft, and we proceeded along at the rate of nearly five miles an hour; we touched once upon a rock at a noted ripple, in which is lodged a huge boulder called Kepétan-

Kamen, "Captain Stone." The current here is very swift, the channel narrow, and the "Captain Stone" right where he ought not to be. The expenditure of a few hundred rubles in the winter, when the water recedes and the river becomes frozen solid to the bottom, would dislodge this famous "Captain," and rob the place of all its terror.

At 9 P. M. we landed at the village of Krugenskah, twenty-five miles by water from Ataman, and twenty-eight by post road from Chetah. Here we found Colonel Oushakoff, the chief of the Russian military expedition to the Amoor this year. He had "posted" from Chetah since we left Ataman, to look after a government raft and its cargo, wrecked upon the "Captain Stone" the day previous. We went up into the village and drank tea with Colonel Oushakoff, after which we retired to our boat to spend the night.

I had passed over the same river in a sleigh but little over a month previous, and had visited this post station twice before, and, after travelling in open sleighs and telyagas, and sleeping in them on the road, night and day, during the coldest mid-winter, I had no new hardship to encounter in sleeping in an open boat. Wrapping ourselves up in our cloaks, either on the floor or along the sides of the boat, on benches of planks, we slept well and comfortably.

Our party consisted of the owner, Mr. Zemin, and his clerk, Captain Fulyhelm and servant, Evan, Mr. Raddy, and a Cossack huntsman, a pilot from the river Lena, ten boatmen, and myself. Mr. Raddy was a naturalist employed by the imperial government, and especially by the Geographical Society of St. Petersburg, and was going to spend a couple of years in the great southern bend of the

Amoor in the region of the Sangahree River. We had no cargo but our provisions and baggage; this, however, made a very considerable bulk, quite sufficient to occupy most of the covered space of the barge.

We found the river of nearly uniform width, about two hundred yards, with occasional bars, composed of small boulders and gravel. We grounded twice during the day, but both times out of the channel. We were only detained a few minutes each time. We were under way at 4 A. M. The day proved bright and agreeable, though the night had been frosty, and the icicles hung to the oars on the shady side till near noon. The shores are generally mountainous, well timbered with pine and birch, with an occasional opening or receding of the mountains, sufficient for a Cossack village and ground for cultivation.

We passed a number of villages during the day; we did not succeed in reaching the post station of Oroolgah, and, it coming on to grow dark, we landed for the night upon the right bank of the river, where there was an extensive prairie and signs of cattle and horses. The men soon had a blazing fire on the shore, seated or standing around which they prepared their supper; we had our *samovar* and tea. The night was bright and beautiful, and we spent some time walking and in conversation upon the shore, till the sharpness of the air and the lateness of the hour drove us to our planks and cloaks.

May 21. We were off as soon as it was light in the morning; the day proved unpleasant, harsh, and cloudy, with much wind, which compelled us to land for a short time, or rather our pilot found the labor of steering too great; he now commenced giving us lessons in Lena barge navigation.

There was not a soul on board who had ever before seen the Ingodah, so that we had to depend entirely upon the experience of our Lena helmsman in river navigation. He was a good-natured, ruddy, stout, hearty specimen of a Siberian, proud of his knowledge as a navigator, as well as of the boat and live cargo intrusted to his care and under his sole direction.

I must say that he had quite a good idea of the draft of water in a current river, but not always as good judgment of the effect of the current upon his craft—a sad defect in a pilot. We made but a poor run, and landed for the night on the right shore, with a village on our left.

The country during the day became more and more open, with extensive high rolling prairies, the shores beautiful in natural scenery; the forests are leafless, except the pine, though the first flowers of spring are seen, and the willows are budding along the shores. Mr. Baddy was perfectly enchanted with the beauties of nature, and anxious to find some new plant to add to his herbarium.

May 22. The country to-day is still more open, handsome rolling prairie, with mountains in the distance; on the left, destitute of timber; on the right, the country is well wooded, and generally mountainous; the river is deeper and more sinuous, with fewer bars and higher banks. We have made a good run to-day; our speed is estimated, with oars, at five miles per hour. We stopped for the night at the village of Klutchefskyah. All the villages along on the river are Cossack, under the old frontier system of settlement, first adopted in this country as a fence against Chinese or Tartar invasion, and to protect and regulate the convicts in the mines.

These Cossacks are a distinct class in Siberia, having a very singular constitution, with laws, regulations, rights, duties, and privileges separate from other classes of the population. Their constitution is strictly for military purposes, though they are cultivators (ever so poor) of the soil.

CHAPTER XXIX.

A MINERAL SPRING.

MAY 23. Early this morning we passed the river Onon, coming in from the right (south); we are now in the Schilkah. This river is formed by the junction of the Ingodah and Onon, the latter coming in from the south and draining all that section of country lying between the Ingodah and the Mongol-Chinese frontier.

These two rivers must have each a course of three hundred or four hundred miles; the accumulation, therefore, of the drippings of the watershed of the Mongol frontier has given our new river greater breadth and depth; more breadth, perhaps, than depth in proportion, for the sand-bars begin now to be a regular feature in the Schilkah, growing more and more like some portions of the Ohio river. There are evidences of much fluctuation in its rise and fall; the banks are sandy and cut in places.

Some forty miles below the Onon, the Narga, or Nertcha, enters from the north. The old city of Nerchinsk is situated upon this stream, a few miles before it enters the Schilkah. On the left, the country is open, rolling, and bare of timber; on the right, the mountains are well wooded, with some very beautiful open spots and hill sides; the bends of the river are more sweeping, and the banks in places crumbling; the soil looks rich. We passed, on the right, the monastery of Nerchinskay. It is beautifully situated on rising ground, some distance from the river, with lofty mountains in the back-ground, and a fine scope of good agricultural and grazing country around. It is a lovely spot, and well chosen as a retreat for religious meditation.

We reached a small village, just below Nerchinsk, on the left, before dark, where Mr. Zemin had several barges building. We went on shore and had supper at the house of Mr. Z.'s agent, who had the charge of the construction of the barges. The village is built in a hollow between two mountains, and, on the opposite shore, the country is rugged, but well timbered—a suitable place for boat-building.

May 24. After supper we retired to our boat, and, resting well, were up at 5 A. M., and crossed the river in a skiff to another village, a little higher up, on the opposite shore, in order to visit a mineral spring, some two miles distant, up a mountain gorge.

We were conducted by the head Cossack of the village along through and up a deep rocky glen, through which a small creek was running, on which, near the village, there were several simple mills for grinding grain. On reaching the spring, we found it surrounded with a rim of ice, and the ground along the creek was frozen. Upon dipping the water with a glass, we found it sparkling and effervescent, like champagne. It was very sharp and pungent to the taste, but wonderfully palatable and pleasant to drink, having the flavor of the purest soda-water, slightly acid, and sweet enough to remind one of hock and soda-water before breakfast "the next morning." We drank as much as possible of it, though it was intensely cold; all regretting that we could not spend a week at the village in order to drink this delightful water. We filled some bottles to take with us, and returned to the village.

There was no care taken of the spring; it was just as fashioned by Dame Nature, surrounded by trees, bushes, and rocks, bubbling and sparkling up from the depths below. We asked the people of the village as to its medicinal properties, upon which they replied that they had not remarked any thing in particular in it, they only drank it when they were sick; this was, of course, entirely satisfactory, and gave us all the light on the subject supposed to be required by us from the villagers.

Captain Fulyhelm compared it to the Seltzer water of Germany. I thought it quite equal to our own Saratoga. After drinking of this water, and while our bottles held out, we all felt a peculiar vivifying effect from its use, with increased and healthy action of the viscera.

On the western side of the mountains, on the waters falling into Lake Baikal, there are several mineral springs, both hot and cold, one of which is very remarkable. This spring contains so much gas, and the effervescing properties are so powerful, that the vapor from it ascends like steam in a considerable column, and, when closely approached, makes you catch your breath. It is quite difficult to drink at first. In the winter it freezes; but the strength of the gas constantly elevating the water through the ice, it forms a column of several fathoms in height, which is giving off vapor the whole winter. This column continues increasing until the mild weather of spring looses its bands, when, the force of the confined gas expanding, the mass bursts, with the report of a heavy cannon, scattering its fragments far and wide.

In the mountains of Mongolia, on the waters of Baikal, there are also reported numerous mineral waters, hot and cold. That region is essentially volcanic, though I could hear of no mountain in an active state.

We returned to our boat, on the opposite side of the river, and, pushing out into the stream, reached Bankin by 9 A. M. This is the place previously spoken of in my visit to the mines. Here Mr. Zemin was to stop for the present to attend to the loading of some of his barges at this point, but he kindly proffered us the use of his barge to convey us to Schilkah. This we very gladly accepted, as it would save us the procuring of a boat in which to proceed thence, the removal of our baggage, and perhaps two days delay. Mr. Raddy also left us here, proposing to visit the Nerchinsk mines, but both himself and Mr. Zemin would overtake us at Schilkah.

CHAPTER XXX.

FROM BANKIN TO SCHILKAH.

WE left Bankin about 11 A. M. It was a pleasant sunny day, and contrasted very favorably with the last day I was here, on my previous visit, about a month since. The river at this point is four hundred and fifty yards wide, the shores mountainous, with occasional prairie and bottom land. The scenery is picturesque; and nothing is wanting but an occasional steamboat puffing along, with more cultivation, scattered farm-houses, and pretty villages, to give it a strong resemblance to some portions of the Upper Mississippi.

We glided along very pleasantly, and, having lost our Lena pilot at Bankin, we were left to our own resources for the navigation of a river unknown to us all. We, however, got on well, and enjoyed ourselves very much with the scenery, and in piloting our craft and sounding the depth of the water on the bars. We landed for the night at the village of Bolovsk, where we were very kindly treated by the people, and had our supper on shore.

May 24. We were off early, and reached Straitensk during the morning, where we landed to learn the whereabouts of Governor Korsackoff. We had expected to have met him at Bankin, but, when we arrived there, he had previously departed from Schilkah, but was looked for daily on his return, perhaps to Chetah. We now feared that we might miss him entirely. Captain Fulyhelm called upon the military commandant of the station, from whom he learned that the governor had passed up the day previous by land, on his way to Bankin, but that he would return in a very few days to Schilkah. We also learned from the commandant's secretary, that an order had been given at Schilkah, before the governor left that place, that a boat should be prepared for us there. This gave us much satisfaction, for we had feared that, in case of the absence of General Korsackoff, we should have some difficulty in procuring the men for the expedition down the Amoor. His presence at Schilkah, or his order to provide us with the necessary men, being absolutely requisite, Captain Fulyhelm had determined, before we reached Straitensk, in case General Korsackoff had gone up, to return himself by land to Bankin, in order to procure his requisition on Colonel Oushakoff for the complement of men necessary for our boat's crew, but the information being satisfactory that the governor would return, we, therefore, remained but a short time.

There is a communication by wagon-road from this to Nerchinsk mines and the Argoon. It is very handsomely situated on the right shore of the river, with bold, beautiful mountains in front. The commandant of a battalion resides here, and there are several good-looking buildings, and barracks for a thousand men, and a station-house for passing exiles. The battalion musters here once a year for exercise, inspection, and drill, gathering from their villages to spend a month perhaps each year, a few only being retained on duty the year round.

We floated and rowed along the beautiful shores of this river. The day proved very delightful, and, after a good day's run, we landed for the night at the village of Botovskah. We were kindly and hospitably entertained at a worthy peasant's house, but preferred to sleep on our boat, fearing that warm rooms would unfit us for our river life. Having a long voyage before us, we must become accustomed to sleeping in our little ark. We bathed in the river, and then turned in.

We departed from our resting-place before the sun was up. The morning was delightful and the river beautiful, with superb shore scenery. I lay upon the deck of our boat, hour after hour, admiring it as we glided along, like the shifting scenery in some grand spectacle, as bend after bend, and point after point, opened upon our view landscapes and vistas of surpassing beauty.

We made all possible speed though, being very anxious to reach Schilkah as early in the afternoon as possible, as we were now only fifty miles distant. Our men pulled at the oars with a will, and, aided by the rapidity of the current, we swept merrily past these lovely shores. We struck heavily against a sunken rock (at the Devil's Elbow), in what our helmsman had selected for the channel, but we soon perceived that the deepest waters lay in quite another direction. No damage was done, and we floated on without further obstruction.

We arrived at Schilkah at 4 P. M., and, as we had to deliver Mr. Zemin's barge to his agent at this point, we procured lodgings, to which we moved our baggage.

We found the boat intended for us undergoing the necessary repairs, with the probability of its being completed within a few days. General Korsackoff had not yet returned, nor had Colonel Oushakoff arrived, but they were both looked for daily. The Amoor expedition being ordered to rendezvous here, and General Korsackoff being, by virtue of his office, hetman of the Cossacks in this province, the whole detail and organization of the expedition is under his immediate supervision.

Schilkah is the seat of an old convict silver mining establishment. The working of the mines is now, however, discontinued. "Schilskenskey Zavad," as it is called in Russian, is now the dock-yard and the naval and military depot for the Amoor. Two steamboats have been built here, besides many barges, boats, and rafts, and it has been considered to be the head of navigation for the Amoor, three thousand three hundred versts, or about twenty-two hundred miles to the sea.

Many barges are in course of construction and preparation, troops being drilled, barges and rafts arriving from the villages above, provisions and munitions being shipped, and different minor and independent expeditions and companies being fitted out and prepared for the descent of the Amoor, viz.: Captain Arnosoff, on a mining expedition, Mr. Raddy, the naturalist, Captain Chickachoff, to take charge of the steamship America, now at Nikolaivsky, to convey Admiral Count Puchachin to Pekin, the admiral's own barge, Captain ——, with a corps of topographical engineers, to establish a line of telegraph between De Castries and Nikolaivsky, several merchant barges, and our own little volunteer exploring expedition.

Schilkah is on the left bank of the river, has a population of one thousand souls, and stretches for some two miles along a narrow strip of table-land between the mountain and the river. The town is evidently in a state of decay from its former prosperity, when it was the theatre of silver and gold mining.

The river in front of the town has a breadth of six hundred yards, with a current of four knots, and a depth of seven feet on the shoalest bars, which is said to be low for this season of the year. During our stay in this place, we were engaged from day to day in perfecting our outfit and in laying in additional stores and provisions, to which were added a few notions to barter with the natives for provisions, or with which to make them presents, and smooth our way.

On the 28th there was a review of the battalion. Six hundred men were under arms—the Russian battalion is a thousand muskets. The following day they were blessed by the priest, on the shore near where they were to embark. This is a religious ceremony observed throughout Russia in the movement of troops. It is also observed in private undertakings. A priest was brought from Chetah to bless the boats built at Ataman, before their departure, the one we sailed in as well as the others.

After the conclusion of the ceremony the battalion embarked, the two gun-boats firing a salute as they were pushed off from the shore and swung into the current. The flotilla was soon rapidly carried down the stream, and lost to view behind a projecting point. This was the advance-guard of the Amoor expedition for 1857, under Colonel Oushakoff as chief.

General Korsackoff arrived on the 30th. This gave spirit and activity to every thing, and added much to the pleasure of our stay, as, at his hospitable board, we met the officers of the great and little expeditions on their way to the Amoor.

CHAPTER XXXI.

FROM SCHILKAH TO OUSE-CHERNEY.

TUESDAY, June 2, 10 A. M. Our boat was now ready, our baggage and stores on board. Captain Fulyhelm had gone out in the town to make his adieus to his friends. I remained to give sailing directions, and to stop for him opposite the quarters of General Korsackoff.

Our boat was built here two years since, and had been a voyage down the Amoor as far as Igoon, with General Korsackoff. It is thirty feet long, seven feet wide, and three feet deep. Twenty feet of the centre is housed in and divided into two compartments, one for sleeping, seven feet—the other for stores and luggage. Our sleeping apartment has a bunk on each side, two feet wide. The centre is open to admit free passage fore and aft. Two oars, a mast forward of the cabin, a small square sail, a flag at the stern, (a blue cross on white ground,) sundry poles, a steering oar, and two spare oars. For our crew we have five Cossacks; Captain Fulyhelm and his servant Evan, and myself, made up the sum total of the party—eight in all.

We pushed out into the stream, and, rowing along the shore, landed opposite the lodgings of General Korsackoff, where Captain Fulyhelm was awaiting my arrival.

We proceeded at once to the general's, to bid him farewell.

General Korsackoff had been so kind to me, added to which his general suavity of manners and agreeable conversation had rendered my stay at Chetah so agreeable, that it was with pain I took his hand to say good-by. He came with us to the beach to take a last look at his old craft, now about to descend the entire Amoor. He stood upon the shore to see us under way; waving to him our final adieus, we were once more fairly afloat upon our downward voyage.

General Korsackoff is one of the handsomest men I have ever seen. He has performed some wonderful journeys in Siberia, and made the quickest trip from Kamschatka to St. Petersburg ever achieved. He was in the first Amoor expedition, and is identified with the final occupation of the Amoor. He is still a young man, active, sagacious, hardy, and accomplished, and capable of performing prodigies for his country whenever an opportunity presents itself. He has, within a few years, advanced rapidly from a captain to be governor of a province, and now general, but deserves all, and I hope his future may be as bright as he is eminently worthy.

It is perfectly incredible, except to those who witness it, what one week of sunshine will do in this country. When we arrived at Schilkah the forests were leafless; now they are in full leaf, the shores gay with flowers and blooming shrubs, and the air at times filled with fragrance.

The country is mountainous, and the bottom-lands upon the river not of much extent, but, as you ascend the small streams that fall into the river, the country opens out into beautiful farming and grazing land. At 12 M. we stopped at Ouse-Skoro, ten miles below Schilkah, on the left shore, in order to visit some gold mines a short distance in the interior. We found a conveyance waiting for us. This we owed to Captain Ornosoff, who had preceded us, and, knowing our desire to visit the mines, had informed the superintendent, who had kindly sent his own vehicle. It had been waiting for us since the day previous.

In a few minutes we were seated in the vehicle, and proceeding rapidly along the road which led up the creek in the direction of the diggings.

The chief, or superintendent, was not at home, but we were politely received by his officers, who showed us every thing connected with the washings.

Like all mines in the province of Trans-Baikal, the labor is performed by convicts and under military authority. Every thing is on the basis of a great camp. The carting and wheeling of the superincumbent earth, the removal and digging of the dry dirt, and canalization, to elevate the water, are all identical with like operations in California mining, but the washing of the earth is by machinery, propelled by water, as previously described at the "diggings" on the Onon.

I could not ascertain the annual product of the mines, but was told that the yield was one *solotnick* to the one hundred poods of earth washed. The mines extend for some miles up the creek, and give employment to about fifteen hundred convicts. There was quite a large village in view, and the government establishments; but as all the washings were of the same character, we were satisfied with the inspection of one company. The men worked with alacrity. The system appeared well devised, each one knew his place, and consequently there was no confusion.

We returned to our boat, and were under way again at 4 P. M. The day was really beautiful, like one of our best summer days, and we enjoyed it very much on this beautiful stream, with scenery as fine as any on the Ohio.

We reached the village of Ouse-Cherney, the mouth of the Black River, at 8 P. M. This river, which comes in from the north, a little below the village of the same name, is a very rapid stream, at times so violent as to dash the passing boat or raft a wreck against the opposite rock-bound shore. So, in order to avoid wreck, if danger there was, we spent the night at the village. The people were very kind. We had tea on shore at a peasant's cottage, with fresh cream, milk, black-bread, and boiled eggs—sumptuous fare indeed.

After landing, we soon learned from the head peasant of the village that there was no danger, as the Cherney was not high, and we could pass without the least risk. We found ourselves so comfortably situated, however, and, wishing to see every inch of the river by daylight, that we remained till morning. We considered, too, that we had done a very good day's work, having accomplished twenty-eight miles by water and twenty by land since we left Schilkah at 10 A. M., and arrived at Ouse-Cherney at 8 P. M. The river being measured here, we find that our speed, with oars, is five miles per hour.

CHAPTER XXXII.

FROM RUSSIAN INTO CHINESE WATERS.

JUNE 3. Cloudy and cool at sunrise, with rain and high wind from the east, so that we did not get off as early as usual. At 7 A. M. the wind lulled, and we shoved off. We found the Cherney quite docile and not the least threatening, and, rowing on, reached Gorbitza at 8 A. M.

As this is a point of some note, historically and geographically, if not in point of size or commerce, I will give it a passing notice. This village is situated a short distance to the west of the little Gorbitza river, which appears on the maps as the boundary in this region between Russia and China. It has some fifty or sixty houses, and is prettily situated on a high flat of table-land on the left bank of the river, and stretches along for over a mile. It afforded me food for serious reflection. After entering Russia at its western gate, Cronstadt, between bristling cannon and frowning fortresses, and having become accustomed to the checkered sentry-box and striped gate-bars on the shores of the Baltic, and wandered amidst that wilderness of palaces at the imperial city, called into existence by the Great Peter, and afterwards passing through such cities as Moscow, Vlademir, Nijne, and Kazan, witnessing the grandeur and the power of this vast empire, and not having lost sight of the checkered sentry-boxes and striped bars, for the distance of five thousand miles, I felt like parting from an old and tried travelling companion and friend, when I looked upon that little frontier sentry-box beyond the last house of Gorbitza, near the mouth of the Little Gorbitza River, dividing the "Central Kingdom" from that of the "Northern Bear."

"There it is; I see it yet. Look! look!" I exclaimed to Captain Fulyhelm, "we have passed through the eastern gate of the mighty Muscovite Empire." I still gazed from the roof of our boat as we passed the little river dividing the two empires. The gate and sentry-box were still to be seen, but the force of the current was sweeping us along, and we were soon carried beyond a projecting point, when the town of Gorbitza was lost to my view, perhaps forever. The last white man's house, the last log cabin, the last civilized dog even, sitting upon the shore and wagging his tail, as we whistled to him from our boat, has been passed on the left shore, and on the right is one solitary village, and that is the last of Russian civilization until you reach the sea.

Twelve M. Cool, with rain squalls. Thermometer 50°. Two natives are poling a canoe up along the shore. In view is a Tonguese hut, with reindeer feeding, on the left shore. We asked the men for milk. They answered, "*Nyat, nyat,*" no, no, in good Sclavonic.

The country is well wooded with pine, birch, larch,

and spruce; mountainous, but occasional level tracts. We landed, and found abundance of wild onions, or garlic, which our Cossacks gathered for use. The river all day has been quite like a large canal, beautiful to navigate, with a steady current, about three miles per hour—bends elongated, with reaches of five miles in extent, giving very delightful views. A Ge-lak boat passed us, rowed by four Cossacks belonging to the battalion of the line. They had been left behind at Schilkah the previous year, and were going on to overtake their comrades near Igoon.

Towards evening, the breeze being fair, we hoisted sail. On the right bank we saw a small cabin. As there were no inhabitants, we supposed it to be built for a station or stopping place in the winter for persons going to Ouse-Strelkah. A short time after dark we passed the gun-boats, barges, and rafts of the Amoor expedition. The cattle were turned on the shore to graze. Last year there were over a thousand head of cattle taken down the Amoor on rafts, with but very trifling loss, and, as they got their food nightly along the shores, with little or no expense.

The night being moonlight, and, as there was no special object of interest in this part of the river, we concluded to float on during the night. Captain Fulyhelm set the watch for the night. The men were to get their supper and retire. I was to steer till 12 P. M., while himself and his servant, Evan, would divide the morning watch; the Cossacks to be called at daylight.

The night proved beautiful, the current swept us along picturesque reaches, and close under and in the shadow of high mountains. An occasional night-bird flitted along these mysterious savage shores, while nought disturbed the profound stillness of nature but the mournful notes of the cuckoo, or the hooting of some amorous owl calling to his mate.

CHAPTER XXXIII.

FIRST VIEW OF THE AMOOR.

JUNE 4. At 5 A. M. we grounded on the head of a middle sand-bar, but our men were overboard and worked us off into deep water.

We made good progress during the night, floating clear of the shores and not touching bottom. Captain Fulyhelm reported the river if any thing more beautiful than heretofore; the soft moonlight of a lovely night in June gave it additional charms. We saw four men in a canoe going up, supposed to be from Ouse-Strelkah going up to Gorbitza. In a short time we passed a new house on the right shore. Near by we saw three women and one man, and on the left shore there were horses feeding. There is fine bottom-land here, on both sides of the river.

At 9 A. M. thermometer 68°. We now proceeded along the right shore. We saw two Cossacks on the right, with oxen and cart, hauling timber. We learned from them the distance to Ouse-Strelkah—ten miles.

We now became very anxious to see the Amoor—to behold which we had journeyed so far. The right bank continued level, with not very high mountains, while the opposite shore was skirted at times with rolling land, susceptible of cultivation for some extent from the river.

The morning was really delightful, the thermometer indicating 70°. We rowed along assisted by the current, watching every opening in the bends of the river, to catch a glimpse of the Kara-Amur. We were not kept long in suspense. Rounding a point, we saw the opposite mountains of the Argoon, between which and ourselves a low point made out, behind which, as we supposed, was the Argoon; consequently the sheet of water before us beyond the low point of sand on the right, must be the Amoor. We pulled in under the right shore, and, skirting along a low willow island that forms between the Schilkah and Argoon, landed on the Schilkah side, a hundred yards above the point of a bar at their junction.

It must be confessed, as I stepped on shore I felt a high degree of exultation. I had not been the first to discover this river, neither was I the first white man, like De Soto on the bank of the Mississippi, but I was the first live Yankee who had seen it, and, as the road had been a pretty long one, and some of it rather hard to travel, I felt, I must admit, a little proud of the American people, inasmuch as I had perseveringly set my face towards it two years since, and had never, for a moment, turned my back upon it, and had confidently looked, with hope and faith, as well as works, to the day when I should stand at the head of the Amoor.

I felt proud of the day and the hour on which I set foot on that little point of land—Thursday, June 4, 1857, at 10 A. M., about fifteen thousand miles from my starting point.

The two rivers came together, much as the Russian name indicates, Ouse-Strelkah—the "Arrow's Mouth"—forming a point of land like the head of an arrow. We crossed the point to the Argoon side, and, after walking some distance along the beach, returned towards the point and bathed at the head of the Amoor. I swam to and beyond the extreme point. We found the water too cold to remain long in. The water was 54°, while the air was 68°. I took a run along the beach, in order to get warm after our cold bath, and, returning to our boat, was now ready to proceed.

The village of Ouse-Strelkah, a Russian post or watch-station, is in view on the Argoon shore, about one mile up. Not far above the river bends to the left and high mountains close the view. Standing on the extreme point of the tongue of land, where the waters of the Argoon and Schilkah meet and form the Amoor, looking to the north-east, the view is very pretty. On the right heavily wooded mountains abut upon the river for the distance of two miles, while on the left a strip of bottom-land reaches along, with gently sloping hills in the background. To the front the river is sparkling in the sun, rejoicing in its new and beautiful birth, amid scenes so lovely and picturesque. Flowing gently along, for the distance of several miles, it sweeps gracefully to the right, and is lost behind a projecting mountain. The horizon beyond is closed with densely wooded, but not very high, mountains. Turning on your heel you see the Schilkah and Argoon flowing joyfully on to meet in that conjugal embrace from which springs a mighty river.

The Argoon serves as a boundary between Mongolia

and Siberia. It is a fine river of the third class. Its course is nearly south, for about three hundred and fifty miles. It then inclines more to the west. At this point, just before you reach the lake of Dahlay-mer, or Choolun, the boundary takes the ridge of mountains dividing the waters of the Schilkah from the Argoon, while the latter river pushes its head waters to the south and west, draining a large extent of country up to the Pekin and Maimat-tschin road. Three hundred miles from this, where I saw the Argoon not far from the Great Nerchinsk mines, it is a fine river and susceptible of navigation with boats of four feet draft.

After making our acquaintance with the Amoor and bathing in its waters, we cast our boat adrift, and, in a few minutes, we were gaily afloat upon this new river that was to conduct us to the ocean—two thousand miles to the east.

CHAPTER XXXIV.

FROM OUSE-STRELKAH TO ALBASIN.

THREE miles below Ouse-Strelkah, the Amoor is four hundred and fifty yards wide, and capable of floating a vessel of five hundred tons burden. The country bordering upon the river is well wooded with birch, pine, and larch. The bottom land is somewhat extensive, and the soil good. Five miles below we saw reindeer on the shore, and were about to give them the contents of our guns, congratulating ourselves upon savory venison steaks for supper; but as we approached them in full view, and observed them more closely, we came to the conclusion that they were private property, and not, as Blackstone says, *feræ naturæ*, but *domitæ naturæ*, for upon a nearer approach we perceived a band around the neck of one of them. A yearling fawn was kicking up his heels in great glee, quite unconscious of his danger. These animals evidently had strayed from their wandering Tonguse masters, and were enjoying themselves upon the rich pasturage of this section.

At 4½ P. M. we passed the river Amahzar, where we observed deserted Tonguse huts. At 5 P. M. we were visited with a severe squall of snow and hail, with the thermometer at 51°. It soon passed over, and at 8½ P. M. we halted opposite the river Toumahcha, where we found an extensive prairie, with rich black soil, and luxuriant grass eighteen inches high.

Several natives came to us in a canoe (dug-out). They were rather a miserable-looking lot of mortals, and sadly in need of somebody more capable than themselves to provide for them the necessaries of life, with which their country absolutely teems. Whether they were the subjects of the Celestial Empire or of Russia I do not know, but they evidently wanted a master. We gave them some bread and salt, although it was rather early in our voyage to be over-liberal, because we did not know to what strait we might yet be brought ourselves, before we reached the ocean; but the particular object of their visit was to get a drink of "arrack," or "rak-ke." They made the motion of crooking the elbow, and saying "arrack," or "rak-ke!" which we would not understand, and they got no whiskey. They paddled off, evidently much disappointed, and disappeared behind an adjacent point.

We continued floating on during the night. The shores were alternately rocky bluffs and wooded bottoms; the river sweeping in great bends along highly beautiful and picturesque shores. The night was cool, and white frost formed on the deck of our boat.

June 5. The weather was cool and clear this morning. At 8 A. M. the thermometer in our cabin 54°. The shores are well wooded and mountainous. The river is very crooked, flowing in great sweeping bends, with a current of four miles to the hour, and neither bars, islands, nor shoals. We reached Kamenskoy at 11 A. M.

This is a post station, settled by the Russians, in consequence of the grounding of the steamer Schilkah, built at Schilkah the previous year, which on her way down grounded near this point; and as she needed some additional machinery, she remained here during the winter. She is expected to be ready to proceed on her way in the course of ten days. We were kindly entertained by Captain Lasofsky at comfortable quarters on shore, in a neat, well-built log-house, not destitute of furniture or civilized-looking table-gear, nor was a bottle of wine wanting at dinner to wash down venison steaks and black bread.

Captain Ornosoff was here, having only preceded us a few minutes. There were quite a number of workmen engaged upon the steamer in making the necessary repairs and in adjusting the machinery. A band of the native Tonguse were here, and I had the first trial of a ride upon a reindeer. They move very awkwardly under the saddle, and must be very uncomfortable to a new beginner in that style of riding. The saddle is fastened right on or over their fore-shoulders or withers, which makes the motion very unpleasant, particularly when in a gallop. My impression was decidedly adverse to reindeer for the saddle. Before a sleigh they would do better; but as I did not reach the reindeer country till sleighing was over, I had no opportunity to test their qualities in that respect.

We departed at 3 P. M., in order to reach Albasin before night, eighteen miles distant. From this point the river has greater breadth and crumbling banks, high and extensive sand-bars, and many islands. Immediately below Kamenskoy there are middle and shore bars; the current runs with increased rapidity; extensive prairies are noticed on the left, with evidences of overflowed banks. The extremes of rise and fall of the river here are twenty-four feet. Trees are torn up by the roots, and drifting with the current, form rafts on the heads of islands and bars. Island chutes are numerous, and the navigation begins to need good pilots.

We reached Albasin, or where it once stood, at 7 P. M. It was a lovely evening, and while the keel of our boat was yet grating upon the pebbly beach, we leaped on shore. The location for a town is really beautiful, and was well chosen. It is on the left shore, upon high table land, with an elevation of fifty feet, overlooking an extensive country to the front and left. An island of several thousand acres lies in front of it, on the opposite side of the river, behind which enters the river Albasin from the south. The mouth of the Albasin is amid a cluster of islands, and the arm of the Amoor, which makes off from the head of the island above, spreads out into a lake, and with the accumulated waters of the Albasin where it joins the main river, becomes an important stream. The country back of the old city stretches off into a plateau, half prairie, half woodland, rich and luxuriant in its young summer garb, and with but little labor, ready for the plough. The remains of walls, moats, ditches, and mounds, showing the site and extent of the city, are to be distinctly traced, while the curious antiquary will find bricks, shreds of pottery, broken mill-stones, arms, etc., by digging.

Albasin is one hundred and sixty miles below Ouse-Strelkah. We remained till near dark, and walked for some distance around and behind the old city, following what apparently must have been an earthwork of circumvallation, and probably the mode by which the Chinese starved the Albasinians into capitulation.

We camped on an island a few miles below Albasin, not liking the appearance of the river for night navigation. We saw a light on the opposite shore, and Arnosoff passed us after dark. We built no fire, as we did not wish to notify the natives of our camping place.

CHAPTER XXXV.

FLOATING ALONG.

We were up and under way at 3 A. M., and floated along until near six, when we grounded, having taken the wrong side of a middle bar. The current was very swift, and forced us down some distance over a rather rough bottom. Our men thought that there was plenty of water nearer the shore, and that we could still go down on the inside by towing our boat in that direction; this proved unavailing, however, and our only resource was to force her back against the stream above the head of the bar, where the current would set us on the opposite side.

This we found pretty tight work, but our Cossacks were all overboard, tugging at the boat to force her up, which was finally accomplished, and, the current catching us on the opposite quarter, we slid off over the stones into deep water.

A canoe, with a number of natives, came to us from the right shore, having skins for sale. Captain Fulyhelm said these were Orochon or Mangoon Tartars. One, a fine-looking young man, might have been taken for a Chinese. They had the Chinese pipes and hats of Mai-mattschin, and were well dressed.

We afterwards became satisfied that some of these were Chinese, or the descendants of Chinese convicts, or emigrants, who had settled in this country. Afterwards, as we advanced, we became quite familiar with the same Chinese face and dress, met with every day in the streets of San Francisco, or in the mines of California.

At 12 M. the thermometer was 72° in the shade. The country was generally mountainous, with prairie and meadow land, near the river and on the islands, which are numerous. There are also many sand-bars and island chutes, which must render the river difficult to navigate, except it be previously known in which of the many channels the deepest and best navigable water is to be found. There is not less than eight feet of water on the bars at this time.

The wind has been contrary all day; several boats, with Mangoon and Orochon Tartars, have visited us during the day, seemingly out of curiosity, or perhaps to beg tobacco and whiskey. These people are all evidently of the Mongol race; they have the Mongol face, and wear the tail. We bartered blue cotton cloth for fresh caviar, which we found excellent, not unlike that from the Volga, not quite so dark colored, nor of that richness of flavor, but nevertheless very good. This caviar is taken from a large sturgeon, abundant in the Amoor. We found ice in shaded ravines to-day on northern exposures. The river has been tortuous, with many islands.

June 7. We continued floating on during the night, meeting with no difficulty. Captain Fulyhelm reported, after 12 P. M., during his watch, many islands, with bars and chutes. At 6 A. M. the weather was clear, with the prospect of a summer day. At 10 A. M. the thermometer stood at 68°, 3 P. M. 73°, and 5 P. M. 80°.

We have had a fine river all day, with large islands, alternate rocky bluffs, and fine bottoms, shores well timbered with birch, spruce, and pine ; no ice seen to-day. We saw many Tartar camp-fires last night. They are now congregating on the shores to fish. We were hailed several times during the night, but returned no answer ; but during the day, up to near sunset, we saw not a human being. We made some use of our sail ; the navigation during the afternoon has been delightful—the shores often beautiful and romantic.

June 8. At 5 A. M. we came in view of high, yellow sand cliffs on our left, crowned with birch and pine, one of the most beautiful points yet seen. About two miles before reaching the cliffs, a pair of antelopes came dashing down the adjacent shore and across a bar on our right, and, plunging into the river, five hundred yards ahead of us, pushed for the opposite shore. We gave chase in our skiff, but they were too quick for us, and reached the opposite bank before we could approach near enough to give them a shot. They went out at a deserted Tartar lodge, and disappeared in the rank vegetation just above the foot of the cliff.

While the barge was floating on, I landed in the skiff, attracted by the singular appearance of the cliffs. I found on the beach chalcedony, carnelian, and agate. The cliffs were composed of amygdaloid sand, decomposed matter, and sandstone, much of it highly colored with iron. The current sweeps past the foot of these cliffs very rapidly, and, being turned from its course, shoots off towards the opposite shore, forming a large eddy under the point below. Our barge was drawn into this eddy, and, the current being reversed, our crew became completely confounded at the sudden change in the direction of the barge, and commenced rowing for the shore. By this time I came up in the skiff and directed them to row into the stream. We soon pulled out and were floating on again.

This is a very charming point; the scenery is very fine, and the river winds along its shores with many a graceful curve, the deep green of the larch and pine contrasting beautifully with the yellow cliffs, and the whole forming a lovely picture.

CHAPTER XXXVI.

A MANGOON CAMP.

At 9 A. M, thermometer 72°, wind ahead and cloudy. The river is over a mile wide in places unobstructed by islands. The wind has rendered our progress very tedious during the day, and, at 4 P. M., we were blown on shore near a camp of Mangoons. They had horses, very sleek, plump-looking, bay and iron-gray little animals, very gentle and docile. These people had recently camped for the purpose of fishing.

As soon as we came near the shore several of the natives came along the beach and directed us where to push our boat so as to reach the bank. Their camp was in an adjacent thicket of willows. We walked to their lodges. Some of them were apparently pleased with our visit, while others seemed rather surly. I discharged five shots from one of my revolvers into the trunk of a willow, some paces distant, in order to let them know that they must keep on good terms with us during the stress of weather. One of them, running up to the tree, and seeing five holes in it, shouted to his companions, one of whom ran to a lodge and brought a hatchet and commenced cutting into the tree, in order to see really if there were any bullets in the holes, which they evidently doubted. Four of the balls were found, each of which were tasted of by the party, trying them between their teeth, in order to see that there was no *hocus pocus* about the shooting.. The fifth ball could not be found, having passed through the tree. This they sought for, and succeeded in finding a twig cut by it several yards further on. This seemed to satisfy them, and they became more friendly.

In consequence of the tossing of our boat, we had our *samovar* and tea on the shore, sheltered from the wind by a thick clump of willows. Several of the natives came to our boat. Among them was a woman having very beautiful teeth, to which I called the attention of Captain Fulyhelm. One of the "lords of creation," standing not far off, noticed our attention to the red lady, who, as it turned out, was his wife. He spoke to her, and they both immediately left the beach, going in the direction of the camp. Not long afterwards Captain Fulyhelm passed along to the camp again, and found this man beating the woman with a heavy stick. Captain Fulyhelm exhibiting his revolver made the brute desist. The woman sat in the lodge, taking the cudgelling without a murmur.

In the course of a few minutes I came up, not knowing what had taken place. I found the woman covered with blood. Captain Fulyhelm had left before I arrived, and she was sitting in the lodge, the man opposite her. By the blood on the woman, and her streaming eyes, and the dark scowl of the man, I saw that there was something wrong, but did not know what had happened. I returned to the boat, where I found the captain, who related to me the particulars of the affair, and gave as a solution the jealousy of the husband on account of our

9

admiration of the wife's teeth. Out of compassion to woman, I admired no more teeth while among this tribe on the shores of the Amoor—at least, not while in the presence of the men.

Captain Fulyhelm would have chastised the fellow on the spot, but he did not think our party quite strong enough to set up a reform society for the amelioration of woman in these parts, as possibly there was a village not far off, from whence reinforcements might have come, while the stress of weather might have rendered our retreat out of the question if about to be overpowered.

These people had the pipes, hats, and ornaments of Mai-mat-tschin; their clothing was principally of skins. Upon giving sugar and copper coins to a little urchin, the father of the boy spoke to him, whereupon the little savage clasped his hands behind his back, and, bending forward on the right knee, bowed till his forehead touched the earth. This mode of obeisance we found to prevail generally among the Tartar tribes.

These people resemble the Chinese much, and, without knowing who or what they were, I should have pronounced them *wild Chinese.*

The Managres and Orochones appear to mix along in this section, as we found, upon inquiry, several of the latter among them. They inhabit indifferently both sides of the river, and both have horses and reindeer, both of which they eat. They had recently killed a deer, or colt, we could not tell which, as the hide was not to be seen, of which they offered us. They had not yet commenced to fish, but were preparing to do so.

At 7 P. M. the wind abated sufficiently for us to proceed, but we were driven ashore on the right bank not long afterwards.

We found ice in a ravine on the left shore, and chalcedony on the beach. A quartz ledge, with indications of gold, was traced up a small creek, where there was every indication of gold in the sands, and I have no doubt that, with a few hours' work, gold could have been found.

The natives along this portion of the Amoor have a very remarkable and novel mode of fishing. Three poles, of eight to ten feet in length, much the same as those used for tent poles, are placed in the water on a shoal, or near the shore of a bar, spread at the bottom, as if for a tent, and tied together at the top, in the cross of which a man takes his seat to fish. Here you see them sitting, perched along the shores, as if they had been left there during a flood and were waiting for means to get off. The hook is dropped, or the spear is used, as the unwary sturgeon comes nosing along the shoal seeking food. The stirlet and sturgeon abound in the Amoor, and in the spring and summer salmon of good flavor run up; in fact, this river is bountifully supplied with fish.

Many native camps have been seen during the day; the country is level on both shores, with prairie and forests, good soil, and most excellent for grazing; the river of fine navigable depth, with many islands, and occasionally mountains in the distance.

We gave a native a glass of *vodka* at a camp where we stopped to-day, but, before he put the glass to his lips, he placed the tips of the joined thumb and middle finger in the fire-water, and, withdrawing them, snapped them over each shoulder, to his forehead and breast, very much like making the Greek cross. This ceremony I took to be a counter-charm against the spirit of evil, if any, in the white man's drink. When we came to ask them questions about the Amoor, they could not comprehend, but when we spoke of Sak-hah-lin they at once understood—the river is called Sak-hah-lin by them, never Amoor.

CHAPTER XXXVII.

MANCHOO VISITORS.

June 9. We departed from our camping ground at 4 A. M. We had both rain and wind during the morning, at 9 A. M. the temperature was 62°, with rain. We passed the Kah-mah-rah river, where there is a Russian post being established—a log-house, men, horses, and a raft on the shore, told their whole history. They had floated, bag and baggage, to this point on the raft out of the Argoon or Schilkah, and were here planting one of the outposts of civilization, as their ancestors had three hundred years since, just at the foot of the Ural mountains. Here, as there, cultivation, commerce, and civilization will take the place of wild and roving Tartar hordes.

It is now one hundred and seventy miles to Igoon. We have had mist and rain the greater part of the day, the river beautiful, with points of fine scenery, and the shores suitable for grazing, with rich land and luxuriant grass. Pine and birch are becoming less general, and trees of other species more frequent.

June 10th. We floated on during the night, rain continuing to fall, but I managed with a thick coat to keep my under clothing dry during my watch at the steering-oar. Herds of elk were frightened during the night as we floated past the shores, where they had congregated, standing in the water to avoid the insects so troublesome at this season. We also saw during the day tracks of a large animal, apparently a panther, upon the sand, and also signs of bears. Ducks have been plenty heretofore, but now we have plenty of geese. They are breeding on the islands and shores of the lakes in this region.

At 8 A. M. temperature 60°. The river is very beautiful and the country well adapted to settlement.

A party of Manchoos came to us from a Chinese post station, or watch-house, on the left shore. The leader of the party wished us to land, saying harm would come to us if we persisted in proceeding down the river. As we did not seem to be much alarmed at their fears, they soon left us and pulled to the shore, but, seeing that we were not going to land, two of them came running down along the bank, calling to us, and making signs and gesticulating. We, however, went on, rather choosing to seek a camping place for ourselves. The "post" consisted of three log cabins, thatched, and on the shore were three large three-plank boats, called by the Chinese "san-pan." Our visitors were not armed, but they undoubtedly had arms at their station.

The faces of the mountains are frequently bare of timber, gently sloping, with a fine carpet of grass, well calculated for the grazing of sheep. The bottoms are sparsely sprinkled with timber, or are entirely bare, ready for the plough.

The Chinese-Manchoo and Russian "posts" are only about seventy miles apart, on the same side of the river. There is a sort of joint occupancy of the Amoor of an ill-defined nature, but the probability is that the exact *status* of the parties will be determined before long, and those who navigate these waters will not long be troubled by Manchoo "watch-boats." Steamboats will take the place of the canoe and barge, and the swarthy Tartar will view with wonder and admiration the progress of Russian power here, as his ancestors did upon the Caspian three hundred years ago. But it will be more rapid here now than there in the sixteenth century, because steam, artillery, and revolvers give to civilized man an irresistible power. Commerce, navigation, the arts and sciences, will develop this stupendous country, and add, as it were, a sixth continent to the domain of civilization.

At 9 A. M. there are Manchoo huts on the right. Three men are standing near wood, prepared for shipment, on the bank. We have fair wind, and, with our sail spread to the breeze, are making fine progress. At 12 M. we landed on the left bank on a rich and luxuriant prairie, where we found lilies of the valley and wild apple. The wind was ahead and we remained for hours rambling over the prairies. At length we put our sail into the water for a current sail, and made some headway, but were finally blown ashore about seventy miles above Igoon.

Here were Manchoos cutting wood for the Igoon market, which they form into rafts and float with the current down the river. We have passed two watch stations to-day. It is raining, and the wind is too high to proceed. We lay to all night under the lee of a lofty mountain, well sheltered from the blast.

Last night troops of reindeer, or *esuber*, frightened by the approach of our boat, fled up the mountain side, loosening the stones as they scampered, which came rolling down into the river. A curious kind of gull was seen for the first time yesterday, with black head and wings, under part of the body and tail white, a long distance from the sea, but they follow the rivers to their very sources. I had seen the common white gull at Chetah, and I have no doubt but that these birds cross the mountains and seek the waters of Siberia flowing into the Frozen Ocean, and that the gulls from that ocean visit the Pacific in turn.

The cuckoo is constantly repeating its unmusical notes upon the shores by night and by day. It has been our constant companion from Schilkah. The nightingale has frequently relieved the stillness of the night by its song. This bird is much like the mocking-bird of the Southern States in its variety of note. It is a small grayish-looking bird, not so large as the mocking-bird, whitish on the under part of the body. Great and little owls hoot and screech on the mountains, while a kind of crow repeats a call like the stroke of a hammer against the rocky face of the overhanging cliff. Flights of water-fowl, alarmed by the approach of the boat, or the occasional splash of the steering-oar, start hurriedly from their repose upon the beach and islands, while great cranes come flapping past, like evil spirits from the Dead Sea shore. But our bark floats rapidly on its way to the great ocean, a thousand miles to the east. It is really enchanting thus, at night, when all is hushed and still, except the occasional heavy snore of a sleeping Cossack, to glide, like a phantom bark, along the shores and among the majestic mountains and through the prairies of this wonderful country upon the silent tide of this vast river.

CHAPTER XXXVIII.

A MANCHOO GUARD-BOAT.

June 11, 9 A. M. Temperature 62°. We got off from our last night's camp at 4 A. M. It had rained the whole night, and was still raining. We landed about thirty miles above the river Zea on the left bank. The mountains in the distance are not a continuous chain, but broken into rounded masses, with valleys intervening. Neither are they abrupt, but sloping, and susceptible of cultivation or grazing. Woodland is scarce upon the river, and it is only upon distant mountains that we observe forests.

We have seen many natives to-day and also Manchoos and Chinese making rafts of wood, already prepared and piled up along the shores. We passed four Manchoos in a plank-boat, covered with a matting made of grass. They were smoking the everlasting Mai-mat-tschin pipes.

As we descend, the country is more rolling, and not mountainous, and timber scarce and small.

We landed at the Russian post of Zakhsky on the left shore, at 4 P. M., in a heavy rain. The situation is very beautiful, twenty miles only above Igoon. It was settled last fall by a company of Cossacks. The officer in charge requested our rank, names, and number of men, in order to announce, as agreed upon with the Chinese-Manchoo authorities, the arrival of officers wishing to stop at Igoon.

At this point last year the river was frozen on the 27th of October and open on the 23d of April. The rise and fall of the river is from twenty-five to thirty feet. It is a thousand yards wide, and flows with a rapid current.

At 6 P. M. a Manchoo boat, with officers, came along side from a town and military station on the right shore, called Sak-hah-lin. The chief, or captain, of the party, was an old man, who stood in the boat, with an umbrella over him. Two others occupied the centre, seated. They were all well dressed. One of them had a kind of oil-cloth mantle over his head and shoulders, made of a black material and lined with red silk. They were all three good-sized men, and whether Chinese or Manchoos we could not tell, but most probably of Manchoo race. They hailed us to stop, but the captain was not inclined to obey Manchoo orders, saying, "if they wish to see us, let them come to us." They then came along side, and two of their oarsmen, obeying the orders of their chief, came upon the bow of our boat, and laid hold of the oars in the hands of our men. We were sitting on our bunks, observing all, and prepared to meet any act of violence, when it became necessary. Our Cossacks did not relish the intrusion of the Manchoo boatmen, and one of them, Evan, seized a heavy pole and used it pretty freely over the heads and shoulders of the intruders, which caused them to retire rather precipitately, either into their own craft, or into the water. We now interfered to quell the combat, while the officers were keeping up a terrific volley of words, like discharges of small arms, from their boat.

So soon as order could be restored among the combatants, and words came to be the only weapons, the chief, making signs to express forcibly his meaning, sawing with his open hand edgewise upon his bare neck, said, "that if we proceeded without his permission, or before the news of our approach was announced at Igoon, that we would be very likely to lose our heads."

This threat made our Russian captain really indignant, and he replied warmly to the old Manchoo, telling him that he must use other language to a high Russian officer, and repeated to him the word *Polkovnik*, which the old chief seemed to understand perfectly. It worked like a charm, the chief pulled off his skull-cap and made a polite bow to our captain, while the rest of the party sat chattering and muttering in the rain.

Captain Fulyhelm then explained to him that it was not our intention to proceed to Igoon until morning, but to stop for the night at the next village, or at the mouth of the river Zea. This seemed to satisfy the party, for they soon made their best bows and shoved their boat off from ours, and pulled for the shore. We had carried them some distance below their post; their disappointment was evidently very great, and I was of the opinion that we ought to have stopped when they hailed us. Of course, after they seized our oars, it became a matter of compulsion to which we did not choose nor think it politic to submit.

The wind being now favorable, we hoisted our little sail, in order to reach the Zea before nightfall and stop at the nearest village. At 7 P. M. we approached the Zea, and, after sailing across its mouth, attempted to land at a village on the left, where it joins the Amoor; but we found the water so shoal in nearing the shore, with a bottom of boulders, and the wind so high, that we could not approach to land. Having struck the bottom, our boat was thumping rather heavily against the rocks; but we succeeded in pushing off again, and rowed out into the current against the wind, in order to try a landing further down the stream. After several ineffectual attempts, the wind now blowing a gale and the rain descending in torrents, we finally succeeded in making a landing at a more favorable spot, where we could approach the shore. By this time it was dark. To have reached the opposite side would have required several hours' hard rowing, if not impossible; so we were compelled to content ourselves with a windward shore, however uncomfortable it might be.

We therefore lost, what I so much desired, the first peep into a Manchoo town, after running the gauntlet of the "watch stations" and "custom-house officers." For my part, I would infinitely have preferred to have been captured at Sak-hah-lin, and shown in a cage to the delighted Tartars, than have missed seeing their town. But all regrets were useless: the storm had us on a windward shore, and there was no help for it.

The river Zea, or Zayah, enters the Amoor from the north-west, being the first great tributary entering from the left, or mountain region, that divides Dahoureya and Manchooria from Siberia, about seven hundred miles from Ouse-Strelkah, by the course of the river.

The Zea has many Manchoo villages on its shores, for some considerable distance up from its junction, as well as a considerable native population; and it is reported to be a good country, the river being navigable for several hundred miles, well stocked with fish, and its forests and mountains with game and fur animals. The people have also cattle, horses, and reindeer. The main course of the river is north-west, but it receives two large tributaries some distance up, one from the north-east, the other from the west: consequently, there is a large intermediate valley between the Amoor and the dividing mountains, whose northern shed feeds the rivers which flow into the Frozen Ocean.

The Zea enters the Amoor with a turbid, yellowish current, forcing itself, by its volume and velocity, into strong competition for the mastery of channel with the black waters of the Sak-hah-lin. This continues for some miles below Igoon; but finally the "black dragon" swallows up his yellow neighbor, and flows on majestically towards the ocean.

The shores of the Amoor here are level, with extensive prairies. Mountains are only seen in the distance, in the direction north of the Zea. Villages are scattered along its banks at every few miles, while the buildings and clothing of the people indicate Tartar civilization. The Amoor is now truly a large river, and strikes the voyager as one of the great rivers of the world. Nearly opposite our camp coal is found, samples of which we saw at the "post" above. It is a poor species of cannel; but, having been taken from near the surface, it may not be a fair specimen of quality.

At 10 P. M. the thermometer was 61°, wind high from the south-east, with rain.

CHAPTER XXXIX.

ARRIVAL AT IGOON.

JUNE 12, 6 A. M. Thermometer 56°. We departed at 5 o'clock, the wind still blowing in our teeth, and it took a long pull and a strong pull for us to reach the opposite shore, in order to float along it to the city of Igoon. As we approached, a boat from a watch station came out to us, in which there were three officers, the chief distinguished by a white ball surmounting his cap, with a peacock feather hanging from the centre of his cap behind, and two black squirrel tails, one on each side of the feather. The under officers had only brass balls on their caps. We invited them to come on board of our boat, which invitation they accepted; and, seating them on the sides of our bunks, entertained them with *vodka*, tea, preserves, and biscuit. They had their own little brass or copper pipes, which they filled and smoked at every spare moment.

Their great anxiety appeared to be as to the number of men we had and our arms, if any. They looked at every thing, poked about our baggage and provisions, examined our guns, and talked incessantly. They already knew that we were not traders, because, by this time, our arrival at the Russian post, and our affair with the guard-boat at Sak-hah-lin, had been communicated along the line. We made no objections to their search, giving them full opportunity to satisfy their suspicions or curiosity. They were very polite, and smiled and bowed and shook hands with us, and made themselves quite agreeable.

We rowed along very near the shore, with the guard-boat in tow, drinking tea and smoking pipes with our friendly visitors, or captors—for which they were we hardly knew. There were two large villages, and many people on the shore. In front of the villages were platforms, built for fishing, where nets were suspended. Just at the upper side of Igoon our boat grounded. By this time a second guard-boat, with another instalment of officers, had come on board. The boatmen of the guard-boats shoved us off, and we were soon at the place of landing, in front of the city.

One of the officers from the second boat, a very polite, good-featured, pleasant person, took great interest in our clothing as we began to dress to go on shore. Captain Fulyhelm was dressed in full uniform, with sword and gold epaulets, and made a very stylish appearance; my suit being plain, not even so much as a metal button to set me off, seemed to give sad disappointment to the Tartars, as they were evidently anxious that we should make a brilliant appearance. One of them insisted that I should strap on, outside of my coat, to make up its lack of buttons, a pair of revolvers and a bowie knife and the captain's gold watch and chain, which he had handed me to take care of. This demonstration I, however, declined, rather wishing to conceal my artillery. One of the under officers smoothed and brushed my coat with his hands, being determined that I should look as respectable as possible. By this time Captain Arnosoff had arrived with his Burat interpreter ; and, as the captain sported regimentals, our grand entrance into Igoon would be more imposing, as I could walk between my two military and naval friends, and thus borrow a little of their lustre.

All being now ready, and the Manchoo officers having preceded us on shore, as a kind of escort, or guard of honor, we walked the plank laid for us by our Cossacks, and were soon in front of the Manchoo city of Igoon. It was a curious spectacle, and one not readily forgotten.

Igoon is built upon the right bank of the Amoor, where it bends gently to the right, sweeping, with its broad and rapid current, the whole front of the city. The elevation is not great, as it stands on a plain, there being no greater elevation than the natural banks of the river, some eight or ten feet, apparently, above the highest floods. This table-land stretches off to mountains, which show themselves as a background to the picture, in a serrated chain upon the southern horizon. Immediately opposite our boat, upon the shore in front of the town, was a pavilion of dark blue cloth, surmounted by a flag. On both flanks of the pavilion were crowds of people—men, women, and children. Adjoining the tent the crowd was very dense, and swayed to and fro, pressing, with impatient curiosity, to get a glimpse of "the outside barbarians ;" but police officers, with sticks in hand, kept them back and within a line parallel with the pavilion, except some few stragglers, who had been allowed to steal along the beach and approach our line of march from our boat to the hall of reception, or audience.

Thus escorted and guarded, we proceeded up the bank by a path to the front of the pavilion, the people crowding and jostling to get as near as possible to the line of our approach. The front of the tent was entirely open. Here we paused a few moments, while the crowd of officials and servants within seemed to be agitated by some unfinished act of preparation. Soon every thing was calm and all stationary within, when a tall, aged, and fine-looking man came forward, just as we entered the threshold, shaking his own clasped hands at us, after which he gave us his left hand to shake, and seated us upon benches on the left. This was the governor of Igoon. He was dressed in rich-figured silk robes, with the cap and peacock feather, surmounted with a crystal ball. After we were seated, he occupied a sort of high-backed chair, or tribunal, raised about a foot from the ground. Upon a platform in front of him was a small table, covered with cloth; behind him, ranged along the back of the tent, was a row of various petty officers and servants, standing. Upon his right and opposite to us, were seated, upon benches, similar to those we occupied, along the side of the tent, the higher dignitaries of his government, while the front and flanks were swarming with common mandarins.

A small table was now brought and set before us, upon which servants placed small dishes of dried fruits and comfitures, followed by tea in China cups. We were warmly pressed to eat and drink. Small cups of *samchoo*, or rice wine, were brought, which we were pressed to drink. Behind us were squatted several scribes, with strips of paper and writing materials, who were noting down the conversation through Captain Arnosoff's Russo-Mongol-

Burat interpreter. The questions were put in Mongol to the interpreter, by him rendered in Russian to Captain Fulyhelm, who answered in Russian; then reduced to Mongol by the Manchoo interpreter, and by him in Chinese to the governor, and written down by the scribes.

CHAPTER XL.

DEPARTURE FROM IGOON.

THE general drift of the questions, after getting our names and condition, of which, by the by, they were already informed, turned on the movements of the Russians on the rivers above, the number of men, guns, boats, etc., on the way down the Amoor, or expected during the year, where they were going, and what they were going to do. They could not understand what an American consul was, or what he could be doing in Manchooria. Captain Fulyhelm said they probably knew of America, but of that he was not certain; but a consul—what that was, seemed to perplex them much.

In the meantime, several fat and portly dignitaries came in, shook their clenched hands at the governor, made an inflection of the body by bending the knees, and, seating themselves on the right, paid great attention to what was passing. When my name was again brought in question, and the interpreters rendered the answers in Manchoo, there was a general casting of eyes in my direction. They seemed puzzled by the term consul as given by Captain Fulyhelm, and were anxious to understand its import; but the impatience of the captain, I am inclined to believe, failed to satisfy them. More tea was brought, and we were invited to renew our cups of *samchoo*, but all further parley was cut short by Captain Fulyhelm, who now rose and said, inasmuch as we were not allowed to enter the city, he should leave instantly.

At this juncture, I requested Captain Fulyhelm to renew, through the interpreter, our desire to visit the city; to say to the governor that we had come a great distance from the west, had heard much of the Manchoo nation and of the city of Igoon, and were, consequently, very desirous to visit the largest city upon the Sak-hah-lin. Upon this there was a consultation among the dignitaries, and, at one time, I thought leave would be granted; in fact, I think there was no positive refusal, and permission was at present given to walk upon the beach in front of the town.

This, however, only irritated Captain Fulyhelm, and he immediately rose, and I had no choice but to follow, because with him also went the interpreter. All further parley was at an end. We shook hands with the governor, and, bowing to him as politely as possible, withdrew to the vicinity of our boat. The crowd and bustle at the flanks of the tent were intense. We walked down along the bank near the water, where a dozen of war junks were moored to the shore, but apparently not manned. They had each a single mast, high sterns, and bulwarks on the sides—were painted a reddish-brown color, and were probably sixty feet long and fifteen feet wide. We then turned and walked up along the shore for some distance, followed and conducted by several mandarins, having short sticks in their hands, with which they drove the people off.

Many well dressed women and girls were standing in

a group a little above us on the bank, near where we were walking. I stepped off a little, as if intending to pass directly to them, but the jealous officer interfered in my movements, and I returned to my companions. The females stood their ground bravely, and seemed not the least alarmed or disconcerted at my approach. I was, however, near enough to become satisfied that the females of Igoon are not without some traces of beauty.

We passed along, the crowd pressing as near to us as the police, with their sticks, would allow. We again, but in a direct line of our march up the beach, advanced towards a group of females and children; but the "brass balls," shaking their sticks and shouting at them, advancing to our front, sent them scampering up the bank towards the town. As we returned along the beach towards our boats, we perceived that the councils still held their sittings in the pavilion, and that the crowd of people had not diminished upon the bank. At this juncture, while we were standing upon the shore of the river, pondering what steps to take, a messenger came running from the council to invite us to renew our visit and partake of refreshments. This Captain Fulyhelm abruptly declined, and sent word back by the messenger that if we were not permitted to visit the city we would depart immediately. After some delay, the messenger returned to say that permission to visit the city could not be granted, as the governor feared we might be insulted, or not receive proper respect from the people. We then proposed to take all unpleasant consequences upon ourselves, acquitting the governor, in advance, of any blame on our part; but it was all to no purpose.

The threat of debarkation was kept, much to my disappointment, for I would have revisited the governor and given him answers to a thousand questions, and drank as many cups of tea and rice-wine as he wished.

Admiral Puchachin, of the imperial navy, as I am informed, is the only Russian who has defied the authorities and entered the city of Igoon, as it were, sword in hand. Having requested permission of the governor, and being refused upon the plea that he would not be safe against the insults of the people, the excitable and nervous admiral, taking with him four armed men, marched into the town, surrounded and pressed upon by the curious people, much to their gratification and greatly to his own; for he not only had a good view of the city, but a review of the whole population during his promenade.

I proposed to follow in the footsteps of the brave admiral, but was not seconded in the movement; and, as the Cossacks would not move without the sanction of Captain Fulyhelm, there was an end of it. To be excluded from the city I felt to be a severe blow after so long a journey to it, and I was quite ready for a desperate effort.

We stepped on board of our little bark, the plank was hauled in, our Cossacks pushed her into the downward current, and we were soon floating along the front of the city. And thus we left the grave and reverend council of the governor of Igoon, seated in their blue pavilion on the shore of the Amoor, smoking their pipes, and sipping their tea, with every mark of Oriental gravity and decorum, wondering and speculating, I have no doubt, as to why we came, and, still more, as to why we went away so suddenly.

CHAPTER XLI.

MANCHOO SPIES.

I FELT much depressed in leaving our hospitable friends so sagely seated, and in having lost all hope of seeing the interior of Igoon. I attributed our failure to the excitable and nervous temperament of Captain Fulyhelm, because these people, like all the red nations, are not to be dealt with hastily. They have their customs, forms, and ceremonies; their civil and religious institutions are rigidly fixed and regulated by laws, custom, and immemorial usage, and strangers should conform to them, or take the consequences. What we met with at Igoon was not more unreasonable, or a whit less exacting, than a foreigner would meet with at any of the continental cities or countries of Europe, and even at the imperial city of Peter the Great, where none can hope to enter without formal passports; and the exactions of the police of Western Russia were more annoying than Manchoo jealousy; for, in entering Manchooria, we were not searched in our baggage or persons—no passports were required of us. The want of them would have been fatal at Cronstadt or Calais. We had forcibly resisted the execution of their police regulations in not landing at the guard-house, which is nothing more than a kind of toll-gate to Igoon, as Elsinore is to Cronstadt, and not more than what is exercised in our own ports by the boarding officer.

We were kindly, hospitably, and honorably received, with great respect and all prescribed ceremony and politeness—all that it required was patience and ordinary common sense to have won these people to our utmost wishes. After the ceremonies, if we had given them full audience, answered their questions and retired quietly to our boat, the crowd having dispersed after satisfying their curiosity, we might, either in the evening, or early next morning, have gone over the entire city and have seen all we desired.

Capt. Fulyhelm tried to console me for the loss of my visit to Igoon, by saying that we should see all in the villages below that we should have seen in the city. This is true in one sense, as to the common people and their way of living, but I wished to see the higher style of buildings, their shops, trade, markets, customs, population, numbers, &c.

But the captain's caution and nervousness arose entirely from the wish and determination to do nothing that might compromise his government or himself as an officer and a man. He acted from the best and most prudential motives, and consequently I was not inclined to act in opposition to his wishes.

The town stretches for about a mile along the shore, but the low stage of water and height of the banks prevented us from observing much of it, except the immediate water's front. At the lower or eastern extremity we observed well-built barracks, capable of housing several thousand troops, but not a single soldier was to be seen—

even the sentry-boxes were vacant. My impression was that the troops had been ordered out of view of the river in order that their numbers might not be known to the passing Russians.

The Manchoos are playing a timid and temporizing policy with the Russians. They are instructed to carry no arms, to offer no force, but not to permit their people to hold any communication with the Russians, and the people are punished if found disobeying those injunctions. I saw a poor disconsolate-looking individual seated on the bank near the river, with his head sticking through a great wooden collar, or movable pillory, as a punishment for holding intercourse with the foreigners.

The buildings fronting the river are generally small, one story, either of logs or daub, with high wooden chimneys, standing detached from the house, into which the smoke is conveyed by an underground pipe after the heat from the furnace has performed the circuit of the house in other pipes.

Soon after we were fairly off into the stream a small boat came rowing after us, with several persons in it, making signs to us, as if wishing us to stop and let them communicate with us. We ceased rowing, and allowed them to come up. I suggested to Captain Fulyhelm that it was a spy-boat following to watch us in the villages below, and to prevent us from having any intercourse with the people, if possible. But he thought otherwise. The boat contained, besides the rowers, a "white-ball" officer and two attendants. We invited the white-ball into our cabin and regaled him with *vodka*, or, as he called it, "*Ruskee arracke*," preserves, biscuit, and cigars. He did not like cigar smoking, and had recourse to his own pipe and tobacco, which he very politely offered to us from his *own lips* from time to time. We soon found that my conjecture was right, and, after showing him all the civilities of our boat, we civilly asked him to take a seat in his own boat again, which, by the by, he seemed to be in no great haste to do. However, he finally very politely shook hands with us and reëmbarked in his own cutter, but still towing along on our side.

We determined to land at the first village, now in view on our left, and to try some expedient in order to rid ourselves of this pest, if possible, by any fair means. We soon came to the village and went on shore, where the white-ball, having his mat brought from his boat to the beach, was soon squatted upon it, smoking his everlasting pipe.

It was really a beautiful place, covered with grass and wild flowers, and the country stretching out as far as the eye could reach in green and luxuriant pasturage. We were a little below the village, and, passing up the bank, came to a house, enclosed with a fence, made of small poles and willow branches interwoven, the same as you will find in many parts of Eastern Siberia. The man of the house came out to us at the fence, and offered us a basket of light red dried beans. A woman and girl, with a young child, retreated hastily into the house as we came up, but turned and gazed upon us from the door. We wished to pass into the yard, but the man shook his head, and, closing the opening with a pole, stood before it. Seeing that he was averse to our entering, we passed on towards other houses a few hundred yards distant. Coming to a house, fenced much like the first, two girls and an old woman retreated hastily upon our approach. We walked up to the fence and stood there, looking over. Soon the girls came to the door, and stood looking at us. We beckoned to them, and, calling out "*mundah, mundah,*" asked for fish in Russian, without making any attempt to force the barrier. The girls soon seeing that we were not very dangerous characters, came out to us at the fence, and finally through the gate into the opening where we were. The old woman now brought garlic and broken grain in a basket, which she offered to us; but we were now occupied with the girls, and beans and garlic became a secondary consideration.

We made the girls some little presents of coin, &c., and Captain A. got a very pretty ring, set with small pearls, with Manchoo characters engraved on it, as a *souvenir* from one of them, giving her, of course, half a dozen times its value. We were getting on very good terms with our red friends, but, at this juncture, up came the two satellites of the white-ball, and drove the girls into the house, to which they retreated very reluctantly.

These girls were evidently sisters, very much alike, and possibly twins, or, at most, not more than a year's difference in their ages. They had small delicate hands, and fine teeth. Their color was red, to be sure; yet the color of the peach-bloom was in their cheeks, and they were very sprightly, and well formed. Being of Mongol blood, their hair and eyes were black.

We now passed on more towards the upper part of the village, where there were people fishing upon the beach; but the spies being on our trail, these men were shy, and we concluded to return to our boat, and rid ourselves of the spies, if possible. As we returned, the two sisters and grandmother came out to meet us, offering us some broken grain and dried fish. We invited them to our boat, but the spies coming up, drove them back with shouts and the shaking of their sticks.

We passed along in front of several houses, making the children small presents, but the spies returning, after we had driven them back the third time, put the people to flight, and prevented us having further intercouse with them.

Returning to our boat, we found the old white-ball seated, apparently very contentedly, upon the beach, smoking his comfortable pipe, as if quite satisfied to remain there an indefinite period of time. We were all terribly provoked, and, as for myself, I felt like ducking his highness in the river, just to try if it would not cool his ardor a little, and induce him to return to Igoon for reinforcements, or further orders. We, however, all came to the conclusion that he must be got rid of in some way, or else we should lose all opportunity to see and know more of the people in the villages below.

CHAPTER XLII.

A MANCHOO VILLAGE.

We launched our boat once more upon the tide, and, making signs and gestures to the white-ball, told him to go back to Igoon and not follow us any further, and fired a few pistol shots—not at him, however—to see what effect the smell of villainous saltpetre might have on his nerves, and let him know that we were armed. But it was all to no purpose, except to keep him at a very respectful distance; for, as soon as we were fairly out in the stream again, he seated himself in his boat, and followed, hugging the shore very closely.

Much to our relief, a breeze sprung up, and, hoisting our sail, we hoped to give our Manchoo friend the slip and a long stern chase. We sailed joyfully along, anticipating an uninterrupted visit to the next village, but, as we found it so near at hand, and the white-ball still in sight creeping along near the shore, we concluded to pass along while the breeze continued to facilitate our escape, in order to put as great a distance as possible between us.

We passed three villages in quick succession, and, in about two hours, landed at the fourth one upon the right shore. Looking back upon the broad expanse of the Amoor, we could see nothing of our pursuer, having fairly out-generalled him by the fortunate assistance of the wind. Very soon quite a concourse of people were gathered upon the beach to witness, perhaps, the first landing of white men upon their shores. They brought beans, red pepper, Indian corn, or maize, dried beans, round cakes of white bread, leaf tobacco made up into small parcels of two to three ounces weight, and a kind of millet, pounded or broken.

Several of the young girls and women were well-favored, generally round-faced and fleshy, and of a very red complexion. There was one girl, of some ten or twelve years old, much fairer than any of the others, who was quite pretty. She was blind of one eye. Several of the old people and younger children were afflicted with sore eyes, and among the women I noticed several cases of goître. The people were generally well clad, much in the Chinese style.

In their houses, many of which we visited freely, we were welcomed with pipes, which were filled and lighted by the females, who took first a few puffs themselves, and then handed them to the guests, not, however, without wiping the mouth-piece with the hand, or upon the dress, first. Mats or carpets were spread upon the dais, or divan, which generally extended around three sides of the family room. Here we were invited to sit, squat, or repose, as we might fancy. The houses are generally divided into apartments, one of which, the first you enter, is the kitchen, where you will frequently find sucking pigs, or young calves, comfortably housed, to say nothing of dogs, chickens, or children. The next apartment is the sleeping, eating, smoking, and reception room Here live, eat, sleep, smoke, talk, and drink, the entire household and their guests, in separate groups, around and upon the divan, according to their social relations, by night and by day. The dais is generally raised about two feet from the ground floor, and about six to seven feet deep, to the wall. It is their bed by night, their seat and table by day. Different kinds of mats or carpets are spread upon this divan, with a small round pillow for each person. These pillows, with the matting, and such covering as they have, consisting of light coverlets of cotton fabric, we saw carefully packed in a kind of clothes-press, against the wall, in one corner of the room, where they are arranged by the careful housewife in the morning, after the night's repose. The room is warmed by the hot air from the furnace, conveyed in wooden pipes along the perpendicular wall of the divan, going out at the side of the house, and ending in a high wooden chimney, sticking up in the yard adjacent to the house, which carries off the smoke.

After we had visited this village pretty freely, the white-ball came up, evidently chagrined at our success, for he found the people perfectly content with our visit, while we remained unharmed and free from insult. The governor of Igoon had given as a reason why he placed officers near us, that it was to preserve order and decorum, and to see that we were respected by the people. But the fact was, that jealousy prompted it; either that the people should not become enamored with foreign fashions or faces, or that we might not observe the strength or weakness of their defences in a military point of view. After the white-ball came up, we still continued our intercourse with the inhabitants, and he was quite content with having his mat spread upon the beach, upon which he was soon seated, cross-legged, smoking the everlasting pipe. Of all the people that I have yet seen, these are the most inveterate smokers. The Russians, I had thought, were very fair smokers, before I saw the Mongol-Chinese population of Mai-mat-tschin, but I was then compelled to give the palm to the latter; but now, since I have visited the Manchoos, all other smokers must be accounted novices—men, women, and children, all smoke, smoke, smoke. The spy, seated on his mat, consoled himself with a small flask of *arrake*, of which he offered me a drink, and also gave me half a dozen cakes of sweet white bread as a peace offering. Having broken bread with him, and drank of his cup, we at once were established on the most friendly relations.

We invited him on board of our boat, and tendered him refreshments of vodka, preserves, and biscuit. A few silver rubles and pieces of blue cotton cloth were shown him, in order to see what effect they would have on his propensity to dog our trail, and to see if the present would not induce him to permit us to proceed without his special attendance; but he very politely declined any substantial present, and pointing to his own and the captain's breast, and shaking his long and bony fore finger before his face—all of which seemed to give us to understand, or to convey to us the idea, that his honor would not permit him to receive presents, or his eyes to be blind to his duty. This, certainly, was much more than many more civilized guardians of customs would have withstood.

We again went on shore, and remained in the village

until our curiosity was fully satisfied, and seeing as much of the people as possible, after which we departed, followed at a respectful distance by the guard-boat.

During our stay at the village we had given many pieces of Russian silver coin to the children, of which they appeared to have no appreciation, except as ornaments. Our Cossacks drove quite a thriving barter with them, giving copper coin for silver, at about one-fourth its relative value; in fact, copper seemed to be much more esteemed than silver. At 12 M. the thermometer stood at seventy-two degrees in the shade; it was a lovely summer day, the air soft, pleasant, and balmy. Apple trees of eighteen inches in diameter were growing in the commons in front of the village; men were ploughing in the small fields attached to the house, with bullocks yoked by the horns, much in the Mexican style; the soil was a rich black loam, while the vegetation along on the sides of the fields and in the open grounds back of the village, bore unmistakable evidences of its fertility. We were offered fish and broken grain, or millet, cooked in small earthen bowls by the women, who seemed to be anxious to make our visit pleasant and agreeable; nor was there, except in one instance, any mark of jealousy on the part of the men, and that was soon allayed, and harmony and good understanding reigned supreme.

Several other villages were visited, but nothing new or striking was noticed, except that we were less closely watched the further we departed from the atmosphere of Igoon, and the people less respectful to the spies who accompanied us.

Passing several other villages, and having no breeze

to fill our sail, we rowed or floated with the current, followed by the spy, who kept us in view. Coming to an island where the river made a great sweep to the left, we followed the main channel, while our white-ball rowed over towards a village behind an island, where a point soon intervening between us, we saw him no more.

The night proving calm, we continued to float with the current; the islands were numerous, the shores low, running off into vast prairies, covered with luxuriant grass. The men having retired, I steered on until 2 A. M.. The current is about four miles an hour; some of the bends are deep, with caving banks, and trees, undermined, have fallen into the river. We swept along several of these caving and crumbling bends, the boat frequently brushing the shore. It was a lovely night. Many wild fowl were started from their repose as we wound along among the shaded island shores and grassy banks.

CHAPTER XLIII.

A TARTAR BEAUTY.

JUNE 13. We continued to float on during the entire night, moving amid a labyrinth of islands fringed with rank grass and tangled growth of willows and vines. In the afternoon we landed, to look at the country on the north or left banks. We found the soil rich, with a growth of oak, apple, pea-vine, grass, and blooming with many beautiful flowers. During the day we have passed much fine country, and several very beautiful situations for settlements. We landed at a Goldee-Manchoo village on the right bank, and found the people kind and hospitable. They had much of the Chinese-Manchoo style in their houses and clothing, and cultivated the soil, having horses and cattle.

They offered us dried fish, caviar, broken rye or barley seed, and jerked meat; but whether horse-flesh or beef, it was difficult to determine. We purchased some milk, and made the children presents, paying for what we bought with blue cotton cloth.

We saw here a native girl, whose appearance struck us with admiration and astonishment. She was from sixteen to eighteen years old, and was exceedingly beautiful.

As we entered the house, she was standing in the shade of rather a dark room, which was only lighted by the open door, and we only got to see her in a more favorable light as she passed out of the door and across the yard, to an outbuilding on the opposite side of the enclosure. We were endeavoring to procure fresh caviar, but failing to make the man understand, when the girl returned into the house. She seemed at once to comprehend the word "*rebah*"—Russian for fish. She led us across the open space in front of the house to the storehouse, or magazine. Her arms were bare to the shoulders, and beautifully formed, and she wore only a very light single chemise or kalat, tucked up on one side under a girdle, which gave her limbs free motion; her head thrown back with a light elastic step, that would grace Diana, she hastened towards the store-room. When in the room she stood with one hand clasping a beam overhead, and occasionally showed a pearly set of teeth, in trying to make us understand the names and uses of the various articles stored within.

These were dried fish, caviar, sturgeons' entrails, dried herbs, meat, skins of various kinds, seeds and grain, with an indescribable medley of half-savage, half-Tartar gear, with implements of the chase, nets and fishing spears, mixed in great confusion. But we were now less interested concerning the caviar, and more than interested in our Goldee belle, who was indeed a jewel for which barbaric princes would have given thousands, or have shared a throne to possess, and which made the civilized wanderer from far distant lands wish that she could have been transplanted to a more genial soil, where cultivation and art could have developed, perhaps, a mind more than equal to the charms and graces of her person. Our memories will often go back to that wild green shore, where dwells the Tartar maiden on the banks of the Sak-hah-lin.

The river during the day has been much like portions of the Mississippi. The plains are extensive, and frequently neither mountains nor rolling lands are in view. The whole country is susceptible of cultivation or stock-raising.

June 14. Thermometer 10 A. M. 72°. We have a fair breeze; partially cloudy; river a mile wide, with islands; high land in the distance, with extensive prairies. At 12 M. we landed at a white sand cliff on the right shore, where Captain Fulyhelm found, after walking some distance along the shore, a seam of coal three or four inches thick, and upon trying some pieces of it upon the fire, we found it to burn well, with but little smoke or smell, leaving but a trace of ashes; it had much the appearance of cannel coal.

I observed two kinds of oak, and the common wild rose of our Northern States, growing here. The country below was very beautiful. We saw a man with dogs herding cattle and horses. As we proceeded we overtook a Manchoo trading-boat, which had just left a village on the left shore, near which there were four canoes, with men drawing fishing nets. The natives in this region appear to be exclusively engaged in fishing at this season of the year, with nets, spears, and hooks. The large fish are cut into thin strips, and exposed in the sun, on poles and wooden cross frames, to dry.

We landed at a fishing camp a little lower down,

where the people had quantities of fish curing in this way. We went on shore to see if they had any sables, but found none. They offered us cooked fish in bowls, as an act of friendship and hospitality, repeating the universal salutation, "Mendow! Mendow!" used by all the natives under Manchoo influence.

We gave them some fathoms of cotton cloth in exchange for fish for our Cossacks. Several girls and women came running to us after we were on board of our boat and about to leave, with more cooked fish in wooden bowls, their hands all dripping with grease. We shoved off, though it was raining, and blowing quite fresh, but went only a short distance, when we were blown violently on a rocky shore below, and our men had to get overboard to force the boat into deeper water, in order to save the bottom from severe shocks. Two of the natives came running into the water to assist us, one of whom was very drunk.

The storm soon blew over, and we made sail with a fair breeze. The Manchoo merchant we overtook would sell us nothing, making signs with his hand across his neck, as much as to say, "If I trade with you I will lose my head." Captain Fulyhelm, however, succeeded in exchanging one of our Russian hens for a large, fine-looking Manchoo chicken, giving him about twice the value of the fowl in cloth, to boot.

We were blown on shore twice during the evening, but succeeded in rowing and poling off. At 11 o'clock, the men being asleep, we were blown ashore again, and as the boat rested easily against the bank, under some overhanging trees, we remained till morning, when the men were called to their work.

The river has been much like the Mississippi to-day, with many islands. The main river has washed but two bluffs in the course of the day, and both of them on the right. There was a ridge of high land in the distance, to the south, most of the day, and on the left (north) a boundless prairie.

CHAPTER XLIV.

MANCHOO JUNKS.

June 15, 8 A. M. Thermometer 68°. There was fog early in the morning, and it is now partially cloudy. We saw antelopes on the right shore; the river is bounded by mountains on both shores. We had strong head wind during most of the day, and put our sail in the water as a current sail, so that we were enabled to make headway, though very slowly. The waves were so high that rowing was of no effect. The mountain scenery has been very pleasing; the forests mostly ovate-leaved, with scattering fir, pine, and spruce.

At 5 P. M. we met ten Manchoo merchant junks or barges, out of the Songahree river, which enters the Amoor about one hundred miles below. They were on their way to Igoon, with the first instalment of merchandise from Pekin for the current year. These junks were about sixty feet long, twelve to fourteen feet wide, with a large mast amidships, forty or fifty feet high, high bows and sterns, and drawing three to four feet of water. There were ten men to each junk—eight at poles or cordels, one steering, and one on the bow, (the pilot,) sounding, and crying the depth of water to the steersman. They all saluted us, crying "Mendow! Mendow!" It seemed like slow work, as they laboriously poled along the sand-bar, or cordelled along the shore, and reminded me of the early barge and keel-boat navigation on the Mississippi and Ohio, and the old flat-boat song,

> "All the way from Shawnee-town,
> Long time ago,"

when it occupied six months to make a voyage from New Orleans to Cincinnati. These junks were unquestionably from the highest point of navigation on the waters of the Songahree, at a point where the commerce overland from Pekin finds its way to supply the wants of the Amoor trade. The distance from Igoon by land direct to Pekin is not probably more than eight to ten hundred miles, for I was informed that couriers performed the distance in twelve to fifteen days; but by way of the Songahree and Amoor, and thence overland to Pekin, the distance must be double. I wished for a good steamboat, that I might have taken these junks in tow and landed them at Igoon, in order to have shown the Manchoos the great advantage of steam on their magnificent rivers.

A short distance below we went on shore, at the foot of a lofty promontory that ran jutting out into the river, forming a very beautiful point. We found a high table-land rising above the bottom, next to the river, running off into gently rounded hills, sparsely wooded with indifferent red-oak and black-birch. The grass was good, with strawberry and grape vines in abundance. A red doe started from her lair within ten steps of us, as we were walking along in the tall grass, and went bounding off, turning in a circle, stopping occasionally to look at us, and snorting like a high-pressure steamboat. We were unarmed, and consequently she escaped.

It began to rain very soon, and as it was growing late, after wandering some time in this sylvan Paradise, we returned to the beach, partly by the bed of a small creek, where there was strong indication of gold. As we had fortunately hit upon a good landing for the boat, and the night looking threatening, we concluded to camp until morning, as we wished to see every inch of the country to the Ousuree. Rain continued to fall during the night, and for the first time we were troubled with mosquitos. There was vivid lightning, but no thunder; though we wished for a regular thunder-storm, hoping thereby to have a clear day on the morrow.

June 17. We left our camp at 4½ A. M., with drizzling rain; but by 10 o'clock we had sunshine, and landed on the left bank, where the country had the appearance of the oak orchards of California. We found the soil good, with grape and pea-vines; many varieties of flowers, among which the lily of the valley was so abundant as to impregnate the air with its delicious fragrance. We were not mistaken in our judgment of this being a choice location for a settlement. The prairie and table-land were extensive, with a rich growth of grass, extending back to the sides of gently sloping mountains, some ten to fifteen miles distant, whose sides were bare of timber, but covered with grass well adapted to sheep or cattle, the higher portions and summits covered with dense forests. After wandering about for some hours, we discovered remains of former habitations, containing broken bricks and shreds of pottery, from all appearances of the same age and quality as found at Albasin. We therefore conjectured this to have been one of the Cossack or fugitive settlements of the Russians from the mines of Nerchinsk, of the same period as Albasin; and as it was well known at the time that the Cossacks passed down the whole length of the Amoor, and even crossed over to Kamschatka in quest of furs, we came to the conclusion that this was one of the links in the chain, and served as a supply station or post of defence.

Leaving this, we landed several times during the day, and found the country one well calculated for the herdsman or agriculturist. Besides the grape and pea, we found apple, asparagus, peony, poppy, and a variety of lilies. We passed the most of the day as near the left shore as possible, but the main land was so masked with islands covered with a tangled luxuriant growth, that we were compelled to take many island chutes, where our boat frequently grounded.

We have seen quite a number of natives fishing today, generally on the lowest points of islands. We landed at 10 P. M. for the night, so as not to miss the Songahree, which we must now be approaching. Slight showers during the day, but mild, pleasant weather.

CHAPTER XLV.

THE SONGAHREE.

June 18, 10 A. M. Temperature 62°. We departed at 3 A. M. High wind from the north-east. The night was clear up to 2 A. M. During the morning we were blown on bars and on shore several times. Being very anxious to reach the Songahree, which, according to the information received from the natives, must be now near at hand, we strained every nerve to proceed; but island after island was passed, and our men, with oars and poles, worked us off the lee shore and bars time after time. We were now approaching the head of an island on the right, which we wished to avoid, fearing to be driven into the chute by the force of the wind. Our Cossacks rowed, and poled, and tugged to avoid this, but all to no purpose. The wind took us a-beam, and the rushing suck of the eddying chute fairly swallowed us up; and rushing down this deep, narrow passage, we soon found ourselves in a very narrow, tortuous, miniature river, going quite in a contrary direction from the main Amoor. But I consoled the captain by telling him that the flat-boatmen on the Mississippi river said, "that if the current is sufficient to suck you in, it will be found strong enough to puke you out;" so that we must come out somewhere in the course of time. Along this chute we passed hour after hour, till we almost came to the conclusion that we had, much against our own consent, found a new channel to the sea, or that we would, perhaps, enter the Songahree some distance from its mouth, or that the higher water of the Amoor was sending us into some vast inland lake; but after some six hours spent in this wild labyrinth of islands, we were ejected into the main river once more, to our great delight.

Following the right bank as closely as possible, and then an immense sand-bar of some miles in extent, we saw to our right a large sheet of water, but at first we were not sure whether it was the Songahree or the entrance of the concentrated waters of other island chutes we had passed on our right. We rowed around under the point of the bar, looking to discover if, by any possibility, we might not be mistaken in our conjectures. We saw evidently a decided change in the color of the water, and now began to see quite a marked line of separation between the two waters. In a few minutes we saw a line of foam and light drift running off towards the opposite shore, and upon rowing still further into the channel, soon saw the two rivers taking their first embrace.

The color of the Songahree is lighter than the Amoor, and upon dipping a tumbler, I found it clearer and much warmer. In fact, the Amoor had, up to this, been cold enough to drink pleasantly, but the Songahree was insipid and warm, coming as it does from a southern source.

We rested our oars to observe the force of the current, and found it feeble in comparison with its great northwestern neighbor, for while we were in a two-knot current, on looking out upon the Amoor, it was sweeping past at the rate of four or five knots.

The Amoor is certainly the noblest river of the two at their junction, but the Songahree bears every evidence of being a river equal to the Ohio. The height of its banks, the breadth and extent of its bars, its width, and force of current, all indicate a river of great magnitude.

We now pulled over near the right and proper shore of the Songahree, and found the current somewhat stronger as we reached the middle of the stream.

A boat had been seen rowing along the right shore for some time, and, having reached a point opposite our boat, came off towards us. It proved to be a Chinese-Manchoo guard or custom-house boat, with the officer of the post on board. He had a brass ball on his cap. We offered him *vodka*, preserves, and biscuit, of which he partook. He saluted us frequently with the now familiar "*mendow! mendow!*"—friend! friend! His greatest curiosity seemed to consist in knowing how many and what kind of arms we had, and the number of men. As it was convenient to do so, we exhibited several six-shooters and a couple of shot-guns, and counted, with our fingers, the number of men. Another boat soon came alongside, with another functionary, who seemed to outrank our first boarding officer. We offered him the hospitalities of our barge also. The new dignitary seemed to be satisfied with the discoveries already made by his predecessor. Each of these officers were accompanied by a secretary, who noted down the result of their observations. They had each four Goldees for boatmen.

Having, by this time, drifted nearly opposite the post, or custom-house, they took their leave and rowed to the shore.

This post of Zend-Zoon-Jelend consists, as far as we could observe from our boat, of two principal houses, some half a dozen smaller ones, and a number of tents or huts, with an open tent or pavilion of blue cloth, standing immediately in front of the buildings on the banks of the river. This we conjectured was for the reception of strangers, in case they landed, as at Igoon.

Three junks, of the same fashion of those seen at Igoon, were lying at the shore. This seemed to be the entire guard to control the navigation of the Songahree and Amoor. As we floated now along upon the united waters of these two great rivers, the scene was truly grand. To the south and west we saw the separate volume of each before united; to the east the great Amoor lay broad and sparkling in the sunlight, bounded by its verdant shores stretching for many miles in the distance. Blue mountains, to the north, stretched like a great wall against the horizon; the air was warm, and filled with the freshness and fragrance of early summer; the declining sun gave a rich and mellow tint to the outstretching prairies on the north, while the southern shore was clothed in a deep dark forest—a scene truly worthy of an artist.

About seven miles below, another guard-boat came to us from a watch-house on an island to the left of the main river. It continued with us until we saw a boat from the left, manned by Russians, coming out to us. This proved to be from a Russian post recently established, apparently for the purpose of providing wood for the steamboats expected up the river this year. We found here also the camp of a corps of Russian topographical engineers. There seems to be a joint occupation of this section of the country by China and Russia, both on the left of the main river, and but a few miles apart. We were informed that the Manchoos have occupied this post since the Russians came here, as a counterpoise to Russian occupation.

At the post above Igoon a Manchoo officer came last year to inquire if it was the intention of the Russians to settle a village there. They told the officer that they did not know. The Manchoo officer then said that they were informed that the Russians intended to settle three hundred families there. He said the Russians might settle that number, but, if more than the three hundred came, a great misfortune would happen them. They are evidently temporizing with the Russians, and, the moment they think themselves strong enough, the attempt will be made to expel them. The Manchoos are now evidently a very timid people, and ill-prepared to oppose force to their powerful Muscovite neighbors.

CHAPTER XLVI.

RUSSIAN PROGRESS.

IGOON was settled by the Chinese government soon after the conquest of Albasin, to serve the double purpose of a frontier guard and penal station, and to prevent any further settlement by the Russians on the Amoor.

Watch-posts or houses have been located from time to time for purposes of communication, vigilance, or safety, and the wild tribes have been subjugated to serve the purpose of a frontier guard; in fact, the natives have been enslaved by the Chinese-Manchoo government, and are seized upon in their villages whenever wanted for purposes of government. The Chinese officers are instructed to prevent the Russians from settlement and the navigation of the Amoor, but are not allowed to use force.

The Russian officers are very kind and just in their dealings, and conciliatory in their manners with all the people along the Amoor, paying them roundly for what they purchase, and frequently making presents of cloth, tobacco, and trinkets. When the first Russian vessel came up the Amoor they knew nothing of the river, and, in order to procure pilots, they were forced to enter the native villages and take by force two of the oldest men in order to be informed as to the channel. Thus they came from village to village, treating the men kindly and paying them a hundredfold for their services. So soon as the natives saw that they were not to be harmed, were treated well, and richly rewarded, the Russians found no difficulty in procuring men to show the navigable parts of the river. These natives are found to possess quite an accurate knowledge of the navigation, and would generally tell in advance the depth of water to be found in difficult parts of the river. In this they rendered an important service to the Russians.

The Manchoos say that the Songahree is the real Amoor and that the Sak-hah-lin empties into it. This is readily credited at this particular juncture, as Russia would be quite willing to have the Songahree as the more southern boundary; in fact, it is now said that the real Ya-blo-novey mountains cross the Amoor and run off far into Tartary, and that the location of the boundary along the ridge that divides the waters of the Frozen Ocean from those of the Amoor was a fraud and a deceit of the Chinese, practised knowingly by them at the time of the old treaty of Golovin, and, therefore, not legally binding on Russia; in fact, recent events have gone far to establish this.

But it remains to be seen how successful Russia is to be in making the Ya-blo-novey, or Hingan mountains cross the Amoor, take in the country to the south, down to Corea, through Manchooria, cross the Gulf of Tartary, or Sea of Japan, and include the whole of the island of Sak-hah-lin to the boundary of Japan.

But Russia, having possession of the upper waters of

the Amoor, she now also needs the Ousuree, because this river runs off to the south, towards Corea, and approaches the Sea of Japan at a point where there is a good harbor (Pahseeat Gulf), in about north latitude 42°, which remains unfrozen during the winter—a *desideratum* "devoutly to be wished" by Russia on the Pacific, and which she will find necessary in her growing affairs in this region. I do not see why she should not have this port as well as England and France their islands, ports, and harbors on the Pacific and in the Indian Ocean. The possession of this point would be one of the best steps Russia could take, perfectly proper and justifiable in view of her future position on the coast of Tartary and the necessities of her commerce. The occupation of this wild uninhabited coast by her will be alike beneficial to civilization, to commerce, and to Christianity. She is now willing to pay China a reasonable price for these wild Tartarian coasts and harbors, rivers and mountains; and morally there is no more wrong to-day in the conquest and acquisition of these countries than there was, some centuries since, in the conquest and settlement of America.

The climate of Pahseeat Bay and the country of the Ousuree is quite mild. Little or no ice forms in the winter to obstruct navigation seaward, which makes it still more desirable to Russia for a seaport and harbor for her fleets, such as she has not as yet on this side of the world. While England, Holland, France, and Spain have colonies in the Pacific and Indian Ocean, open the year round, Russia has nothing but frozen seas and ports closed for six to eight months in the year.

A few miles below the mouth of the Songahree the

two rivers become so thoroughly mixed, that but little change in the color of the water can be observed, though it was sensibly warmer. The river is now over a mile wide without islands, and, in places, wider, including islands and chutes.

June 19. High wind from the east. Shoved off, but were blown on shore a few miles below. We went into the country; an extensive prairie, with some oak near the river bank. Strawberry vines, in astonishing abundance, peony, two varieties of pea, and asparagus and clover; good pasturage; mountains to the north, distant ten miles. After some hours delay, the wind still blowing fresh, we shoved off and rowed with much difficulty into the current, put down the sail into the water, as it was impossible to keep her head to the wind with the oars, but our progress was short-lived. Coming to a bend of the river, the wind blew us to the shore again. Here we rested some hours, but seeing no likelihood of the wind abating, we shoved with our poles along the shore. After two hours of hard work we reached the head of an island-chute, into which we pulled under a lee shore, thereby avoiding the wind which was sweeping up the main river. Being now quite sheltered in this narrow channel, we got on quite well until 7 P. M., when a violent rain-storm came on, which, after a struggle of an hour and a half, drove us on to the lee shore, where we were forced to tie up for the night, though it was an exposed situation. The rain descended in torrents; our boat thumped very severely against the shore and bottom. Our Cossacks, thoroughly wet and fatigued with the hardest day's work they had yet, had erected a temporary camp on the shore, which was well wooded, and kindling a huge fire, cooked their supper and dried themselves. A little *vodka* was distributed to comfort the wet bivouac. The whole day's toil has only advanced us eighteen miles—the poorest day's work yet accomplished.

CHAPTER XLVII.

FLOATING ALONG.

JUNE 20th, 8 A. M. Thermometer 60°. It rained and blew violently all night, with occasional flashes of lightning, without thunder. This is the third time, since our departure, that lightning has occurred. At 5 A. M. the wind was too high to depart, but at 7 we were enabled to get off. The weather was still foul, with wind, fog, and mist. The beautiful mountains that had been in view for the last four days were now hid from us, and we only caught a glimpse of the foot of a very high peak, which we had seen in the distance, as we glided past it, the river sweeping its base, and, at the same time, a little lighting of the weather gave us a hasty view of the spurs of the great chain of mountains bounding the northern horizon.

As the day advanced, the clouds partially lifted, so as to give us a fine view of the mountains now forming a background to the view, as they had a foreground at the mouth of the Songahree.

The evening proved windy, and we were again forced to land on a desolate island. This we regretted the more, as we had anticipated during the day to have reached an Indian village, where to have spent the night. It was now very dark, the wind blowing a gale, and we had great difficulty in making a suitable landing place, as we were on a lee shore and the water rough.

At 11 P. M. a severe rain-storm, accompanied with heavy claps of thunder and lightning, the first thunder heard on the Amoor. The severity of the storm made our boat pound very unpleasantly on the sand of the shore, but there was no escape for us; we had to take it as it came; but in the course of two hours the storm passed over, and we slept a little towards morning.

June 21st, 10 A. M. Thermometer 70°. The morning looked unfavorable, and we were blown on shore soon after our departure, but, the wind shifting a little, and coming to a less crooked part of the river, we used our sail, and the wind beginning to blow again quite fresh, we made good speed. We kept our sail till about 6 P. M., when, a rain-sqall coming up, we ran into an island-chute, where we were protected under the lee shore of an island, but the squall was soon over and with it our fair wind.

We rowed on till 10 P. M., and landed on the right bank at the foot of a mountain covered with forest. Some Goldees who had rowed out to us as we passed their village an hour previous, came to overtake us and to trade sables for silver. They asked two rubles for them. Captain Fulyhelm said they were indifferent; but, as we had no silver, and they wanted nothing else, we made no trade with them.

The country on the right has been very interesting today; mountainous and well timbered, reminding me of mountains in the tropics from the variety and richness of the foliage of the different species of trees. Some twenty miles above the Ousuree we took to the left shore, or island-chute, a part of the river perhaps never before descended by white men, and, with a fair breeze, we passed along this unknown river, amidst innumerable islands, complicated chutes, and darkly-wooded banks, alarming the quiet water-fowl and startling the timid fawns in their sylvan abode. We saw neither man, nor the marks of any human being, until we entered the arm of the river, some fifty or sixty miles below, usually travelled by those navigating these waters.

Two barges, not far astern of us, took the Ousuree channel, and I was curious to see which would come out first at the meeting of the two arms of the river, but as yet we have seen nothing of them.

During the night several canoes and three-plank boats filled with men passed up and down between two villages, and about 1 A. M. a boat came along near us, hailing several times with the usual "Mendow! Mendow!" as they came rowing up merrily against the current. The rowers were uttering a kind of brisk, lively cry, keeping time with their oars, while the steersman, perched upon the stern, was chanting a wild melody. In the stillness of the night, and under the shade of a huge mountain, which gave back from its rocky sides a half-repeated echo, the effect was wild and strange in the extreme, and filled me with romantic feelings.

The night proved pleasant, though it had threatened both wind and rain. We were, however, in a favorable situation, in a kind of cave, under a high mountain, where only one direction of the wind could reach us, and being to the windward of the threatened storm, we rested quite secure.

June 22, 10 A. M. Thermometer 63°. Head wind and cloudy, with drops of rain, at 4 A. M. The wind was fresh during most of the day, but by putting the sail in the water, we succeeded in making a little headway against the storm; but we were finally driven on the shore at 5 P. M.

With the help of our poles we crept along very slowly until about 7 P. M., when the wind freshening, rendered further progress out of the question. The wind blew quite a gale during the night.

The country where we have landed is prairie, rich and luxuriant, with grass to the height of my shoulders—a choice country for raising stock. There was a dim trail along the shore, showing a path traversed by the natives, and clumps of timber off in the distance. I walked some distance out into the prairie, until I came to a long lake, with oak and aspen on its banks, and signs of elk and deer or antelope. There were also geese and ducks in the distance, but too shy for a shot.

CHAPTER XLVIII.

FLOATING ALONG.

JUNE 23, 10 A. M. Thermometer 61°. The wind blew a gale all night, and it was past 9 A. M. before we were able to get under way. The weather was cloudy and cool, with the wind ahead. We struggled along all day with poles and current-sail, and being driven at length near to the head of an island chute, we were drawn into it with great swiftness by the current, though we struggled hard to keep out of it. We wound along its banks of tangled woods and rank undergrowth for many hours, turning point after point, and rounding bend after bend, hoping every moment that we might see our way out of this labyrinth.

We finally landed at a deserted Tartar village, to examine the forest trees. We found elm, ash, oak, poplar, maple, walnut and gum, with a tangled and luxuriant undergrowth of vines and shrubs of various kinds.

Though a mountain-side, and rocky in places, the soil was exceedingly rich. The rocks were evidently plutonic. We finally succeeded in reaching the main river again. Though we had not advanced much in our direct course, we had visited a wild and beautiful country, never before, perhaps, seen by a white man. We stopped several times during the day to look at the country, and penetrated the forests for some distance, but found them so rank and dense with undergrowth, as to deter us from going far. We saw extensive woods of aspen. The climate and soil here are certainly very favorable to agriculture, as is shown by the vigorous growth of timber and herbage.

We were now on the southernmost bends of the Amoor, below the Ousuree, and about eight hundred miles above its mouth. The main river is so broad, and the shores so masked with islands, that the navigation, with only oars and the current, is very tedious; for when the wind is blowing, as it does nearly all the time at this season of the year, if it happens to be adverse, you are confined to the lee-shore, and pretty much at the wind's mercy; the river being so wide, that to reach the opposite shore with oars is out of the question. The river is truly a grand one, and since we passed the Zea, more and more resembling the Mississippi; and since we passed the Songahree, and now the Ousuree, in many places with its cut and crumbling shores, falling-in timber, and the muddiness of its waters, and its huge sand-bars, the resemblance had become almost perfect.

From the Songahree the Amoor is certainly a more considerable river in breadth than the Mississippi below the mouth of the Ohio. The expanse of water, the numerous islands, and the many navigable chutes, some of them thirty miles in extent, must give it more breadth than the Mississippi. As for instance, above the Ousuree the river is divided into two parts; one—the right—usually navigated, into which falls the Ousuree, deep, and about the size of the Ohio; the other, broad and filled with islands, bars, and chutes, certainly as large as the Mississippi above Memphis, and looking very like it.

We have seen but two Tartar villages to-day, and only a solitary old man came to us in a canoe. We showed him our map of the river, and asked him for certain villages which were indicated on it, at which he was much surprised. We found, through him, our position, of which we had been ignorant since yesterday.

We passed in the afternoon a range of elevated land on the left, which was truly such a country as a farmer would select for healthiness of locality, richness of soil, and beauty of scenery. He would have timber and prairie land at his option, with abundant grazing for cattle, horses, and sheep.

The natives dress usually in the summer in clothing made of fish skins. I saw a woman to-day preparing some of these garments, which are durable, and well adapted to the necessities of the fishing season. They shed rain as well as an india-rubber coat, and are light and pliable, while some of them are quite becoming in style and finish. The young girls, dressed in these new, shining fish-skin *robes*, trimmed off with shells, beads, and trinkets, laughing and frolicking along these wild shores, are doubtless quite as attractive to the young men around them as are their crinolined sisters of Broadway or Pennsylvania Avenue to the youth of New York or Washington.

June 24th, 10 A. M. Thermometer 60°. High wind. We lay all night, the bottom of our boat pounding rather unpleasantly upon a rocky beach, as our landing was after dark and upon a lee shore, badly chosen, or rather not chosen at all. The wind blew quite a gale all night. We lay at the foot of a mountain densely covered with forests of poplar, aspen, elm, and small oak. The river opposite was over a mile wide, with several islands masking the opposite shore. We pushed off at about 6 A. M., for it certainly was better for our boat to breast the waves and winds, than to have her thin ribs in such close proximity with occasional thumps from volcanic boulders.

We struggled all day, with current-sail, oars, and poles, along a lee-shore, frequently grounding upon the bank, and seeing no likelihood of the wind abating, and having been unable all day to make the opposite shore, which we wished to visit, or gain a windward island, under whose lee we might have some shelter from the wind, we at last landed. We found a soft bank, where we were somewhat sheltered by the bend of the river, and bringing a point of land a little to the windward, we tied up for the night. The shore was a vast prairie as far as the eye could reach, with grass shoulder high, where perhaps the foot of man never before had trod. We were again out of the accustomed channel, and on water not laid down on the charts, but I must still believe on the main river, for it was at this point certainly a mile wide, with a current of four miles an hour.

The shores to-day have been somewhat hilly, with some rocks and high sand-cliffs, wooded with aspen and elm. The islands and bottoms are subject to overflow, and either prairie or covered with willow. Wind north, and north-east by east. This is the third day of this storm of wind without rain, cloudy by day and clear by night. We have not seen a human being this day on the shores, or the sign of habitation. The grass was so luxuriant, and the country so flat, that we did not undertake to penetrate more than a few hundred yards from the water. Up to 2 o'clock A. M. the wind was still blowing fresh and cool over the broad expanse of the river, but the bank of the river was soft and crumbling; consequently our boat did not suffer much, though she was "bobbing round" all night.

CHAPTER XLIX.

THE NAVIGATION AND FEMALE SAILORS.

June 25, 10 A. M. Thermometer 64°. Head winds and clouds. We got off at 8 A. M. Wind still ahead, but somewhat abated in violence; the weather cloudy, with indications of rain. We made more progress to-day, the wind being more directly ahead, which made our current-sail of more use, though we were again driven by the wind into deep bends, but had no detention, nor were we forced to resort to our poles except occasionally.

The river all day broad, with numerous islands; the banks covered with a dense growth of willow. We therefore conjecture that we have not seen the main shore to-day. Towards night the peak of a distant mountain was seen, which gives us hopes of seeing *terra firma* some time to-morrow, as the wind now (11½ P. M.) had nearly subsided, and we are lying without being tossed by the waves, which has not been the case for the four last nights past. Just at dark we saw lights, and attempted to pull in to them, but were swept past by the force of the current, and landed on a high gravel bar, below a village, with an island chute intervening. The captain's servant, Evan, and two of our men, have, however, gone with the skiff to the village, to try to procure fish.

The night is cloudy, with drops of rain, and bids fair to drench us before morning. It is a most extraordinary fact, and proves this to be one of the safest navigable rivers in the world, that last year (1856), out of six hundred and ninety-seven barges and rafts which descended from the upper waters of the Schilkah and Argoon, only one failed to reach its destination, and that one was not wrecked, but abandoned in an island chute, where it had grounded, and the sudden fall of the water rendered it impossible to get it afloat again; so the cargo was reshipped on other barges or rafts.

There has as yet been no instance of the loss of a barge. Several rafts have been broken or abandoned. Last year there were fifteen hundred head of beef cattle transported on rafts. All these cattle but seven reached their destination. These rafts are more than two months descending, landing every night to graze the cattle, and frequently in the day-time, on account of storms; yet see the little loss! One government barge, loaded with cannon, was stove at Nikolaievsky, by coming in contact with a ship. This was no fault of the navigation. The steamer Schilkah grounded, not for want of water in the river, but because she was not in the channel. Of course, in such an immense river as the Amoor, some time must elapse before the channel, at all stages of the water, becomes well known. Till such time, much caution must be observed in navigating by steamers, particularly in descending, in order to know that they are pursuing the channel or chute in which the greatest depth of water is to be found; otherwise it may happen, as in the case of the Schilkah, that entering the improper channel and grounding, the sudden falling of the water renders it impossible to get afloat again, and may leave the steamer high and dry on the inside of a sand-bar or island chute, where a rise in the river must be awaited.

In my opinion, the Amoor river will not prove as difficult or as dangerous to navigate as the Mississippi, because there is not so much shifting of the bars, nor but a very limited number of snags. In the upper portions of the river, the flow of ice in the spring effectually clears the river of all fallen timber of the previous year, while in the central and southern portions, the immediate banks are not timbered to much extent, while again, low down on the Amoor, the heavy timber is most generally on high or rocky shores, not subject to be washed into the river.

Friday, June 26, 12 M. Thermometer 78°. We got off at 4 A. M., with very little wind, but during the day it blew sufficient to make the current-sail available. We succeeded in reaching the northern shore, along which we coasted, landing and looking at the country during the morning. We found the soil fertile in grasses, with pea-vine and strawberry, but generally destitute of timber. In the afternoon, as we were approaching mountains on our right, we pulled over to the southern shore, and coasting along it, landed and examined the forests along that shore. We found oak, ash, elm, and aspen. The oak was frequently two feet in diameter, but the trees were generally imperfect, being hollow at the butt or partially decayed at the sides. We saw marks of elk or reindeer on the beach along the shore, as well as tracks of a large cat or panther, which had probably prowled along the night previous in search of sleeping water-fowl, which are abundant here. Walking along the shore while our boat was floating along in the stream, we came to a creek, which was the boundary line of mixed timber; far below, for some distance, we saw nothing but a dense forest of aspen.

It came on to be dark before we entered an island chute which bore us to the right of the main river. The banks were low, and the chute so narrow, that in turning some of the bends, the stern of our boat swept the willows. After proceeding near an hour along this chute, it divided, when we again took to the right. Not being sure that we were going with the current, as it was now quite dark, we ceased rowing in order to observe the effect of the current. We found that we were floating but slowly down the chute. We rowed and floated on. It was now pitch dark, and past 10 P. M.; cloudy, and threatening a storm. We again came to a division of the channel. Again we pulled to the right, but we found that we had entered into a large and apparently circular space of water, though the entrance was not fifty feet wide. By stopping the oars this time, we found that there was no current.

We now concluded that it was time to stop for the night and await the coming daylight to guide us either out of this apparent *cul de sac*, or into some chute leading into the main river, or rather to be guided by the de scending current. We therefore pulled up to the shore, and made fast to some overhanging willows; upon which one of the men took the skiff, and rowing out upon the dismal waters of this seeming dead lake, returned in the course of half an hour with the intelligence that the only outlet was the one by which we had entered, and reported hearing the barking of dogs down the chute which we had passed on our left.

At 12 P. M. the night was warm and perfectly calm. The mosquitoes sung a very merry tune over our mishap, as if they were delighted with the prospect of a rich repast from the full veins of their hyperborean visitors. Our Cossacks boiled their brick tea, hoping with smoke, fire, and tea, to come to a parley with the leeches. They fought them off for a couple of hours, and finally, under the joint protection of our sail and their sheep-skin coats, with the woolly side turned out, in which they hoped the bloodthirsty swarm would become entangled in presenting their bills, resigned themselves to slumber.

In the course of the day we were visited by two boats, mostly *manned* by Goldee girls. In one of the boats there were two very old men, one of whom performed the office of steersman, while the other sat on the floor in the centre. The girls were capital rowers, and handled their oars with great ease and dexterity. The old men had some fish for barter, but the main thing they desired was a little *arrakke.* Captain Fulyhelm made one of the girls a present of a number of pieces of Russian coin, of which she seemed very proud as she passed them to her companions to look at. Not to be outdone in gallantry by the captain, I distributed a few coins among her companions.

They were all habited in short tunics of fish-skins. Around the lower edge of the skirts were rows of small pieces of brass or small sea-shells. One of them had as many as three sets of ear-rings, two of which were very large, and a ring in the nose, with a small piece of white metal like an ear-drop on the ring, which hung in the centre of the upper lip. These are the first natives that I have seen with ornaments in the nose; all had ornaments in both ears and nose. Their whole wardrobe consisted of a single garment of fish-skin, which was not too long or too full to impede the free movement of their limbs, nor yet so closely fitting or transparent as to reveal nature unadorned; but yet one could see, as they stood gracefully in their boats, resting upon their oars, that they were not destitute of either shape or form; and one of them in particular had a well-developed bust, though yet young—perhaps fifteen or sixteen. After satisfying their curiosity they pushed off into the stream, and striking their oars regularly and gracefully into the water, were soon lost to sight behind an adjacent island. We saw no habitations or camp, and concluded that they were out on a pleasure excursion, or perhaps a *pic-nic.* We learned from the old men our whereabouts, of which we had been ignorant since we left the Ousuree settlements.

It was really refreshing to find these laughing, frolicking damsels, in this wilderness, enjoying themselves, apparently without fear or restraint, approaching the uncouth stranger and *barbarian* with all the confidence, and yet the delicacy, of the sex, seemingly quite as unabashed as any well-bred lady of London or Moscow, and evidently tittering at our uncouth appearance, manner, and address, as a fashionable belle would at the first essay of a country cousin in a city drawing-room.

CHAPTER L.

NATIVE VILLAGES.

SATURDAY, June 27. We were up at 4 A. M. to look at our location. We were indeed in a lake; the mountains not far off and well wooded. Among the trees we saw cedar. The mosquitoes and black sand-flies were very annoying during the night, but, by closing the door and windows of our cabin, we kept out the more hungry swarms. We pushed our boat out through the narrow passage, by which we had entered this lake, into the chute we had left, and found a gentle current to assist our oars in our onward progress.

At 6 A. M. we grounded on a sand-bar, but our Cossacks, now converted into good watermen, were soon stripped and overboard, towing our boat into deeper water. Some natives came to us in canoes and pointed to the part of the river where the best water was. We were soon again afloat. Two miles below we landed at a Goldee fishing station. We found the men well provided with nets and spears and with plenty of fish. We saw them here building one of those peculiar three-plank boats found on the Amoor, called by the Russians Gel-ack boats, from the name of the tribe who use them also at the mouth of the river. These boats are made of cedar boards or plank, the trees from which they are made growing here to great perfection and of excellent quality and large size. The tree is felled and split of the requisite length and width. They are then floated to the village or fishing station and fashioned into boats. They are of various sizes, but the Goldee generally uses one of the smaller size—say fifteen feet long. The sides or gunwales are well raked fore and aft, and not brought quite together at bow and stern, into which pieces are fitted. The bottom plank extends beyond the bow, and, having a good rake, stands clear of the water in the form of a tongue, into which a ring is placed, or a hole made for a rope, by which the boat is fastened to the shore. This tongue answers also a useful purpose, as a means by which to leave or enter the boat over the bow, while the great rake it has, with its flat bottom, allows it to go in very shallow water and readily approach the shores over shoals and bars, so abundant on the Amoor. This allows the bow of the boat to shoot quite on dry land, while the stern is still afloat. The tongue projecting affords a steady means by which to gain the shore dry-footed, or to regain the boat.

A native was constructing one of these boats here. He used an iron adze, not a good instrument by any means, but he nevertheless used it with much skill. I conjectured that the adze was of Chinese make. The fastenings of the boat were wooden pins, some with heads like bolts; but they use iron nails, when they can procure them from the Manchoo traders.

These people make ropes and nets of the bark of a

tree, as well as a kind of grass, also of hemp or flax procured from the Manchoos of the Songahree. The women were very busy preparing the fish for drying, and also quantities of a large species of wild garlic, very strong and of a rank smell, which they were cutting up with knives and drying in the sun. This garlic, together with a bitter herb, seemed to be all they had in the way of vegetable food, which they had cooked with fish, of which they pressed us to partake. Fish and garlic was the bill of fare for breakfast. They had several young foxes confined in cages, but whether for pets or preserved for some religious ceremony, I could not determine. Admiral Wrangel, in his Polar explorations, mentions the fact of young foxes being caught and tamed by some wild tribe, through whose country he passed, and probably kept from some religious motive, or as an offering or sacrifice upon some religious ceremony.

All that these people had of foreign clothing, ornaments, or utensils, was evidently of Chinese manufacture. Their dresses, except those of a few of the younger women, were of fish-skins, or entrails of fish. One woman had a kind of mat made of bark, which she seemed very anxious to sell or give me, and, bringing a skin skirt or tunic from her lodge, on which to place the garlic, which was spread upon the mat, offered it to me. I passed on down the beach to some other lodges, and, as I returned, the mat-woman came running to meet me from her lodge, with her hands full of garlic, which she offered to me. Two other women then came up, who were rather inclined, as I could perceive, to laugh at her. I, however, gave her some small pieces of silver coin, which seemed to compensate for the disappointment in the sale of her mat. These women, seeing that I was not a dangerous character, but inclined to be friendly, now gave my clothing a very minute and scrutinizing inspection; my shirt, shoes, and stockings seemed to attract the most attention. In turn, not to be less curious, I looked at their dresses and ear-rings, and finally entered the lodge of my mat-woman, in order to observe their household economy. It was very poor. The interior of a lodge on the Amoor, as well as on the Columbia, is a very sorry and filthy place, and takes from savage life what little of outward romance there is attached to it. It was well stocked with fish and garlic, of which my hostess offered me some already cooked in an earthen bowl. At another lodge I observed a young woman with many ornaments in her ears, having her hair carefully dressed with ornamented hair-pins thrust through it. The hair was brought on the back part of the head in a large knot. She also had a dress of Chinese cotton-cloth, worked with embroidery at the edge of the skirt. Her complexion was a deep brownish red, with full cheeks and fine teeth. She was busy cleaning fish, and was at first inclined to be offended at my close scrutiny of her personal ornaments, but the first friendly squaw came up, and, after some words of conversation between them, she ceased from her work and was inclined to be on more friendly terms. I afterwards visited other lodges, and found iron pots, in which they cooked their fish, and some few earthen jars and bowls of pottery.

We proceeded along down this seemingly interminable chute, along portions of which the shores were beautiful, and above overflow covered with grass and scattered groups of trees. It was not till 5 P. M. that we again floated out into the main river at Mount Chalahtzve. Here we met sixteen row-boats and a small barge going up containing Russian soldiers, whose term of service had expired, making their way back to Siberia or Europe. Each boat contained from ten to fifteen men—the barge the officers. It seemed a tedious process, thus to force these boats over two thousand miles against a current of three and a half to four miles per hour, but even this seemed preferable to the route by Ayan, where the land route was of nearly equal distance to Irkutsk. But this party expected to be overtaken by one of the iron steamers building at Nikolaivsky, which is to take them on board and convey them to the head of the Amoor or to Schilkah. They had left Kezee, one hundred and fifty miles above the mouth, on the 13th inst., and were now some two hundred miles on their way. If not overtaken by the steamer, in case of accident or otherwise, they will have a hard pull to reach the Russian settlement at Ouse-Strelkah before the freezing of the river, in which case they may suffer much hardship.

These men and officers had been serving at Petro-Paulosky, De Castries, and at the mouth of the Amoor during the war, and in erecting fortifications since. They had withstood every sort of hardship and privation, and were now joyfully, though laboriously, wending their way to homes, parents, and wives, after toil and suffering sufficient to bow any but the most hardy and resolute.

The river Nooch-koo-che falls into the Amoor here, and it must be a desirable spot, for there are seven villages in the vicinity. The shores are very handsome, the mountains well timbered. The river is grand and majestic, with beautiful shores, which nature has done much to fit for the abode of man.

We proceeded till 10 P. M., when we landed at the lofty mountain or promontory of Sahr-koo-Book-ke on the right bank. This was one of the high points seen on the previous day before entering the long chute, and in which we were lost in the lake. The mountains are well wooded with larch, pine, birch, and cedar, while oak, ash, and aspen are found on the bottoms and foot hills.

CHAPTER LI.

THE HONGAHREE.

SUNDAY, June 28. We were off early in the morning. The weather was cloudy and threatening rain, with head wind the whole day. We passed into another of those long chutes, making but little headway. Late in the afternoon we reached the main river.

We have been in view during the day of lofty mountains covered with forests, and near night came in view of the loftiest yet seen. They were on the left of the river, to the north of a stream called the Ahl-benn, distant some thirty miles. After a long unsuccessful struggle against wind and tide, in order to reach the main shore on the left, we were compelled to take shelter under the lee of an island at 10½ P. M. In order to cheer our desolate bivouac we fired the old dried grass and bushes of the previous year still standing. It soon spread far and wide and lighted up the dark shore for several miles, making our camp more agreeable. The warmth of the fire was not unpleasant, as the evening was cool, with a heavy dew falling. Many birds, either driven from their cover by the fire or attracted by the light, flew over the shore, among which we observed ducks, quail, snipe, and curlew.

We found to-day, as usual ever since we left the Zea, the river too wide to be pleasant or agreeable for our mode or means of navigation; there are so many islands, bars, chutes, and channels, that one becomes lost in their labyrinth, and, when the wind prevails, you are thrown on one shore or the other, without the possibility of crossing the river or visiting such objects on an opposite shore as may be of interest. We often wished for a little steamer in which to go where we pleased, not regarding wind or tide. There are many beautiful lakes that communicate with the river, that we wished to visit, or sometimes ascend a tributary stream, but, with our boat, we found it out of the question.

The natives use here, as well as all along on the Amoor, the birch-bark canoe, very lightly and beautifully made, which they use in hunting and fishing excursions. They usually carry but one person, and are readily transported over portages. They sit in the centre, flat on the bottom; both ends are shaped alike. Two kinds of paddles are used, one double, with a blade at each end, which is used with both hands, first striking on one side and then on the other with very rapid strokes, which sends the canoe along with great speed. The other paddles are small, one used in each hand, like the fins of a fish, and used much in the same manner. They manage these canoes with much adroitness, and proceed with great speed, and, being so light and easily managed, they are a great *desideratum* in hunting and fishing excursions, where the game is taken by surprise, as they approach without noise or float negligently along the shaded shores. These canoes are like those used by our Indians on our northern lakes and rivers, only these are mostly for a single person, or two at most, while those of Michigan, Huron, and Superior, are frequently constructed to carry the whole family, their provisions, and lodges. They are constructed like those of our Indians.

Monday, June 29. We were under way by 4 A. M. The fire we had kindled was burning far and wide, the weather cloudy and threatening rain. Thermometer, 7 A. M., 63°. The wind had increased during the night, so that as soon as we had passed the island and came to the open river, the water was quite rough and our progress slow. We were finally driven upon the shore, a mile below a Goldee village, under a lofty mountain, well wooded, with cedar and other trees. Our Cossacks went up to the village to procure fish, but returned without any.

The natives, except some old men and a dozen women and children, were absent at a fishing station. In a short time the whole remaining population came along the beach to where our boat had landed to take a look at us. We threw some biscuit on shore, which caused an animated scramble among the younger women and children. There was one man who understood a few words of Russian, from whom we derived some information concerning the river. We wished to keep along the left bank, and, as there were many islands intervening, we wished to learn from him if it was possible to pass between them and the main shore. He indicated that we could, all but one, which we found by experience to be correct. We were now nearly opposite the Hon-gah-ree river, which comes in from the south; but as the Amoor here divides into two large branches, from two to three miles broad, a high wind prevailing right in our teeth, rendered it impossible for us to cross to look at the country at its mouth, where it falls into the Amoor.

The country during the day has been more interesting than for several days previous, there being much fine mountain scenery. We progressed but slowly, however, having to pole along the shores and bars and resort to the current-sail from time to time. We wished to reach a village, at which to pass the night, near which exceeding fine cedar is said to grow ; but the wind was too strong and contrary for us, and, at 10 P. M., we were compelled to land on a sand-bar to the left, with high wooded mountains opposite on the right.

The Hon-gah-ree river drains the coast range of mountains to the south of the Amoor, up to and within a short portage of Emperor's Harbor, on the coast of Tartary, in 49° north latitude, at which point the Russians have now a settlement, and it is their intention to make it a harbor for their ships upon this coast. From this point easy communication can be had with the Amoor by way of the Hon-gah-ree, without making the long and tedious navigation of the Amoor and then through the Straits of Tartary to reach the sea-coast. Though Emperor's Harbor freezes in winter, yet it is open much longer than the mouth of the Amoor or De Castries, and a much better harbor in the winter than the latter. My companion, Captain Fulyhelm, had visited Emperor's Harbor, and he described it as very safe and easy of access. Two months later I had a very good view of the approaches to it myself, as we sailed along in view of its entrance, in September, on our way to Hakodadi. There is also another gulf or harbor more to the south, on the coast of Tartary, nearly opposite Hakodadi, in about 42° north latitude, called by the Russians Pahseeat Gulf. The French and English visited this gulf during the allied war and gave it the name respectively of Napoleon and Victoria Bay, the French naming a group of islands, near, Eugenie Archipelago. To Russia this would be the most desirable acquisition next to the Amoor, because here communication and entrance may be had the year round, the harbor not being frozen during the winter, added to which communication can be had by a short land transit to the navigable waters of the Ousuree, which communicates with the Amoor by two mouths, about one thousand miles from the sea. There is also, at the head of the Ousuree, a large navigable lake, which, as well as the river, is well stocked with fish, while fine pine, oak, ash, and cedar timber, suitable for ship building, are found in great abundance upon their shores and mountains. The land transit might be very easily opened by railroad to the lake, and steamboats thence into the Amoor. The Russians, as yet, have made no settlements there, but it is the point towards which, in my opinion, they should direct their attention immediately, if they wish to secure a harbor on the coast of Tartary available to them the year round, where their ships can be repaired and refitted without submitting to the tedious process of a six or seven months' imprisonment in the Amoor.

Timber for ship building may not be considered good on the Amoor, though the cedar, pine, and spruce may be rated as fair. The oak upon the immediate shores is not good, but it is reported that the Hongahree and Ousuree, with some small streams coming in from the south, are well stocked with good oak. Pine and cedar may be considered the best timber; birch is plentiful for fire-wood, and pine, larch, and spruce for building purposes. It is perhaps upon the Ousuree, next to the Songahree, that the Russians will have to look for oak timber, and this, of itself, is sufficient inducement to explore the Ousuree to the lake, and thence to the sea, for, at this point, good timber, according to climate, ought to be found.

CHAPTER LII.

A GOLDEE VILLAGE.

TUESDAY, June 30. We were under way at 4 A. M., with head wind, and made very slow progress till midday: when the wind abated we dispensed with the current-sail, and took to our oars. We stopped to visit a village on the left, behind an island, about a mile from the main river. We landed some distance below the village, and walked along a very nice gravel beach towards it. Not a human being was to be seen as we approached. Just below we came to a number of newly-placed stakes set in the ground, leading from the beach in two rows six feet apart, and at intervals of twenty steps, up to a small frame house on the bank, in quite a thicket of bushes and wild undergrowth. It proved to be a tomb of some patriarch of the tribe. I passed along the path, guided by the stakes, up the shore to the house. A kind of flask and an earthen vessel of Chinese make, or such as I had seen among the Manchoos, were suspended at the gable of the tomb. A small square opening of twelve inches was the only means of observing what was within. There were some rough-hewn planks loosely laid together on a kind of frame, with coarse matting partially covering it. It was evidently a tomb of some years standing. The recently-placed stakes were most likely a religious offering, placed by the tribe or friends of the deceased to propitiate some evil spirit, and turn away his wrath from the departed chief.

We passed on into the village, and were finally greeted with the howls, growls, and yelps of a score or two of dogs of every size and color. Entering a house, the door of which was open, we found a woman the only occupant. She was not apparently the least disconcerted by our abrupt entrance, having been prepared for our visit by the uproar of the dogs. She was engaged in dressing a skin, and only ceased from her labor as we approached her to look at her handiwork.

The house was thirty-five or forty feet square, built of small posts set up and plastered with mud. The roof was supported by heavier posts at the corners and sides, with cross pieces and stringers, from which the rafters rose, and upright pieces supported the roof. It was of larch bark, with heavy poles and stones laid along, and pinned to keep the bark in its place and from warping in the sun. The cross-beams and joists overhead were the receptacle of nets, skins, dog sledges, light canoes, dried fish, herbs, and in fact the wealth and precious stores of the half-dozen families to whom this was evidently a comfortable home during a long and severe winter. Around three sides of the house was a raised platform, sufficient to seat and lodge the whole household. At the vacant side was the fireplace, where the utensils for cooking, and various fish, intestines of fish, and skins, were drying for use.

From this we passed into several other houses. The only persons there were one sick man, and several women and children. We found the women employed mending or making nets, or in dressing skins and making mats from splints of wood. The men of the village were off fishing. The dog sledges we saw accounted for the number of dogs which greeted us upon our entrance into the village. These people along this portion of the Amoor use dogs in summer to tow their boats along the shores, as well as to draw their sledges in their winter excursions.

Finding no fresh fish, nor a man who could go with us to guide us or procure us a sample of the cedar said to grow in the mountains ten miles from the river, the quality of which is said to be very fine, we were compelled to return to our boat. We were soon under way again. The afternoon was really pleasant—the first for the last ten days, and one of the most agreeable in the last fortnight, while the river and the country were all, as to scenery and natural objects, that one could wish.

Towards night, on the left, we saw snow-capped mountains fifty miles to the north. The scenery is truly beautiful, and the river one of the grandest in the world; the vegetation all a farmer could ask.

I sat for hours on the deck watching the shifting scenery, as we glided along with oars and current, like a fairy bark softly and silently along some mystic stream. A few sea-gulls were skimming lazily along the shore; a monster sturgeon occasionally darted out of the water for an instant, and with a heavy splash as soon disappeared; a solitary blue heron was seen upon an adjacent sand-bar or the point of a low island; the mournful cuckoo repeated his monotonous notes of love ; a solitary fisherman paddled his light canoe along the shore ; and in this you have the sum of animated nature seen of a warm summer's evening on one of the greatest rivers of the world, and amid natural scenery scarcely surpassed.

We stopped after dark at a native village on the left shore, where we found some Russian Cossacks, who were here for the purpose of making a settlement near this point. From them we learned that one of the iron steamers (the Lena) which had been sent out from Philadelphia by the Russian government, and put up at Nikolaivsky (mouth of Amoor), had passed up eight days previous. This we very much regretted. We had unfortunately missed her when in one of those interminable island chutes, through which we had been descending, while she was ascending the main stream. We had been congratulating ourselves all along on the passage, that we should meet her and obtain an inkling of news from the outside world, to say nothing of some little creature comforts that we might obtain for the inner man, and above all, to have seen the first successful steamer ascending the Amoor, American make (and perhaps a live Yankee engineer on board), puffing and blowing like a true Mississippi craft, against the current of its prototype ; but fate had ordered it otherwise.

We have been to-day in a country abounding in fine forests of fir, larch, and spruce, on the bottoms and upland, and cedar, ash, and pine on the mountains. This country is not so well adapted for farming settlements as higher up on the river, in the vicinity of the Songahree, because there is scarcely any open country here, and consequently it is much more laborious to clear away the timber to make the soil ready for the plough; but for timber it surpasses any section of country yet seen. The natives here use sails, for their large fishing boats, made of the skins of fish dressed and sewed together. We landed on the left bank, a few miles below the last village of Tsyan-Kah, kindled a fire of drift-wood upon the shore, and bathed at 10½ P.M.

CHAPTER LIII.

KAH-OOR-ME.

WEDNESDAY, July 1. At 12 M. the thermometer indicated 81° in the shade. We were off at 4 A. M. The wind still ahead, but the river being here more confined within solid shores, we made better headway. The scenery has been beautiful all day. In the afternoon we had fair wind for a few hours, and hoisting our sail, we made fine progress; but at 7 P. M. it hauled ahead again, and continued so during the night.

We stopped at the village of Kah-oor-me, a little below the mouth of the river Ger-en, on the left shore. We found here a few Cossacks, from whom we learned that it was the intention of the Russian government to form a settlement at this point. Fine spruce and larch are found here, as well as cedar on the mountains, three feet in diameter. There were several Manchoo merchants with their junk-like trading-boats on their way to Keezee, a Russian military station, two hundred and fifty miles above the mouth. They had furs and a variety of Chinese wares, with tea and arrakke, for trade with the natives. Their junks were manned by Goldee Tartars, and one of the merchants had a tent spread on the shore, where he was drinking tea, smoking his pipe, and ready to strike a trade. The captain's man Ivan purchased a few sables; they also had a number of good black bear-skins and other furs.

We are now about five hundred and fifty miles from Nicolaivsky. We observed to-day a number of canoes being towed along the shores by dogs. This I thought to be a very good use made of these howling, wolf-like curs, so troublesome and annoying at the camps and villages of the natives. These dogs are invaluable to these people in winter, when they use them to draw their sledges, generally having twelve to each loaded sledge. They are fed on fish, and have, when worked, a dried salmon each day. They are rather indifferent-looking animals, but their skins are also valuable, the hair being long and dense, and when dressed, make warm and excellent winter boots or garments; so that after all, these animals that seemed so worthless and annoying to us at first, are in reality a choice gift of the Good Spirit to these people.

Having a moon and not much wind, we concluded to float with the current during the night. The men having been dismissed from the oars at 9 P. M., I steered till 1 A. M., when I gave way to Captain Fulyhelm, who stood till daylight, when he was relieved by his servant. When I gave way we saw on our left a distant mountain peak, from which smoke was issuing apparently. 'Tis said that there are active volcanoes near the Amoor. This may be one of them, though we might have been mistaken, or possibly deceived by some other cause producing the apparent smoke or vapor; it however ascended in a column to a very great height, and had a light, steam-like appearance. We afterwards, however, saw another, and since seeing the burning mountains of Japan and Kamschatka, I am satisfied that they were volcanoes. The peaks were lofty and covered with snow, and I should judge, fifty to sixty miles distant.

Thursday, July 2. At 12 M. thermometer 79°. We floated on during the night, making fair progress, the river being less sinuous, and the current quite four miles per hour. The wind is adverse, but not so violent as on previous days. On the right we have snow visible on high mountains—a long and elevated sierra—in the deep gorges of which the snow lies like so many bright lines of silver reflected by a noonday sun. Some of the peaks are bald, but their sides are generally wooded.

At 12 M. we found frozen snow on the sandy point of an island. It had been preserved in this manner: In the winter a great drift of snow had taken place, which in the spring had been covered from the adjacent bar, by a drift of sand covering it, several feet thick, and thus preserved from the action of the sun. We landed and provided ourselves with a bucketful, which made the river water very cooling and pleasant. It was a great treat. We saw on the main shore of the river, opposite this island, evidences of a great and peculiar current of air, which had piled up ridges of sand ten to fifteen feet high.

During the afternoon we had occasional fair wind, and the river being straight, we made good progress. More lofty mountains on the right, with snow in the gorges. We kept as near the right bank as possible towards evening, in order to enter the right hand channel at a village, where it is separated by an island or a succession of islands from the main river, leading into the lake of Kee-ze, on which there are Russian settlements. The main river leads far to the left, with a broad and rapid current, and if entered, would sweep us past the lake and station at which we wished to halt. We hugged the right shore, because boats are frequently drawn by the current or drifted by the wind past the post, in spite of all the exertions of their crews.

We went on till 12 P. M., when it came on to blow very hard, and the moon being obscured by clouds, and again hid behind lofty mountains, under whose base the river run, we concluded best to land and await daylight. We landed on the right shore, in the shade of a dark forest. The scenery has been grand during the day, the river noble, the country densely wooded, but mostly of pine and aspen. Some of the more lofty mountains are bare of timber. Upon these it is said great numbers of animals congregate during the summer, in order to avoid the flies and other insects so troublesome in the low lands and forests. These mountains are celebrated for the resort of great numbers of mountain-sheep of large size. During the afternoon we had showers, and during the day squalls of rain, accompanied with lightning, have been seen on the mountains.

CHAPTER LIV.

LAKE KEEZEE AND MARINSKY POST.

FRIDAY, July 3. About 1 A. M., the weather looking more favorable, and the barge of Count Admiral Puchachin, the Russian Ambassador to Pekin, coming along, we cast off from the shore, and proceeded on our way. We had not gone far when the barge of the admiral grounded; we kept more to the right, and escaped the bar; within a short time, however, his barge came on, and passed us again.

The night proved pleasant, with but a light wind, and when I retired, at 2 A. M., we expected to find ourselves in the lake near Keezee, by 8 A. M. The fates were, however, against us, for about daylight, Captain Fulyhelm having also retired, leaving Evan to steer our boat, he rowed into a small right-hand chute, which ought to have been passed, and which proved a perfect labyrinth. We meandered, turned, and twisted in this miserable place till about 2 P. M., when we finally emerged into a lake, which also proved to be very bad navigation. We rowed out into it for some distance, when we sighted a remarkable rock, which Captain Fulyhelm at once recognized, he having been here the year previous, by way of the river from its mouth. This decided our latitude and longitude, but how to get out was the next question. The water now became too shoal for us to proceed by rowing, and the opposite shore was four miles off. Our Cossacks were soon overboard, wading in different directions to find deeper water, while I took the skiff to sound out a channel of escape. We were several hours, however, in getting to the opposite shore, near which we discovered the deep water to be—our Cossacks towing our boat by main strength through the mud and water into it, some eight miles from where we had entered the lake.

While in the chute we had heard guns saluting Admiral Puchachin at the military post of Marinskey. We reached the post at 5 P. M. This place was first settled in 1851–'2, by the servants of the Russian American Company, as a trading post with the natives. Afterwards the Russian government selected it as a military station, and erected earthen batteries on a point nearly opposite the junction of the lake and river. The two places—Keezee and Marinskey post—are little more than a mile apart, on the right shore, and both military stations with a village attached.

The importance attached to this settlement arises from the fact that from this there is a communication by the way of the lake, with four to seven feet water, to within twelve miles of the bay of De Castries, which is the best harbor near the mouth of the Amoor, and easy of access, and through which much communication has already been had.

De Castries is situated on the main coast of Tartary, one hundred miles south of where the Amoor enters the straits, and two hundred miles to the mouth by way of the river and lake. De Castries has good water and anchorage for any ship, with fresh water convenient. It is not considered safe in the winter, when the ice is running, but it is said that a breakwater can be erected within the bay, so as to render it secure at all seasons.

At the two posts there are accommodations for two thousand soldiers. One battalion is now stationed at Marinskey. It was from this point that the Russian troops came who repulsed the Allies at De Castries during the war. It is about forty miles from the Amoor to De Castries, and the whole distance could be traversed by a railroad, or by steamers on the lake and a railroad of less than twelve miles, thereby avoiding the difficult navigation of the Straits of Tartary. A telegraph is to be erected from De Castries to Nicolaivsky this year, an engineer being now on his way down the river to survey the route.

The country around Keezee is generally mountainous, except on the side next the Amoor. A very high mountain, with much snow upon it, is seen to the south-west. The lake is a shallow, irregular body of water, fed by many mountain streams, some of which have their sources in perpetual snow. It extends sixty miles in length by ten to fifteen in breadth. About this lake and the adjacent parts of the Amoor there is a perfect labyrinth of islands, lakes, chutes, and channels, all communicating with the main river, so that one is perplexed which way to go, and without other knowledge, must float with the current.

The season has been wet, raining almost daily during

the spring and summer, in consequence of which their gardens are quite ruined. The people do not look healthy. I have no doubt the climate, added to all the wants and lack of conveniences of new settlements, make it an uncomfortable place. Admiral Puchachin remained but a short time here, and had left before we came up.

We departed at 7 P. M. Light favorable wind, and raining. The wind soon, however, hauled ahead. We passed a Russian village on an island to the left, with gardens facing the river, and a little lower down, in a chute, an encampment of Manchoo trading-boats, with quite a large number of natives. Their boats were hauled to the shore, and bark tents erected along the banks. It continued to rain and blow, and at 11½ P. M. we were blown ashore upon a willow bar.

CHAPTER LV.

A NIGHT OF DANGER.

SATURDAY, July 4. The rain and wind continued during the night. We were under way, however, at 4 A. M., struggling against a head wind with oars and current-sail. At 10 A. M. we overtook the barge of the Archimandrite Avvokomb, with others of the suite of Count Admiral Puchachin. This reverend gentleman is one of the returned fathers of the Russo-Greek mission at Pekin, now on his way to join Count Puchachin's embassy. He is well versed in the different Tartar dialects, and speaks Chinese like a native. During his ten years' residence in China he visited Canton overland, and from his travels in China and Tartary, understands the Celestials well politically, religiously, and strategically. This is the same gentleman whom I had visited at Irkutsk, and from whom I gathered much valuable information in relation to Tartary and China.

They had left Schilkah seven days after us, and had passed us while we were in some island chute. Their barge was a large, roomy vessel, with a large crew, and managed both by oars and sail. They had not rested at all on the way, but were straining every nerve to reach the sea. From them we learned that General Moncarieff had proceeded with the regular military expedition as far as Igoon, and was encamped opposite that city, determined to have a talk with the Chinese authorities, but as yet nothing of moment had transpired in regard to the question of boundary.

The day proved a very boisterous one, with the thermometer at 60°, and much rain. We rowed on, however, till near dark, when Captain Fulyhelm thought it best to land for the night, as we were in a part of the river liable to high winds and rough water. In fact, during the afternoon the waves had so tossed us as to make it any thing but pleasant. The stowage of our baggage and stores was all deranged, and the boat not too dry for comfort. We were now nearest the left shore, and concluded to make it, in order to effect a landing for the night, before dark. We rowed on, but before we reached the shore our boat grounded, five hundred yards off. It was now dark, the storm increasing, and not being able to discern the nature of the shore below us, we concluded to push out into the stream, and try to make the right shore, where we had a mountain in view. We now hoisted sail, the waves being so high that our men could do nothing with the oars. In the course of half an hour we reached near the opposite shore, but found no better success in approaching it to make a landing than we had on the left. After much time lost, and coming upon a bar where the ground swell was rather high, we found that the shocks were too violent for the safety of our boat. We pushed her out into the stream again, but the wind was so violent, that with all hands at the oars, we could not breast it. I now took the skiff, with one man, and rowed along near the shore, which was here a sand-bar, to see if within any reasonable distance water sufficient to land our boat could be found ; but having gone near a mile, found the water still shoal, and the bar extending, with a heavy sea on it. I then returned to the barge and reported progress. Captain Fulyhelm still thought that we must be going with the current, but after half an hour steady pulling with the oars, and the current-sail down, we came to the conclusion that we were making no progress. I now wished to hoist sail and run before the wind up along the right shore until we found a place upon which to effect a landing. The captain was, however, still of the opinion that we could go with the current, and did not like to turn back. Another half hour passed, and the men by this time were fagged out, proving the impossibility of further progress in a downward direction. It was 1 A. M. ; the storm on the increase, with squalls of rain. Finally the captain said, " You may do as you choose." I then had the sail hoisted, and putting her before the wind, with a man on the bow sounding the depth of water, and taking the steering oar myself, run her up along the shore as near as the depth of water would permit, and in half an hour we found a good landing on a dry beach at the foot of a lofty mountain.

The men were absolutely wearied out, for they had been pulling very hard all day, besides the extra fatigue of the night, so that when we struck the shore they expressed themselves much pleased with my skill in navigation. Nor had they relished much the force of the wind or the height of the waves. They soon sunk to rest on the fore part of the boat, while Evan watched till daylight.

This is a part of the river subject to high winds; at times dangerous to small craft, owing to the peculiar formation of the mountains, which creates a current of air sweeping in this direction from the Okhotsk sea.

After all our toil we have only made to-day ten miles. The fact is, we had escaped shipwreck by the merest chance, and I not only felt relieved, but truly thankful to a higher source for our preservation and a safe harbor under the shadow of this friendly mountain. I laid down, but not to sleep; for my mind was too busy with the escape and excitement of the past night.

Sunday, July 5. We were off at 5 A. M. Wind still ahead, driving clouds, rain and fog, with the thermometer 59° at 12 M. The wind was so severe, and the waves so high at times, that we sought to keep as near the shore as possible. This part of the river is quite straight, and rock-bound on both shores. The scenery, of a fine day, would be of the most agreeable description, as the mountains rise on all sides grand and lofty; but such miserable weather makes one feel more like suicide than like admiring scenery.

The river is a mile wide. We struggled on till about 6 P. M., when the storm abated, and at 8 we had a glimpse of sunset upon the distant mountains, which was gorgeous in the extreme. I do not recollect seeing a mountain scene more richly painted—the different shades of the forests, the deep gorges with their tangled undergrowth, the high peaks, the bare and precipitous cliffs, all were lighted up in rich and mellow hues. This, added to the fact that the day had been so disagreeable, made it still more enchanting. It was not long before the wind began to blow again. We, however, struggled on until 10 P. M., when it came to blow a gale, and we were compelled to seek a landing.

We made a lee shore, the windward being out of the question. We landed on a low, rocky bar, with loose boulders scattered on the bottom. The shore was wet and boggy in places, and we had to go some distance to procure wood to make a fire to dry ourselves, and for the men to cook their supper. It proved a very uncomfortable night. It was 2 A. M. before I laid down, but not to sleep; for the ground swell was so heavy, and there not being sufficient water under us, our boat pounded so heavily against the rocky bottom that sleep was quite out of the question; added to which, the roar of the waves breaking upon the beach, made one think of shipwreck more than slumber. I was glad when daylight came, so that we might leave our uncomfortable quarters, rather preferring to breast the waves than be pounded to pieces on the beach. We were off at 3½ A. M.

CHAPTER LVI.

ANCIENT MONUMENTS.

MONDAY, July 6. We departed at daybreak. The weather was dreary and wet, and the wind still high, and blowing in squalls from the north-east. The river being very rough, we made miserable progress till about 6 P. M., when the wind lulled, and we made all haste to reach the Russian village of Michaelovskey. We rowed on until near 10 P. M., when the lights in the village were seen. We soon reached it. We had proposed to pass the night at this village, but upon landing, learned that Mr. Bodisco, a Russian officer from Nikolaivsky, was there. We hastened up the bank, guided by a peasant, to find him. We were both anxious to learn something from the outside world—Captain Fulyhelm, of the Russian American Company's ships expected at the Amoor on De Castries, and myself, to learn if there were any chance vessels arrived from China or California.

We soon found Mr. Bodisco, and were delighted to learn that four American vessels had already arrived either at De Castries, or were on their way to Nikolaivsky. This encouraged us so much that we determined to push on during the night, in order to take advantage of

ANCIENT TARTAR MONUMENT ON THE AMOOR

Page's 293-300.

the calm which now prevailed, hoping, if the weather proved favorable, we might possibly reach Nikolaivsky the following night.

We pushed off into the stream at 11 P. M. in high glee, keeping two men at the oars by turns during the night. It was very dark and cloudy, threatening rain; but the shores were at times discernible. We pulled on, keeping in mid-river as near as we could. I continued to steer till 2 A. M., the weather rather improving as the morning advanced. At 6 A. M. thermometer indicated 59°, and at 12 M. 69°. The river here is broad and majestic, with a current of four miles per hour; the shores generally covered with forest.

Tuesday, July 7. Thermometer at 6 A. M. 60°; at 12 M. 65°. We continued on rowing during the night. It remained quite calm, the first for many nights past. The morning proved pleasant; the sun shone out warm at 10 A. M. The river and surrounding country are on a magnificent scale. The vast stream is like a sea of glass. The shores and mountains are beautifully variegated by the different-colored foliage of the various species of trees growing in distinct belts, according to the nature of the soil or the elevation. At 12 M. we came to a rocky promontory on the right shore, one hundred and thirty miles above Nikolaivsky, where are to be seen some ancient stone monuments, commemorating Tartar supremacy centuries since in these remote regions. The cliff rises abruptly from the beach, which forms in a beautiful little sandy cove, between the two points of the overhanging cape, which arises to the height of one hundred feet, upon the summit of which there is table land extending for some distance, covered with oak, aspen, and fir, with a rich undergrowth of grass, flowers, and shrubs. Landing at the cove and ascending by a steep and difficult footway, between where the rock became solid and perpendicular, we reached the summit. On the westernmost point stand two of the monuments, and about four hundred yards to the east, upon a more elevated point and on a bare rock foundation, stands a third. The cliff faces the south.

Looking up the river, you have a very extensive view of the Amoor, with a large island to the left, opposite to which, on the right shore, there is a Ge-lak village, two miles distant. Far to the west, on the opposite side of the river, stretch extensive plains, with streams of water or outlets of the Amoor and Amgoon meandering through them. To the north, the river is seen stretching in the distance till the shores are lost to view, with a snow-capped sierra rising against the horizon. On the west, the horizon is bounded by ranges of lofty mountains, while to the east the gradual rising of the woodland obstructs the view. It is a very beautiful landscape, and seen under a bright sun and on a lovely summer day, is hardly surpassed by any I have ever seen.

On the table-land, back of the two first-mentioned monuments, are several excavations or pits, both within and without the remains of a wall or the fallen and crumbled ruins of a large building—these remains being now from six to ten feet above the surrounding soil. Near these monuments are to be seen several stones, nearly square, with a groove cut through their surface from side to side to a depth of an inch. These are supposed to be

ANCIENT TARTAR MONUMENT ON THE AMOOR

Page's 293-300.

altars of sacrifice, the groove serving to conduct the blood of the victim into the proper vessel. These altars undoubtedly were once elevated and within the temple.

The ground was richly covered with green sward, and a number of plants and flowers were springing up around. One large fir tree, which had withstood the devastating effects of fire, yet visible in the adjacent forest, had been felled by the occupants of a Russian post station for firewood or some other purpose. This we thought a desecration of this holy mount. Between the first two monuments two poles, forty feet high, trimmed and the bark removed, except near the top, were planted in the ground. At the top were a few branches decorated with wreaths and bound together with vines or bark. Upon the monuments were wreathed garlands of finely worked splint or the stripping of some tree, bound together at intervals with willow twigs. The base of the monuments, as well as the altars of sacrifice, were also dressed with shavings of wood, worked to represent flowers, thickly planted around in the earth. At a far jutting point of the rock, some broken moss-covered stones indicated the remains of another monument; here also the reverent hands of devotees had wreathed the wooden flowers. This work of pious remembrance bestowed upon these ancient remains of former Mongol power, were evidently devotional offerings of the natives of the country, who have for the place and its ancient uses some vivid tradition, sacred and lasting, and this was undoubtedly the annual offering, accompanied perhaps by the sacrifice of an animal in propitiation of the spirit of the place.

Standing upon this remote wild spot, where more than

six hundred years previous, the agents of Genghis Khan had stood, or perhaps himself, erecting these monuments or laying the foundation of the structure which they commemorate, calling upon God to "give grace to his empire"—I could not but reflect upon the westward progress of that vast Tartar horde for many centuries afterwards, until finally the grandson of the Great Mogul himself made the very heart of Russia bleed, cities to smoke in ruins, whole districts to be laid waste, and men in tens of thousands to be dragged in chains to slavery and death. Then came ages of the decline of those restless and ruthless Tartar hordes, and the gradual but steady advance of the Sclavonic power, and now the Russian finds himself master of the easternmost limits of the ancient dominions of Ghenghis; while at the same time he rests secure in his citadal of the Kremlin or in his winter palace on the shores of the Neva, while Tartar power and Tartar supremacy have become almost annihilated before the retributive sword of the Czars. Six hundred years have sufficed to wipe almost from memory the vast power and world-wide conquest of the Moguls, who had empire from the shores of the Pacific to the gates of Moscow; and now Moscow, then weak and tributary, has stretched forth "the force of her hand every where" from the shores of the Baltic to the coasts of the great Eastern Ocean. Nay, from Cracow to Sitka, over a longitudinal distance of two hundred and ten degrees, you may now travel under the protection of the Sclavonic eagle and upon Russian territory—more than half round the globe. What is left to be done in Asia? Only to place the second son of the Sclavic Czar on the throne of Ghenghis.

It would be a vast step in the progress of the Mongol race and of civilization and worthy the great advance and the great epochs of the nineteenth century, and the only means by which nearly half of the inhabitants of the earth can be Christianized and brought within the pale of commerce and modern civilization. May we not look to this as a solution of the Chinese riddle? for without Russian interposition the Mongol race must go down in intestine religious wars, pestilence, and famine, pressed as they now are on all sides by the irresistible force of Christian powers.

These thoughts came, as if the spirits of the slumbering dead beneath my feet, on the Cape of Ghenghis, were holding up to me a mirror, in which the past and future of these two contending forces, Sclavic and Tartar, were shadowed and revealed. They have been wrestling for a thousand years. The blood of Japhet has triumphed over that of Shem. The curse of Noah is about to be accomplished, the prophecy fulfilled, and Asia Christianized.

CHAPTER LVII.

THE MONUMENTS.

The following interpretation of the writing upon the monuments was given to me from the Russian by Captain Phillip Ayers, a Russian officer at the Amoor in the service of the government there under Governor Kosakevitch, a gentleman learned in languages. Archimandrite Avvokoom, by whom it was rendered from the original, is the prelate previously spoken of, now going to China as the interpreter of Count Puchachin's embassy.

CONCERNING THE STONE MONUMENT AND THE INSCRIPTIONS UPON IT.

"Every thing proves that the spot where the monument is standing was once the site of a temple devoted to the worship of Budha, which, in Chinese language, was called '*Youn-nen-se*,' *i. e.*, 'The Temple of Eternal Repose.' This denomination is testified to by two inscriptions on the stone—one in Chinese, the other in the Mongolian language. The irregular disposition of words in both inscriptions shows that they have been made by some

ANCIENT TARTAR MONUMENT ON THE AMOOR

Page's 293-300.

unlearned Mongolian Lama who had been living at the temple.

"The inscription in Chinese, written in the copy in the middle in the upper part, is read horizontally from the right hand to the left, as follows: '*Tsen-youn-neen-se.*' According to the Chinese construction, these words ought to be placed in the following order: '*Youn-neen-tsin-se,*' *i. e.* 'Deed concerning the Temple (or Monastery) of Eternal Repose.'

"In the Mongolian inscription, consisting also of four words written vertically, it is difficult to decipher the first word from the left hand. It certainly ought to correspond to the first Chinese word, viz.: 'to remember,' 'to recollect,' 'to inscribe,' 'memoranda,' etc. But, according to the manner in which it is written, it is impossible to indicate positively a Mongolian word that has a similar signification. Leaving the honor of interpreting it to persons better acquainted with the Mongolian language, I will only speak of the other three words. That they are quite indistinctly written, so that they would not be correctly deciphered and interpreted without the assistance of the Chinese inscription, is also true.

"These words are the following: '*Youn-nenn-soomah.*' The two first words are Chinese, left without being translated. The last is Mongolian, and means pagoda, temple. All the three words together signifies 'temple,' '*Younn-nenn,*' *i. e.*, 'of eternal repose.'

The inscriptions on the sides of the monument are as follows: 1st. On the left hand, in the first line, are the Sanscrit words, '*Ott-mane-badd-ma-choon*' in Thibetian letters, *i. e.*, 'Oh! mane badma, give.' The inferior part of this line incloses the Chinese words, '*Dai-youan-schoochje-le-goon-boo,*' *i. e.* great Youan (the Dynasty of Youan), 'may the force of the hand be extended every where;' or, in Russian, 'may the power of the great Youan (Mongolian) dynasty be extended every where.'

"On the same hand, in the second line, the same Sanscrit words, first in Chinese letters: '*An* (*Omm*) *ma-ne-ba-me,*' and afterwards, in Ooygoonian letters: '*Ott-ma-ne-bad-me-choon.*'

"2d. On the right hand, in the first line, the Chinese words: '*Dai-youan-schou-chie-lee-goon-boo,*' *i. e.*, 'The power of the great Youan Dynasty extends everywhere.'

"In the second line, the first letters are Chinese: '*An,*' after that, in Ooygoonian letters: '*Ott-ma-ne-bad-me-choon;*' further, in Thibetan letters, the same words: '*Ott-ma-na-bad-me-choon.*'

"There is nothing more.

"ARCHIMANDRITE AVVOKOOM."

M. Huc gives us a further solution of this inscription. In his recollections of a journey through Tartary and Thibet we find the following:

"The Thibetans, as we have before said, are eminently religious.

"There exists at Lha Ssa a touching custom, which we are in some sort jealous of finding among infidels. In the evening, as soon as the light declines, the Thibetans, men, women, and children, cease from all business and assemble in the principal parts of the city and in the public squares. As soon as the groups are formed, every one sits down on the ground, and begins slowly to chant his prayers in an under tone, and this religious concert produces an immense and solemn harmony throughout the city, powerfully affecting to the soul! The first time we heard it we could not help making a sorrowful comparison between this pagan town, where all prayed in common, with the cities of Europe, where people would blush to make the sign of the cross in public.

"The prayer chanted in these evening meetings varies according to the season of the year: that which they recite to the rosary is always the same, and is only composed of six syllables—*Om mani, padmé houm.* This formula, called briefly the *mani*, is not only heard from every mouth, but is everywhere written in the streets, in the interior of the houses, on every flag and streamer floating over the buildings, printed in the Landza, Tartar, and Thibetan characters. Certain rich and zealous Buddhists even entertain, at their own expense, companies of Lamas for the propagation of the *mani;* and these strange missionaries, chisel and hammer in hand, traverse field, mountain, and desert, to engrave the sacred formula on the stones and rocks they encounter in their path.

"According to the celebrated Orientalist Klaproth, *Om mani, padmé houm* is nothing but a Thibetan transcription of a Sanscrit formula introduced into Thibet from India, and which has, in that language, a complete and indubitable sense not to be found in the idiom of Thibet. *Om* is with the Hindoos the mystic name of the divinity, with which all prayers commence. This mystic particle is also equivalent to the interjection Oh, and expresses a profound religious conviction; it is, in some sort, the formula of an act of faith. *Mani* signifies jewel, precious thing; *padma*, the lotus (*padmé* is the vocative case of that word); *houm*, is equivalent to our Amen. The literal sense of this phrase is then:

> Om mani padmé houm!
> O the jewel in the lotus! Amen!

The Lamas assert that the doctrine contained in these marvellous words is immense, and that the whole life of man is insufficient to measure its depth and extent. We were curious to know what the regent thought on this subject. This was his explanation: animated beings are divided into six classes—angels, demons, men, quadrupeds, flying creatures, and reptiles. These six classes correspond to the six syllables of the formula, *Om mani padmé houm*. All animated beings revolve by continual transmigration, and, according to their merits or demerits, in these six classes, until they have attained the height of perfection, when they are absorbed and lost in the grand essence of Buddha—that is to say, in the eternal and universal soul whence emanate all other souls, and to which all others, after their temporary evolutions, will reunite and become one. Animated beings have, according to the class they belong to, particular means of sanctification for ascending to a superior class, obtaining perfection, and of final absorption in the divine essence. Men who recite very often and very devoutly *Om mani*, &c., avoid falling after death into any other of the six classes, and are immediately absorbed in the soul of Buddha. The jewel being the emblem of perfection, and the lotus that of Buddha, these words may perhaps be taken to express the desire of acquiring perfection, in order to be reunited to Buddha ; and the symbolic formula, 'O the jewel in the lotus ! Amen,' may be paraphrased, 'O that I may attain perfection, and be absorbed in Buddha ! Amen.'

"According to the explanation of the regent, the *mani* may be, in some sort, the *résumé* of a vast Pantheism, the base of all Buddhist belief. The educated Lamas say that Buddha is the one necessary being, independent, the principle of all things. The earth, the stars, man ; all that exist, is a partial and temporary manifestation of Buddha. All has been created by Buddha, in the sense that all proceeds from him, as the light from the sun. All beings emanating from Buddha have had a beginning, and will have an end ; but as they proceeded necessarily from the universal essence they will be reabsorbed also necessarily. Thus as Buddha is eternal, his manifestations always have been and always will be, although taken separately—all have had a beginning and will have an end."

We remained some time upon the promontory of Ghenghis Khan, as I named it, because it seemed to be but just to the Great Mogul that this far eastern point of land, made historical by these long-preserved monuments, denoting perhaps the limits of his conquests east, should receive his name, in accordance with the inscription—as the Youan dynasty was that of Ghenghis. On a Chinese map that I have seen this point is called Toon; the Russians call it Teer or Tver, or rather that is the name, perhaps native, (Gelack) of the village just below the promontory. Just above the village on the side of the mountain there is a solitary loghut, built and occupied as a Russian post station. The island of the river from the promontory is called Veder-Bahl. The river ten miles above divides into three branches, two of which unite at this point, while the other passes off to the left, where it unites with the waters of the Amgoon—a considerable river coming in from the north-west. Several chutes, forming islands and lakes, again make off lower down to the north, which do not unite again until within ten miles of Nikolaivsky.

While standing upon the promontory we saw in the river several large grampuses, for the first time, making their way up stream two hundred miles from the sea. We descended reluctantly from this beautiful spot, rather commending the reverend Lamas for the selection of it as a site for their pagoda. Our boat was ready at the beach, and pushing her into the stream, we floated along with the current, as near the right shore as possible, casting lingering glances back towards the cape, and enjoying the wild but beautiful scenery of the shore. Mr. Bodisco overtook us at 6 P. M., but as he was in a whaleboat with five oars, and on official business, we could only keep company for a short time.

It coming on to blow about 8 P. M., and being unable to reach the right shore, which we wished to do in order to cross the river at the most favorable point above Nikolaivsky, we hoisted sail in order to gain the shelter of an island on the opposite shore, two miles distant. We, however, sailed too far, the wind and current both setting us towards another island chute, that would have carried

ANCIENT TARTAR MONUMENT ON THE AMOOR.

Page's 293-300.

us thirty miles out of our direct course. We had now to sail against the current, added to which, our men pulled slowly with their oars, and with both sail and oars we had a hard pull before we were able to reach the friendly shore of an island. We, however, touched land at 11 P. M., where we had a comfortable night, free from wind.

CHAPTER LVIII.

ARRIVAL AT NIKOLAIVSKY.

WEDNESDAY, July 8. Thermometer at 12 M. 79°. During the night we heard the mournful notes of the cuckoo—one of the birds that we have found inhabiting the shores of the Amoor from its head to its mouth. We were under way at 3 A. M., in order to take advantage of the early part of the day before the wind rose, the mornings being generally calm on the lower part of the river. We got on quite well till 3 P. M., when the wind again became high. We contended with it till 10 P. M., making but little headway, when we were finally blown on to the right shore of an island. Our men were perfectly exhausted. As we were on a lee shore, we lay pounding all night—the waves at times breaking over our boat, and making it rather uncomfortable.

The waves dashed against the shore with much force, and the boat tossed so that the men preferred to sleep on shore. The night was bright starlight, and but for the wind, would have been quite warm. We are not more than fifteen miles above Nikolaivsky.

THURSDAY, July 9. Thermometer at 12 M. 77°. We were under way at 2 A. M., in order, if possible, to get the benefit of a lull in the wind about daylight; it was still blowing, but we conceived it better to be afloat than pounding against the shore, though the shore was soft mud. After a great struggle we succeeded in crossing to the opposite side, but found it quite out of the question to make any headway. After trying both oars and poles, and coming on to shoal water, our men got overboard and essayed to tow our boat; but this seemed also to be a difficult process, so we finally concluded to sail out into the main current, and try if we could not succeed against the wind with the current sail.

The waves were rolling too high for comfort, or safety to our style of craft; for we soon found that neither oars nor sail would manage her, and we were at the mercy of the wind, broadside to in the trough of the sea, perfectly beyond our control. Our only safety lay in hoisting sail, with the danger of capsizing; but it was our last resort, for it now seemed probable that we might be under the disagreeable necessity of swimming to shore, not very conveniently near. However, we hoisted sail; she came round before the wind, and after an hour's sailing as near the wind as we could hold her, we effected a landing. The men were quite worn out, and we rested on shore to cook dinner.

While we were here a whaleboat, rowed by six sailors, sent by Captain Chickachoff of the steamship America to Captain Fulyhelm, came up to invite him to proceed in it to Nikolaivsky, but he declined, as we expected to be able to reach it in the course of the night.

We got under way again at 4 P. M. The captain wished again to try the channel, but to this I objected, having determined, if possible, not to leave the left bank again, as it was that on which the point we wished to reach was situated. We wished to try the current sail, but finally concluded to make what progress we could with poles, and the men in the water towing, for it was too shoal to approach the shore as we proceeded. We kept on this way till 10 P. M., when the wind increasing in force, we were compelled to land at the first convenient place where the water would permit, as well for shelter as to rest the men. We have made through the whole day only about six miles.

As we toiled slowly along the shore we came in view of several square-rigged vessels, lying at anchor opposite the port of Nikolaivsky. My reflections were certainly very pleasurable, after a journey of over a year's duration from the shores of the Baltic Sea to the very verge of the Pacific Ocean, whose tides, waves, and winds we were already under the influence of—the approaching termination of a voyage not always very agreeable or comfortable, with the probability of a speedy passage in one of these winged messengers that would land me once again at the point of my departure, after an absence of two years, all contributed to fill me with heartfelt thanks to a protecting Providence for my safe arrival so nearly to that ocean whose opposite waves washed the shores of my own country, and upon whose bosom I could float to my home.

FRIDAY, July 10. Thermometer at 12 M. 78°. We were comfortable during the night, the wind having abated very much before midnight, to which must be added the reflection of the near approach of our present journey's end, with ships and the fort of Nikolaivsky in view. Our Cossacks took the masts of the ships for church steeples.

They could imagine nothing but a church steeple so tall, and were surprised when told what they were.

The wind abated during the night, and when we attempted to shove off at 3 A. M., we found our boat hard aground on the sticky clay of the shore. The subsiding of the wind after a storm of some days duration, together with a tide of something like a foot, had left us firmly embedded. Our crew, after several ineffectual attempts to launch the boat, stripped, and took to the water cheerfully. They tugged and toiled for an hour, so deeply was the keel sunk in the mud, before they succeeded in getting her afloat. I was so worn out, and we glided along so quietly after we got off, that I fell asleep, and did not awake until our keel grated upon the beach at Nikolaivsky.

At 8 A. M. we paid our respects to Rear Admiral General Kosakevitch, governor of the sea coast of Eastern Siberia. He received me cordially, and welcomed me to his house and to the province of the "sea coast." I delivered to him, from Governor General Mouravief, a package containing letters in my behalf. I remained but a short time, as the governor was about to go on board the steamer Amoor, on her first trial trip. This was one of the iron steamers constructed at Philadelphia and shipped here in a sailing vessel, and put up during the winter and spring, destined for the navigation of the Amoor to its head.

The governor informed me that he had ordered a room to be prepared for me—the best to be obtained in the place—which Mr. Bodisco had the kindness to conduct me to. I was rather unwell after the fatigues and excitement of the voyage, and chose to remain on board of our little bark for a day or two. After taking a hasty look at the water-front of the rising city, I retired to our boat to rest for the day. It was pleasant and clear, with the usual sea breeze.

In fact, I was really sick, and when the excitement and necessity for further action was over, I found that the wear and tear of the voyage, particularly the last fifteen or twenty days, had rather used me up, and I required rest and physic. My head ached, my stomach was topsy-turvy, my bones ached, my back ached—I ached all over—good indications of approaching fever. But it was no place, nor no time to be sick; therefore I must give it up. My little stock of medicines that I had laid in on the other side of the world were not exhausted, and I swallowed twenty grains of quinine, then a blue pill the size of a bullet, and a pill of opium, and went to sleep.

CHAPTER LIX

NIKOLAIVSKY

SATURDAY, July 11. Temperature 12 M. 78°. The morning was fair and pleasant, the usual sea breeze blowing, white-caps dancing, and a very considerable surf breaking upon the beach east of the post. I called upon General Kosakevitch at 10 A. M., this being his name's day. It is a custom in Russia for persons to keep the anniversary of the day on which they were baptized and received their name, as a holiday, and for their friends and acquaintances to call upon them. Particularly, all persons in authority receive calls from the officers of government. I also called, in company with Captain Fulyhelm, on Admiral Puchachin, at his lodgings. I found him very affable and agreeable, speaking English with a slow and measured tone, and with the slightest possible French accent. The ambassador was only awaiting the signal of Captain Chickachoff (steamer America), "ready for sea," to embark on his mission to Pekin. The Russian government is willing to compensate the Manchoo inhabitants on the left shore of the Amoor for their improvements and property, in case they do not wish to remain under Russian rule. The interference of the Manchoo authorities in the free navigation of the Amoor by Russia must be stopped. The river was more necessary to Russia than to China. It was only preserved by the Chinese in a wild state, neither useful to themselves, to mankind, to civilization, or to progress—while from the geographical isolation of Siberia, the Russians absolutely needed this only natural means of egress to the navigable waters of the ocean. Nor would Siberia alone be benefited by the navigation and settlement of this river—Manchooria would be vastly interested in the commerce that would immediately spring up and the money that would be expended upon its shores.

The admiral had experienced also much head wind on his passage down the Amoor, and Captain Chickachoff was under the necessity of cutting the cover of his boat off and casting it adrift in order to get on. He was twenty-five days in descending from Schilkah with a large crew and very light boat.

I dined with Governor Kosakevitch; the ambassador, Admiral Puchachin, and many other Russian officers were present, most of whom I had met before in Siberia or upon the upper waters of the Amoor or in Russia. The dinner was excellent, with wines of different kinds, winding up with champagne—the Russian custom. Although the only foreigner present, I found eight of the party speaking English.

I find at anchor in the river, opposite the post, the following American vessels: Schooner Lewis Perry, Captain Turner, from San Francisco, California, with assorted merchandise to Carlton & Burling, who are establishing a commercial house here; schooner General Pierce and bark Burnham, with assorted merchandise to Mr. Ludorf, from Hong Kong via Hakodadi ; bark Messenger Bird, Captain Homer, from Boston, with assorted merchandise to Pierce & Co., both of which are establishing houses here permanently ; bark Bhering, Captain Morse, from Boston, via Sandwich Islands, Kamschatka, and Hakodadi, to Mr. Cushing, of the house of W. H. Boardman & Co., of Boston, for many years in the Pacific trade, with a house at Petropaulosky of many years standing and the first to enter with the Russians into the Amoor, having established a house here also. The Bhering had also machinery and stores for the government and general merchandise.

This certainly was an unexpected and agreeable surprise to me to find the stars and stripes floating from the masts of so large an American fleet in these, until recently, unknown waters. The Russian steamer America and a small Russian schooner, with the new steamer Amoor, and the hulk of the steamer Argoon, built at Schilkah, but now dismantled, made up the entire fleet. Scattered along the shore were the remains of various barges, rafts, and vessels, which had found their resting place here, either from the waters above or from the waters outside. Anchors, chains, guns, hulks, engines, and machinery lay along the beach or preserved in temporary magazines, all going to show the importance of the rising post.

Sunday, July 12. Temperature at 12 M., 80°. A fine fair day, with sea breeze. Admiral Puchachin and suite embarked on board the America. On the morning of the 13th the America sailed. Governor Kosakevitch and suite embarked on the steamer Amoor to escort the admiral to sea. A salute in honor of the occasion was fired from the shore battery. The flags of the American vessels were displayed in honor of the occasion. The steamer and steamship proceeded down the river, returning the salute, and were lost sight of behind the projecting point of land, or Fort Point.

The day proved really lovely and of that pleasant and agreeable temperature just suited to frail humanity. I walked down upon the beach beyond Fort Point and bathed in the beautiful Amoor, where it was a luxury to walk along pebbly shores, with fine overhanging old pine trees sighing in the gentle sea breeze, and just enough surf to make the shores musical.

This place, "Port" Nikolaivsky, is situated about thirty miles above the entrance of the Amoor into the Straits of Tartary on the left shore, having for its defences two fortifications, a few miles below, one on each side of the river; one upon a low sand spit forming the eastern point of the bay, on which the town is built, and one opposite raised from the water on the shoal edge of the bank, which commands the approach to the town from up the river. A small bay makes in from the river, with a depth of seven feet of water, which makes a convenient and secure landing for small craft. The town is built on the shore of this bay, which rises to the height of fifty feet and extends off in a heavily-wooded plain to the foot of mountains, several miles distant.

The post was first established in 1853, as a military station, but has, by emigration from Siberia and Kamschatka, acquired about fifteen hundred inhabitants. The river opposite has a breadth of near a mile, while the current rolls broad and deep towards the sea. Though the tidal wave from the Straits of Tartary is felt here, yet it has no perceptible effect upon the current which flows at near four miles per hour. It is the seat of government for the eastern coast of Siberia and head-quarters of naval and military affairs for the regions round about. The site is not well chosen, either in respect to the land or water, for a commercial city. In the first place, large vessels must lie out in the stream, half a mile distant, from whence their cargoes must be lightered to the shore, while the land is wet and swampy and very difficult to reduce to a state of cultivation. The proximity to the straits renders it bleak and subject to terrific storms in the winter, and there are no very good lands for cultivation in its vicinity. On the whole, it is badly chosen, except perhaps for a post of defence. The commercial city should be built higher up on the river, where bold water and good land can be had, with comparative shelter from the winter storms.

CHAPTER LX.

AMERICAN RESIDENTS.

DURING my stay at Nikolaivsky the weather was remarkably pleasant, though the general complaint was that the spring had been very backward. The gardens also attested that; for the cabbage plants were yet small, and, after my arrival, potatoes were planted and plants set out. The best garden is at the governor's country residence, two miles to the west, upon the shore of the bay, where lettuce and radishes, under glass, were ready for the table. Here also the soldiers have gardens, to which the governor gives his special attention. A little further on is a Russian village, from whence grass and timber are procured, and where are beginning to be also poultry, eggs, and butter.

Governor Kosakevitch treated me very kindly while here, and gave me a permanent seat at his board during my stay. We also had a pic-nic at his farm in company with several ladies. We proceeded by water in the admiral's cutter, rowed by a boat's company of Russian sailors. The day was very pleasant. The governor had provided quite a beautiful surprise to us at his country seat, giving us a handsome repast. We looked at the garden and enjoyed ourselves seated or standing in front of the house, which is situated on the elevated shore of the bay, out of the port, having a fine view of the country to the west and south. The governor did every thing in his power to make me comfortable during my stay, and his officers and staff were also very agreeable gentlemen and treated me with much kindness. The American merchants and Mr. Ludorf also tendered me the freedom of "pot-luck," of which I readily availed myself.

The weather remained generally pleasant. The steamer Amoor steamed up on the 18th, and departed for the upper regions of the river at 6 P. M., with four small barges in tow. It is expected that she will ascend to Schilkah. She has some cargo, with officers and soldiers returning to Russia and Siberia. During the month of July the steamer Schilkah arrived from the upper waters. She remained until the 5th of August, when, taking Governor Kosakevitch on board, she steamed up the river. I was informed that the governor was going to select and settle upon the point for a new city between this and Kezee, and that perhaps this post would be abandoned to the soldiers and sailors, and for workshops for the fleet. The country about this is generally mountainous and densely wooded. Between this and De Castries, by way of Kezee, there are scattered a few Russian villages, which answer for post stations, the whole Russian population amounting to perhaps four thousand. Then there are the Gelack villages, including those also below and on the coast, which make up the whole sum of population.

The climate is certainly a harsh one in winter, the soil cold, wet, and poorly adapted to cultivation; while the spring is tardy and wet. The summer is too short for producing any thing but the hardier grains and vegetables. Timber is abundant, but not of the proper species for good ship-building, though for lighter river craft and building purposes it can be made to answer.

The several vessels were busy discharging and housing their cargoes of merchandise, while various store-houses were being erected in which to transact business permanently. The establishment of Messrs. Boardman & Cushing, built last year is the best, and very comfortably arranged, and, under the hospitable charge of Mr. Cushing, is very convenient for a hungry or dry soul, or for one seeking a readable book or paper from his well-stocked library, to be read lounging on a sofa in a pleasant sitting-room. Their buildings have been erected in this wooden country, at a cost of over seven thousand rubles, with iron roofs, and are really most excellent log buildings, well calculated to withstand the climate, and defy both cold and wet.

Messrs. Pierce & Co. have brought with them, in California style, a frame-house from the Sandwich Islands, with shingle roof—the first in the country, and it looks curious enough, with its high-peaked roof, trim, neat sides, and rakish appearance, among its massive log neighbors. The Russians think it impossible that this house can be made habitable for the winter, with its thin sides only, to resist the cold.

Messrs. Carlton & Co. have purchased a log-house, which they are refitting to suit their views of comfort, with San Francisco furniture, wide bedsteads, and white sheets.

Mr. Ludorf has a large commodious log-house, with zinc roof, nearly finished, for his head-quarters, and, with his assorted cargoes of Japanese, Chinese, German, English, French, and Yankee notions, can not fail to suit the tastes as well as drain the pockets of his customers.

Mr. Otto Esche, of San Francisco, whose vessel, the Conrad De Savin, I met coming up just within the river, as I was on my way out, is also about to establish a house here, and intends to reside permanently next year. He had landed at De Castries, and was on his way, via Kezee and the river, to Nikolaivsky.

The Russian-American Company have an establishment here, dealing generally in Russian merchandise and controlling the fur trade among the natives. They send out trading parties during the winter and spring. The head-quarters of the company will be removed from Ayan to this port next year, as the communication and supplies will come by way of the Amoor in future instead of overland by way of Yakutsk. Governor Fulyhelm will then reside here permanently, and perhaps the company will have a steamer or two upon the river to facilitate the transportation of their supplies down and furs up the river.

The schooner Lewis Perry sailed on the 30th of July. The General Pierce was sold to the Russian government, while the other vessels began to talk of departure. However, as neither the Burnham or Messenger Bird were prepared to take a passenger, I was left to the "Hobson's choice" of the only remaining vessel, the Bhering, without any particular port of destination, but an even chance of Hong Kong or Honolulu, via Hakodadi and Petropaulosky.

The departure of steamers and vessels, with the absence of the governor, tended to render the post a little dull, while the near approach of the departure of the remaining vessels began to make me pack up once again for one more movement eastward. The 8th of August was finally determined upon by Captain Morse, of the Behring, wind permitting, to sail, and upon her I was to traverse the Pacific for some months to come.

CHAPTER LXI.

VOYAGE TO JAPAN.

On the 8th of August, 1857, at sunrise, I was ready to embark, but the wind proved unfavorable till about 10 A. M., when we went on board. It was not long before the captain gave orders to weigh anchor, and in less than half an hour we were sailing down the Amoor.

From Nikolaivsky to the straits the channel changes from the left to the right shore, the river widening to some three miles at its mouth. We were provided with a pilot and eighteen Russian soldier-sailors, with a large launch and anchor, to assist us through the Leman, as they call the upper part of the Straits of Tartary. We came to anchor in the river before night the first day, the wind having shifted to the south, which prevented us from sailing out. The distance to De Castries is only about one hundred miles; but, in consequence of adverse winds, the crookedness of the channel, and the slight depth of water, we did not reach De Castries until the 27th of August, making the passage occupy nineteen days. We were frequently aground, becalmed, or detained by head winds. This, however, to vessels of the proper depth—not over thirteen feet—can all be overcome by the assistance of steam. A steam-tug of the proper construction would.

have taken us to De Castries, that is to sea, in twelve hours. Much detention must occur till steam is provided for this purpose. This must, however, speedily take place; the wants of the government alone will require it. The necessary coal for steamers is found in the greatest abundance on the island of Sak-hah-lin, just in view of the Amoor.

De Castries is accessible and commodious, with wood and water convenient and good holding ground. At this point vessels going into the Amoor will stop for a pilot as well as to forward despatches by way of the post to Kezee and Nikolaivsky. De Castries freezes in the winter and becomes inaccessible, and, in consequence of drift ice in the winter and spring, vessels would be in danger; but it is said that a breakwater can easily be constructed in the southern site of the bay that will render it perfectly safe during the winter.

We passed De Castries on the 27th. The coast of Tartary is everywhere rugged and flanked with mountains. The opposite coast of Sak-hah-lin is also mountainous, and in the region opposite this, good coal mines are found. The coal has been tested by the steamers here and found suitable for sea-going steamers. The steamer America has used it and is now on her way to China, burning this coal. The mines are convenient to the coast, and veins of eighteen feet in thickness have been found. They are said to be inexhaustible, ranging for a great extent along the island.

We coasted along the Gulf of Tartary to Emperor's Harbor, and then made the opposite coast of Sak-hah-lin, where the mountains are very lofty. On the 4th of

September, in the afternoon, we made the Japanese island of Jeddo or Matsmai, and, sailing near the islands of Oh-semah and Cosemah, off the entrance of the Straits of Sangar, the wind being contrary, we stood to sea until morning, when we entered the straits and sailed along the coast near to the city of Matsmai. This city, the residence of a prince, is very handsomely situated, facing the straits upon land sloping gently from the mountains to the sea. We coasted along, passing numerous Japanese junks of large size, entered the bay of Hakodadi, sailing in with a moderate breeze, cast our anchor in front of the city at 3 P. M. on the 5th September, nine days from De Castries and twenty-seven from Nikolaivsky, the whole distance not being more than eight hundred miles, or seven hundred from De Castries. At this season of the year the winds are from the south, which makes the voyage in a sailing vessel tedious and lengthy; while a steamer would make the voyage in three days from anchor to anchor.

It was a very agreeable surprise to us to find the stars and stripes floating at the top of a high pole on shore, for we had not been apprised of the appointment of a United States consular officer to this port. The custom-house officers came on board soon after our anchor was down, having an interpreter who spoke English after a fashion. The first question asked was, "What you want here?" Answer: "Trade, provisions, and water." This was not specific enough for Japanese purposes. We were then requested to specify what particular articles and the specific quantity of each. Mr. Cushing then furnished them with a list of the objects desired, adding one thousand *piculs* of rice. This made the officials open their eyes, and their mouths too, they absolutely declaring that there was no *lice* (rice) for sale; and from the number of persons on board—seventeen in all—thought it impossible that we could eat such a quantity—about sixty tons.

The captain treated them to wine and brandy, of which they partook—the champagne being their favorite. The chief of the party became sea-sick, and, drawing a very capacious pocket-book from the bosom of his dress, commenced swallowing silver-coated pills; but they did not seem to have the desired effect, for he soon had to leave his champagne and retire to the deck. They smoked their thimble-like brass pipes, filling them from their handsome pouches with very soft fine-cut tobacco, which was exhausted in about three puffs. They were handsomely dressed in silks and rich brocades, carrying fans, pipes, pouches, tobacco, flints and steel, and two swords each. The Japanese wear no tails like the Chinese or Tartars. They shave the head and face, with the exception of a small circle on the back of the head, between and behind the ears. This is carefully dressed and brought to a point on the top and centre of the head, and there confined by metallic rings or tied in a little queue the length and size of a finger. For pocket-handkerchiefs they use soft yellow paper, wiping their faces or hands and depositing the soiled pieces in the capacious sleeves of their garments, where it remains until a convenient opportunity presents to throw it aside. They are polite and courteous in their demeanor, making their bows with their hands upon their knees, and shaking hands with you, if you will, in European style. Their boat was rowed or sculled by nearly naked natives. In the stern was carried two banners, denoting the quality and functions of the officers.

The following morning Dr. Rice, Commercial Agent of the United States, came on board; he had only been here a short time, and came by the way of China. From him we were made acquainted with more recent affairs in China and our own country.

The doctor is housed in a very good and commodious residence in one of the Temple yards, and provided by order of the Governor with some half dozen soldiers, who perform the functions of boatmen, cooks, servants, compradores, barbers, washerwomen, &c. He has them already speaking several words of English, and they are engaged every day in taking lessons, which they reciprocate in teaching the doctor Japanese, in which he has made also some progress. The town is well situated, having in its rear a high promontory making into the straits, which breaks the force of the wind and waves and protects the inner harbor and port; a low strip of land unites the town with the main land to the north and protects the harbor in that direction; the shores of the bay sweep around forming the half of a circle, which makes it a very commodious and secure harbor, with good holding ground within four hundred yards of the town. The capacity of the bay is sufficient to accommodate several hundred ships. During our stay there were from four to five hundred junks in the harbor, frequently fifty arriving or departing in a day according as the wind or tide favored them. Their import cargoes consist of rice, and articles of the growth, produce or manufacture of the southern islands, while their export cargoes consist principally of fish, sea cabbage, soy, furs, skins, lumber, and timber, and various objects the produce of the sea and forest. Their domestic trade is all regulated by the proper officers through the custom-house, and all their affairs appear orderly and well regulated. In their shops you find a considerable variety of objects well adapted to their wants, habits, and climate. Cooper shops, blacksmiths, tinkers, barbers, bath-houses, ply their various vocations ; silk mercers, shoe stores, fruit and vegetable stalls, fancy shops, tea and tobacco venders all find customers and occupation ; trains of horses or bullocks with their cargoes strapped upon their backs, tied head to tail pass in long trains through the streets ; dogs bark and run with tail down away from the uncouth foreigner, while women gaze and children scamper from the approach of the red-haired white-faced man. The shaven priest looks askance with fan in hand protecting his bare skull from the hot sun, wondering in his mind who may be the God of such an outlandish uncouth set of barbarians with unshaven chins, leather-cased feet and legs, stove pipe hats, and candle-mould breeches. God be praised ! the priest ejaculates. God is great ! He has created many wonderful things.

During our stay the weather was pleasant ; the country looked fresh and verdant ; we procured potatoes, onions, tomatoes, rice, eggs, chickens, fish, apples, pears, tea, lacquered ware and silks.

A company of wrestlers were exhibiting in a square kind of rough enclosure back of the town ; the sides were enclosed with boards and cloth, and the top with bushes and cloth ; a range of boxes ran around the sides raised a few feet from the ground, which were occupied by the aristocracy, while the people were squatted on the ground around a platform of earth raised some three feet from the ground in the centre. The wrestlers entered from the rear and ranged themselves by nines on opposite sides of the platform or ring, in a sitting posture; they were naked except a girdle about the loins; they awaited the master of ceremonies, who now ascended the platform and announced in a loud singing tone and with many flourishes of his elegant fan the order of performance and the manner of the entertainment; he then descended making his bow to the audience; soon another attendant who appeared to be the property man of the establishment came upon the ring, and in a loud voice, with a peculiar flourish of his fan announced the names of the wrestlers by pairs, who immediately, one from each side, stepped upon the arena; the last attendant remained to direct the exercises and regulate the contest. The wrestlers walked back and forth, took a sup of water from a small wooden vessel, squatted upon their haunches, smoothed the sand upon the arena with their hands, rubbed their bodies and armpits with the sanded hand, scattered pinches of salt or some other charm from a little bag hanging to the corner post of the arena, faced one another half squatting, half standing, and at the word agreed upon between themselves or given by the master, sprang like tigers at each other's throats, with the guttural growling of bears. Now they tug and strain, bending every muscle to the combat, first at arms' length, then at under hold, again at back and side hold—they are well matched, and are blowing and puffing, and reeking with perspiration. The attendant arrests them as they stand, unlocking their muscular and brawny arms from close embrace to give them a few minutes respite—they take a sup of water, spit it out, stretch their limbs, squat upon their hocks, spread the sand with their hands, wipe their faces with sheets of paper handkerchiefs hanging to the corner posts of the arena, throw the soiled paper upon the ground, spit, blow the nose, and wipe their faces again with paper. The attendant now places them in exactly the position they held at first, and the combat is renewed with fierce and excited zeal; a feint, a forward bend of the body, one knee upon the sand, head thrust against the chest, and the victim is flying over the head of the victor, and in an instant his brawny body is rolling upon the sand or hurled from the arena, amid an approving murmur from the audience; the attendant elevates his fan, the victor bows with his hands on his knees and leaves the ring.

This is repeated not only by the nine pair, but by a second nine pair who make their appearance after a short interval and who go through quite a similar performance. During the play a variety of refreshments were hawked round within the "*Smo*" as it is called by the Japanese; tea and fruits were served in private boxes, and families partook of their meals during the performance. Our party had tea served with some rice cakes and fruit; and all smoked who chose. Two-sworded soldiers served as policemen during the entertainment, which was conducted with decorum. Children played, laughed, and occasionally imitated the wrestlers; old people smoked, drank their tea and gossiped, while black-eyed, betel-chewing, red-lipped girls looked a little curious out of the corners of their eyes.

CHAPTER LXII.

HAKODADI.

SEVERAL hundred persons visited the "Smo" daily. An elevated box in one corner was appropriated for the *barbarians* having benches to sit upon, a luxury not much practised by the Japanese; they sit upon their hocks or squat upon the ground; shoes wooden-clogs and bark-sandals are worn in the street, but taken off when entering a house or temple, left at the door or carried in the hand; fans, pipes, tobacco and tea are in constant requisition. Betel-nut* is chewed by the women, who

* The chewing of this preparation seems to be quite common among the females of Japan: it colors the lips and mouth quite red; and the manner of stuffing the quid outside of the front teeth gives their mouth a puffed (not to say pouting) and unnatural appearance, and frequently when they open the mouth or rather the lips, a roll of this preparation will be seen protruding from their lips as if they were sticking the tongue out from between the teeth, while the lips are fairly dripping with the red juice from the masticated betel. They appear to be quite as determined chewers as any of our male admirers of the "honey-dew" or "Mrs. Myers' fine cut," and seem to be devoted to it, and consider it more fashionable than *dipping* or snuffing appears to be among our females, as they make no concealment of their quids. With the Japanese belle, there is no disguise; they chew on all occasions; there is nothing however in the flavor of it at all unpleasant, but on the contrary it tends to sweeten the breath, and it is that quality perhaps with its stimulating properties that has given it such wide and extensive consumption in the East.

have rather agreeable faces and good forms, the effect of which however is spoiled when they walk, their gait being very ungraceful. Many of the girls and young women have good teeth, white and regular, while the teeth of the married women are all colored black. Prostitution is licensed and regulated by strict laws; houses of ill-fame are painted red with gratings in front, and latticed on the verandas. Poor parents who cannot support their female children, apprentice them to houses engaged in this traffic; they are educated, and accomplished in music, dancing, singing, conversation, embroidery, &c.; and after the years of their bondage have been served out, they are free to choose their future position. Many being chosen for their high accomplishments and beauty by respectable persons as wives, their former life is never spoken of; they now enter the society of their husbands, and a person casting any reflection upon them in consequence of their former life is considered rude and unmanly. They are said to make the best of wives. Licentiousness is carried to the highest pitch in Japan. The system of tea-houses is one of the most notable features of this extraordinary country; the road side inns and post stations are *red* tea-houses, all regulated by law.

While we lay at Hakodadi the bark Messenger-bird came into the bay and anchored. The captain's wife was on board with her two children, one a fat little cherub, a baby of only a few months old, born on the passage since leaving the Sandwich Islands.

I shall never forget the day on which the first American woman and her baby appeared on the streets of Hakodadi.

The population, men, women and children, priests, soldiers, barbers, merchants, all seem to have deserted with one accord their various callings to gaze upon Mrs. Homer and her infant. The baby excited the most intense curiosity among the women and children; with gaping mouths, outstretched necks and piercing eyes they followed it through the streets; every turn, every movement, was watched; police officers would occasionally drive them off but it was only to give place to more eager faces; at the turn of every street troops would dash off and seek to get a better view by appearing through other streets to intercept her at the next corner. As we turned the corner of the street leading to the temple, on one side of which the foreign bazaar was held, the crowd, men, women and children, made a rush for the inner court to gain the temple. There was a perfect stampede; the clattering of wooden-shod feet over the rocky pavement with the hum of a thousand voices filled the air; they piled upon the steps, rushed pell-mell into the temple and crowded the court, hoping to get a better view. In this they were doomed to disappointment, except a favored few who reached a back balcony, from whence they had a full view of the lady and baby as they sat within the bazaar.

Upon her return the streets were again filled with curious people following her to the gate of the custom-house which led to the boat, in which she reached the ship, eyed as she passed through a labyrinth of junks by the curious Japanese sailors, who beheld for the first time a white woman.

The bath-houses are also a curiosity in their way in Japan; men, women, and children bathe promiscuously.

They use the steam bath, retiring behind a screen into a room reeking with steam, and then emerging to an outer room, where they sit or squat, wiping, rubbing, combing, and pouring bowls of water over their bodies, and again retire to the steam or hot bath, and return, wipe and dress.

The people being strictly prohibited from trading with foreigners, any article or commodity selected in the shops or stalls must be sent to the bazaar of the temple, where officers of government arrange with you for payment. Here also was opened a shop or market for lacquered and fancy articles under the superintendence of officials, who also had a word in arranging the price, which was certainly high—the supposition is that the officials pay the merchant his ordinary price and pocket the difference paid by the purchaser. The mart opened for commerce with foreigners during our stay was in the Carp-fish-Temple buildings to the right of the main entrance, rather dark, but opening in the rear to the temple grounds, where miniature lakes and mountains, dwarf trees, and beautiful, trimmed shrubs and gravelled walks attest much taste and art in gardening. Many people with a large sprinkling of children rushed before us into the temple yard, upon our first vist to the bazaar, scampering out of reach of the soldiers, who seemed to be conducting us *unasked.* Many of the younger fry rushed through the temple and took post behind paper screens on the rear porch, to get a better view of us, while the officials, with the interpreter were seated on a bench near the rear wall, looking out on the tiny lake and the miniature mountains in the garden. The merchandise was ranged along in tiers on the floor, while the sober mute merchants, with their clerks, were on their knees, awaiting in this humble posture the command of the officers; at a word one or more were at the feet of the officials with a "hick"! "hick"! and head to the earth in humble reverence. It turned out that the prices only were to be arranged between the officers and merchants, and that the wares would be for sale on the morrow; but it was worth an hour's loss of time to witness the figuring and adjusting of the prices. I strolled into the temple, looked at the images, the altars, the tablets and miniature tombstones arranged on shelves, the paintings, the figures, the screens, the inscriptions; passed up through a long back street, looked at another temple, walked into a graveyard, returned to the "hall of trade," and found them as busy as ever. Tea was served, and innumerable pipes smoked, and upon walking into an adjoining room I found cooks busily preparing rice-cakes, offerings for the gods, and motley dishes for the priests.

We adjourned to Dr. Rice's quarters, talked over the programme for the evening, went on board for dinner, returned at 2 P. M. to the "Smo," where, in drinking tea and looking at the wrestlers and fashions, we spent most of the afternoon.

A lofty conical volcano was smoking steadily some twenty miles to the north, the weather was mild and pleasant, with occasional showers, and fresh sea breezes; the adjacent country looked pleasant; fishermen daily and hourly plied their arts in entrapping the scaly denizens of the bay; gulls and ducks, were attending industriously to their dinners, heavy lug-sailed, tub-bowed, and two-story sterned junks were passing in and out or bobbing up and down at anchor in the harbor; boats with crews singing and tugging at their oars were skimming along the shores or towing some dull junk to sea or to anchor; the dull heavy sounding bells, and wooden tomtoms were warning the devotees to prayers, the dead to their graves or funeral pyres, or the young and happy to the hymeneal altar; shaven priests and mendicants solicited the copper cash from the more charitable, shopmen vended their wares, barbers were busy with shaven pates and shining crown tails, pretty girls peeped from the interstices of the latticed verandas, and two-sworded *samrays* watched our strollings along the less frequented streets.

CHAPTER LXIII.

TO KAMSCHATKA.

September 14, 1857. Our stay was drawing to a close. Mr. Cushing had satisfied himself as to commercial affairs; our little trade was nearly finished, all but paying the bill, which Mr. Cushing arranged; our chickens, potatoes, soy, and fancy boxes were on board. Doctor Rice wished he could sail with us, as we said good-by; our anchor was atrip, and our graceful bark with bellying canvas glided gaily out of the bay into the Straits of Sangar—the broad Pacific was before us, and Petropaulosky our next destined port. We sailed that evening along the northern coast, and had a good view in the morning of Volcano bay and a smoking cone.

We had a fair voyage of eight days to the coast of Kamschatka opposite the Bay of Avatcha. The burning mountain of Avatcha was sending up a considerable column of vapor, the sides were covered with snow, while a coating of dusky brown covered the immediate cone of the volcano, probably snow discolored by ashes thrown up from the crater. The shores of the coast looked beautiful, clothed in their fall gear of variegated foliage, while bare and precipitous mountains assumed according to the shade various colors.

The whole country is evidently plutonic and presents the appearance of a great caldron which has boiled over, and cooling quickly, left the mountains in a solid state of all forms and shapes. The gate or entrance to the bay is really a gem in coast scenery, and will compare very favorably with the Golden Gate of San Francisco.

We sailed up the same evening we came in view of the coast, towards the entrance of the Bay, hoping that we should be able to enter before night with a slight breeze which we hoped would be found constant enough to waft us into the harbor. Our Captain did not like to lie too near the coast during the night for fear of foul weather and a lee shore, and was determined if he could not pass the heads before night, to stand off and await the coming morning and perhaps more favorable breezes.

We stood up towards the heads with a very slight breeze or rather just a breath of air, and were fanned along to within two miles of the entrance before dusk, and probably could have entered, but the tide was found to be against us as we neared the shore, and as in this state of things we might be becalmed under the southern headland, our Captain very prudently turned his bow sea-ward and stood off for more favorable breezes in the morning.

The look-out at the watch tower on the northern head had lighted up a beacon which was repeated within the bay and harbor in order to light and guide us on our way, but the wind and tide which "waiteth for no man," rendered his kindness of no avail.

The next morning we were standing on towards the

land again in the direction of the entrance to the bay. The day was bright and pleasant with but little wind; we had made considerable offing during the night, and without favorable wind and a little more of it as the day advanced we became fearful that we would not be able to reach the port of destination before dark, and would consequently be compelled to stand to sea again.

We had ample leisure however, to study the wild and majestic scenery of the coast, with three or four smoking volcanoes in the foreground. We fanned along very slowly and lazily until quite late in the afternoon, when a more favorable breeze springing up we worked along very slowly, and gaining the entrance we were carried clear of the headland, which made available the breeze from the west, which filling our sails, we stood joyfully up the Bay towards the Port of Petropaulosky, and cast anchor just outside of the harbor after sunset on the 23d of September, 1857.

Two Americans connected with the house of Messrs. Boardman & Co. of Boston, came off to us, accompanied by the Governor of the country, and the next morning with the assistance of several boats from the town furnished by the Governor, we were towed into the harbor of Saint Peter and Paul, Kamschatka, N. L. 53° E. L. 158° 16′ thirteen thousand three hundred and thirty-six *versts* east of St. Petersburg by land; one thousand miles north-east of Hakodadi and about the same distance east of the mouth of the Amoor River, and about three thousand three hundred north-west of San Francisco, California; population since the war about two hundred and fifty, previously one thousand. It is a regular Russian town, population, language, manners, customs, dress, buildings, manner of living, church and religion—so closely resembling European Russia that one could scarcely credit the fact, or realize that he was near nine thousand miles from the seat of government, and that this was the same race of people he had conversed with on the shores of the Baltic Ocean a year and a half since.

The peninsula of Kamschatka was not discovered by the Russians until near the commencement of the eighteenth century, and then only nominally taken possession of, by rendering some of the native tribes tributary. Not long afterwards, however, a small detachment of troops penetrated from the north and establishing posts, the whole country was quickly subjugated and rendered tributary. The peninsula is generally very mountainous, yet there are some considerable valleys, and fine rolling uplands, with mountain sides yielding excellent pasturage where the soil is good; but being liable to frequent frosts even in summer, grain is not produced—yet cabbages, turnips, radishes, beets, cucumbers and potatoes are grown in favorable locations with great ease and in abundance; hemp and flax of late years have been introduced which are likely to succeed well also.

The principal trade of the country is, however, in its furs and skins; the sable and ermine of Kamschatka are considered equal if not superior to any, while the black and silver-grey fox to the north and on the adjacent islands are the best and rarest in the world. The fisheries yield most abundantly; game is found in the forests, and several kinds of berries grow in the valleys and mountains; while good hay to any amount can be cut from the natural meadows.

The people are very hospitable, not much inclined to labor, but prefer mostly to hunt and fish; the women generally cultivate the small gardens, assist in making the hay, drawing the seines and rowing the boats.

The population about Petropaulosky are mostly full blooded Russians, yet there are many who have a mixture of the native Kamschadale blood in their veins. In the interior there are yet considerable numbers of natives who live in their primitive mode.

There are also at Petropaulosky some Russian-English and Russian-American mixtures, the offspring of persons settled there from either English or American trading or whaling ships.

The population of the Peninsula is set down at about eight thousand, how accurately I do not know. The whole trade is confined to a few vessels yearly, which bring assorted merchandise, taking furs and money in exchange. There are at this time two American and three Russian commercial houses at Petropaulosky; these keep up the trade and furnish the foreign supplies to the interior, sending out in summer small boats loaded with merchandise, which coast along the shores or ascend the rivers, supplying the interior villages, receiving furs and skins in return. In the winter the more difficult interior portions are visited with dog-sledges, and the natives from a great distance also visit Petropaulosky, where the year's catch is bartered for cloth, whiskey, and tobacco, powder, etc., etc.

During my stay of a fortnight, I made several excursions into the adjacent country; one of which was to visit a celebrated warm spring about fifty miles to the west. After making all the necessary arrangements we started early one morning in a whale boat; the party consisted of Messrs. Hunter and Burling, recently from San Francisco, having established a trading-house here, Mr. Smith in the employ of Messrs. Boardman & Co., Captain Morse, and myself—all Americans. We had four oarsmen from the town and a pilot from the opposite coast. We pulled right across the bay of Avatcha to the mouth of a small river which comes in from the north-west. We rowed and pulled up this river, in places against a strong current, for several miles until we came in such shoal water that our boat touched the bottom, near which were a party of men and women making hay; the wife of our pilot was one of the party. We landed on a large meadow, and the whole hay-party joined us and walked up to the village about two miles distant. We were ferried over the river by a female *ferry-man* just below the village in a very shackling pair of canoes, fastened together by poles laid across, on which we sat to keep them from upsetting.

CHAPTER LXIV.

A WARM SPRING.

ARRIVING at the village, we soon had the whole population around us to provide the necessary horses for the expedition to the springs, fifteen or twenty miles further on. Having a good supply of provisions along, including tea and sugar, we made, with the assistance of milk and black bread furnished by the wife of our pilot, a hearty dinner, and started off, well mounted on fat frisking little horses, under the guidance of our river and bay pilot, now turned pioneer, and two other peasants of the village, with provisions, guns, and blankets.

The road, or rather path, led up and across the same stream we had ascended in our boat, and then through well-wooded bottom land, gradually rising into beautiful table land, covered with fine birch trees, rank grass, and high weeds. We had several shots at the black pheasant of the country, which our pilot said were very abundant in the interior, as well as partridges and bears.

The road was a mere track, along which we passed in Indian-file, getting an occasional view of lofty snow-covered mountains to the south; from the growth of the vegetation and the size and quality of the forest trees, the soil must be of superior quality; and in these sheltered valleys I should judge grain certainly could be produced; the country looks as well adapted to grain growing as in similar latitude in Russia. We rode along briskly, coming to a very beautiful country of rolling woodland, which extended for several miles to the edge of a considerable valley destitute of timber, stretching up among the mountains for many miles. After halting a few minutes to enjoy the open view presented to us here, we rode on, and turning down along the edge of the valley, soon came to a single house, and then a long low building. This was the hot springs and bath house; it had been erected by a former Governor of Kamschatka, for the accommodation of those visiting the springs for health. Our men secured our horses, unpacked provisions, and prepared every thing for our night's rest. By this time it was dark.

We entered the house and found two men, the only occupants. We took possession of a vacant room where there was a table and some board frames against the wall, answering the purpose of bedsteads. While our men were busy preparing our supper, to which we all thought we could do ample justice, we visited the bath. There is a covered way leading from the main building down to the springs, at the end of which there is a small dressing-room; this opens immediately into the springs which you reach by a few wooden steps. There is a screen of planks extending on each side for twenty or thirty feet, open at top as you enter the water, beyond which there is no inclosure. The bath or basin, which has been formed by a small dam to retain the water after it boils up just under the bank where it runs off to unite with a little creek not many paces distant, is some thirty or forty feet in diameter and from one to three feet deep. When you first enter the bath and step into it, the sensation is as if the skin was about being removed, while the stones and mud on the bottom fairly burn your feet; added to which the steam and gas, ascending from the caldron, fairly take away your breath; yet in a short time you turn red and get used to it; when the sensation is remarkably pleasant and refreshing. The aches, jolts and thumps of the day's excursion were all speedily removed, and the whole party pronounced the bath the very quintessence of luxury. Smith, one of our companions, called it "ecstatic," all were highly delighted, and after a thorough scalding we retired to our lodgings to drink hot tea, and after the necessary delay to partake of our supper.

Captain Morse was the most sadly disappointed of any mortal I had seen lately, in regard to a pan of baked pork and beans that he had attempted to transport from the cook-house of his ship to the interior of Kamschatka—he had packed the delicious dish as he thought very carefully and securely as well as some sea-biscuit, and gave the package in charge to our worthy commissary and pilot, who had transferred it, with bread, ham, boxes of sardines, bottles of porter, etc., all into a capacious leather bag which he had lashed hard and fast upon his sumpter-horse, without paying very strict regard to the hay used in packing. We were all counting on the delicious pan of pork and beans to be served up in the wilds of Kamschatka, but the Captain had in particular set his heart on it, and the ride and fast during the day had not lessened the force of his desires.

We all looked with interest to the opening of the sack—out came a porter bottle minus the neck, contents vanished, then came a ham badly jammed, next a loaf of bread, *a la flapjack*, boxes of sardines all right, other bottles sound, tea and sugar damaged with porter; but worse than all, and under all, the pan of pork and beans was a mass of hay, straw, pork, beans, and bread, in a conglomerate jumble, which if pressed and dried from the amount of hay intermixed would have made good adobes. The two Captains Hunter and Morse took turns about in picking the straws from the mass. I was quite satisfied with tea, ham, and bread.

I had neglected to take my thermometer along with me, and consequently cannot state the temperature of the water, but where it boils up out of the ground, the heat is sufficient to scald a chicken—it certainly is hotter than the celebrated Arkansas hot springs, and probably possessing the same or quite similar medical properties—scorbutic, rheumatic, scrofulous and mercurial diseases being relieved or entirely removed by the bath.

We slept in our cloaks and blankets, some on the floor others on the wooden frames; the number of roaches and other bugs were beyond computation; but the day's journey and fatigue, winding up with the hot bath, ensured us a good night's rest notwithstanding the vermin. I slept well and soundly, and we were all up early in order to enjoy the bath before our departure.

The view in the morning was very fine. The spring is just on the edge of a great meadow, with forests in the rear, and a large valley stretching off to the right and left; lofty wooded mountains in the foreground and to the left. In the distance, in several places in this meadow, columns of steam were ascending, marking the locality of other hot springs. The morning was cool and cloudy, but not unpleasant, with indications of rain.

CHAPTER LXV.

STAY AT PETROPAULOSKY.

SEPTEMBER 27. We saw but one woman about the springs. She occupied a hut near by and furnished us with tea. She and one of the men probably were the custodians of the establishment. No compensation was demanded. We, however, paid for the tea, black-bread, and fish, furnished.

After breakfast we had pistol and rifle-shooting at a mark, as we found no game. Our horses being saddled, we started for town. The grass and bushes were wet from the frost over night, and a slight shower of rain rendered the road a little unpleasant, but we hastened on to reach the village of Nikolaivsky, near which our boat was waiting to take us over the bay, for we feared that as the weather appeared unsettled that we might be detained in case of a snow storm, as the bay would be very rough. We had an unsuccessful grouse hunt on the way back. We saw a flock and pursued them in the woods some distance, but they were too shy for us, and we gave up the chase.

Two revolvers were lost on the road, but found again. We arrived back at the village where we had procured our horses, and the wife of our guide had plenty of milk, fish, and curds for us. This, with the ever-ready *samovar*, and black-bread, gave us a good dinner. We were visited by many of the villagers, among whom there were two girls, quite good-looking—one a blue-eyed rosy-cheeked lass, the other a brunette with black eyes and hair. Pistol and rifle-shooting and crow-killing were practised after dinner, and, after paying for our ride and provisions, we took our departure to where our boat was, some distance below. The day was now warm, and the walk through the rough ground, over a boggy meadow-land, gave us a perfect sweat-bath. We were all glad enough to sit down on the bank of the river and take a rest while the men were preparing the boat. We were soon under way, and, assisted by the current of the river, glided along down towards the bay, with the volcano of Avatcha in the north presenting a very beautiful view. We also had some very pretty scenery on our way down on the right—high cliffs, where two bald-headed eagles were perched. The captain saluted them with his rifle, but without effect.

We entered the bay and rowed along the beach, and among some low islands were flocks of ducks and thousands of gulls fishing, while in the deeper water of the bay many seals were showing their heads above water and as quickly disappearing. As we came out into the open bay the scenery was truly very beautiful. There were four volcanoes smoking, three to the north and one to the south-west. A large valley stretched far away to the north of Avatcha, bounded by high snow mountains, while the wooded hill sides and grassy valleys immediately upon the bay were clothed in the variegated hues of autumn. We pulled on stoutly across the bay and landed at Petropaulosky. Captain Hunter and Mr. Burling of the party gave us a nice supper at their residence. We spent a very agreeable evening after our day's work and retired to the ship, where we lodged.

The next day Captain Morse and myself went plover-shooting along the beach in the direction of a small village a few miles up the bay. We killed a number and stopped at the village to rest and refresh ourselves. We asked permission of the good woman of the house to enter, which was readily granted. The samovar was soon steaming, ready for tea. We had provided ourselves with tea and sugar before we left town, to which the hostess added raw turnips, milk, curds, black-bread, and some berries. We dined most sumptuously after our exercise and took several lessons in Russian. Many of the words used here I found to differ from those in Russia. There is, of course, a provincial idiom, and some little native language mixed up with it. We made our way along the mountain side, as the beach would not be practicable at night. There was a well-beaten mountain path, and the walk was agreeable, until we came within half a mile of the town, when we had to ford the outlet to a lake that communicates with the bay ; but as it was not more than two or three feet deep, we only got moist to that extent.

Mr. Cushing was arranging his business affairs and having his cargo discharged, while I determined to make use of all the lay-days granted, and so the captain and myself, through the cleverness of Mr. Whitfield, procured the only two horses in town, one belonging to the priest, the other to the acting-governor, Captain Gubaroff. We mounted, and rode in the direction of the bottom of the bay and by the village of Avatcha to the foot of the volcano, or as near to it as we could proceed. Our route lay along over the spurs and foot-hills skirting the bay, through the same village we had visited before. There is plenty of timber and meadow-land, and the soil on the hill-sides looks as though it would produce grain if cultivated. We passed up beyond Avatcha until we came to water and a dense tangled wood, beyond which we did not think it safe to proceed without a guide. Here we sat down and had a fine view of the mountain, which was belching forth great volumes of dense white smoke. The volcano had been in a state of eruption for several days, and had sent forth flames and lava. We could now see distinctly the stream of lava which had issued from the crater, where it had taken its course down along a deep gorge, which it nearly filled, and, having cooled on the top and sides, formed a tunnel through which the hot lava was pouring, some two thousand feet down the side of the mountain, where, as it burnt out, a dense column of smoke arose and went curling off along the side of the mountain, until it formed into a cloud. We sat gazing for some time, and saw two eruptions while there, the earth trembling as if in an ague fit.

We rode back to Avatcha, and entering a cottage, soon had, with our own tea and sugar, such a meal as a Kamschatka peasant's cabin would afford. There was a very old man here, once of stalwart frame, but now sickly, to whom the contents of our teapot, and a little from a black bottle, gave much relief. His daughter, a stout, buxom damsel, or dame, I don't know which, did the honors of the house smilingly and pleasingly and seemed to be much taken with the captain, who was really a handsome man. I joked the captain with taking away the maid's heart. I asked her if she would like to take a voyage to sea. She laughed and said, "*pajanlst*"—if you please. We had a very pleasant day. The people had been fishing, and there were several canoes on the beach, loaded with fish, all alive and kicking. The dogs were being fed bountifully on them.

All through this country dogs are used in the winter in the place of horses. At every village you will see scores of dogs tied about, generally a little outside, or along a creek near the village, where they are fed on fresh fish during the summer and fall, and not allowed to hunt, as that spoils them for draught, it being necessary to break them from the pursuit of wild animals. They are fed on fish the year round, which are caught in the summer and dried for their winter use. Six to twelve dogs are generally used to a sleigh, and, when well fed and trained, make most capital journeys. Government officers are conveyed from Kamschatka entirely up around the Sea of Okhotsk by Okhotsk and Ayan on the road which leads by Yakutsk to Irkutsk, with dogs, until they strike the reindeer or horses near Okhotsk.

I have seen two officers who have performed the journey from St. Petersburg to Petropaulosky by land, a distance of some ten thousand miles—Captains Martinoff and Ayers. But it takes stout hearts and sturdy frames to perform these journeys. Martinoff is now aid to General Mouravieff at Irkutsk, and Ayers is government interpreter to Governor Kosakevitch at the Amoor. They are always detailed on difficult and arduous service, and must rise to high employ in Siberia. They deserve it. Both speak English well—Capt. Ayers perfectly—besides French and German. We made our way back towards St. Peter and Paul, but stopped to drink tea with our friends in the little village of Serra Glaska, and rode into town after night, not fearing the water this time, as our horses did not mind wet feet.

The weather was very pleasant, and I spent the most of the time in walks about the country and in hunting birds.

CHAPTER LXVI.

THE BURNING MOUNTAIN.

We had several beautiful exhibitions of the burning mountain of Avatcha at night, when it burst forth with columns of bright flame and a fiery river of lava pouring down its side. On several occasions the earth shook considerably, sufficient to make the houses crack and the crockery and bottles rattle on the shelves and the bedsteads to move. One night, while we were watching it from the ship's deck, a great explosion took place, and an immense ball of fire was seen to roll down the mountain. Next morning we perceived that a section of the cone to the north had been broken off, making a large notch, where before it was rounded.

One evening, as we were walking towards the lake near the town, we were arrested by a tremulous motion of the earth and a rumbling noise beneath our feet, with a kind of indistinct report in the air, like the discharge of small arms, and, on looking up, the mountain was belching flames and smoke. 'Twas said that the volcano had been quiet, until since our arrival, for many years, and I think it was in 1838 that the inner harbor was made dry then by the quakings of the earth during an eruption.

We were very much delighted at the fortunate occurrence, which we construed to be especially for our benefit, as we had never before seen a veritable mountain belching flames, fire, and smoke, and rocking the earth like a cradle. We therefore watched it very closely, and sometimes to a late hour at night, in order not to be cheated of any of the extraordinary exhibitions of fire-works. The mountain has never been ascended by man—that is, the crater has not been reached—owing to the great fissures and the rugged nature of it at the top. It has a base of twenty miles and a height of ten thousand feet. Kamschatka is volcanic, and has now the distinct craters of sixteen burning mountains, many of them in action from time to time—as before stated, within view from our ship's deck, there were four smoking at once.*

* "Many traces of volcanoes have been observed in this peninsula; and there are some mountains which, at present, are in a burning state. The most considerable of these volcanoes is situated near the Lower Ostrog.

"In 1762, a great *noise* was heard issuing from the inside of that mountain, and flames of fire were seen to burst from different parts. These flames were immediately succeeded by a large stream of melted snow water, which flowed into the neighboring valley, and drowned two Kamschatdales, who were there at that time upon a hunting party. The ashes and other combustible matter thrown from the mountain, spread to the circumference of three hundred miles. In 1767, there was another discharge, but less considerable.

"Every night flames of fire were observed streaming from the mountain; and the eruption which attended them, did no small damage to the inhabitants of the Lower Ostrog. Since that year no flames have been seen; but the mountain emits a constant smoke. The same phenomenon is also observed upon another mountain, called Tabeet Skinskain."—PALLAS.

The town is in rather a dilapidated condition. The Allies burned all the public buildings, broke the glass in private dwellings, mutilated the church, the people having all withdrawn to the country, in 1854. When the fleet came there first, the Russian frigate Aurora guarded the port, and batteries were erected to protect the town. Finding they could not take it in front, they landed a force upon the beach to the west of the town, where there is a lake upon the left, which leaves a very narrow passage between the foot of the promontory lying between the town and the bay. Along this narrow pass the Allies attempted to enter the town by a flank movement, but, just as they turned the point of the lake, a masked battery from the ravine opened upon them, and the Russians posted in the bushes gave them a warm reception. They now made a flank movement to the right up the mountain side, in order to avoid the raking fire from the battery; but here they were met by bullets from every bush. The mountain was inclined towards the town, but, on the sea side, precipitous. They retreated up and along the side until they reached the top, where they again found leaden messengers from every bush. They were now seized with a panic and threw themselves down the mountain-side in the direction of their boats, the Russians firing on them deliberately as they were fleeing and gathering on the beach, and getting into their boats. Many were killed and crippled in the hurried descent over the craggy precipice, while numbers were killed in the fight. The Allies abandoned the beach as quickly as they could gather the stragglers, took to their ships, and their ships to sea, leaving Saint Peter and Paul in the possession of the Kamschatdales. Some three hundred Allies, it is said, perished in the fight and flight and about ten or fifteen Russians. The Russians, however, abandoned the place and retreated to the Amoor, which they fortified effectually. The following year the allied fleet returned and entered without opposition, burning the public buildings, etc.

The captain of the port gave a dinner party while I was there, which was quite a pleasant affair. We also had other social parties. The time was very agreeably occupied ; the weather mostly fine, but growing very frosty at night ; Avatcha being covered with snow.

On Tuesday, 6th October, we took our last ramble in the country. We were to leave with the first fair wind. We were late getting into town that night, having walked some distance in the country and stopped at Serra Glaska to take tea and rest, so it was not till after night when we started in. The bark had been hauled out into the bay and we went immediately on board, but I fully expected to have had another day on shore. Morning came ; it was cold and cloudy and scattered flakes of snow falling. In a short time a breeze sprang up from the north. The captain sent the boat on shore for Mr. Cushing, and orders were given to unbend the sails and get the slack of the chain in. This looked like a start. In the course of an hour Mr. C. was on board, the anchor was a-trip, and we were bound out of the Bay of Avatcha for the Sandwich Islands.

Of all things in the world to me a sea voyage is the most tedious. Waiting upon men in office ; waiting for a rich uncle to die ; waiting for the decision of a suit in chancery ; or for your turn at the post-office window of a rainy day in San Francisco in 1849; waiting for fame at the foot of the ladder, with one hand upon the first round, looking up, but not daring to climb; waiting for a handsome girl to pop the question to you, are all insignificant in comparison to a voyage at sea. We had a boisterous passage, head winds, head-beat seas, wind-storms, squalls, rain-storms, and calms, but we had a good ship, commanded by a real sailor; one who loved his profession and who studied it; careful of his ship, faithful to his owner's interest.

We reached Honolulu on Monday, the 2d day of November, 1857, after a passage of twenty-seven days—that is, it was Monday on land, so the people said, when we arrived, but, according to my reckoning, it should have been Tuesday; but we had crossed the 180° of longitude east from Greenwich, and consequently had gained a day in the economy of sunrising.

CHAPTER LXVII.

CHARACTER OF THE AMOOR COUNTRY.

The Russian name "Amoor" is derived, I believe, from the Tartar name of the river *Kar-Amur-an* or *Kar-amur-an-Oula*, which signifies, I was told, the "Great River of the Black Dragon."

The country bordering upon the Amoor has been very imperfectly explored, but apparently it may be divided into three sections in accordance with its vegetation.

First.—The upper or western section, commencing at the head of the Amoor, Ouse-Strelkah, and extending down or south-east to the river Zea. This country resembles the better portions of the Trans-Baikal country east of the Stanovey mountains, but evidently grows milder in climate as you proceed to the south-east by the course of the river. The extent of this region may be roughly stated at one-third of the whole distance.

In this, the great western division, we find the river running much of the way through a mountainous country in numerous bends, having considerable fertile bottom lands, first on one side and then on the other, covered with excellent grass, and well, but not heavily, timbered, with white and black birch, pitch pine, fir and larch, inferior oak and linden.

With the rapid advance of summer you find the climate, soil, and productions evidently changing for the better, while the mountains are gradually receding from the river as you descend, and large extents of country are spreading off into extensive plains, and by the time you have reached the Zea you find a country certainly adapted to both agriculture and grazing purposes, with sufficient timber for all necessary wants.

Second.—The southern division or the region from the Zea to the Ousuree, again about one-third of the whole distance. This country has extensive prairies, with plenty of wood upon the mountains. Here the Amoor has made an immense sweep to the south, receiving the mild air from that quarter unobstructed by mountains and also the warmer waters of its more southern affluents, and being besides well protected from the cold blasts of the Frozen Ocean by the distant barrier of the Altaï, and the country assumes quite a southern aspect. From the Zea to the Songahree the mountains recede to the south, forming an extensive plain, though which the Amoor flows like a second Mississippi.

The soil is generally good, and though nearly all the varieties of timber heretofore enumerated grow in this division, yet they are not so plentiful. The forests consist principally of birch, oak, ash, maple, cork, and elm ; good timber for building purposes is only found upon the distant mountains, where cedar, pine, and larch grow to great perfection and in abundance. But the best mode of supplying this section with timber is to cut it on the streams above and float it down in rafts, as practised on our western rivers. Innumerable flowers of rich and varied hue, grape-vine, pea, clover, and grass, rich and luxuriant, attest its fitness for the abode of civilized man.

Third.—From the Ousuree to the Straits of Tartary will constitute the eastern division, again about one-third of the whole distance from the head to its mouth. This region, on the south of the Amoor, is mostly covered with dense forests ; the country gradually rising from the Ousuree to the Ocean forms a mountainous district, which declines abruptly at the coast. This accounts for the fact that no river of any considerable size enters the Sea of Japan, for a distance covered by 15° of latitude south of the Amoor towards Corea.

The left or north bank is, on the contrary, comparatively speaking, an even or gently rolling country, and in this part of the Amoor the growth and climate is so varied that, in order to correctly understand and review it, it must be subdivided as follows :

1st. The tract of country along the sea shore to the south of the Amoor from Emperor's Harbor to Petrofsky, north of the Amoor, and along the shores of the Amoor to the high mountains lying in the neighborhood of the villages of Dary and Havandah, a distance by the coast, sea, and river of about five hundred miles.

2d. The middle tract to the mouth of the Hongahree River, or to the mountains of Bokee, a distance of one hundred and sixty miles.

3d. The southern tract or region of ovate-leaved forests, from the Hongahree to the Ousuree two hundred and seventy miles.

In the first subdivision, or the region of pinnate-leaved forests, the climate, particularly on the coast of the Sea and Straits of Tartary, and on the Amoor almost to the village of Michailovskey is very severe; in the winter snow falls to the depth of seven to ten feet, and the storms are terrific and blinding, so that it is absolutely at the risk of one's life to be caught in one of them, the air being so perfectly filled with snow before a driving wind that progress is impossible, and the only resort is to bury yourself up in the drift and wait for it to pass over. The country is mountainous, hence the shores of the Amoor are abrupt and rocky, and for cultivation few favorable spots are found. The forests consist of pine, a peculiar kind of pitch pine, and larch; cedar only grows in stunted bushes, mostly on mountains, and small red oak, maple, and birch are found only on the borders or skirts of the forests. The soil which produces the fir and larch forests is generally clayish and wet; meadows on open spots are rare, except on islands and in partially mountainous valleys. Above Michailovskey the country becomes lower, leaving rather extensive even spots covered with groves of aspen and birch. Small meadows are often met with. The soil of the aspen and birch forests is less marshy, and in the birch groves is covered with a rich carpet of grass suitable for hay. All this country abounds with berries peculiar to northern and middle Russia; Turk's cap, wild garlic, and a peculiar kind of hazlenut. On the opposite side of the Iise-kee mountains, linden and cedar are found, but they grow only in the second subdivision.

2d subdivision. The right bank of the Amoor here is generally mountainous, but there are a few even spots at long intervals. The left bank is mostly masked by a chain of low islands. Here the country begins to partake of the region towards the Ousuree and higher up the Amoor. It is low and flat, with meadows cut up by small creeks, bayous, and lakes, here and there crossed by chains of hillocks covered with trees. Here cedar is the principal forest tree, and it is found on hill and valley, though the tree is always larger and of better quality on the hills or upland. Linden, ash, elm, oak, four kinds of maple, birch, and aspen are found in abundance, while grapes and berries, found occasionally in the first subdivision, begin here only to grow in abundance. In this tract may be included the country on the Hongahree and Gehrin, as well as the upper parts of the river Tonjah.

3d subdivision or southern tract. The banks of the Amoor form here a plain, only occasionally a mountain ridge or spur from some distant ridge approaches the river. The Amoor divides itself into a multitude or labyrinth of branches, channels, or chutes, forming islands, lakes, and deep bays. Larch and fir are seldom seen, and are met with only on mountains distant from the river. Here dense forests are found, two species of elm, ash, oak, four species of maple, white and black birch, two species of linden, walnut, aspen, and poplar. The undergrowth of hazel is such and the grape-vines so interlaced with grass and weeds, that it is quite impossible to penetrate into the country without cutting a track. On every open spot a luxuriant growth of grass attests the richness of the soil and the mildness of the climate. Though in this section there are plenty of locations suitable for colonization, yet the clearing of the forests must be difficult, requiring great labor, with the loss perhaps of the first year.

On islands above overflow and on the shores of lakes and bays there are comparatively extensive meadows, and here the natives begin to cultivate small gardens.

The principal trees in the forests of the Amoor are:

1st. A peculiar kind of peach. 2d. Spruce-fir, or the common fir of Siberia. 3d. Larches grow everywhere on the shores of the northern Amoor and on the mountain ridges of the southern section; on plains and valleys protected from the wind and storms, they obtain considerable dimensions. Trees of three feet diameter are often found, particularly in the environs of the Gaseren River and Bogarotskey village and on the right shore of the Hongahree. 4th. The Siberian pitch; but this is found only on the Hingan mountains in abundance. 5th. Cedar grows in bushes on the mountains of the upper Amoor and has a diameter of five inches. (Where the diameter is mentioned it is always four feet from the ground.) As a tree the cedar is found at Sam-ah-hag-due, a village eighty miles from Kezee, three hundred and fifty miles from the mouth. From this to the southward and westward it appears in every forest of the middle subdivision, but prefers high land, where it constitutes entire forests without other timber. The natives build their boats of this timber. It attains a diameter of twenty-eight to thirty inches with a straight limbless trunk to the height of thirty feet. This valuable tree grows in great abundance and is seldom found defective. 6th. Yew grows in small numbers, on mountain ridges in the middle subdivision. On the shores of the Amoor it is seldom found, and not more than two inches in diameter; but, according to the statements of the natives, it attains on the mountains the thickness of a foot. Its wood is dark, resembling the cypress, and very hard. The Mangoons call it kin-dah-lah. 7th. Mongolian oak; Mangoon name, ho-ron-choo-rah; Goldee, ho-ron-ko-lah. This oak is met with on the sea shore south of De Castries Bay, in the northern part on the skirts of woods and on high stony declivities or mountain slopes; but always of small growth. It is found oftener in the middle section and frequently at the south. Its trunk is seldom straight. At the height of one to two fathoms it divides in crooked branches and attains a thickness of eighteen inches, but generally hollow or defective. In the north it is quite small, not more than five inches; grows oftener on the skirts of forests in the middle division, but attains its full growth in the southern subdivision, where it often reaches two feet in diameter. It is found in the greatest abundance, particularly in forests between the villages of Khogds, Gowan, and Doloy, as well as some forty miles above the mouth of the Hongahree on the right bank, where it attains enormous dimensions. 8th. Walnut, Goldee, kotch-dah, is met with at the mouth of Hongahree about the village of Jong-doe. It is found exclusively in ovate-leaved forests of the south, where it sometimes abounds, as well as ash, from which it is difficult to distinguish it, their barks being quite the same. It has a diameter of eighteen inches. 9th. White birch grows everywhere on the shores of the Amoor, but not so plentifully in the southern subdivision as elsewhere; diameter eighteen inches. 10th. Black birch is scarce in the middle, but abundant to the east. 11th. Linden, Goldee, kill-dah, is found of two species, with small and long leaves. The latter grows only about Ousuree, the former is found at Iise-kee mountains, as well as further south, where it has a diameter of three to four feet. 12th. Selp-heal attains a diameter of several inches, and is found in the northern and middle divisions. 13th. Elm of two species, long and small leaved. Both have hard and dark wood, and can be used where oak is required. Grows but seldom in the northern subdivision, and then small, but is found in the middle subdivision, having four feet diameter. 15th and 16th. Apple of two kinds, the common Siberian and a better kind having a fruit of one inch diameter, grows only in the most southerly bend of the Amoor. The first is found everywhere. 17th. Hawthorn or whitethorn grows along the whole length of the Amoor, and has a thickness of ten inches. 18th. Service-tree is occasionally seen with a diameter of six inches. 19th. Common birch or rock cherry grows everywhere. 20th. ———, Goldee, hat-too-lah, grows on the islands and on the main shores in the middle subdivision, five inches thick, with a straight trunk of five fathoms. 21st. Buckthorn, Goldee, a-mal-lah, grows in the southern bends of the Amoor, where it is often found a foot thick, the color a deep red, very hard, excellent for cabinet work. 22d. Cork-tree; Goldee, koch-tah, grows in the most southern bends, has a diameter of one foot. The bark is rough, with a thickness of something over one inch. The natives use it on their fishing nets. 23d, 24th, 25th, 26th. Maple; of which only one species is found at the mouth of the Amoor; the others grow in the middle or southern division. Has a diameter of one foot. 27th, 28th. Alder, gray and black; the first small;

the second grows in bushes on the more northern portions of the Amoor. 29th. Aspen grows everywhere, best in light soil. It is found in the central district in groves, and attains a diameter of two to four feet. 30th. Poplar is found mostly in the southern bends. 31st. A great variety of willow. Between Ouse-Strelkah and the sea shore are found more than thirty different species of this tree. Eighteen belong to the northern Amoor. For building purposes pitch, fir, and larch are considered as the most useful. Though larch is considered good for ship timber, it seldom attains the necessary thickness. In the eastern section we find twenty species of trees, while in the more southern parts we find twenty-nine species of all kinds, of which seven are suitable for building purposes, to which may be added walnut, ash, and elm.

CHAPTER LXVIII.

NATIVES ON THE AMOOR.

THE upper Amoor, from Ouse-Strelkah to the mouth of the river Zea, is inhabited by a people resembling the northern Tonguse. Though they bear the name of Managre yet they do not differ materially in language or in habits from the great Tonguse family of more Northern Asia. They are evidently a branch of the same stock, having, from dissensions within the tribe, passed the great Altaï range of mountains that separate them from the waters of the Frozen Ocean; and an immense inhospitable wilderness intervening, they have, in the course of many generations, or perhaps ages, lost their original name, and coming in contact with the Mongols or Manchoos, received from some local or accidental circumstance a new name. It is not attempted to enumerate this tribe; in fact, I could get no data from any Russian officer in relation to them. They are essentially nomadic, and not of much force, though they are somewhat dangerous and treacherous in their disposition, and require to be cautiously dealt with, but not at all formidable to parties, even of our number and strength. They are great beggars, fond of whiskey and tobacco, and not inclined to labor.

From the Zea to the Hingan Mountains, the shores of the Amoor are occupied by Manchoo and Chinese. Both are agriculturists, but the Chinese are either exiles or their descendants, for this part of the Amoor or Dahoureya was erected into a penal colony by the Chinese government soon after the evacuation of Albasin by the Russian forces in 1680–'85.

Along the Hingan mountains to the north of the Amoor wander a nomadic tribe, who possess horses. They are also a branch of the Tonguse family, the Solonsee.

Two hundred miles above the Songahree, and from thence to below the Geren on the right, is inhabited by the Goldee. Their language is a mixture of Manchoo-Tartar and Tonguse, though partaking more of the former tongue. Like all the tribes inhabiting the middle and lower Amoor they subsist mainly upon fish. In the winter the men resort to the distant mountains to hunt for fur animals, and do not generally return to their families until the approach of spring.

It is only noticed that between the Songahree and Ousuree rivers they cultivate gardens to any extent, and also have horses and cattle, though there is some cultivation for a short distance below the Ousuree.

The Olcha or Mangoon inhabit both above and below the river Geren, which comes in from the north. In language and habits they resemble the Goldee, have their villages and regular houses, and make some provision against both climate and starvation. They probably have also horses and cattle, but resort to the use of dogs in the winter.

Between the Amoor, the Ousuree, and the coast of Tartary, south of De Castries, are a semi-nomadic people, calling themselves Oh-roch-cha, or natives of the coast. They are sparsely scattered over a wild and extensive country, and were never brought under the absolute dominion of the Manchoos, but are probably like the north-eastern Chuck-chi, who have maintained their independence of the Russian yoke; the supposition is, that they are influenced in their social relations by the Corean tribes to the south, and have little or no affinity with the real natives of the Amoor.

North of the Amoor along the river Geren are a tribe known as the So-mah-gar-see, and still further to the north, on the Amgoon, some one hundred and fifty miles from the Straits of Tartary, are the Ne-ga-dal-sey, who are, from the best information, settled Tonguse. The latter tribe particularly are considered an important and valuable tribe, as they are tractable and inclined to civilization and Christianity. I saw at Nikolaivsky a Greek priest and a Russian artist who had been among them, and who reported very favorably as to their gentleness and kindly disposition. The priest was very much encouraged with his prospects of evangelizing the whole tribe and inducing them to cultivate the soil and raise cattle and horses. The country of the Amgoon was also described as being really a very beautiful country, and one well adapted to agriculture and stock. Seeds had been distributed and inducements held out by the governor to bring them to the cultivation of the soil.

Along the coast of the Amoor, from the Russian village of Bogrotskey half way between the Amgoon and the Geren to the sea, and along the coasts of the Leman to De Castries south and the village of Petrofsky north, as well as along the northern coasts of the Island of Sakhahlin, the country is inhabited by the Gelack or Gelan, a tribe in power perhaps more formidable than the Goldee, though not so numerous.

This tribe differs entirely in language and in many of their habits and customs from any of the tribes upon the Amoor.

The southern coast of Sakhahlin is inhabited by I-nee or Kou-rel-see, who are quite similar to the inhabitants of the Kurile Islands; and on the mountains of Sakhahlin are a nomadic people having reindeer, probably of the Tongusean stock—the Oh-ro-ka-te; but as they are very shy little is known of them.

The traits common to all the tribes inhabiting the valley of the Amoor and adjacent coasts and islands of the sea, are idolatry and Schamanism, independence of every male person, polygamy, slavery, and oppression of females and purchase of wives. Upon the females devolve all the labor and drudgery incident to the lowest state of savage life. The lords of creation only hunt, fish, and trade.

The Goldee, and people having consanguinity with them, rank in intelligence above the Gelack, who have not had much intercourse with the Manchoos or Chinese. This intercourse with the Manchoos has given to the Goldee some notions of God as the supreme ruler of the universe; yet they worship idols representing certain visible living evil creatures; as, for instance, the tiger, the panther, a large snake, and a fish represented as living upon human flesh.

The Schamans, or priests, are considered as powerful mediators between the people and the evil spirits, while the true God is adored or worshipped without the assistance of the Schamans; but this act of adoration takes place but once in each year—in the autumn—and then by the whole community in mass.

The soul of the dead is represented as passing underground, lighted and guided there by its own sun and moon, and continues to lead, there in its spiritual abode, the same manner of life and pursuits as when in the flesh of this life.

There exists no hell or place of torment or punishment for the common people; but the Schamans are not so fortunate; they have a place of torment awaiting them, if in case they have abused or misused their power over the evil spirits, whereby a fellow-being has suffered misfortune or evil. In this case, the wicked Schaman descends into hell, dark and damp, filled with gnawing reptiles.

In their funeral rites among the Goldee and Mangoon, the dead body is deposited in a coffin, which is placed on a low frame, while with the Oh-ro-ka-te three posts are buried in the ground upon which the coffin rests. So soon as the relatives of the deceased have been able to gather means commensurate to the solemn occasion, they make *po-inn-kee*, offerings, upon the grave. They then deliver over the tomb prayers for the the tranquillity and happiness of the soul of the deceased, eating and drinking at intervals, and making presents to their neighbors.

In character, the Goldee resemble the Tonguse. They are cheerful, but timid and lazy, and but little given to enterprise or adventure. They occupy themselves in the summer in fishing, while in the winter they hunt fur animals, principally sable and ermine, upon the mountains. They live in houses resembling those of their Manchoo masters, each house containing generally four families. In the spring, they remove into huts or movable bark or skin lodges, conical in shape, situated in locations near the river or upon the shores of islands desirable for their fishing stations. The Oh-ro-ka-te live constantly in these huts.

The Gelack, it appears, have no idea of the true God, for they worship only idols representing evil spirits. These spirits or demons they endeavor to bribe by the aid of their Schamans, in order to avert their wrath. Unlike the Goldee, they consider the bear a personified evil spirit, keep it alive, feed and bring it up from the cub with great care, and finally kill it with much ceremony. This curious custom prevails also among the Mangoon and Inees on Sakhahlin.

The Gelack have the same idea of future life as the Goldee; they, however, burn their dead on funeral pyres, and build a low frame house over the carefully gathered ashes. The ceremonies over the tomb differ in some respects from those of the Goldee.

The Goldee, after the death of relatives, make a wooden idol under the belief that the soul of the deceased enters it. They then place food near the idol, besmearing its face with oil, offering up prayers and other ceremonies upon the tomb, and after some peculiar service has been performed by the Schamans, the soul of the dead is supposed to have departed from the idol to Paradise, whereupon the idol is broken and cast away.

The Gelack, on the contrary, take the favorite dog of the deceased, feed it with choice food for some time, and after the prayers of the Schamans, when it is supposed that the soul of the deceased has departed out of the dog (where they believe it had been residing up to this time) and gone to Paradise, they then sacrifice the dog upon the grave.

The character of the Gelack is harsh and austere. They are active, fond of gain, enterprising, and disposed to trade—except those living on Sakhahlin, who are inclined to pillage and murder, and are in a very rude and barbarous state. The probability is that the Gelack on the Amoor, though now free from the Manchoo yoke, were formerly under their control, or, if not, have either been taught by straggling Manchoos, or borrowed from them or their serfs, the Goldee, the art of building their houses.

The houses of the Gelack on the Amoor resemble those of the Goldee, while those on Sakhahlin have conical huts half buried in the ground, with an opening in the top for the smoke to escape, all going to prove that those on the Amoor, being on the borders of Tartar civilization, have very likely borrowed a little from them.

In the summer, the Gelack are exclusively occupied in fishing, but in the winter they make trading voyages to Sakhahlin with their sleighs, drawn by dogs, in order to trade with the Inees and Japanese, as well as to the coast of Tartary, to the south of De Castries. Sometimes they also proceed by the Amoor to visit the Manchoos in order to trade their furs for Chinese merchandise, which they again barter with great profit to their more southern neighbors.

The number of native inhabitants upon the lower Amoor (I use this term native in contradistinction to the great khans or hordes of Manchoo and Mongul) may be deduced from the following facts :

From the mouth up, to the distance of two hundred and fifty miles, occupied by Gelack, there are, on the right side, twenty-six, and on the left thirteen villages, containing in all about one hundred and forty houses. Counting four families to each house and three persons in each family, will give twelve persons to each house. It is true that in some houses as many as twenty-five persons are found, but in others only five or six. Therefore, multiplying one hundred and forty by twelve will give the total population of the Gelack sixteen hundred and eighty.

In the distance of three hundred miles from Bogortskoy to Geren, occupied by Mangoon, we find forty villages, thirty-six on the right and four on the left shore, with a total of one hundred and ten houses; but the number in each house is less than with the Gelack; but we must take ten to each house, and we have as the number of this tribe eleven hundred.

The Goldee, in a distance of eight hundred miles, until you come to the borders of the Manchoos above the Songahree, have one hundred and fourteen villages, containing three hundred and twenty houses; but their houses are smaller than those of the Mangoon, so that only eight persons reside in each house, which will give twenty-five hundred and sixty as the sum total.

These villages are so distributed that in the distance of three hundred miles from Geren, up and between Ousuree and Songahree rivers, the greater portion of the population is found, while below the Ousuree, for two hundred and fifty miles, it is much less, according to distance.

From De Castries, south to Emperor's Harbor, in about 49° north latitude, it is calculated that there are no more than five hundred souls. The So-mah-gar-see and Ne-ga-dal-sey, one thousand souls; roving Tonguse seventy-five families of four each.

RECAPITULATION.

	Number.	Houses.	Villages.
Gelack	1,680	140	39
Mangoon	1,100	110	40
Goldee	2,560	320	114
Coast Indians	500		
Ne-ga-dal-sey / So-mah-gar-see	1,000		
Tonguse, roving	300		
	7,140	570	193

The population increases as you approach the mouth, and the right shore is more densely settled than the left. The first circumstance can reasonably be ascribed to the fact that the lower Amoor is richer in fish than higher up the stream; and again, the population being greater between the Ousuree and the Songahree, may be attributed to the fact of their planting gardens and keeping cattle and horses, and the possibility of procuring grain for breadstuff from the Manchoos of the Songahree, which makes them less dependent upon fish for their subsistence.

But again, where fish are scarce there also the population is small; as, for instance, from the entrance of the river Hongahree to the entrance of the Ouldjah, a distance of one hundred and fifty miles, only one hundred and twenty persons are living; while on the lower Amoor, in the same distance of coast, there are more than nine hundred and eighty Gelack inhabitants. The same is the case along Ousuree. The water on the right shore of the Amoor being generally the deepest and better for fish may again suggest another reason for its greater population.

CHAPTER LXIX.

TRADE AND RESOURCES OF SIBERIA.

SIBERIA is comparatively a free country. There are no landed proprietors, no serfdom. The land belongs to the crown, and is given to the settlements or villages in the country or to individuals in cities. Public sentiment and speech are quite free also ; in fact, the reins of government seem to set lightly on her people. The people are hardy and robust, accustomed, like our own frontiersmen, to a rough and active life, have the rifle and use it well, as the mountains of furs and skins seen in the cities and market-towns fully attest.

Though the extent of Siberia is very great—greater than that of the United States—yet the population is comparatively confined to a small portion of her vast territory. Leaving the Ural at Ekatherinburg and penetrating east you find the great proportion of the population settled along between the parallel of 52° and 58° north latitude, while, in fact, the whole population, with but a very small fraction, is between 50° and 60° north latitude, stretching over about two thousand miles in longitude, which will make the country covered by population, in extent one million two hundred thousand square miles. The population being twelve millions, will give ten to the mile square. This population, as to density, is greater than that of our territories; in fact, more than equal to some of our states.

The whole extent of Siberia or Asiatic Russia, according to recent estimates, is seven million two hundred thousand square miles, about double the superficial extent of the United States, or about equal to one hundred and forty-four of such states as New York. Much of this country is susceptible of sustaining a population of fifty to the square mile. I may say, in fact, that two millions of square miles of it can well support a population of fifty to the square mile; that would give a population of one hundred millions to that extent. That the country is fully capable of supporting such a population I have no doubt. But even put it at ten to the square mile upon the whole, and you have a population of seventy-two millions.

Siberia reaches from the Ural Mountains to the Pacific Ocean, a distance of 100° of longitude, and from the Great Altai chain to the Frozen Ocean, about 25° north latitude. To which, in a commercial point of view, must now be added the Amoor country, the whole of Tartary, Bucharia, Thibet, and Northern China. These countries contain more than thirty millions of people, who will become tributary to the commerce of the Amoor. It is the only outlet they have to the Ocean, and foreign commerce will naturally seek that channel in the hands of civilized steam communication.

Persons generally who have drank tea in Russia, if

they have any taste, liking, or partiality to the Chinese leaf, have remarked the richness and flavor of the better sort of teas found in Russia. And here it will be as well to remark, that in western and southern Russia it is not always "caravan tea" that the voyager will find upon the road, as, *par excellence*, the Kyachta tea is called; but the greater probability is that he will be served with the very poorest, meanest, and dirtiest black tea, via London, that has found its stealthy way over the Prussian or Polish borders.

In the first place, it will be well to state that all the tea lawfully entering Russia must come overland from China via Pekin and Kyachta, with the exception of one cargo of seven hundred chests imported by sea yearly by "The Imperial American Company of Russia," under a special and exclusive grant in their charter.

The argument in favor of the superiority of "caravan tea" over other tea in Europe, is, that the sea voyage, with its salt atmosphere, the heat and dampness consequent upon a double passage through the tropics and across the equator, the alternation of heat and cold, the sweating, dampness, and confined air, all tend to exhaust and deteriorate from the delicacy of flavor, and add perhaps to it something of the flavor of bilge water and the double sweat-bath it has gone through. And again, the sea-going tea has grown to such an enormous bulk that less pains are taken in its selection, preparation and quality from year to year, besides which adulteration has stepped in to increase the bulk of the poorer qualities of the leaf.

Again, climate, soil, and air, as we know, in many

vegetable productions produce wonderful changes and operate very singularly on the quality of plants. Tobacco, cotton, rice, sugar-cane, the vine, are all affected by very little change in climate, soil, proximity to the sea, or when withdrawn far inland, and this when reproduced from the same seed, plants, graftings, or cuttings. Havana tobacco ceases to be the delicate-flavored plant when transplanted to Missouri. Virginia seed will not produce the "Old Virginia leaf" in Louisiana; the Gulf Hills' seed loses its texture, color, and silkiness in Tennessee; Carolina seed will not reproduce "Carolina rice" on the banks of the Mississippi, nor will "Sea Island cotton" reproduce its like in Alabama. The cane of Louisiana refuses to produce crystallized sugar further north, while it is widely known that the different faces of a hill from the same vine produce two kinds of wine.

Why should not tea be governed by the same general laws, aside from all other considerations?

But again, this Russo-Chinese tea trade has been, as it were, a kind of monopoly and one of regular and steady growth, not subject to those fluctuations or demands or speculations to which the sea-going commerce has been subjected. The taste of the Russians was formed steadily; perhaps certain districts more adjacent to Pekin, having its peculiar soil and climate, at first engaged this commerce and supplied the demand; the peculiar mode of picking, drying, curing, packing, have all concurred to give it uniformity and quality.

Then if you choose the overland passage, the most of the time in an open dry atmosphere, free from dampness, mould, must, salt air, bilge water, or sweat, and in a very cold atmosphere the most of the time, the outer packages enveloped in raw hide; all these considerations, after drinking real "caravan tea," to one who has a taste for it, will furnish the pros and cons of the argument, and, I think, must determine a judge to decide in favor of Kyachta, Mia-mat-tschin, and Pekin tea.

The tea of Kyachta being the leading article of import from China, becomes the pivot upon which all other trade turns. Formerly the most of the trade was one of barter, by treaty only, one-third of the value being paid in silver; woollen cloths, Siberian and Kamschatka furs in the main settling the balance. This more properly prevailed in early times, when the caravans were composed of camels and made their voyages at stated and regular periods. But as the country of Siberia became more populous and merchants increased, and the tea of China became to be really an article of prime necessity in Russia, a very considerable change grew by degrees to be engrafted into this commerce. What was once considered as a great desert and only traversable at stated and appointed times, and that only with camels, has, as commerce increased, come to be a great thoroughfare and highway, traversable at all seasons of the year, and now by oxen drawing loaded carts across this once great desert, and by degrees the appointed time of trade from a few days has increased to several months, during which the merchandise arrives, and consequently trade has grown to be more a regular business than a fair. Be sure the merchants have their particular seasons, according to the mode of conveyance and the necessities of the trade in which the bulk of their commerce takes place; nevertheless there is always trade at Kyachta and Mia-mat-tschin if you have silver or valuable furs. Now, however, under the late Mouravieff Igoon Treaty the whole trade and intercourse has been remodeled on a new and liberal basis to suit the advanced state of commerce and the more intimate relations hereafter to exist between the two empires.

The road is left open and free at all seasons of the year, and commerce will take its own time and tide to suit its own wants and to accommodate itself to its greatest profits.

A regular monthly mail is to run from Kyachta to Pekin, and merchants from either side will be allowed to visit the different countries. A Russian Embassy has ere this taken up its quarters in Pekin, and their superior power and weight upon the north, their intimate knowledge through their old established religious mission at Pekin, their internal commerce in the provinces of Tartary, and the knowledge and use of Russian merchandise for two hundred years past, must give them an influence in the interior of China that no other nation can attain to; added to which, and perhaps more important than all, and more valuable than all else, a large corps of young Russians speaking the Chinese language like natives.

There is a very great misapprehension concerning the fall of snow in high northern latitudes. The fall in depth is not so great, as a general rule, as in the more temperate latitudes. There are peculiar locations where snow falls to a great depth or where the drift is very great, but take it on an average between the parallels of 50° and 60° north latitude, and I do not think the general snow level will be found to be over three feet. That the fall of snow or the severity of the frost would not interfere seriously with the working of a railroad in these high latitudes is evident from the roads from St. Petersburg to Moscow, over four hundred miles, from St. Petersburg to Peterhoff, St. Petersburg to Luga, completed one hundred and thirty-three miles, on the line to Warsaw, of one thousand and seventy-seven miles, St. Petersburgh to Paulosk and Tzars-ko-Ceilo, and the road from Warsaw to Cracow.

Now all these roads are north of 50°, and those about St. Petersburg in near 60°, yet we find no unusual difficulty in their working or any objection to their building on account of climate or snow ; nay, I have no hesitation in saying that these lines are cheaper and more readily worked than those in tropical countries.

From my own observation in European Russia and an entire winter spent between Moscow and the Altaï Mountains in Siberia along on a parallel not much different from Moscow, I have not the least hesitation in saying that railroads are quite as practicable in Siberia and from Europe across the Ural and Altaï Mountains to the head waters of the Amoor as they are from St. Petersburg to Moscow or from Moscow to Warsaw. A line of railroad striking the Amoor from Moscow via Nijne, Kazan, Ekaterinburg, Omsk, Tomsk, and Irkutsk to Kyachta, would be quite as manageable as some of our lines over the Alleghany Mountains or the more northern roads in Canada ; and if the severity of the climate and the fall of snow as a hindrance to the building of a railroad from the head of the Amoor to the sea is all that is to be taken into consideration, and no other or greater difficulties presented themselves to be overcome, a railroad from Moscow to Pekin and the Pacific Ocean might be considered as a fact accomplished.

CHAPTER LXX.

THE AMOOR RAILROAD.

DURING my stay at Chetah I had many conversations with Governor Korsackoff touching the natural resources, navigation, and future prospects of Siberia as connected with the opening of the country to foreign commerce by way of the Amoor.

In my conversations I proposed the plan of uniting the Amoor by railroad with the city of Kyachta and Irkutsk, thereby connecting two systems of internal water-communication and creating a line of transit to the very heart of Siberia. These conversations, which related chiefly to railroads, telegraph, and steamboats, led to the following correspondence:

CHETAH, March 9th, 1857.

SIR,—Herewith you will find a proposition to construct a railroad from Chetah to Irkutsk. After having passed over the greater part of the country through which the road would naturally pass, and from information which I believe reliable, there can be no doubt but that the construction of a railroad is highly practicable. Chetah, situated on the Ingodah at a point which may be relied upon as the head of steamboat navigation on the waters of the Amoor River, presents a favorable point from whence to cross the country in order to reach Irkutsk by the nearest practicable route. The Stamovey Mountains present no very great obstacle to the enterprise ; in fact the country, generally speaking, so far as I have been able to see myself, and from the information obtained from the most reliable authority, presents very great facilities for such an enterprise. The Amoor must become in the hands of Russia a very important country, through which a great trade will flow, opening Siberia to the commerce of the world. What is necessary then is to assist nature a little, and, by building this road, make the heart of Siberia easily accessible to commerce, so that her products can be quickly and readily exchanged or transported to the ocean by way of this railroad and the Amoor, where a ready market can be found. With steam upon the Amoor, and this railroad constructed, aside from commercial views, the road would be highly valuable to Russia in the development and protection of her possessions on the Pacific coast, both in Asia and America.

But it is unnecessary to enter more at large at present into the great advantages Russia must derive from perfecting speedy and certain communications to the Pacific. All that is necessary is to regard the map, which will at once speak more than I can write.

I remain, very truly,

Your obedient servant,

P. McD. Collins.

To General Korsackoff,

Governor of Trans-Baïkal, Eastern Siberia.

Proposition to construct a railroad from Chetah to Irkutsk, by "The Amoor Railroad Company."

1st. The right of way, with alternate sections of land, six versts deep by three versts long, on each side of the road, to be donated to the company.

2d. The company to have the right to take from the government lands, free of charge, stone and other materials necessary for the construction of the road and its appurtenances.

3d. The government of Russia to furnish the iron necessary to the construction of the road from the Imperial Works in Trans-Baïkal, at a stipulated price, which shall be reasonable, for which amount the government to become stockholders in the road.

4th. All objects for the use of the government to be transported at reasonable and stipulated rates.

5th. The stock of the company to be divided into shares of one hundred rubles each, and books of subscription to be opened in Siberia, where any person may be entitled to subscribe for any number of shares by paying ten per cent. on the value of the stock subscribed for, and the remainder in five equal annual instalments of eighteen kopycks on the ruble.

6th. If it be found impracticable to procure the necessary laborers in Siberia to construct the road, the company to have the right to import them upon contract from China or elsewhere to aid in its construction. The company to be responsible for their conduct, and if, upon the conclusion of the contract, the government is unwilling that they should remain in the country, the company to remove them.

7th. If it should be practicable, and the government willing to furnish the necessary laborers from European Russia, then it may be done on the following conditions, viz.: The company will require twenty thousand effective men. Within the first year after the conclusion of the contract the government must furnish five thousand, to be delivered to the company at Irkutsk, and the remaining fifteen thousand the year following; otherwise the sixth article to remain in full force. In removing the laborers from Russia a man and his family to be counted as two persons. The cost of removing the laborers to be agreed upon at St. Petersburg before the conclusion of the contract.

8th. The government to have the right at any time, by guaranteeing seven per cent. on the cost of the road, to purchase it, payable in twenty years.

9th. The road and its appurtenances to be forever free from any tax or exaction of any nature on the part of the local authorities or of the imperial government.

10th. When it shall occur that there may be minerals on any of the lands belonging to the company, then said company to have the right to work them subject to the laws of the country; and in case the mineral lands are prohibited to be worked, then the company to be compensated in other lands of equal extent in other sections.

11th. In case the government cannot furnish all the iron required by the company, then said company to have the right to construct the necessary works upon such mineral lands as they may choose in order to manufacture the deficiency after the completion of the road, the government to have the right to purchase the works erected by the company at a price to be agreed upon, at which time it shall also be adjusted what compensation the government shall receive for the use of the mines, which shall go towards the payment of the purchase of the company's works.

P. McD. Collins.

Chetah, Eastern Siberia,
Government of Trans-Baïkal,
March 9th, 1857.

In order that the contract may be concluded as early as possible in 1858, it will be necessary that I shall receive a favorable answer in July at Nicolaivsky.

P. McD. Collins.

Translation of General Korsackoff's Reply.

City of Chetah, 14th March, 1857.

Dear Sir,—Having received your letter of March 9th, with the propositions for the construction of a railroad from the city of Chetah to that of Irkutsk, and fully recognizing all the advantages that must result from such an enterprise to the Trans-Baïkal province under my administration if your proposition might be realized by our government:—I reported on this subject by a special courier to the governor-general of Eastern Siberia, Lieutenant-General Mouravieff the III.

I shall not fail to transmit to you His Excellency's answer so soon as it reaches me.

Receive, Dear Sir, the assurance of the distinguished consideration with which I have the honor to be,

Your obedient servant,
Michael Korsackoff.

To Mr. Collins,
Consular Agent, &c., U. S. A.

From General Mouravieff.

IRKUTSK, March 26th, 1857.

SIR,—It is to my greatest satisfaction that I have received from General Korsackoff the project of a railroad which you have the intention to build in the Trans-Baïkal country.

I have already sent it with a courier to St. Petersburg, and I do not doubt that you will receive an answer to your proposal before your departure to America.

I sincerely wish our government may give its consent to an enterprise in which I take the most lively interest, and in which I wish you all possible success. * * *

May I take the liberty to pray you, Sir, to have the kindness of rendering to Rear-Admiral Kosakevitch the papers I have written to him in relation to you.

In hopes that I shall see you on the Amoor next year,

I have the honor to remain, Sir,

Your obedient servant,

NICHOLAS MOURAVIEFF.

TO PERRY MCD. COLLINS, &c.

To General Mouravieff.

CHETAH, Trans-Baïkal, April 4th, 1857.

SIR,—Your favor of the 26th ultimo was received by the hand of Captain Booeved a few days since, after my return from a visit to the mines of Nerchinsk. * * *

I should have forwarded by return of the courier the acknowledgment of your favor, but a sudden illness prevented.

It is with great satisfaction that I receive the advice under your own hand of the favorable estimate of the Amoor railroad project, and of the despatch that you have given it to St. Petersburg.

In looking over this vast and truly interesting country, one is more and more impressed with the necessity of communication by the Amoor; without this it is a country closed to the commerce of the world.

After my arrival here and a sojourn of some days with our truly noble friend, General Korsackoff, and having made all possible inquiry and investigation concerning the navigability of the Ingodah from this point to its entrance into the Schilkah, I came to the conclusion that it is entirely practicable to navigate the Ingodah with steamboats to this city.

I also became anxious to see the whole length of the river from this place. In anticipation of my wishes, and to facilitate the voyage, General Korsackoff generously proposed that I should embark from this point, and has had the goodness to order the construction of a boat for this purpose, so that I am now here awaiting the breaking up of the ice in the river and shall absolutely embark at this point.

This gives me the most profound satisfaction, for I shall then be able to see with my own proper eyes this whole system of navigation to the ocean. Having now seen myself that from the navigable waters of Lake Baïkal to those of the Amoor it is less than four hundred versts direct, which absolutely comes within my estimate before I visited the country, I feel entirely certain that a railroad will be built—for within a few years, with the Amoor open to commerce, the imperious necessities of the country will demand it.

So that, even if we find it cannot be accomplished through our efforts, we shall have the remembrance (satisfactory to ourselves) of having known the wants of the country only a little in advance of the times.

Of course the road must reach Irkutsk, from whence would be distributed the whole trade and enterprise of Siberia, making Irkutsk a great city, as it is justly entitled to be—the centre and capital not only of Eastern Siberia but of Northern Asia—from whence in a very few years after the completion of this enterprise, a commerce of fifty millions of rubles would flow annually.

The papers you have had the kindness to forward to Rear-Admiral Kosakevitch concerning me I will deliver in person, and for them you have my thanks.

I have received this day, by the hand of your courier, the letter to my address from St. Petersburg as well as your note of 2d instant. Rest assured, Sir, that I have not the least uneasiness in regard to the accidental opening of the letter; it is readily to be perceived that it arose from the manner of its superscription by the person who addressed it to you at St. Petersburg. America has no secrets she would conceal from so noble a friend as she finds in you.

In conclusion allow me to subscribe myself your much indebted and

Very obedient servant,

PERRY McD. COLLINS.

To His Excellency

LIEUTENANT-GENERAL MOURAVIEFF III.,

Governor-General of Eastern Siberia, Irkutsk.

APPENDIX.

COMMERCIAL PROGRESS IN EASTERN ASIA.

At about the epoch of the accession of the present Manchoo dynasty (1642) over China, the hardy Russian exiles, gold-diggers and fur-hunters, led on, probably, by some daring Cossack, who had emigrated, either with or without his own consent, to the head waters of the Amoor, began to extend their hunting and fishing excursions, mixed, perhaps, with a little freebooting, along the shores of the Amoor to the east. Most probably the whole course of the Amoor to the sea was well known to these hardy pioneers, and that some trade was even had with the Kamchadales.

The boldness and audacity of these Nerchinsk hunters soon brought them into conflict, upon the southern shore of the Amoor, with the constituted authorities of the Manchoos; for their appropriating propensities did not always allow them to distinguish, with the precaution of good neighbors, between the absolutely wild herds of deer and elk and the half-wild herds of cattle, horses, and camels of their Manchoo neighbors. Serious conflicts soon took place, and complaints were made to the supreme authority of China against the marauding Russians. The progress of these free hunters of the Nerchinsk was, however, so rapid and so successful, that fortified camps or towns began to be established upon the north shore of the Amoor, several hundred miles in advance of imperial Russian title to the soil.

Escaped convicts, desperate and hardy adventurers, with the riff-raff of a convict, Cossack, and mining population, joined heartily in the fortunes of these new and distant settlements, where Russian power and law for the punishment of crime had not yet reached.

The Russian government unquestionably sympathized with these enterprises on the high-road to the Pacific, and was willing enough to let them go on, watching its own opportunity to make them legitimate.

CAM-HI, a Manchoo, coming to the throne of China about this time, saw plainly enough, that if the Russians were not promptly restrained but little of the vast territory of the Amoor would remain to China. He accordingly set on foot an expedition to drive the Russians from their comfortable quarters at Albasin, which was the chief point of Russian strength.

The Albasinians, finding they were to have serious trouble, perhaps a bloody conflict with organized Chinese troops, repaired to the Russian authorities of Nerchinsk, after the example of Yermack to the Emperor, to hand over to the government all the newly-acquired territory and possessions, together with themselves, on condition of receiving aid to repel the expected Chinese troops—the Russian government granting a full and free pardon to all of her subjects found upon the Amoor who had taken a hasty leave of absence on their own authority.

The two governments were thus soon brought into armed conflict, but CAM-HI's soldiers were too numerous on the Amoor; Albasin capitulated, the Russians retired within their stipulated borders, and the Chinese power ruled supreme on the whole line of the Amoor to the sea; and not long afterwards Chinese embassadors, escorted by a numerous and well-appointed army, with a train of artillery, presented themselves before the gates of Nerchinsk, and constrained GOLOVIN, the Russian ambassador, to conclude a treaty, by which Russia abandoned all claims to the Amoor country, or navigation upon its waters. Since that day, 27th August, 1689, up to about 1853–'4, the commerce and military operations of Russia to the east, toward the shores and coasts of the Ohotsk, Kamschatka, and her American possessions, have been conducted by an immense detour to the north, by way of Yakutsk to Ohotsk or Ayan, and thence distributed, the furs returning to Kyachta and St. Petersburg over the same road. Thus for near two centuries has Russia awaited patiently the development of her power and the right opportunity to seize upon the Amoor and hold it.

Up to the close of 1860 we have reliable information of the following steamers and steamships either navigating or preparing to navigate the Amoor and its approaches: AMERICA, MANCHOOR, JAPANESE, sea-going, built in the United States; two river steamers, LENA and AMOOR, constructed in Philadelphia, iron, shipped and set up at the Amoor; one on private account, at Boston, and two at San Francisco. The Russian government built two at Shilka, over two thousand two hundred miles by the course of the Amoor and Shilka rivers from the sea, and steamed them to the Straits of Tartary. The Russian government has also partly organized a force of ten small courier or mail steamers, which are to keep up postal and military communication along the whole course of the Amoor, Shilka, and Ingodah rivers, and connect with the Chinese and Siberian system of overland communication at Irkootsk.

The Amoor Company (Russian) have had constructed in Europe one steamer, sea-going, and five river steamers. The Russian American Company has two sea-going steamers which visit the Amoor, where the headquarters of the company for the Pacific is now located.

From the fact that Nicolivsky, the port of the Amoor, is a

military post, and not a commercial port, under custom-house regulations, no exact return of merchandise entered can be given. The papers, manifest, and bills of lading of vessels are handed over to the captain of the port, and by him retained until they sail. There being no custom-house, or duties, the value of cargoes stated cannot be relied upon, because it is the policy of merchants frequenting the Amoor to conceal as much as possible from rivals the nature and extent of cargoes taken there for sale.

In 1856, first year of foreign intercourse, only two foreign ships entered the Amoor—both American. In 1857 seven merchant ships arrived in the Amoor, with cargoes amounting to 500,000 silver roubles. In 1858 four ships entered with 805 tons of freight for government, and merchandise amounting to 174,650 silver roubles, including 72,444 roubles in value of Russian production. In 1859 thirteen foreign merchant ships arrived at the Amoor. The total traffic from foreign countries and from the upper Amoor, amounted to 1,090,714 silver roubles; at Nicolawsky, from the upper Amoor, 140,114 silver roubles, while the total import and export amounted to 1,230,829 silver roubles.

The port of Nicolivsky has 2,183 male and 369 female inhabitants. There were forty-nine government houses and two hundred private residences, besides twenty-seven government houses uninhabited. There were twelve stores, of which five were American, making in all two hundred and eighty-eight houses.

Among the inhabitants were, 1,518 military, of all grades, with their wives and attachés.

In 1859 there were seven foreign merchants, five of whom were Americans.

In 1860 the amount of merchandise received was greater than the previous year, though the sales, owing to temporary causes, had not been so profitable. One American house had withdrawn, but three others had been added. One of the Amoor Company's steamers had ascended the Amoor, but to what point it is not stated.

The number of vessels entered is not stated, but supposed to be ten to fifteen.

Again, in regard to the commerce to the Amoor in American bottoms, we can get no returns of clearances from American ports, because, with but two or three exceptions, vessels intended for the Amoor have cleared for "ports in the Pacific;" consequently, the true returns are not to be had.

In the figures given above we have only a partial statement of the actual value of commerce at the Amoor. The great probability is that neither the transactions of the government in the purchase of machinery, naval stores, and provisions, nor the commerce of the Russian-American Company, are included. During 1856 and 1857 fully 700 barges and rafts descended the Amoor from the Trans-Baikal province of Eastern Siberia, freighted with munitions, provisions, merchandise, and live stock. The most of them for government account, but the Russian-American Company and private parties had some share in the expedition.

The Amoor is formed by the junction of the Schilka and Argoon, in 121° 40′ E. L., and 53° 30′ N. L., and, after a very tortuous course of two thousand miles, falls into the Straits of Tartary, in about 140° E. L., 53° N. L. The Amoor is navigable for steamers its whole length.

The winter is severe, but not much more so than Moscow, or in equal degrees of latitude on the Volga. The natural floral and cultivated productions of the country indicate a good grain, fruit, and grass country, being also well adapted to the rearing of flocks and herds.

The province of Trans-Baikal (Eastern Siberia), which

lies in part upon the head-waters of the Amoor, viz., the Schilka and Argoon, contains a population of 340,000, and is the chief source in Eastern Siberia from whence the Russian government procures its silver; the mines are rich and extensive. These mines are, however, worked only by the government, but it is reported that they are soon to be opened to the public.

The Amoor is free from ice, and navigable from May to November, which will compare favorably with the navigable season at St. Petersburg.

There is plenty of time and plenty of water, with properly constructed steamers and barges, or keel-boats, to conduct the commerce, during open water, to such points upon its head-waters as convenience and experience may decide upon, where the overland conveyance will be ready to distribute it to the remotest points of the interior. During the winter all the return produce of the country will be concentrated at these depots, ready for shipment to meet the sea-going vessels arriving at tide-water in the spring, and thus the commerce will be regularly and conveniently conducted much on the same plan as at St. Petersburg.

To what extent, or how advantageously this new field of Oriental Asiatic commerce is to be occupied by Americans, depends upon the sagacity and nerve of our merchants.

At first the commerce to the Amoor will be most profitably conducted by sailing vessels; barks of two hundred and fifty to three hundred and fifty tons burden being, in my opinion, the best fitted for that trade. Schooners of one hundred to one hundred and fifty tons may also be employed, for special voyages to Japan, China, or San Francisco. Vessels should be of good beam, and not more than ten to twelve feet draft.

Upon the Amoor there should be two classes of steamers: 1st. Side-wheel, of three hundred tons, with a draft of six feet. These would navigate to the mouth of the Zea, or about two-thirds of the distance, and may, in the early summer, reach the head of the Amoor. 2d. Stern-wheel steamers, having twenty feet beam, one hundred and thirty to fifty feet long, with four to four and a half feet hold, and ample power. These steamers would reach the head of navigation, and place their cargoes at available points, from whence sledges, wagons, and pack-trains would distribute them throughout the interior of Siberia and Tartary.

Steamers on the Amoor are absolutely necessary to its commercial development. We cannot look, at first, to the immediate shores of the river for any large development of commerce; it is to the Siberian and overland trade from whence we are to reap the first great results. This can only be accomplished by a regular, certain, and well-organized system of steam navigation throughout the whole length of the Amoor, Schilka, and Ingodah rivers. Depots of merchandise must be established at points upon the head-waters of the Amoor, where the Siberian, Chinese, and Tartar tradesmen may resort at all times, and where they may, beyond peradventure, find a full supply of such commodities as they desire. There must be no failure in the supplies on hand at these depots, because Moscow, Nijne, Novgorod, St. Petersburg, Pekin, and Irbit are at great distances, and a failure of supply on the Amoor would be the loss of a year's supply to the trader, and consequently he would lose faith in the Amoor, and seek other marts for his supplies.

The kind of merchandise at first introduced must conform to the choice of experienced Siberian and Northern Chinese merchants. As we progress, we may introduce new articles and more extensive varieties, as well as to manufacture for them goods of such exact pattern, finish, and style as they may order, which will become a very important branch of commerce.

By penetrating at once to the head of the Amoor, we tap a regular, well-established, and systematic commerce, both Asiatic and European, a commerce that has been conducted with great success and much spirit for a long time. Here we may take our stand and build upon a sure foundation. The increase, development, and extent of this commerce depend much upon the class and calibre of merchants who initiate it; they must neither be wanting in mind nor in dollars. It is a wide field, and a distant one; its cycle is a year, consequently patient capitalists only can enter it with any hope of success.

The lower Amoor and Manchooria are not to be forgotten; but, as they are on the high-road to Siberia, and always within our grasp as we are passing along with our well-freighted steamers, to supply them is a very easy matter.

The favorable and enlightened policy of the Russian government has already given us free trade for five years, and Count MOURAVIEFF, who is the father of the annexation of the Amoor to Russia, is in favor of a prolongation of this liberal policy; in fact, the progress and importance of Russian interests in Asia, under Count MOURAVIEFF's administration of the government of Eastern Siberia, has given him great power and influence, and his views are very likely to prevail.

As evidence of the importance that Russia attaches to her new possession upon the Pacific, we have only to mention the fact that the government is now constructing a line of telegraph, which is to connect St. Petersburg with the mouth of the Amoor and other points upon the Pacific coast, and along the whole northern border of Chinese Tartary. The line will be in operation this year as far as Omsk, in Western Siberia, one-third of the distance from St. Petersburg to the Pacific; in another year it will reach Irkootsk, or probably Kyachta, and so on, in the course of the third year, we may expect it to reach the ocean.

The project now on foot, to tap the Russian line at the Amoor, and carry a line of telegraph *via* BEHRING's Straits, to unite with the California overland line, will give us telegraphic union with Europe; in fact, with the whole world. Nor is it a project so difficult, upon investigation, as it at a first glance appears; the climate presents no impediment, and there is but forty miles of ocean to cross.

The extent of country opened to commercial contact through the Amoor is a matter of interest.

The valley of the Amoor covers from west to east about 40° longitude, and north to south about 13° latitude, probably nearly a million square miles of territory, with a population of some five millions.

Mongolia, Songaria, Northern and Central Tartary, cover a vast extent of territory, six hundred miles wide by two thousand long, with a population of probably ten millions.

These people are rich in cattle, sheep, horses, and camels; a barter of merchandise for their hides, skins, pelts, wool, hair, and tallow would be large and lucrative.

Eastern Siberia, which would be tributary to the commerce of the Amoor, is also a vast country, covering a million of square miles, with a population of two millions to three millions of European blood.

This immense country is dependent, to a great extent, on Europe and China for its fabrics of cotton, silk, flax, and wool; to estimate the value of commerce on the specific supply and demand is quite impossible from present data. We know that the Kyachta tea trade has developed a commerce of fifteen to twenty millions of dollars per annum; what amount of European merchandise Siberia consumes we have no precise knowledge, but we may safely put it at ten millions.

The fair supposition is, that every inhabitant will consume six yards of cotton cloth yearly; and we only put this as an illustration of the value of commerce in one single item, which must govern us in making up the future of this commerce. This would give us 102,000,000 yards of cotton cloth, worth, delivered, certainly ten cents a yard, amounting to $10,200,000.

A very reasonable and important question to be answered is: How are we to be paid for what these people want? Where are the millions of hard dollars to come from out of this wild and distant country, to compensate or equalize this commerce?

To begin with Siberia: she is the California of Russia; her mineral wealth is absolutely beyond any reasonable array of figures. She exports to Russia about $15,000,000 of gold yearly; need more be said?

She has copper, plumbago, tin, silver, marbles, iron, salt, bitumen, and precious stones.

She has hemp, flax, furs, skins and peltry, wool, tallow, wax, honey, and ivory.

She has tar, pitch, and turpentine. All these are elements of wealth, and the contact of an extra-territorial commerce, proffering articles of necessity, convenience, and luxury, must excite her population to make an exchange.

Mongolia and Tartary have their skins, pelts, wool, camels' hair, hides, and tallow. To these must be added Thibet musk, Bucharian rhubarb, pearls, and precious stones.

What can be the amount of these articles that these people will have for export? I do not know—but one item I can suggest. Mutton is the chief article of diet, and I suppose, from my own experience and a knowledge of Tartar appetite, that three sheep *per capita* per annum to the whole population would be a very reasonable allowance. Here we have thirty millions of sheep skins, with the wool included, as one item of the production of this country.

Manchooria and the Amoor River country come next; here foreign commerce has, up to within a very recent period, been absolutely excluded. It is only since Russia has made this eastward step that outside barbarians have been permitted to look into this country. While Mongolia is strictly a pastoral country, Manchooria is both agricultural and pastoral; yielding, besides, all the more northern grains, corn, rice, silk, and ginseng.

Heretofore the commerce of this country has been, of necessity, all directed toward Pekin and Corea; but may we not hope that in a contact along the whole northern border of the Manchooria that a very large and lucrative commerce can be introduced? Like the Mongols, the Manchoos have abundance of cattle, horses, and sheep, but having bread, their diet is not so strictly carnivorous as the Mongols.

The Manchoos have, however, many fine furs, beside the skins and pelts of wild animals.

The wilder portion of the Amoor country, which now belongs to Russia, that is, all north of the Amoor River, and all east of the Ousuree, from its confluence with the Amoor, and following the Ousuree to the south through Lake Hinka, and on to the border of Corea, forms again a distinct subdivision of this part of Asia, in extent covering, probably, not far from 300,000 square miles. This country has an aboriginal population of some sixty thousand; what the Russian and Manchoo population may be is difficult to state with any degree of certainty.

The Russian government has already commenced a system of colonization both from Europe and Siberia, and is actively engaged in fortifying its approaches seaward, and in planting military posts and opening post-roads in order to protect the frontier and afford facilities for certain and rapid overland communication at all seasons of the year.

The demand for foreign commerce is of course restricted to mere necessity, and to the actual population of the coasts and borders of the river, because, as yet, steam has not succeeded in presenting to the upper and distant populations stores of merchandise to save them the necessity of the overland, European, and Chinese supply.

This country is rich in fur animals, the rivers abound in fish, and gold is found in the mountains to the north of the Amoor. The forests, both upon the Upper and Lower Amoor, are fair and abundant, with ample resources for naval stores and timber for all economic purposes.

The island of Sak-ha-lin, opposite the mouth of the Amoor, abounds in extensive deposits of coal suitable for steam vessels, accessible and already worked by the Russian government.

The steady and onwark progress of the present Emperor of Russia, ALEXANDER II., in ameliorating the condition of his people, and in encouraging internal commerce and communication, will open a vast field to American enterprise and commerce.

The Mouravieff-Igoon Convention, ratified by the Ignatieff-Pekin treaty, has annihilated all of those ancient border restrictions against free intercourse between the Chinese and Russians.

Under this treaty, merchants and traders may freely cross the frontier and establish themselves in such towns and cities as they choose, the police authorities being specially directed to protect them.

This liberal policy will give great stimulus to the Siberian and Amoor merchants, and must lead to the introduction of European and American merchandise and manufactures into the interior of the whole length and breadth of Tartary.

We have also a recent ukase of the Emperor, granting to foreigners equal privileges with the native Russian merchants in all parts of the empire. This ukase will explain itself, is one of great liberality, and must lead to most important results, opening, as it does, this vast empire to the merchants and bankers of the world.

On the 7th–19th July, 1860, the Emperor addressed to the Senate the following ukase:

"The Imperial manifest of the 1st January, 1807, has set certain restrictions to the commercial rights of foreigners estab lished either permanently or temporarily in Russia. Now, with the improvements introduced in the means of communication, and the rapid development of the international commercial relations, said restrictions do not agree any longer with the necessities of the present times. On the other hand, the principal European powers allow our subjects, as in general to all foreigners, to carry on commerce in their countries on the same terms as their own subjects.

"Taking into consideration the useful influence that would result to all branches of public wealth by an extension granted to the facility of profiting by use of foreign capital in all kinds of enterprises, and desirous to give, at the same time, a new proof of our particular solicitude for the general prosperity of trade, agriculture, and of industry in the Empire, and show, at the same time, a just reciprocity toward foreign powers, we have thought proper to grant, in this respect, to foreigners residing in Russia the same rights as our subjects enjoy amongst the principal European nations.

"Consequently, and in accordance with the opinion of the Council of the Empire, we decree:

"1*st*. It is allowed to foreigners to inscribe themselves in all the guilds of merchants in like manner as the subjects of the Empire, and to enjoy all the commercial rights that those guilds give to Russian merchants. (*Art.* 87, *à* 107 *du reglement sur le commerce, tome xi., du corps des Lois, de* 1857.)

"*First Observation.*—The foreign Israelite subjects, known by their social position and by the great extent of their commerce, who arrive from abroad, can, according to the order established—that is to say, on a special authorization each time by the Ministers of Finance, of the Interior and of Foreign Affairs—trade in the Empire and establish banking-houses on procuring a license of merchant of first guild. It is also allowed them to establish factories, buy and take on lease real estate, according to the resolution of the present ukase.

"*Second Observation.*—The commercial rights granted to Asiatics are resolved by the articles 227 to 233 of the commercial regulations. (*Tome xi., corps des Lois, edition de* 1857.)

"2*d.* The safety of the domicil and of the magazines of foreigners, as well as of the lands that appertain to them, are placed under the protection of the common law; no search can be made in their dwellings, nor in their commercial books, but in accordance to the regulations prescribed in such cases to Russian subjects of the same condition.

"3*d.* Foreigners can acquire—be it by purchase, be it by inheritance, legacy, donation, concession of the Crown, etc.—all kinds of movable and immovable property, with the exception, however, of that which the hereditary Russian nobility and foreigners who have obtained the right can alone possess in virtue of laws in force.

"4*th.* Foreigners, with the exception of Israelites, can direct, under title of clerk, inhabited lands, if they have the procuration of the proprietors to that effect. It is also allowed them farms, according to agreements allowed by the laws, real estate occupied, and of any other kind, inhabited or not, by conforming only to the condition and restriction imposed upon the subjects of the Empire. (*Code Civil, livre iv., cest. iii., ch.* 2.)

"The Senate will take the necessary measures for the execution of the present.

"ALEXANDRE."

In order to make this subject more readily comprehended by our readers, we annex in full the report to the House of Representatives in February last. It is one of the most important commercial subjects of the day.

[U. S. CONGRESS OFFICIAL REPORT.]

SURVEY OF THE NORTHERN WATERS, COASTS, AND ISLANDS OF THE PACIFIC OCEAN, &c.

Mr. JOHN COCHRANE, from the Committee on Commerce, made the following report, February 18, 1861:

The Committee on Commerce, to whom was referred the memorial of PERRY McD. COLLINS, asking the aid of Congress, in order to make a thorough exploration and survey of the coasts, islands, and seas of the Russian possessions, both in Asia and America, from the mouth of the Amoor River, in Asiatic Russia, to the confines of the Russian possessions in America, adjoining the possessions of Great Britain, in view of the construction of a line of telegraph, which shall unite the city of New York, in the United States of America, and consequently the whole of the United States, Canada, and the British possessions in America, with not only London, but with all the great capitals of Europe and Asia, respectfully report: That the committee have had under consideration the said memorial, and, after mature reflection and a study of the importance of the proposition, have been deeply impressed with its great value to commerce.

In the first place, what is it that Mr. COLLINS proposes?

"The telegraphic union of Europe with America, overland, *via* Asiatic Russia and BEHRING'S Straits."

Can this be accomplished? Let us see.

It is already known to practical working telegraphists, that high latitudes add to rather than retard the electric current. During snow-storms the escape of electricity over the common wire and pole telegraph is essentially diminished; thus, while rain and moisture are good conductors, snow, ice, and a dry, cold atmosphere are good non-conductors, or insulators; consequently, high latitudes are favorable to the free and rapid passage of the electric current.

But in this connection we do not have to depend upon theory alone to substantiate the truth of the foregoing proposition; we have existing lines of telegraph stretching from Berlin to Vienna, from Vienna to St. Petersburg, from St. Petersburg to Moscow, and from Moscow eastward to Perm—all to the north of 47°, and as high as 60° north latitude. Here, then, we have positive and irrefragable proof of the practicability of telegraphic communication in very high latitudes.

Being satisfied that telegraphic communication can be successfully maintained in high latitudes, we will, in the next place, inquire as to the country over which it is proposed to construct this line, in view of its practical maintenance.

It is well known, that from Moscow to Kamschatka the Russian government hold absolute sway, and have a continual system of overland communication, absolutely free from interruption, so far as the inhabitants of the whole intervening country is concerned. There is not on the whole line a single hostile tribe or nation. The absolute, the peaceful, the patriarchal sway maintained by the imperial government over this vast extent of country might be a profitable, a humane, and a practical study of our own government in the control and government of the red tribes inhabiting the great interior of our own country, from the borders of Missouri to the Sierra Nevada Mountains and the Pacific Ocean.

The accompanying papers indicate more precisely the different routes by which it is proposed to reach the American shore. Therefore, we do not propose to examine them in detail. We will not refrain, however, from expressing our conviction, in view of all the difficulties, physical, mechanical, and experimental, that the route which involves the least amount of submerged cable should take preference. Up to the present time experience has proved that submerged cables of any great length are, practically, of no value for telegraphic purposes. Without going into lengthened or tedious detail, we have sufficient evidence of the truth of this proposition, not in isolated or unimportant cases, but in gigantic and costly efforts to unite continents.

First in time and place were the efforts to unite Europe and Africa, next Europe and America, and lastly Africa and India. All these great schemes have failed, apparently from physical difficulties; for if science, ingenuity, hardihood, and indomitableness ever gained a victory by their united efforts in a great cause, we certainly should have had, ere this, telegraphic communication nearly around the earth. We all know the history of the Atlantic cable, and of other long, deep-sea cables; but perhaps the facts in regard to the Suez and Kurachee cable, or, as it is more familiarly known, "the Red Sea cable," because quite recent, may be instructive.

The British government, being very anxious to establish telegraphic communication between her own insular shores and her far-off Indian possessions, determined either to construct or to encourage to be constructed submerged lines from England to Gibraltar, from Gibraltar to Malta, thence to Egypt and overland to Suez, from whence a cable was to stretch along the bottom of the Red Sea to Aden, along the Arabian coast to Muscat, and thence under the Arabian Sea to the mouths of the Indus.

This gigantic work was to place Bombay, Calcutta, and Singapore in the immediate and visible presence of the Foreign Office, where in peace or in war, by night or by day, secured from friend or enemy, from accident or design, the premier and viceroy could hold council over the destinies of India, six thousand miles distant.

Under tenders to the British government a company was

formed, with a capital of £1,000,000 for the construction of the line from Suez to Kurachee, in India. Four and a half per cent. interest per annum was guaranteed by the government for fifty years upon the capital; provided, only, that the company expended the money in good faith, whether the cable proved permanently a working telegraph or not. These were the best terms the government could get; the contract was made, and the cable has been submerged; it worked for a short time, and then, like its great predecessor, the Atlantic cable, ceased to speak.

Very recent accounts tell us, that after every effort upon the part of the most able and efficient practical telegraphists, like the Atlantic cable, it has been abandoned to the fishes, and remains only another gigantic monument to the perseverance and liberality of the English government and nation in works of public utility and national importance. Thus we perceive that, up to the present time, some ten thousand miles of deep-sea submerged cable has been lost or abandoned, costing, in the aggregate, not far from ten millions of dollars. We therefore consider, that without some new plan by which a telegraph can be constructed, or the application of some new principle in electricity by which the known difficulties can be overcome, Europe and America must remain as far asunder as if electricity had never been discovered, or MORSE, WHEATSTONE, AMPHERE, and SIEMENS never had lived.

But must mankind, by the intervention of the Atlantic Ocean, be forever barred from the advantages of this agent? We hope not.

Mr. COLLINS has, we think, demonstrated the practicability of the construction of a telegraph line from Moscow to the shores of the Pacific Ocean. Here he was compelled to pause in the personal inspection and exploration of the proposed route, for want of adequate means to cross to the American coast. We perceive, in tracing the route over which it is proposed to construct this line of telegraph, that there are many elements of success in it, besides the fact that no very large bodies of water obstruct its pathway.

The Russian government is now engaged in pushing forward a line to the East, which has already reached Perm, one thousand miles east of Moscow, and is to be continued to the mouth of the Amoor. This line, with its system of lateral branches, unites the whole of Europe, taps the Caspian provinces of Russia, Circassia, Georgia, Persia, and British India, and, consequently, whatever telegraphic connection may exist between Europe and Africa.

Penetrating eastward through the extensive mining districts of the Ural, it leaps from town to town and city to city, until Omsk is reached, from whence a branch will penetrate to the frontier of Chinese Tartary and Kokhan, on the route of the great central caravan trade, vibrating through that immense country between Persia on the west and Manchooria on the east.

Pausing for a few moments at this point, we should take at least a hasty glance of a country which may in a few years figure as one of interest. Russia has been steadily pushing at this point to the south, until she has touched, as it were, British India; not that she has as yet joined territory, but that she has tapped Indian commerce. Turkistan to the west, Thibet to the south, Bucharia, Koko-Nor and inner Mongolia to the east, all combine to make this *southern central wedge*, driven by Russia into the very heart of *Central Asia*, a point that must eventually gather around it an extended and lucrative commerce.

This *central gate of inner Asia*, through which the whole commerce of a vast and populous country must flow, is renowned in history as the pathway of nations—the only practicable pass between Eastern and Western Asia as a central route. Through this *gate* the Great Mogul, GENGHIS, led his victorious hosts, under the banners of a thousand chiefs; where OCTAI and TIMOUR followed, and where MARCO POLO saw an Asiatic Italy, rich in fruits and vines, wines and silks, and all the marks of wealth and luxury.

The approach of Russia to the centre of *Northern India* is really a matter of interest to the civilized world, because it will evidently open that hitherto sealed country to the knowledge of the world and to commerce. It is only a little to the south of the point gained by the late Russian-Chinese treaty that the great pioneer in Asiatic exploration, MARCO POLO, passed, on his way to the court of KUBLAI KHAN.

Yarkand is but five degrees south of the Russian post of Varnoë. MARCO POLO describes the countries through which he passed on the line of Casgar, Yarkand, Hoton, and Pein. He says: "That these countries contain many castles and cities; that the people, besides much merchandise and manufactures, have fine gardens, vineyards, and orchards, with a good supply of silk, and all necessaries in great abundance; cotton is also grown, and the artisans are most skilful; they have also many precious stones."

In fact, MARCO POLO's description of the countries passed through in these central regions makes them quite a second Italy in climate and productions.

The province of Hoton alone is estimated to have (now) a population of two millions and a half. It is through this country, which is, as it were, a gate, in consequence of the approach of the Altai chain of mountains from the north and the Himalaya from the south, without uniting, that an easy passage is found from Eastern to Western Asia, and may be compared, physically, in some respects, as a means of communication, with the Gila route, in traversing our continent.

At the Gila the Rocky Mountains have been broken down, while the Sierra Madre have not yet raised their formidable barriers. Now, suppose the Atlantic side had a population of some three hundred millions, and the Pacific side two hundred millions, even without railroads or steamboats, one could very readily conceive that there would be a very large commerce between the two sections through this pass, even if it had to be carried on the backs of animals, or even of men. But with the hardy Bactrian camel, a train of which is nearly equal to one of our great freight trains on a railroad, the commerce would of necessity and naturally be very considerable. Such is the gate of *Central Asia* now.

The most southern outpost of Russia in this section is in about 43° north latitude, and 78° east longitude; Yarkand is 5° southwest; Samerkand, Kokan, and Bucharia, west by south; on the high caravan route to Persia *via* Yarkand, Laddak, and Cashmere, you reach Cabul; while through Hoton and Murgen the Koko-Nor is reached on the navigable waters of the Ho-ang-ho.

Laddak, it must be remembered, is on the waters of the Indus, and consequently on the high road to British India, and only 8° southwest of the Russian frontier. A glance at the map of Asia will at once show the importance of this gate; and if Russia should will to set up a great national fair there, an Asiatic Nijne-Novgorod would soon spring into existence.

It is not necessary to follow very closely the route proposed to be traversed by the main trunk line of telegraph; we see that it follows along the great post and caravan route, reaching from Moscow to the heart and centre of Russo-Chinese commerce at Kyachta, about four thousand miles to the east.

After leaving Omsk, we have found many towns and cities besides Irkootsk, the capital of Eastern Siberia, at which point concentrates the commerce of a vast country. Irkootsk holds the keys and unlocks all that is to the east for the west, and all that is to the west for the east—a beautiful city, half barbaric, half Asiatic, where refinement and civilization and the energy of Europe have met, subdued, and utilized the fierce hordes of the Steppes.

From Irkootsk to Kyachta, and from Kyachta to Pekin, Nankeen, Shanghai, Amoy, and Hong Kong, seems to be the natural route, all by land, which shall place China, from the great wall to the sea, all under magnetic influence. (*See Note on page* 467.)

From this, *via* the Amoor River, to the shores of the Pacific Ocean, though a new field, is one of much interest; and though but recently brought to the knowledge of the country through the report of Mr. Collins' explorations, recent events have brought it prominently before the commercial world. By the treaty between China and Russia, concluded at Pekin on the 14th November, 1860, it is provided:

"ART. 1. Henceforth the eastern frontier between the two empires shall commence from the junction of the rivers Schilkah and Argoon, will follow the course of the river Amoor to the junction of the Ousuree with the latter. The land on the left (north) bank of the river Amoor belongs to the empire of Russia, and the territory on the right bank (to the south), to the junction of the river Ousuree, to the empire of China. Further on, the frontier line between the two empires, from the point of the issue of the river Sou-gat-chu, divides the Lake Hinka, and takes the direction of the river Be-lin-ho (Tour); from the mouth of the river it follows the mountain range to the mouth of the river Houp-i-tou (Hop-tou), and from thence (that point) the mountains situated between the river Koun-choun and the sea, as far as the river Thou-men-Kiang. Along this line equally the territory on the seaside belongs to the empire of Russia, and that to the west to the empire of China. The frontier line rests on the river Thou-men-Kiang, at twenty Chinese versts (li) above its mouth into the sea."

"On the whole of the frontier line established by this treaty trade free of all duties or restrictions is established between the subjects of the two empires. The local authorities are bound to give special protection to such trade, and to those who exercise it."

Free intercourse is also extended to the citizens of both nations. Thus, at one stroke, the barrier of Chinese exclusiveness has been broken down along the whole northern boundary, and the Amoor River has been opened to free trade from its sources to the sea. This new liberal commercial and boundary treaty must soon work a wonderful change in the interior commerce of that vast country, and must make the Amoor River a great commercial highway.

Tributary to this river there are many millions of people, whose trade and commerce must be vastly augmented by steam, railroads, and telegraphs. This commerce must naturally find outlet to the Pacific through the Amoor, where our merchants may congregate, and with their ships distribute it to the markets of the world.

From the mouth of the Amoor another lateral line of telegraph is proposed, to extend to Yeddo, the capital of Japan; this is accomplished by crossing to the island of Suk-hah-lin, to Jesso, to Niphon, upon which Yeddo is situated, with about only fifty miles of submerged cable. Thus we have progressed from Moscow to the shores of the Pacific Ocean without meeting with more than the ordinary physical difficulties on great lines of telegraph, and have, in a very hasty manner and to a very inconsiderable extent, touched upon the trade, commerce, population, and resources of this vast country, yet, in the main, locked up from the approach of exterior contact and commerce.

We have shown how, by its own local and intrinsic merit, *this route attracts* and *attaches* to itself the whole European system of telegraphs, and also how naturally the Caucasian, Persian, and Indian nations are made tributary to it; and, as we progress to the east, other nations, including China and Japan, are all, as it were, embraced in its ample folds. Having, therefore, as we conceive, annexed Europe, Asia, and Africa, we have yet America to reach, in order to encompass the whole earth.

From the mouth of the Amoor, in order to reach America, there are several routes proposed. Whichever may be the most practicable should most unquestionably be selected. We do not propose to enter into any lengthened argument for or against any of the particular routes; but we have come to the conclusion that until the route *via* Behring's Straits shall be, upon full and fair investigation, pronounced impracticable, to be the route to which we should give our attention. By this route submarine cables are dispensed with, except at one point—the crossing of the straits—and then only to the extent of forty to sixty miles, which may be divided into shorter sections by using islands lying in the straits.

The advantage of this route over all others is so patent, in view of the necessity upon any other line of long submerged cables, that it has only to be stated to be at once fully appreciated. We do not, from all the light before us, believe that the physical difficulties in the way are of such a nature as to be insuperable, though they may be very great. Our greatest apprehension arises from the presence of savage tribes along a portion of the route as you approach Behring's Straits, over which, as yet, the Russian government has not exercised *absolute* control. This objection may, however, be very materially modified when we come to know, by actual contact, how far these tribes are to be controlled, even without force.

It is not apprehended that any unusual stubbornness or difficulty will be encountered, not incident to most of the red tribes, both in America and Asia. However, the cause is worthy of the trial; and until it is known that they cannot be controlled sufficiently to permit the passage of a telegraph through their country, we shall be in favor of the attempt.

It is not considered that on the American side much difficulty will be encountered, except in a portion of British Columbia; but it is to be hoped that the importance of the object in view will bring sufficient power to bear upon the difficulties to be overcome as to dissipate them all.

What are the probabilities and the prospects of the ultimate success of an overland telegraph to unite Europe with America? Let us see: In the first place, we have come to the conclusion that it can be done; and, in the next place, it is infinitely more practicable and likely to succeed than by any other route or mode yet suggested. In fact, we have come to the conclusion of its entire practicability, and that it is only a mere question of how much will it cost, and can it be made to pay as an investment? In an international, in a commercial, in a political, in a utilitarian point of view, it soars above all mere questions of cost, of profit and loss, of dollars and cents. It is one of those great works which very properly commends itself to the attention of all governments, because its value or importance cannot be measured by a mere money standard.

If it were possible, we think that the commercial nations of the world should unite in its construction, and donate it to progress and civilization. But as such a plan would be impracticable, the next thing to be done is to encourage the construction of it by private parties by all the means at our command.

Already, while we are writing, the work of progression is busy at both extremities; Russia is constructing her line eastward across the Urals, while the United States is engaged in pushing to the west over the Rocky Mountains and to the shores of the Pacific. Thus these two opposite forces are constantly diminishing the intervening space, and solving most effectually all doubts and difficulties as to the possibility of telegraphic communication overland between America and Europe.

Telegraphs, tending ultimately to unite America with Europe by the overland route, *via* BEHRING'S Straits and Asiatic Russia, are in progress of construction on both sides; Russia is determined to build her line to the Amoor, while the contract made by Colonel HIRAM SIBLEY with the United States government, to construct a line to California, insures a line from the Mississippi to San Francisco. Nor is this all; a line is in course of construction from California to Oregon. Consequently it will be perceived that there remains only the intervening space on the American side from Oregon to BEHRING'S Straits, some seventeen hundred miles, and on the Asiatic side from the Straits to the mouth of the Amoor, some two thousand two hundred miles, in all, say about four thousand miles, to complete the circuit of the earth. It would seem a small matter to fill up this intervening gap, when we take into consideration the immense interests involved.

We have already seen many millions of dollars expended in experimenting with long deep-sea cables, upon theory alone, in order to unite distant continents. It certainly looks to be but a small affair, to carry out this plan of connecting the Old with the New World, when we see that success is certain with our present knowledge of working telegraphs, and at a less cost than was incurred in laying the Atlantic cable.

Four thousand miles of land telegraph is no very great distance, when we see what has already been constructed and in progress of construction in America and Europe. The California overland line will be two thousand miles long, and will be constructed for about three hundred and sixty thousand dollars. In fact, the proposed line from Oregon to the mouth of the Amoor can undoubtedly be built for less than the Atlantic cable cost.

There are now in Europe some one hundred and fifty thousand miles of telegraph, and in America fifty or sixty thousand miles, producing a revenue of probably ten millions of dollars annually. Unite all these lines, and make them subsidiary to the great world-encircling telegraph, and it must become one of the most lucrative investments possible.

If this line should be finally constructed, it leaves nothing more for human enterprise to achieve in telegraphic communication, except to fill up gaps and construct lateral lines. It will encompass the earth over a route formed by nature, and to which there can be no rival. It accomplishes every thing, satisfies every interest, penetrates into every nation and country, pervades the whole earth.

Aside from telegraphic communication, there are other interests which would be materially benefited by this exploration, and survey.

The Amoor is now open to free trade. A number of American ships and merchants have been attracted there already by its rising commerce. A number of steamers and steamships have been built in the United States, either for commercial purposes or connected with its rising fortunes as a Russian colony.

Again, in view of establishing steam communication between San Francisco and China by way of Japan, Hakodadi might become an intermediate station, which would rapidly augment American commerce in the North Pacific and adjacent coasts and seas; consequently a more thorough survey and knowledge of those remote coasts and islands would be highly advantageous to commerce. And, in this connection, a thorough search for the most favorable points from whence a supply of coal for steam navigation could be obtained would not be neglected. Coal is found on the Fox islands, on Jesso and Suk-hah-lin.

Our Pacific whaling fleet, of which more than a hundred sail frequent the more remote coast and waters of the North Pacific, would be vastly benefited by such survey as the one proposed. Shipwreck and loss of life would be lessened by a better knowledge of those waters, which consideration should, if necessary, argue in favor of the proposed survey.

As to Russian America, so little known to our commerce (because of the exclusive grant to the Russian-American Company of its trade and commerce, internal and external) heretofore, we are likely, on the expiration of their grant, in 1862, to have a commerce also in that direction, when it will also be highly advantageous to have a better knowledge of its coasts and waters.

Under all the circumstances of the case, and in view of other benefits to be derived from the exploration and surveys as proposed by Mr. Collins, the committee recommend an adequate appropriation by Congress, in order to carry out successfully the views of the petitioner, and for that purpose report a bill.

STEAM AND THE TELEGRAPH TO INDIA AND CHINA.

Cape Race and San Francisco are united. London, Paris, and St. Petersburg, are now the same distance from San Francisco as Boston, Quebec, or New York. Space has been annihilated; the Atlantic and Pacific are no longer separated by oceans, deserts, or mountains. One hundred and fifty thousand saplings and some five thousand miles of iron wire have done the work. We stand on both oceans at the same moment of time. The Pacific Telegraph Company has conquered time and space, and in an incredibly short space of time united the Atlantic with the Pacific.

It is only about a year since that this gigantic work was

placed upon a working basis; during the winter of 1860–'61 the work of procuring the poles at the most available points was commenced, but it was not until the 20th day of June, 1861, that the actual work of erecting the line was commenced; and on the 25th day of October, 1861, San Francisco spoke to New York.

St. Joseph, in Missouri, is considered the starting point of the Pacific Company—about 2,200 miles to San Francisco. This is properly the Pacific Telegraph, other independent companies occupying the space thence, distant from New York say about 1,500 miles.

The government, by act of Congress, is to pay the Company $40,000 a year for ten years. The line has cost, probably, about $350,000; of this, as yet, we have no positive data, but the cost will be much less than the most favorable estimate, many of the apparent and imaginary difficulties vanishing as they were approached by the workmen.

To HIRAM SIBLEY, Esq., of Rochester, the President of the Western Union Telegraph Company, probably more than to any other one man, we owe this gigantic enterprise. He has pursued it with faith, works, and money, until triumphant success has crowned his earnest efforts.

Here, then, we find ourselves actually in telegraphic union with San Francisco. Are we to stop there? That is the next question. In looking west from San Francisco (for that seems to be our destiny) our eye falls upon the shores of Asia and upon the thousand islands of the Indian Ocean, teeming with one-third the population of the whole globe, and opening up to our view all the dreams, visions, facts, and fancies of all those who have, from the earliest times, contemplated unrestricted commerce with the populous and opulent Orient, India and the further Ind. Thus we find ourselves with the speed of lightning on the shores of the great Pacific Ocean, calmly awaiting a further and a greater stride, still westward; because on our march to the Pacific we have reversed all the old laws and usages of time-honored commerce, and the Orient has now become the Occident.

A telegraph is already in course of construction, connecting California with Oregon, and most probably an independent line, without any connection with a proposed Asiatic line, will reach Washington and Vancouver. This may be considered, then, as the utmost limit of telegraphic enterprise, as far as North America is concerned, at present. In looking west from the shores of the Pacific toward Asia, we find an immense expanse of water intervening, which would seem to preclude the idea of any further progress in the realization of telegraphic union. But brute instinct, as well as the reasoning power of man and the more unerring square, compass, and level, have all determined that it is easier and quite as *direct* to go around a mountain rather than over it. Upon this theory, granting the Pacific Ocean to be a mountain over which we cannot reach Asia, and the distance being too great to *tunnel* it with a submerged cable, we must resort to the only plan left, and go around it. Taking, then, Vancouver as the western *terminus* of telegraphic communication, which is in about 50° N.L., we would ascend the coast to Sitka, the capital of Russian America, in about 56° N.L. Thence, following up the coast to Mount St. Elias, in 60° N., we would proceed northwest to Behring's Straits, 65° N., 168° W.L.

At this point the strait is about forty miles wide; here, of course, submerged cables would unite the American to the Asiatic shore. In order to insure the union of the two worlds, at least four or five separate cables should be submerged, all of which would be united at the shore ends. This would not only tend to preserve the cables from over-work, but render the possibility of breakage or other accident to the continuity of the line quite beyond doubt.

Leaving Behring's Straits, the Asiatic coast would be followed as far as practicable to the Anadir River, whence the line would be extended across the head of the peninsula of Kamschatka to Penjinsk, at the northeastern extremity of the Sea of Okhotsk, and thence around and along its shores to the mouth of the Amoor River, in 53° N., 140° E.L.

Here we stop, because the Russian government not only propose, but is in fact now engaged in constructing a line of telegraph which is to connect Europe with this point on the Pacific Ocean.

Pausing for a few moments at the Amoor, we find, in looking back along our track, that we have overcome the *mountain* of the Pacific by merely keeping the shore line or base of this mountain, and thus reached a point on the Asiatic shore where we can open communication overland to Europe,

We have ascended from 50° N. to 65°, and descended to 53°, having overcome, in the mean time, 95° of longitude and 27° of latitude.

We scarcely need remind our readers, that although in ascending so high north so much out of a direct line from our starting point, in order to reach the opposite coast of Asia, we have in all probability not increased the distance at all.

In doing this we have merely followed a great circle, while the known spheroidity of the earth will prove the hypothesis that it is quite as easy to go around as over it.

By looking at the map of the North Pacific it will be perceived that from a point on the Russian-American coast west of Sitka, at Alyaska, the Aleutian islands form, and separate the North Atlantic from Kamschatka or Behring Sea.

These islands are prolongated toward the coast of Kamschatka, and, with Copper and Behring islands, form, as it were, a succession of steps between the two continents.

Again, from the southern point of Kamschatka, the Kurile

islands enclose the Sea of Okhotsk, and, leading to Jesso or Sak-hah-lin, conduct, by short intervals of water, to the main coast of Asia.

Again, between Alyaska and Behring's Straits there are other islands, such as Nunivak, Gores, St. Lawrence, &c., which might be used as *posts* for submerged cables, in order to reach Asia. But in considering all these island routes, we must look to the practicability and expense of submerged cables, as compared with the almost exclusive land route, *via* the straits.

If we follow the Aleutian and then the Kurile islands we shall have probably two thousand miles of cable, in sections not to exceed probably three hundred miles; or, if after reaching Kamschatka, we should be compelled to cross to Amoor direct, on account of the inexpediency of touching Japanese soil, then we have the Sea of Okhotsk to cross with a cable of 600 miles.

The other island route further to the north, though not requiring in the aggregate so much cable as the Alutian route, would, however, require sections of two, three, and four hundred miles.

The distance over these various routes will fluctuate between four and five thousand miles.

As to cost, take the Behring's Straits route and call it 5,000 miles, at $300 a mile, and we have the cost at $1,500,000.

If we take the Aleutian Island route, where the greatest length of cable will be required, and carry it by the Kurile islands to the Amoor, the cost may be stated at from four to five millions of dollars; in fact, calculations have run up to £1,500,000 or $7,500,000. Thus we have the difference in calculations of cost and distances over the various proposed routes.

In round numbers we have the following distances:

New York to St. Louis, ...	1,100 miles.
St. Louis to San Francisco, ...	2,600 "
San Francisco to Vancouver	700 "

Vancouver to Sitka	600 miles.
Sitka to Behring's Straits	1,200 "
Behring's Straits to Amoor	2,500 "

The distance by the island routes would be nearly the same as by the longest land route.

From this great world-encircling telegraph, as it progresses east from Moscow, lateral lines will in time branch off to the Caspian, Circassia, Persia, and India.

From Irkootsk, in Eastern Siberia, a line following the track of the tea caravans could reach Pekin, thence to Shanghai, Amoy, and Hong Kong. From the Chinese coast, opposite Formosa, a line could, by way of that island, reach Manilla, and thence over islands and straits to Melbourne, Australia.

Tapping the main trunk line at the Amoor, we could reach Jeddo and connect all the Japanese islands, thus actually concentrating the whole world telegraphically upon this great overland route.

At Omsk, in Western Siberia, a branch line following the Russian and Chinese frontier would penetrate the route of the overland caravan commerce, between the Caspian provinces on the west and the Chinese provinces on the east; this branch line might also be pushed still to the south and west *via* Bokhara, Balk, and Cabool, to connect with the lines throughout the whole of British India; but all these lateral lines are questions of time and necessity. The first work in order is to build the great trunk line, after which the construction of these lateral lines will become questions of State policy or commercial necessity.

But enough of telegraphs; let us now turn our attention to steam.

San Francisco must, from her position, climate, and productions, be to the Pacific side of our continent, what New York is to the Atlantic side. Already, telegraphically, San Francisco is, say seven days from London, the shortest time; under ordinary circumstances, ten.

Westward the star of empire has taken its way; let us but carry out its destiny and cause it to shed its rays upon the shores of Asia.

A line of steamers from San Francisco to Shanghai should not only become the first study of our Pacific merchants and bankers, but New York should, by every means in her power, hasten the consummation of such a noble project. Nay, there is not within the legitimate scope of governmental protection and patronage a more important or useful field.

With a line of swift steamers from San Francisco, Shanghai can be brought to within twenty days of New York, and London in twenty-six days. Over this line the current news, the mails, the exchanges and the bullion would soon inevitably find their way, as well as the lighter and most costly of Chinese, Japanese, and much of the Indian commerce, seek a market or eastern transportation.

San Francisco is in 38°, Shanghai in 32° N. L.; the distance is about 5,500 miles. From New York to Liverpool it is 3,000 miles; consequently, with steamers such as the VANDERBILT, the ADRIATIC, and the BALTIC, Shanghai would be but sixteen and a half days distant from San Francisco.

Counting seventeen days from Shanghai to San Francisco, one day's telegraph to Cape Race, and six days thence by steam and telegraph to London, we find that China is only twenty-four days distant from the Bank of England.

This schedule gives us an important advantage over the western mails and steamers leaving Shanghai for Europe *via* the Peninsular and Oriental Company's line.

Considering, as I do, that by no combination of circumstances the centre of commerce and power on our side of the Pacific can ever be removed from San Francisco, I shall consider that as the point from which our contact with Asia shall concentrate.

There seems to be, as yet, no limit to the discoveries of the more precious metals. The field is no longer limited to the foothills and western slope of the Sierra Nevada, but has crossed equally to the eastern slope; while Oregon, Washington, and British Columbia have been added.

The silver deposits of our young and thriving Nevada, now in rapid course of development, must, within a very few years, give to San Francisco the control of supply for India and China of that metal.

It has been estimated by parties engaged in silver mining in Nevada, that there is now sufficient machinery on located mines in the territory to produce, when put in working order, fifty millions of dollars the first year.

Again, the cinnabar of California assures the working of the silver mines, for this metal is found in such abundance that the supply of quicksilver may be considered adequate to all demands.

Amid all this surfeit of gold, silver, cinnabar, and copper of California and adjacent territories, we find yet other elements of prosperity, safety, and wealth.

While the gold-fields are so rich and extensive, the wheat-fields are adequate to all demands; and while the miners in the mountains, ravines, and placers are settling the balances of the world with their yellow dust, the no less industrious cultivators of the soil are distributing to distant nations of the earth their golden harvest.

Not content with regulating and sustaining the commerce of the world by supplying the basis upon which it rests, as well as literally scattering her bread upon the waters, California, with her vine-clad hills and valleys, must soon make herself not only independent of, but will enter the markets of the world with her wines and brandies.

Thus, amid all these elements of wealth, prosperity, and luxury, it is hardly necessary to attempt to foreshadow what position San Francisco must surely hold on the shores of the Pacific, nor attempt to picture her steady and irresistible march to power and wealth.

But these white-winged messengers, that so much delighted and astonished our forefathers, which walked the waters like things of life, and dared the elements to strife, and all that, no longer rule the wave.

In our degenerate times we most delight to see a black but graceful combination of iron and wood, some three to six hundred feet long, belching forth from her great smoke-stack volumes of the densest and blackest smoke, her great paddles dashing the waves to foam, and her sharp prow cutting the ocean asunder, while her track glides away in a sea of light.

It is something like this that rules the ocean now; without it we are fifty years behind the times.

San Francisco must have steam to China, and it is time not only that our merchants, but our government took the question under serious and determined consideration.

Consider at this time the threatening attitude of our foreign relations, the immense extent of our Pacific coast, the absolute necessity, in case of war, for a defensive steam marine, and we should need no further argument to make us act promptly and efficiently.

It is to be hoped that Congress is now, or soon may be, pretty thoroughly weeded of political hucksters, and that instead of legislating for self, that great and [should be] noble body of men will be found legislating for their country.

What an insignificant sum one or two or three millions of dollars a year would be in order to give us the control of the Chinese commerce, while at the same time we would be building up a steam fleet upon the Pacific which would render us secure in case of war.

It is astonishing how easy it is to do a great thing if we only have a very little encouragement; this has been proved very recently, in the construction of the Pacific Telegraph, which everybody has been talking of for the last ten years, yet no one man would, or set of men could be found, either in or out of the United States, to undertake its construction without the help of government.

This miserable pittance of forty thousand dollars a year has accomplished one of the wonders of the age; a sum, I have no doubt, the government will be enabled to save in actual expenditure and economy more than a dozen times this present year.

Again, the government is giving a million a year to the overland mail. Now, as a matter of revenue, I have no doubt it is a bad speculation, or rather investment; but has not the establishment of the overland mail hastened and rendered more practicable the erection of the telegraph? and though the government makes very bad bargains in some cases, yet facilities are cheapened in others. Thus the million given to the overland mail induced telegraphists to undertake their great work for forty thousand dollars; and though the discrepancy, as far as resulting actual benefit is concerned, is so enormous, that one is constrained to fancy that Congress, in its idea of compensation or encouragement, is not always ruled very sagely, yet we rest content on general results. However, we have now the overland mail and the telegraph; these are of the past—now let us look to the future.

Yet we must not forget how easy and rapidly these really great and difficult works were accomplished with only a very little, a mere mite, of that lubricating and efficient government oil—money.

Now, since Congress has set the ball in motion, and rolled both post-coach and telegraph over the grand deserts and mountains of North America, from the Atlantic to the Pacific Ocean, let our wise men, political economists, statesmen, philosophers, and philanthropists, just keep the ball in motion, while they have their hands in, and send the fleet and stately steamer across the gentle Pacific, and, consequently, finish the *last link* in *compassing* the *round earth* with *steam and electricity*.

The space from San Francisco to Shanghai is the last gap that remains to be filled in this world-encircling girdle.

Congress should, within twenty days from the first Monday in December next, pass a bill offering at least one million of dollars to any individual or association who would carry the United States mails to China and Japan, not less than twice a month.

It is hardly necessary to present an estimate of the number of steamers, their dimensions, speed, or cost which should undertake this service. The moment the question is presented to Congress, a dozen competitors for the honor and emoluments would be ready with every detail and specification.

Let it not be said that this is not the proper time to present the subject to Congress, because we are engaged in a war for our national existence, that we are taxing the whole energies and calling upon the whole resources of the nation in a time of great peril, and that the expenditures to sustain the government will reach five hundred millions a year, the bulk of which must be borrowed.

No! let us rather say that the United States still exists; we know our duty and our future; our national flag still floats on every sea, and shall continue to float; and, as an evidence of our faith and determination, we mean it shall float triumphantly on the Pacific as well as on the Atlantic.

Our steam line from San Francisco to Shanghai will strengthen and consolidate that power so necessary to a commercial nation, and evidence to the world that, as a great power, we surrender nothing to the circumstances of the hour, but go steadily, hopefully, and bravely forth in the path of progress, duty, and power.

If Congress will do this we will, amid one of the most gigantic wars that has ever reddened the page of history, prove to the world our vitality as well as our determination to exist.

While there are so many thousands actively engaged in the strife and hazards of war, there are yet many more thousands equally active and zealous in all the arts of peace, and this enterprise would be most readily and quickly undertaken, and carried out successfully.

Now is the time; our commerce wants new avenues—extension, expansion. Thousands of our merchants and ship-owners have been driven from old, time-honored, lucrative, and beaten paths. Let the government, while they are sustaining it with their millions upon millions of money, open up this new field of commercial enterprise, and pour some of the wealth of India into their coffers.

Able navigators should be left to choose the route to reach Shanghai; whether they reach it by the northern or southern route, it matters not to the government.

If experimental voyages should prove that the outward route should be made direct to Shanghai, taking advantage of the northeast trade winds, let it be so, returning up through the sea of Japan, touching at such ports as necessary.

At Hakodadi the commerce and mails for the Amoor and other Russian-Asiatic possessions would be distributed, while our whaling fleet in the North Pacific would make this point a rendezvous for advices from home.

Our steamers, thus making a circuit from San Francisco to Shanghai, thence up the western coast of Japan, and out through the Straits of Sangar on their return, would consolidate and accommodate American commerce, and assure to it all the necessary facilities for rapid and regular communication, strengthen us in the east, and divide the commercial empire of India with Great Britain.

Table of distances from San Francisco to important ports on the Pacific.

To the Amoor,	4,200 miles.
Hakodadi,	3,500 "
Petropavlosky,	3,000 "
Sandwich Islands,	2,200 "
Melbourne,	7,000 "
Calcutta,	9,500 "
Canton,	6,550 "
Shanghai,	5,500 "

Sailing vessels have made the voyage from Shanghai to San Francisco in about thirty days; from the Amoor in thirty days; from Petropavlosky in seventeen days, and from Hakodadi in twenty-two days. These are the short and favorable voyages; generally, a large per cent. in time must be added to these voyages.

The Pacific Ocean being so much more tranquil than the Atlantic, steamers would make much greater speed; and again, there would be no winter coasts to be approached, with north-easters, snow-storms, or icebergs. Consequently, the voyages across the Pacific would be attended with much less risk, greater speed, and more regularity than across the Atlantic.

Again, voyagers bound from China for Europe would find it decidedly safer and more pleasant to reach Europe, *via* San Francisco and New York, rather than by Calcutta, Bombay, and the Red Sea.

Over the Indian route the heat is intense, the seas liable to sudden tempests, while the construction, size, and accommodation of the English steamers compare very unfavorably with ours on the California side.

If our route from Shanghai to San Francisco should be to the north, *via* the Straits of Sangar, and consequently on a great circle, we would make quicker time and avoid all the scorching and broiling that passengers so much complain of on the Indian overland line *via* the Red Sea.

The time from Shanghai to London being about sixty days by

the Peninsular and Oriental Overland Company's conveyance for mails and passengers, we claim that the *Occidental* California route would attract and attach to it a fair, if not a marked number of passengers, as well as the preponderance of mails.

Telegraphically our San Francisco route defies the competition of the Peninsular and Oriental Company, because, under the most favorable circumstances of that company's despatches, we can reach London to the east, *via* San Francisco and Cape Race, in about twenty-five days; whereas it takes about forty-five days from Hong Kong, and consequently about fifty days from Shanghai, for telegraphic despatches to reach London over the Indian overland route.

This time may be reduced, to be sure, if the efforts to *relay or reconstruct* the Mediterranean and Red Sea cables should be permanently successful. But speculation is unnecessary when we have an aërial line that defies the elements, is visible and palpable, and which can only, under the most unfavorable circumstances, be interrupted but a few days at any one time.

Give us, then, our swift, airy, well-ventilated, and capacious American floating, sea-going, Pacific palaces, and, my word on it, we will not only carry our own mails and passengers, but will tap the Peninsular and Oriental line, and divert a large proportion of oriental voyagers and mails to our shores, where comfort, health, and luxury will be increased a hundred fold.

Nor will we be confined to passengers alone. These steamers will carry the specie, the quicksilver, and the higher descriptions of merchandise to China, besides many articles of luxury, fruits, wines, flour, butter, preserved fruits, meats, etc., etc.

In return we will receive not only what is required for the consumption of the Pacific coast of Chinese and Japanese produce and articles of luxury, but we may expect the finer teas, silks, etc., etc., to find their way to New York and even Europe, *via* San Francisco and Panama,

In fact, this steam line once established, we would, like in the case of the Pacific telegraph, be absolutely surprised not only why we had not carried it out before, and the ease with which it was done, but we would be astounded at the new avenues of commerce it would open to us, and the facility and ease with which we acquired so glorious a result.

Therefore, under the various phases of the completion of the *last link* in the *world-encircling* steam and telegraph lines over and around the Pacific, in order to open up to us the vast commerce of Asia, may we not very justly begin to look forward to the day when the transfer of power must be from the far-off seat of power now enthroned in London, to a more genial, approachable, and adjacent seat on the shores of the Pacific itself, viz., San Francisco?

It is a thought that is not vague or vagrant; we have only to grapple with manly souls and willing works, and even before the work shall itself be accomplished, the empire of London over Chinese commerce will be found gradually migrating toward the golden and silver shores of the Pacific.

MR. LATHAM'S REPORT TO THE SENATE OF THE UNITED STATES, FEBRUARY 17, 1862.

The Committee on Military Affairs, to whom was referred the memorial of Mr. Perry McD. Collins, asking the aid of Congress "that a survey may be made of the North Pacific Ocean, in view of overland telegraphic communication with Europe, via *Asiatic Russia," would respectfully report:*

That it appears from the memorial, the accompanying papers, and other information on file in the Department of State, that he personally undertook and accomplished a voyage over land from

St. Petersburg, in European Russia, to the mouth of the Amoor River, on the Pacific Ocean, with a view of proving to the commercial world the value and practicability of nearer relations with the hitherto unknown and unexplored regions of Siberia, the great Amoor River, and of Tartary. Mr. Collins performed his task in a most commendable and satisfactory manner.

He being the first American who penetrated these regions, from him we have reliable information in regard thereto.

Accompanying these explorations special attention was paid to the subject of immediate steam and telegraphic connection with them and our present Pacific possessions. He found a practicable and highly favored route already existing for the construction of an overland telegraph, uniting us with those Chinese and Japanese ports where, even now, is concentrated the great bulk of commerce. At the time of this gentleman's first visit to that country the telegraph had not extended east of Moscow, in Russia, nor west of St. Louis, in the United States.

The original plan, therefore, comprised an intermediate space of 14,000 miles; a portion of this distance, 4,000 miles, at least, nearly due east from Moscow, being along the route traversed by the great Russo-Chinese caravans to Kyachta, on the frontier of Chinese Mongolia; the whole route, from city to city and from village to village, protected from interruption by the vigilance of government and good order of society as safely as in any portion of our own States.

Aside from governmental considerations, the two great centres of Russo-Asiatic commerce, Kyachta and Nijne-Novgorod, would be brought in telegraphic union, and the whole of Siberia in practical contact with Europe.

From Kyachta the route proposed would cross the Yablonoi mountains, reaching at once the head-waters of the Amoor at Chetah, the seat of government for the province of Trans-Baikal, eastern Siberia; thence along its main course to the strait and coast of Tartary upon the Pacific.

When first proposed the latter portion of the above route, from the head of the Amoor to the sea, was considered very difficult; but recently, Russia, having obtained by treaty with China the sovereignty of this river and country to the north, has extended over it the same system of Cossack settlements and post-stations which secure and render communication all through Siberia so orderly and safe; moreover, has already placed a number of steamers successfully on the navigable portion of the river.

The only remaining point is to reach satisfactorily the shores of America, portions of the country remaining still unexplored. The proposed route is to proceed from the mouth of the Amoor up and along the coast of the Okhotsk Sea, from the head of the Gulf of Penjinsk across the head of the peninsula of Kamschatka to the Anadir River; thence to a point under the lea of East Cape, crossing Behring's Strait to the south of the Godenow islands, and reaching the American coast south of Cape Prince of Wales.

From this point on the American continent proceed southerly to Sitka, the capital of Russian America, thence through the British possessions to Vancouver, and thence to San Francisco.

Russians who have given this subject any attention, favor the route from the Amoor to Petropavlosky, crossing either the Okhotsk Sea or following the island of Sak-hah-lin and the Kurile islands to Kamschatka. From Kamschatka to Behring's and Copper islands, thence following the Aleutian islands to Alyaska on the American main land.

This last mode of reaching America, however, involves a very considerable extent of submerged cable. By either of the two routes more than two thousand miles of submerged cable is required, divided, to be sure, into sections of greater or less length.

For instance, if the Okhotsk Sea were crossed from opposite

the mouth of the Amoor River, one cable of 550 to 600 miles would be required to reach Kamschatka; and again, from Kamschatka to America sections of from 50 to 300 miles to reach from island to island.

If the route by Sak-hah-lin and the Kurile islands were followed the sections would be less; in no case, however, could less than 2,000 miles of cable be dispensed with, while the whole line, land and submerged, would be greater than the greatest northern land route by Behring's Strait.

Mr. Collins indicated two other routes, viz.: by the way of Ouloutorskoy to Gore's and Nunivack islands, or by Cape Navarin and St. Lawrence island to Cape Romanzof; either of which would not involve more than one-fourth of the extent of cable proposed by the Kurile and Aleutian islands. Since this subject was first agitated it has been much narrowed by the construction of telegraphs, both in Russia and America. The imperial government has assumed the construction of the whole line, as originally proposed, from Moscow to the Pacific, a distance of 7,000 miles, which is already in course of construction, as will be seen by the following communication from the chief of telegraphs addressed to Mr. Collins:

"BUREAU OF THE DIRECTOR-IN-CHIEF OF PUBLIC WAYS.

"ST. PETERSBURG, RUSSIA,
"*November* 30, 1861.

"SIR:

* * * * * *

"The proposed execution of the telegraphic line from Kazan to the Amoor is divided into two sections. 1st. From Kazan to Irkootsk. 2d. From Irkootsk to the mouth of the Amoor River. The telegraph from Kazan is in course of construction through Perm, Ekatherinburg, Tumen, to Omsk; and the intention is to carry it forward through Tomsk and Krasnoyarsk to Irkootsk.

The line is finished already to Perm, and in the beginning of next year will be opened from Perm to Omsk.

"The construction of the line will not be finished to Irkootsk before the year 1863.

"The line from Irkootsk to the mouth of the Amoor River is proposed to be made through Verchne Udinsk, Chetah, Blagavestchensk, Habaravka, at the mouth of the river Usuree, and through Sofinsk to Nicolavisky, at the mouth of the Amoor.

"Branches will be carried from Verchne Udinsk toward Kyachta, and from Habaravka, by the mouth of the Songotscha, to the port of Novgorod, on the Gulf of Peter the Great.

"The execution of this line of telegraph will be carried out under the supervision and control of the governor general of eastern Siberia, and the minister of the navy.

"Steps have already been taken to expedite the building of these lines with the greatest despatch, as well as the branches from Nicolavisky to Habaravka, and from Sofinsk to the Gulf of De Castries.

"As to the execution of the line of telegraph from New York to San Francisco, for the purpose of joining California to the Atlantic, I learned from you, with the greatest personal satisfaction, and afterward by reading to the same effect in the newspapers.

"Indeed the union of the Old World with the New World we must expect to see executed and obtained through the Pacific, which will soon appear to be only practicable, and which alone can satisfy the general expectation, particularly as the Russian government offers so many inducements, in my opinion, by its vast system of works begun and to be carried on without intermission, both in Russia and Siberia. In order to build these lines of telegraphs in a shorter time than was originally intended, there will be taken certain measures as much as possible compatible with the uncommon rapid growth of telegraphs in Russia.

"There are already in operation more than twenty thousand

versts of telegraph lines, and with branches, almost thirty thousand *versts;* and of this extent, in the last three years, were constructed twelve thousand *versts*, with branches, making almost eighteen thousand *versts;* and besides all these lines there are many more to be constructed to different points *particularly* important to the interests of the *interior of the empire.*

"Accept, dear sir, the assurance of my particular esteem.

"CHEFKIN, *General Adjutant,*

"*Director-in-Chief of Public Communications.*

"PERRY McD. COLLINS, Esq."

Thus while Russia has been progressing eastward, the United States has been progressing toward the west; and 5,000 miles of continuous wire stretch across the continent, connecting the Atlantic with the Pacific.

The two countries, on their own soil, having already nearly connected the two oceans, this question has been reduced to a far less gigantic task than it seemed only a short year ago.

All we have now to consider is the mere uniting of the two systems, and we have a union of all the continents of the globe; the only subject of discussion now being the least length of deep sea cable.

We have already seen gigantic efforts made, and immense sums of money cast, as it were, into the ocean in futile attempts to connect great distances. The Atlantic cable, unhappily, after exciting the enthusiasm of the world, has come to a disastrous end; the great Red Sea and India telegraph (submerged in sections from Suez to Babelmandel and Muscat, crossing the Gulf of Persia to Kurachee, in India, near 3,000 miles) has also succumbed to a fate quite as lamentable.

We name these facts, still not without hope that science, ingenuity, and indomitable will may yet overcome all obstacles.

The recent success of the Malta and Alexandria cable has inspired the friends of long submerged lines with new ardor and ambition for further efforts.

The Malta and Alexandria cable being a three section line (where the length of any one section does not reach 300 miles, and the strength much augmented over similar ones, the size of the conducting metal quadrupled), it is to be hoped it may render its working a permanent success. The telegraph under consideration, although of greater length, meets with fewer local obstructions than any of those named, short distances only of submerged cable being found necessary. The whole of Asia would be practically annexed to Europe, and through the line we propose to America, being to us as a political and commercial nation a subject of great and growing magnitude.

We hold the ball of the earth in our hand, and wind upon it a network of living and thinking wire, till the whole is held together and bound with the same wishes, projects, and interests.

As this Asiatic system penetrates to the east, we may speculate upon probable routes *ad infinitum*. At Kazan, which is considered by Russia as the initial point from whence the Russian Pacific telegraph shall be extended, a line may run south through the Astrakhan, Circassian, and Georgian provinces to Teheran, the capital of Persia, and thence, uniting the cities along the Euphrates and the Persian Gulf, connect with the English-Indian line at Kurachee, adding India to the already established Kazan-Amoor line.

Again, from Omsk, a lateral line can be extended through the central portion of northern Asia, uniting Bokara, Turkistan, Cashmere, reaching Cabool *via* Balk; thus again tapping India through the *northern central* gate of Asia. Progressing east, the *Kazan-Amoor* line, reaching Kyachta, on the borders of Mongolia, can be tapped by a lateral one over the route traversed by the tea caravans to Pekin; thence to Shanghai, Amoy, and Hong-Kong; thus China becomes tributary to the "*grand trunk*" line.

From the Chinese coast to the island of Formosa a line may be projected to Luzon, Manila, the capital of Spanish India; thence from island to island until Australia (Melbourne) is reached, embracing the principal centres of trade in that wonderful, rich, and extensive quarter of the globe.

Pursuing our way along the main course of the Amoor, we have seen what Commander Chefkin proposes in regard to branches to the different points upon the sea of Japan, as far south as 42° north latitude, even to the northern limits of Corea.

At this point, without any telegraphic communication, China and Japan would both be within easy and rapid contact by means of steam vessels, when the commerce of these countries could be regulated for either European or American interests; or, from the mouth of the Amoor, a branch line, involving but three short cables in the whole, to the extent of not more than fifty miles, could be constructed to reach Jeddo, the capital of Japan.

Thus progressing eastward from Moscow to the Pacific, we have prospectively connected the whole of northern Asia, India, China, Japan, Australia, and the islands of the sea.

We now come to the plain point of the report, the practicability of the *Overland Russian-American Telegraphic Union.*

Under authority from the Russian government, Mr. Collins proposes a survey of the waters, coasts, and islands of the north Pacific, and we think it fully worthy the aid and assistance of our own government.

The waters of the north Pacific, which would come under inspection in the general plan, are much visited by our ships, more particularly the Pacific whaling fleet; while the opening of Japan and the Amoor has also attracted, within a few years, a large number of our merchant vessels.

Latterly American vessels having entered this river, the Russian government has also had constructed several sea-going and river steamers in the United States and in Europe, for service here and in the north Pacific, to all of which private enterprise has made an addition of six merchant steamers.

American commerce has then already made its entrance into northeastern Asia; several American commercial establishments have found permanent place within the Amoor at the seat of government, Nicolavisky; American engineers are employed in this so recently unexplored region; American steam-engines, saw-mills, and machine shops have also found in the wilds of Tartary a new field of practical occupation.

Thus, independent of the consideration of telegraphic communication, the proposed survey of the north Pacific would be of much value to commerce in those regions; our whalemen and merchant-ships would be guided by certain and reliable information; safe anchorage ground would be revealed; depots and deposits of coal, new bays and harbors, would be sought and sounded, and generally much information obtained serviceable and interesting alike to commerce and science.

Again, in view of the contemplated steam postal communication between San Francisco, China, and Japan, this northern commerce must increase; and whatever there may be in the waters, forests, or mines, be made available by the enterprise of our people. Coal is known to abound in the north Pacific, and with steam communication the quality, locality, means, and manner of obtaining it, would be valuable and profitable. Entering so largely into our economic life, and adding so greatly as it does to the power of a nation in these days of steam, railroads, and manufactures, information in its regard must be of the highest interest.

The distance from San Francisco to the Amoor River *via* Behring's Strait—the largest and most northern land line—is estimated at about 5,000 miles. The crossing at the strait being the only portion of the ocean lying in the track of the proposed telegraph, is but 40 miles wide, which is all the submerged cable that will be required on the whole route. In fact, from New York to Paris, by the *Russian-American line*, we have but this one expanse of water where submerged cable will be required; and though the distance is great geographically, telegraphically it presents no very serious objection.

The most costly, difficult, and longest line in the world is the Pacific telegraph, yet it has not cost over two hundred dollars per mile. The Behring's Strait route, from San Francisco to the Amoor, being 5,000 miles long, and estimating it, from climate and sparseness of population, still more expensive to construct than the Pacific, say three hundred dollars per mile, will cost in all but one million five hundred thousand dollars. Thus this connecting link, uniting all the subsisting lines over three continents, costs but a small sum, estimating its value. Experienced and able men, engaged in the construction of long lines, think it can be done for even less.

The highest northern point reached by this route will be within 66° north latitude. The two other highest northern routes would be 63° north latitude and 60° north latitude. The highest point touched, *via* the Aleutian Islands route, keeping the land to Alyoska, will be 62° north latitude on the American coast, and within 54° north latitude on the Asiatic side, while the European lines at present in operation reach considerably above 60°, both in Russia and Sweden.

The climate has presented no impediment in their working. In fact, a cold dry atmosphere is favorable to insulation; so that this, though of great length, would work much more surely and rapidly than shorter lines in lower latitudes.

The American government has already given its aid to the Atlantic cable and the Pacific telegraph. The British government is constantly aiding telegraph projects, and but recently gave the use of a public vessel to assist in the survey of their north Pacific route, *via* Greenland and Iceland; consequently, we

19*

have sufficient precedent, if that were necessary, to justify us in asking aid for this proposed survey, and we instance these facts merely to show that the plan is not one of a wild, chimerical character, not only practicable and feasible, but already almost accomplished.

Mr. Collins has for several years pursued, with indefatigable zeal, the construction of this overland telegraph, not only before foreign governments, but in arousing the public mind to the possibility of ultimate success. He has at his own expense pushed this project as far as individual enterprise can go, and he now asks the assistance of his own government to perfect a survey and reconnoissance, with the authority of the Russian government, in regions highly advantageous to us as a commercial nation, and holding within themselves unexplored treasures of science and knowledge.

An extract of a letter from Professor Morse to Mr. Collins, shown to the committee, on the subject of overland telegraphic communication, will afford matter of interest.

"NEW YORK, *November* 29, 1861.
"*No.* 5 *West Twenty-second Street.*

"MY DEAR SIR: Your communication of November 27 is received, and in reply would briefly say, first in general terms, that I conceive there are no *insurmountable* difficulties in the way of establishing a telegraphic communication with Europe, westward from San Francisco. That difficulties of a peculiar character may have to be encountered I do not doubt * * *

"The liability to be injured by climatic changes, such as storms and frost, may be provided against by more than usual substantial material: lower and stronger posts, nearer together, and larger wire, so as to require less frequent and rigid supervision.

"To your fifth question, I answer, I know no reason why they (telegraphs) should not be maintained and worked in high northern latitudes as well as in lower; and my feeling is strong that from the absence of atmospheric moisture, which there congeals into frost and ice, telegraphic wire will conduct better than in warmer latitudes, subject to more rain * * * *

"To the eighth question, I can only answer from the scanty means I have of judging of the peculiar obstacles that each of the two routes present. In ordinary circumstances, the less submarine communication the better; but there may be obstacles to a land route, such as hostile uncivilized tribes, or marshy borders, that would throw the advantage on the side of a longer submarine line.

"This point, therefore, can better be determined by the intelligent observation of those who have visited the regions of the proposed line, and no one that I know is more capable of giving a more intelligent opinion than yourself.

"SAM'L F. B. MORSE.

"P. McD. Collins, Esq."

We also give an extract from a letter, written by Hiram Sibley, Esq., of Rochester, who has been as largely engaged in the construction of lines of telegraph as any man in the country.

"Western Union Telegraph Company,
"*Secretary's Office, Rochester, October* 16, 1861.

"Dear Sir:

* * * * * * *

I can say, however, by way of encouragement to you, that the contemplated difficulties vanished as we approached them.

"The cost of the line will not exceed one-half the lowest estimate made when the contract was awarded to me; and our men are pressing me hard to let them go on to Behring's Strait next summer, and (as you say to me) 'if I had the money,' I would go on and complete the line and talk about it afterward.

"If the Russian government will meet us at Behring's Strait, and give the right of way, &c., through their territory on the Pacific, we will complete the line in two years, and probably in one.

"The work is not more difficult than that we have already accomplished over the Rocky Mountains and plains to California; and, in my opinion, the whole thing is entirely practicable, and that, too, in much less time and with much less expense than is generally supposed by those most hopeful. No work costing so little money was ever accomplished by man that will be so important in its results. The benefit resulting to the world will pay the entire cost of the line every year after completion while the world continues to be inhabited by civilized man; and it is to me a matter of surprise that any intelligent person, at all familiar with building and working telegraph lines in the west, should doubt the practicability of the successful working, after built, of a line to Behring's Strait.

"Respectfully and truly yours,

"HIRAM SIBLEY.

"P. McD. Collins, Esq."

It is astonishing to observe what great enterprises are accomplished with very small and inadequate encouragement; this has been fully proved in the Pacific telegraph, which, although discussed for the last ten years, yet no man would, or association of men could, be found, either in or out of the United States, to undertake its accomplishment without, at least, the constructive aid of government; and the mere pittance of forty thousand dollars per annum has accomplished one of the wonders of the age; a sum, we have no doubt, the government will save to itself more than ten times this present year. Let this not be called an improper time to present this subject to Congress, because we are engaged in a war for our national existence, and because we are already taxing the whole energies and resources of the nation in a time of great peril; let us rather say that the United States is not only able to suppress rebellion at home, but able also to extend her great commercial and scientific power over the earth.

Such an enterprise as this telegraph from San Francisco to Asiatic Russia will only strengthen our power as a great commercial nation, and evidence to the world that we surrender nothing to the circumstances of the hour, but go steadily, hopefully, and bravely forward in the path of duty; that while there are so many thousands actively engaged in the strife and hazard of war, there are yet many more thousands equally active and zealous in all the arts of peace. If aided and countenanced by government it would be most readily and quickly undertaken and carried forward.

Thousands of our merchants and ship owners, having been driven from old time-honoured and beaten paths, want new avenues for expansion and extension of trade; and the opening up of this new source of power will reflect honor upon the commerce and high character of the nation that successfully fulfils it.

All of which is respectfully submitted with an accompanying bill.

New York, *March*, 1864.

Since the reports on the proposition for a survey under the authorization of the Russian government, Mr. Collins has visited St. Petersburg again, and after an absence of two years has received the authorization of the Russian government to construct a line of telegraph from the mouth of the Amoor River in Asiatic Russia over Asiatic Russia and Russian America to the British possessions.

Connected with this grant of right of way over Russian territory, the Russian government agrees to construct and complete a continuous line of telegraph to the mouth of the Amoor, so as to form a junction with the whole European system; thus the Atlantic and Pacific will be united by an overland line from London to the borders of China and Japan.

After having obtained the consent of Russia, as far as Russian territory was concerned, in order to unite Europe and America, or rather the American system of telegraphs, it was necessary to procure the consent of Great Britain to continue the line over the British territory on the northwest coast of the Pacific which lies between Russian America and our northern frontier in 49° N. L.

In order to effect this, Mr. Collins visited London and laid the whole subject before the government of her Majesty, and has received the concession of right of way for the prolongation of the line across British Columbia, so as to unite with lines already established on the Pacific coast.

Thus the right of way has been secured, which in connection with lines already established and in progress of construction in Asia and America, seems reasonably certain to bring us in telegraphic contact with Europe by a westward route, and that nearly the whole distance by land.

As this line, or this combination of lines, which seems destined to solve "the Northwest Passage," at least, telegraphically, progresses to the west, we find Japan, China, Siberia, and India, will all be brought on to one through line, which, as far as dry land is concerned, girds the earth.

The distance from New York to London by the overland route is about seventeen thousand miles; of this distance about nine thousand miles are completed, two thousand miles in course of completion, and six thousand miles yet to be constructed, under the proposition of Mr. Collins.

The basis for the construction of the line from the United States to the mouth of the Amoor, as contemplated under the British and Russian grants, has been agreed upon between Mr. Collins and the Western Union Telegraph Company.

This company, under an assignment of the Russian and British concessions, agree to construct a line of telegraph from some point on their lines not east of Chicago to the mouth of the Amoor River, thus carrying out the enterprise contemplated, by which New York shall be united to Europe by an overland telegraph.

A portion of the line will be constructed this year, and the basis of active operations laid for a vigorous prosecution of the work next year, along the whole Pacific coast and on to Behring's Strait.

It is expected that the whole line can be constructed in three years; simultaneously with the construction of the line on our side to the mouth of the Amoor, the Russian government will construct the intermediate line from Irkootsk to the Amoor. Thus, when the two systems shall touch at the Amoor, Cape Race and London will be in telegraphic union, and the earth will be, as far as practically necessary, belted by the electric telegraph.

INTER-CONTINENTAL TELEGRAPH.—PROCEEDINGS OF THE CHAMBER OF COMMERCE OF NEW YORK.

At the Annual Meeting of the Chamber of Commerce of New York, which was very fully attended, on the 5th of May, 1864, Mr. Samuel B. Ruggles offered for consideration the following preamble and resolutions:

Whereas, The Chamber of Commerce of New York have received satisfactory information:

First.—That the government of Russia has undertaken to establish and maintain a line of telegraphic communication from Moscow to the Pacific Ocean, at the mouth of the Amoor River, a distance of 6,000 miles, of which the 4,000 miles from Moscow to Irkootsk, in Eastern Siberia, are already finished and in operation, with proposed branches leading into China, India, and Persia:

Second.—That the Russian government, on the 23d of May last, in a spirit of wise liberality, and after due conference between the Ministers of Russia and the United States, duly granted to Mr. Perry McDonough Collins, a citizen of the United States of America, the exclusive right for thirty-three years to extend and maintain said telegraph line from the mouth of the Amoor River, along or near the Pacific Ocean, northeastwardly up to and across Behring's Strait, and thence southeastwardly through the American Territories of Russia to the northern line of British America, a distance in all of about 4,500 miles:

Third.—That the British government, on the 9th of February last, in pursuance of a policy alike enlightened, granted to said Collins the further right to extend and maintain said telegraphic line through the British Territories on the Pacific, to the Northern frontier of the United States, a distance of about 500 miles:

Fourth.—That the said Collins, encouraged and supported by such grants, has now applied to Congress for permission to extend and maintain said telegraphic line through the territories and the public lands of the United States, so as to connect the whole telegraphic system of Europe and Asia with the telegraphic system of the United States, by means of which great continental conjunction the Old World and the New, with all their dependencies, will be united by one safe and unbroken chain of intercourse, enabling every civilized nation to communicate daily with all the capital cities of the globe:

Now, therefore, the Chamber of Commerce of New York, in view of the incalculable advantages of such a world-embracing line of communication, not only to the cities and States of the

American continent, but to the whole family of man—do respectfully but earnestly commend the application of Mr. Collins to the speedy and favorable consideration and support of Congress, subject only to such proper conditions as may be required for the security and protection of the government and of the people of the United States.

Resolved, That copies of the preceding resolutions be duly authenticated by the President and Secretary, and transmitted to both Houses of Congress.

In presenting these resolutions, Mr. Ruggles said that the great importance of the subject they embraced would be obvious, without any extended remarks. He wished, however, distinctly to say that they were offered in no spirit of hostility or rivalry to that noble enterprise, the Atlantic Cable Telegraph. Far from it. The world needed both, and he trusted that both would soon be triumphantly completed, exhibiting, as it would, the great moral spectacle of the citizens of a nation struggling for its very life or death, nevertheless finding the means and the courage and the intelligence with one hand to lay the wires in the dark, unfathomed depths of the Atlantic, and with the other to plant them firmly beneath the polar circle, amid all the darkness and desolation of a polar winter. He had reason to know that Mr. Collins, the hero of this great civic achievement, would have ample means at his command with which to combat any physical difficulties he might be compelled to encounter, and that its full completion might be expected within three years from the time when the government of the United States should follow the examples of Russia and Great Britain, and afford the just measure of its countenance and support.

Mr. Ruggles laid before the Chamber a letter from the President of the Company now managing the American telegraphic line from the Atlantic to the Pacific, stating that messages had been repeatedly sent during the present year from Boston to

San Francisco, a distance of 3,000 miles, in *two minutes*. The total distance overland, by way of Behring's Strait, from New York to London, will be about 16,000 miles. The Strait is 39 miles wide. The greatest depth of water is stated to be 160 feet.

The resolutions were unanimously adopted.

COMMUNICATION OF HON. WILLIAM H. SEWARD, SECRETARY OF STATE,

Upon the subject of an Inter-continental Telegraph connecting the Eastern and Western Hemispheres by way of Behring's Strait, in reply to Hon. Z. Chandler, Chairman of the Committee on Commerce of the U. S. Senate, to which was referred the Memorial of Perry McDonough Collins.

SENATE CHAMBER, WASHINGTON, *April* 14, 1864.

Hon. WILLIAM H. SEWARD,
Secretary of State.

SIR: I have the honor to transmit, herewith, a printed copy of the memorial of Perry McD. Collins, representing that he has obtained from the government of Russia a grant of the privilege to construct a telegraph from the mouth of the Amoor River to the Russian possessions in America, and a similar grant from the British government in British Columbia, and praying the coöperation of the government of the United States to enable him to complete his enterprise.

The Committee on Commerce of the U. S. Senate, to whom this memorial has been referred, will be glad to receive from you such information upon the subject as may be in the possession of the Department, together with your views upon the expediency of granting the prayer of the memorialist.

I have the honor to be, sir,

Your obedient servant,

Z. CHANDLER,

Chairman of Committee on Commerce of the United States Senate.

To the honorable the Senate and House of Representatives of the United States of America in Congress assembled:

The memorial of P. McD. Collins, a citizen of the United States of America, and a resident of the State of California, most respectfully represents: That he has obtained from the imperial government of Russia privilege to construct a line of telegraph from the mouth of the Amoor River, in Asiatic Russia, to the frontiers of the Russian possessions in America, adjoining the possessions of Great Britain.

In connection with the grant from Russia, the Russian government stipulate, upon certain conditions, to construct a continuous line of telegraph connecting the European system with the Pacific Ocean, about eight thousand five hundred miles east of London, and on the route of a line which may be projected to Pekin and the great commercial cities of China.

Your memorialist also represents, that after having obtained the Russian grant, and upon a representation of the state of the case and the facts to the government of her Majesty, that he has been authorized by the British government to construct a line of telegraph across the intervening territory of British Columbia.

Thus the grants from Russia and England authorize the construction of a continuous line of telegraph which is to connect Europe with the United States across the whole of Asia and the northwest coast of the Pacific.

The whole country, except a portion of the route in British Columbia over which this proposed line must pass, is sparsely inhabited, and presents no local inducement for the construction of a telegraph.

The sole inducement to the construction of a telegraph over this great extent of country is the union of Asia and Europe with the American system of telegraph lines, and by as nearly as physically possible an overland route.

The great progress of telegraphs both in Asia and America since the proposition was originally made to induce a trial of this northern overland route, in order to unite Europe and America, has cleared away from the path of this enterprise many apparent difficulties suggested in the early stages of the undertaking.

Russia has extended her telegraph from St. Petersburg to Irkootsk, a distance of four thousand miles to the east; and now a line is being constructed along the Amoor River, which is to connect with the line in course of construction from Irkootsk to the east. Thus it will be seen that Russia is rapidly approaching with a continuous line the Pacific Ocean.

On our side of the world we have already reached the Pacific, and up towards the British possessions, and as far as Portland, Oregon.

From our northern frontier, adjoining British Columbia, to the mouth of the Amoor River, in Asiatic Russia, the distance may be stated in round numbers at some five thousand miles.

Previous to granting right of way for the construction of a telegraph, the Russian government authorized your petitioner to survey a route over all that portion of the Russian dominions east of the Amoor on to British Columbia.

On two previous occasions your petitioner presented to Congress the facts of the case, and reports were made thereon, copies of which are hereunto annexed, marked A and B.

The reasons which then existed not only hold good now, but are greatly enhanced by the absolute grant of right of way then withheld.

There is much in the North Pacific valuable to us as a nation in a commercial point of view, aside from the special interest particularly involved.

Our Pacific whaling fleet resort in considerable force to the seas, bays, and sounds, not only of the Pacific, but of the Arctic; in one year more than seventy American vessels have passed through Behring's Strait, and largely over one hundred have visited the waters adjacent, and the Okhotsk Sea.

The commerce of Japan and of the Amoor region, increasing from year to year, makes it requisite that we should have a more perfect knowledge of these interesting regions of the North Pacific.

In view of the premises and furtherance of American commerce and enterprise, and the vast and incalculable benefits to result to us as a great commercial nation out of the achievement of telegraphic communication which shall not only unite Europe to America, but add the whole of Asia, including Japan, China, and India, your petitioner most respectfully asks the favorable consideration of Congress, and that aid for a survey of the proposed telegraph, and a subsidy, in the form of a contract, for the dispatch of government messages, be accorded, so as to meet the concessions of Russia and Great Britain in a coöperative international spirit, and for the general intelligence of all nations.

And, as in duty bound, your petitioner will ever pray.

PERRY McD. COLLINS.

DEPARTMENT OF STATE, WASHINGTON, *May* 14, 1864.

To the Hon. ZACHARY CHANDLER,

Chairman of the Committee on Commerce,

in the Senate of the United States:

SIR: I have the honor to reply to your letter of the 14th of April last, upon the subject of the memorial which has been submitted to Congress by Mr. Perry McDonough Collins.

Mr. Collins is an American citizen, residing in California. He has been, since 1856, commercial agent of this Government for the Amoor River. The public archives, as well as the records of Congress, furnish satisfactory evidence that the country could not have a more enlightened, assiduous, and faithful representative.

The project which he submits for the consideration of Congress is the construction of a line of telegraph from some point on the Pacific Telegraph line, or the northern extension thereof, in one of the Northwestern States or Territories, across the border of the United States and through British Columbia and Russian America to Cape Prince of Wales; thence across Behring's Strait to East Cape; and thence by an inland route around the Sea of Okhotsk to the mouth of the Amoor River.

The telegraph line thus proposed is intended, primarily, to connect at the last-named place with a line to be extended from thence to Irkootsk, the capital of Eastern Siberia. At that important town a line of telegraph begins, which stretches through Tomsk and Omsk, in Western Siberia, Katherinburg on the Asiatic European frontier, Pirm, Kasan, Nijni-Novgorod, and Moscow, to St. Petersburg, the capital of the Russian Empire.

The line projected by Mr. Collins, from the Pacific Telegraph to Amoor River, with its anticipated extension by the Russian government to Irkootsk, would be the one link now wanted to supply direct and unbroken telegraph communication from Cape Race, in Newfoundland, on the eastern coast of America, across the eastern and western continents and the Pacific Ocean to Cape Clear, in Ireland, the westernmost projection of Europe.

When a submarine cable shall be successfully laid between Cape Clear and Cape Race, it will, together with the link I have last before described, complete a telegraphic circuit around the earth between the parallels of forty-two degrees and sixty-five degrees of north latitude.

Three questions arise from Mr. Collins' memorial, namely:

First. Is the enterprise feasible?

Secondly. Would it be useful?

Thirdly. Has it a just claim on the Government to the patronage which he solicits?

I shall examine these points in their order.

First. The feasibility of the enterprise. The difficulties to be surmounted may be classified—physical, political, social, and financial.

The most prominent physical difficulty is the extent of territory to be traversed. The starting point must be chosen in either Nebraska, Kansas, Colorado, Utah, Montana, Idaho, Oregon, or Washington. Thence the distance to the line of British Columbia would be about one thousand miles; the distance to be traversed through British America, to the line of Russian America, about six hundred miles; the distance through Russian America to Cape Prince of Wales, about nineteen hundred miles; the length of a submarine cable across Behring's Strait would be forty miles; and the distance from East Cape, by an inland passage around the Sea of Okhotsk, and through the settlements of Okhotsk, Ayan, and Shantar's Bay, which are well-known stations of the whale fishery, to the mouth of the Amoor River, would be about twenty-five hundred miles. The entire length of the line would be about six thousand and forty miles.

Operative telegraph wires have already been stretched on this continent of the aggregate length of seventy thousand miles; and similar wires have been stretched on the eastern continent of the aggregate length of two hundred thousand miles. Operative submarine telegraph wires have been laid of the lengths, respectively, of three hundred miles, and five hundred miles, from Dover to Heligoland, and from Malta to Tripoli.

Thus it is seen that the *mere extent* of the route to be traversed in the present case does not constitute an insurmountable, nor even a serious difficulty.

The physical obstacle which next presents itself, is, the surface formation of the regions to be traversed. That portion of the route which lies within our own territory is chiefly mountainous; and the projected telegraph line must at least course along declivities of the mountains, even if it should not be found necessary, in one case, to surmount them. British Columbia presents a similar topography. But there the mountains are divided into three ranges, whose courses are from north to south, while intervening valleys invite the introduction of telegraphs and roads. The Pacific coast of Russian America is chiefly level. The portion of Siberia which lies between East Cape and the head of the Sea of Okhotsk is, for a large extent, a steppe, or plain, with gentle elevations occasionally rising into mountainous ridges. At the head of the Sea of Okhotsk a range of mountains must be crossed, and the region lying between that range and the mouth of the Amoor River is of the same character as that before mentioned, which extends from the same range northward to East Cape. The highest elevation to be overcome on the whole line would be found in the Rocky Mountains, within the United States; and this elevation may be estimated at eight thousand to ten thousand feet.

Operative telegraph lines have already been stretched over steppes, in both continents, similar to those thus described. The

Pacific telegraph line, in crossing the Sierra Nevada, rises to an elevation greater than that which is to be surmounted on the line now under examination.

With the exception of timber, all the materials of a telegraph line are light and portable. Metallic wire sufficient for a mile of telegraph, together with the materials for insulation, weighs not more than four hundred pounds. Sufficient timber awaits the builder along the route through the United States and British Columbia. Timber is also found on those portions of the projected line which lie within the Russian dominions, on each continent, with the exception of a timberless steppe five hundred miles wide, on each side of Behring's Strait. There the needful timber can be brought near to the line, either by sea or from the forest-covered shores of navigable rivers.

The temperature of the region, through which the northern part of the line would pass, is very low. Nevertheless, winter is less severe than it is between the same parallels of latitude on the Atlantic coast. The telegraphic line which connects St. Petersburg with Archangel on the White Sea, and also the telegraphic line which passes around the Gulf of Bothnia and connects St. Petersburg with Tornea, are maintained in operation without difficulty, although they cross as high parallels of latitude as those which lie in the way of Mr. Collins' line.

The waters of Behring's Strait are about one hundred and eighty feet deep, and they are frozen through one-half of the year; but the congealed mass, when broken, generally takes the form of anchor ice, and not that of icebergs. Thus, climate seems to offer no serious obstacle to the enterprise; while it is not entirely unworthy of consideration that in cold latitudes timber used in any necessary structure is less perishable than timber used in warm latitudes, while less of insulating material is demanded in high latitudes than is required in more genial climates.

The only political difficulty in the way of the enterprise is the fact that it requires concerted aid from three several States, namely: The United States, Great Britain, and Russia. The two last named Powers have already, with enlightened and fraternal liberality toward the United States, made all the concessions which were demanded. Therefore, if Congress shall grant the application of Mr. Collins, no political obstacle will remain.

That portion of our own country in which the enterprise is to be carried on, is so well known as hardly to require a description more minute than I have already given. It is newly and as yet thinly settled. The case is the same in British Columbia. Indian tribes are found along the American part of the route, but they have been so well subjected to the influences of society and government, through the operations of the Fur Trade, that no serious resistance from them need be apprehended. The inhabitants of Asiatic Russia who dwell inland, are nomadic Tartars, affecting much independence. They are, nevertheless, not savage like the American natives. After centuries of internal war, they have now settled into a state of semi-civilization, in which they are accustomed to barter with whalers, with exploring parties, and with the government agents of Russia, and they are hospitably inclined by that intercourse.

The result of the survey of facts thus far made, is, that there are no insuperable obstacles, either physical, political, or social, in the way of the projected line of telegraph.

In regard to the expense which it requires, I must be content to refer the Committee of the Senate to the estimates which have been submitted by Mr. Collins. They have been made with a view to secure from private sources an advance of the moneys to be expended, and at the same time to obtain from the governments of Great Britain, Russia, and the United States, the necessary political aid. It may be assumed, therefore, that they were prepared honestly and cautiously, and with as near approach to accuracy as is possible in regard to a design in which so much that is to be done must be done under conditions never before tried. Mr. Collins estimates the whole cost at five millions of dollars. A just legislative caution would probably induce Congress to double that estimate. I understand that an association is already formed with a capital of ten millions to be devoted to the enterprise. I am, therefore, of opinion that it is entirely feasible.

I proceed, in the next place, to consider the probable usefulness of the enterprise.

It is needful here to assume that the line of telegraph proposed will be extended immediately from Amoor River to Irkootsk, so as to complete the telegraphic chain over the two continents. The agreement of Russia leaves no room for doubt on this point.

It is quite too late at this day to debate the abstract question of the usefulness of the magnetic telegraph. It would be as easy now to dispense with the steam engine on land or on sea, in the business of commerce, in social intercourse, or in political affairs, as it would be to forego the use of the telegraph. To be without it, is to be isolated. Other conditions being equal, the country that has the largest extension and the most thorough radiation of the telegraph wire, enjoys the most active and profitable system of domestic commerce.

Of the seventy thousand miles of telegraph now in operation on the American continent, sixty thousand miles are found within the United States and the remainder in the provinces of British America. But commerce on the American continent defies political restraint, and centralizes itself within our own country. For practical purposes, we may regard the whole telegraph system of the American continent as our own. But internal commerce imparts life to, and receives new life in return from foreign commerce. In proportion to the extent and variety of its resources, the nation that enjoys the most prosperous foreign commerce exhibits the greatest industrial activity and domestic happiness within its own borders. The vigor which commerce has already attained among us, while we continue to hold our communications with the eastern continent by navigation only, is justly a subject of national congratulation. Can there be a doubt that if our telegraph system should be connected by a trans-oceanic line with the *one* that is now performing its equally isolated part on the eastern continent, new and stronger reciprocity would be exhibited, not only in commercial centres but in every recess of the land? The unremitting exertions which are made by enlightened men in Europe and the United States to connect the two countries by a wire passing through the Atlantic Ocean, as well as the responses which Great Britain and Russia have made to the application for favor and patronage to the line now under consideration, show the existence of a very wide and general conviction that each of the isolated telegraph systems existing on the two continents is imperfect and incomplete, and relatively inefficient, and that a connection between them is a necessary supplement to secure their greatest attainable usefulness.

Setting aside the temporary disturbance of war, the merchant, or the manufacturer, the miller, the farmer, the miner, or the fisherman of Halifax, Quebec, Portland, Boston New York, Philadelphia, Baltimore, Charleston, New Orleans, Galveston, Montreal, Buffalo, Pittsburg, Chicago, St. Louis, Memphis, St. Paul, Little Rock, Denver, Salt Lake City, Carson City, Los Angelos, San Francisco, Sacramento, Portland, with the aid of an inter-continental telegraph, would be in daily and, in case of need, in hourly correspondence with producers and consumers on the Amoor, where the fur trade of Asia is gathered up; with Sovinsk, the depot for the overland traffic between Russia and Japan and the mineral treasures of Nerchinsk; with Kiakhta, the centre of the international commerce of Russia and China;

with Irkootsk, Moscow, St. Petersburg; with all the cities of Western Europe, including Constantinople; with the cities of Alexandria, Cairo, and Suez; and with every other town, city, or hamlet, on either continent, now in telegraphic connection with the several marts of trade which have been enumerated.

Every one knows, however, that neither the American nor the European system has yet attained to its ultimate development. Transient wars now delay the establishment of wires in Pensacola, Havana, San Juan, Panama, Quito, Lima, Valparaiso, Buenos Ayres, Montevideo, Rio Janeiro, Surinam, Caraccas, and Mexico, and the incorporating of them, with all their local ramifications, into one American telegraph system. On the eastern continent neither the domestic disturbances nor the rivalries of States, nor their occasional collisions, prevent a continual expansion of the telegraphic systém. The telegraph construction of Russia at this day, like her system of railroads, presents the frame-work of an imposing structure, the dimensions of which are boldly outlined, while the connections and extensions yet remain imperfect and unfinished. It has been already mentioned that the Emperor has bound himself to extend the main eastern and western line from Irkootsk to the mouth of the Amoor River. This extension is now rapidly advancing. But this is only a single and not very prominent part of the work which the Emperor of Russia has begun. His design embraces nothing less than the following stupendous works, namely: A telegraph wire, with the necessary submarine cables, from the mouth of the Amoor River across the Straits of Tartary, over the island of Sakhalin, across the Straits of La Perouse, over the island of Jesso, through Hakodadi, and across the Straits of Sangar to Jeddo, the capital of Japan.

Secondly. A telegraph wire from the confluence of the Usuri with the Amoor, which confluence is seven hundred miles above the mouth of the latter; thence southward, on the bank of the

Usuri, to Lake Kingka; and thence to the port of Vladi Vostok, on the coast of Tartary, opposite to the port of Hakodadi, on the eastern coast of the Japanese Sea. Vladi Vostok is selected by the Emperor for his naval station on the Pacific coast.

Thirdly. A telegraph wire from Irkootsk, before described as the capital of Eastern Siberia, through Kiakhta, now the entrepot of European and Chinese overland commerce, through the vast territory of the Mongols to the gate in the Chinese wall at Yahol, and thence to Pekin, the capital of the Chinese Empire. American citizens temporarily residing in that country, are now soliciting, with good prospect of success, permission from the Chinese government to extend this last-mentioned line overland through China, to terminate with the needful branches at the ports of Nankin, Shanghai, Amoy, and Canton, on the Pacific coast, opposite to California.

There are already in operation twelve thousand miles of telegraph wire in the continent of Australia. This Australian telegraph system, which now is so purely local and isolated, is nevertheless expected to be brought into combination by alternating submarine and island wires with the Chinese and Russian wires last described.

Fourthly. A telegraph wire from a station on the main continental Russian line at Omsk, near the southern boundary of Asiatic Russia; thence passing through Mongolia and entering China at Huc, sometimes called Illy; thence crossing Turkestan, Bokhara, and Balk, to Cabool, in Afghanistan; thence to capital points in the Punjaub, where it will meet the telegraphic system of India, and thus become a medium of communication between London and the colonial dependencies of Great Britain, the Netherlands, Spain, and Portugal, on the shores and islands of the Great Indian Ocean.

Fifthly. A telegraph wire from Kazan, on the main central Russian line, through Georgia and Circassia, along the western shore of the Caspian Sea, to Teheran, the capital of Persia; thence to the Euphrates, at Bagdad; thence, descending along the banks of that historical river, to its mouth, at the head of the Persian Gulf, there to be connected with the Oriental telegraph system of India last before mentioned.

When we take into consideration the fact that Russia has already brought all her chief inland markets and mines, as well as her principal ports on the coasts of the Arctic Ocean, into telegraphic communication with her capital, it is readily perceived that, by offering to coöperate with us in giving effect to Mr. Collins' design, Russia actually invites us to put forth our national energy from every point within our borders where industry of any kind dwells, and especially from our northwestern and western States, and apply that energy in the great work of renewing and restoring the long-languishing civilization of the regions where our race first impressed its dominion upon the globe appointed for its residence. Certainly it cannot be necessary to say that such efforts belong to the class of human labors which are pronounced to be doubly blessed, because they bless equally those who are the subjects and those who are the performers of them. It seems impossible to over-estimate the direct effect of this new application of the national energy in producing a rapid and yet permanent development of the agricultural, forest, mineral, and marine resources of the United States. Nor is it any more practicable to assign limits to the increase of national influence, which must necessarily result from the new facilities we should acquire in that manner for extending throughout the world American ideas and principles of public and private economy, politics, morals, philosophy, and religion.

In attempting to make such estimates, it is important to remember that the telegraph wire is as yet a newly-invented instrument, timidly employed and clumsily handled, with a very imperfect knowledge of the fulness of the power that resides in it. It costs us now one-half a mill per mile to speak a single word through the cheapest telegraph wire of any considerable length. This is vastly more costly than the average transmission of messages in writing by employing the steam engine, either on land or on water. This great expense of telegraphic communication is due, however, not at all to any inseparable quality of the telegraphic machine, for that machine is easily constructed of very simple and cheap materials. The expensiveness is due to two transient conditions of the telegraph system: First, the charges now justly imposed upon it for rewarding the inventors; and secondly, the fact that, as yet, fixed habits of communication in ancient forms prevent frequent resort to the new mode of correspondence, and customary investments of capital which are sufficiently remunerative cause it to be sparingly applied to the perfection of the new system. When those mere ephemeral embarrassments of the magnetic telegraph shall be removed, the magnetized wire will become, for the chief purposes of social, commercial, and political communication, as practical as, by reason of its adaptation, it is effective.

I proceed to consider the question whether the enterprise deserves the patronage Mr. Collins solicits for it. Throughout the remarks which I have thus far submitted, I have, not without design, called it Mr. Collins' enterprise. It is truly his, because it was he alone who conceived and projected it, and who has clothed it with the substantial form which enables the three great States, whose concerted action he solicits, to cause it to be put in operation. But in another sense it is entitled to be regarded as an enterprise of the government of the United States. During all the time that Mr. Collins has been engaged in maturing and developing it, and presenting it to the consideration of Russia and Great Britain, he has been acting under the instruction and with the approbation of the Department of State, and a knowledge of that fact has not been withheld from Congress.

I think it may be regarded as settled that the United States cannot neglect to employ telegraphic communication with foreign countries and yet expect to maintain a healthful commerce with them; that the United States cannot hope to inspire respect, confidence, and good will abroad, and so secure peace with foreign States, without using the magnetic telegraph when it is possible; and that the United States cannot even hope to preserve peace and order at home, much less to maintain a military and naval police on their inland frontiers and around their ocean coast, without availing themselves of all feasible telegraphic communications.

Finally, it seems to me that in extending dominion over inland mountain regions, and setting up the national flag on the Pacific coast, the American people, however inconsiderately, assumed the duty of diffusing an equal civilization throughout the whole of the great country which they thus included within their borders. Nor would it be wise to shut out from our thoughts the consideration which necessarily results from contemplating calmly the positions and the resources of our new northwestern and western States. It becomes our duty to act upon the conviction that, from this time henceforth, those States are to perform an important part in a great work which shall make the shores of the Pacific Ocean the home of communities that shall be as busy, as prosperous, as free, as enlightened, as powerful, and as happy as those which now cluster upon the Atlantic shores. The Atlantic States, by their intermarriage with those of the Pacific, have come under an obligation to favor this great development.

What Mr. Collins asks of Congress is, the grant of a right of way across the public lands, with the right to take therefrom materials necessary for constructing the line; the use of a national vessel, suitably officered and equipped, to make surveys and soundings along the north Pacific coast, beyond the limits of the United States, and to aid in prosecuting the work; and, finally, a stipulated compensation for the government use of the line, when it shall be constructed. If the views I have submitted are just, this demand for patronage is neither unnecessary nor unreasonable. We could not withhold it without showing a want of appreciation of the liberality and friendship which have been manifested toward the United States by Russia and Great Britain in the proceedings they have adopted toward the same enterprise. I do not know any one object lying within the scope of our foreign relations more directly important than the preservation of peace and friendship with those two great and enlightened Powers. Nor can I conceive of any one measure of national policy that would more effectively tend to secure that great object than the construction of this proposed inter-continental telegraph.

I forbear to urge the project in competition with the proposed line across the Atlantic from Cape Clear to Cape Race, which, notwithstanding past difficulties, I yet hope to see speedily completed. The two lines would naturally aid and strengthen each other. If they should even come into competition, it would be more advantageous to the world to have the use of both than the use of only one of them. One might be expected to operate when the other should be accidentally suspended. Nor can it be reasonably doubted that the great interests of human society will, at a very early period, require more than one, and more than even two, trans-oceanic, world-encircling telegraphs.

I have the honor to be, Sir,

Your obedient servant,

WILLIAM H. SEWARD.

NOTE FOR PAGE 412, LINE 7.

The subject of the adaptation of the electric telegraph to the vast Empire of China has attracted the attention of scientific men. Count d'Escayrac de Lantrue, of the French Embassy to Pekin, lately published an account of a method that he had devised, by which, employing *only* thirteen hundred symbols, the many thousand characters of that language can be telegraphed. Some years previously, however, the American Orientalist, Doctor Macgowan, published a work in the Chinese language, describing an invention of his, by which the same object can be accomplished by the aid of sixteen symbols. (*Journal of American Oriental Society*, vol. iii., p. 195.) Dr. Macgowan's treatise was republished by the Japanese. There seems, therefore, to be no limit to the extension of telegraphs in China and Japan.

CPSIA information can be obtained
at www.ICGtesting.com
Printed in the USA
LVHW022017120422
716028LV00006B/179

9 783752 591262